Barbara Ewing is a New Zealand-born actress and author who lives in London. She has a university degree in English and Maori and won the Bancroft Gold Medal at the Royal Academy of Dramatic Art. She has written six novels besides *The Circus of Ghosts: The Actresses, A Dangerous Vine, The Trespass, Rosetta, The Mesmerist* and *The Fraud.*

Praise for Barbara Ewing:

'Ewing has a light touch, and a vivid sense of era' *Sunday Times*

'A gripping historical novel fusing love, hate, murder and revenge' *Glasgow Herald*

'Ewing writes accessibly and tells a ripping good story, but her passion is also for ideas . . . [she] keeps the pace up right to the dramatic ending' *New Zealand Herald*

'Colourful and gripping' Maureen Lipman

'Compelling storytelling' Clare Boylan

'Deftly written, funny, fastidiously well researched and, above all, features this innately fascinating business of mesmerism' *New Zealand Sunday Star Times*

'Ewing weaves a plot as complex as Fair-Isle knitting . . . [she] fastens off all the threads so the pattern is satisfyingly complete' *Daily Telegraph*

'Engrossing . . . fascinating historical details' *Time Out*

'A good-humoured saga' *Sun Herald*

THE CIRCUS OF GHOSTS

Barbara Ewing

SPHERE

First published in Great Britain in 2011 by Sphere
Reprinted 2012 (five times)

Copyright © Barbara Ewing 2011

The moral right of the author has been asserted.

*All characters and events in this publication, other than those
clearly in the public domain, are fictitious and any resemblance
to real persons, living or dead, is purely coincidental.*

A CIP catalogue record for this book
is available from the British Library.

PAPERBACK ISBN 978-0-7515-4095-6
C FORMAT ISBN 978-1-84744-204-8

Typeset in Palatino by M Rules
Printed and bound in Great Britain by
Clays Ltd, St Ives plc

Papers used by Sphere are from well-managed forests
and other responsible sources.

MIX
Paper from
responsible sources
FSC
www.fsc.org   FSC® C104740

Sphere
An imprint of
Little, Brown Book Group
100 Victoria Embankment
London EC4Y 0DY

An Hachette UK Company
www.hachette.co.uk

www.littlebrown.co.uk

For Bill, one more time.

HISTORICAL NOTE

In the mid eighteen-forties, the somewhat lurid newspaper reporting of a scandalous society murder in London – with links, however tenuous, to both the dubious practice of mesmerism and the eminently respectable young Queen Victoria – forced the main protagonist, a lady Mesmerist cleared of the murder by a jury but nevertheless irrevocably tainted by the reporting of the events, to leave London with the rather odd group of people she called her family, for America.

It is known that with them, for reasons of the heart, travelled Inspector Arthur Rivers, one of the first British detectives, from the newly-formed police division based in Scotland Yard, off Whitehall.

The Fox Sisters, who began the cult of table-tapping and claimed to talk to the dead, were a nineteenth century American phenomenon, fanned by the American press. It is thought that opium always hovered; the alcoholism and the scandals came later.

Gallus Mag was a well-known figure in the underworld of the New York gangs in the nineteenth century. And newspaper reports on the performance of Mrs Ray from the Royal Theatre, New Zealand in 'The Bandit Chief' can still be found.

And although Sigmund Freud is not, himself, part of this story, it is interesting to note that he visited America with his psychoanalytical theories in 1909. The visit was not a great success: Freud afterwards described America as 'a gigantic mistake'.

1

In his large house, in the most elegant part of London, the old and raddled Duke of Llannefydd poured whisky for himself and shouted.

'Find the harlot! Find the whore! Find the actress!'

'Our investigations have shown, my Lord, that she has, some time ago, travelled to America and – I am sorry to have to inform you – joined a circus.'

'What do you mean by "your investigations"? It was there for all the world to see and laugh over in the *Times* newspaper!'

'Indeed the matter was reported in the newspapers, your Lordship.'

'Well, find the harlot!'

'America is a large and unchartered country, my Lord.'

'Well, if it is large and unchartered the whore will be in one of the obvious places, won't she! Washington. New York. Boston. Do you think I do not know the geography of that disloyal, revolutionary land of traitors and Irish clod-hoppers and democrats? Of course she would go there, the actress-harlot! She killed my son.'

Mr Doveribbon senior (wealthy lawyer to the nobility, a large man used to comfort but not invited to sit at this meeting) cleared his throat, exchanged an uneasy look with his son Mr Doveribbon junior (putative lawyer and man-about-town). 'My Lord, you must, I think, disabuse yourself of that notion for it is generally agreed and known that your son was killed by his own wife.'

The duke spluttered and gesticulated, and in doing so knocked the bottle of whisky on to the marble floor where it smashed, ejaculating its golden contents over Mr Doveribbon junior's fine boots, much to the elegant young man's horror. Sickly whisky fumes rose and a manservant appeared miraculously with broom and bottle, and the expression of a Christian martyr.

'Lady Ellis may have killed my son *nominally* and wielded the dagger, but who killed my son *morally*? The whore! The actress!' (It was perhaps incongruous to hear the word *moral* in that Mayfair room of scoundrels, for not only the duke but the manservant, the lawyer, the lawyer's son, and the doctor trying to listen unobserved outside the door, would not have, any of them, recognised the meaning of the word *moral* even if it had come up and punched them on the jaw.) 'I want the harlot actress disposed of and I want the *daughter* – whatever her name is – my blood, *mine*, my grand-daughter, returned to me, *mine*. She is to look after me. She is the daughter of my son even if her mother is a whore.' He imbibed whisky from the second bottle. 'I am alone.' Tears formed in his crafty eyes, ran down his crafty face. 'I want her here with me.' And then the tears dried as suddenly as they had appeared. 'And when I *get* her I can overturn the disgusting, money-grubbing intentions of my cousin's son, the locust, who waits for me to die so that he can inherit Wales!'

Again Mr Doveribbon senior cleared his throat. 'The girl is female off-spring, my Lord. In law she would not be able to inherit any part of Wales that you may own.'

'The ancient and noble family of Llannefydd is above the law! I will change the law! That girl had more sense than her sister for whom I did so much, and the nimsy-whimsy-pimsy *stupid* boy,' (again whisky spluttered) 'and she shall be returned to me as is my right! And the mother disposed of!'

'When you say "disposed of" your Lordship, you mean . . .'

'What do you *think* I mean, you fool? Surely an Irish clod-hopper can be paid to find a dark corner in that traitorous land! Do I have to spell out everything to you?' And then he observed the lawyer and his son with a slow look of cunning and his voice took on a silken tone. 'My purse will – of course – be open to you. All expenses. Any bills paid. High fees. Just find that actress-harlot! And bring me my grand-daughter!'

Mr Doveribbon senior, now that serious money was being discussed, considered. 'I would have to send my son to America. He is a most presentable Englishman.' Mr Doveribbon junior with his whisky-stained boots looked further alarmed. He was indeed presentable, in fact he knew he was even devastatingly good-looking, but he was not stupid and he was (unbeknownst to his father) heavily involved in some dubious land-buying in newly developed housing sites round the Edgware Road, so he had his own plans and they did not include travelling to any part of America. 'It would be a long and arduous and expensive task,' his father continued, 'to find the mother and the girl.'

'Dispose of the mother! That whore with the black and white hair! Nothing will come to any good if she is to interfere. Dispose of the mother and bring me my grand-daughter!'

'We would need a very large advance on expenses, your Lordship.'

Again the cunning, crafty eyes. 'No paltry advance! Dispose

of the mother, bring me my grand-daughter, and I will give you ten thousand pounds!' At this pronouncement both Doveribbons swooned slightly: *Ten thousand pounds? Ten thousand pounds* was unheard of riches, even in the murky world of the legal profession.

Nevertheless, instinct nudged Mr Doveribbon senior to refuse this particular set of instructions. The Duke of Llannefydd was one of the richest and most prominent nobles in Britain, certainly, but he was also known as untrustworthy, even among those who manoeuvred where untrustworthiness was the norm. And 'disposing of' was something Mr Doveribbon left to wilder men. However: *ten thousand pounds* echoed. Also: his son was extremely presentable and – Mr Doveribbon's dreams suddenly leapt higher – might even make an impression on the heiress. Greed and instinct battled in the mind of Mr Doveribbon senior.

Greed won.

2

All classes of people in New York (which called itself class-less) attended Mr Silas P Swift's Amazing Circus: something about the wild, and the exotic, and the vulgar, and the dangerous. In the brash, expanding, crowded, noisy, money-making city of New York Mr Silas P Swift's Amazing Circus was the most notorious – and the most visited; the bright, gaudy pennant flying above his huge Big Top could be seen from Broadway and his circus posters were larger and brighter and more brazen than any other.

ROLL UP! ROLL UP!

MR SILAS P SWIFT'S AMAZING CIRCUS

presents

the Acquitted MURDERESS from LONDON

MISS CORDELIA PRESTON, FAMOUS MESMERIST!

And her daughter Miss Gwenlliam Preston,
STUNNING ACROBAT!

Accompanied by the most talented riders
and artists of the Circus World

And WILD ANIMALS including

A DANGEROUS LION FROM AFRICA!

A HUGE ELEPHANT FROM AFRICA!

A CAMEL FROM ARABIA!

DANCING HORSES!

BEAUTIFUL ACROBATS, MEXICAN COWBOYS!

FEARLESS FIRE SWALLOWERS!

CLOWNS AND MIDGETS!

The most exciting show ever seen in our country!

Only $1.00 (children 75 cents)

Murderess, Mesmerist were the words that echoed, like *Dangerous Lion from Africa*: crowds, and dollars, poured into Mr Silas P Swift's Big Top, with its huge canvas walls and its sawdust floors and its planked wooden seats for fifteen hundred people; hawkers set up stalls nearby to sell oysters and ale and sarsaparilla and big pies.

This afternoon the City Aldermen came, with their children in elegant smocks; not so far from them, but back in the shadows, were members of the most vicious criminal gang in New York, sprawling on the precarious wooden seating and laughing and eating the big pies. They wore dark shirts, and gold earrings in their ears.

The lion-tamer had already escaped certain death (as he did twice daily); the elephant was trumpeting loudly as clowns juggled coloured balls, and the top-hatted, red-coated circus master cracked his whip. Fire-eaters breathed flames at the audience who stank of sweat and excitement and ale, and who in their turn breathed in the thrilling, peculiar circus smells of wild animals and sawdust and canvas and oil-lamps and dung and fire; the brass band played patriotic marches. And all the time the circus troupe kept up, as usual, a running commentary among themselves about the audience, in among the cries of *HOUP-LA!* and *HURRAH!* and the roaring of the lion; the audience came to be entertained by the circus, did not perhaps know that they were themselves entertaining also. Pretty girls and pompous Aldermen and mean-mouthed gangsters alike: they may not have observed they were observed but indeed they were; the performers were calling in their own circus language to each other: a mixture of new American slang – *high-falutin'*, *humbug* – plus theatrical gestures that may have seemed part of the act and Spanish whoops from the *charros*, the wild and clever Mexican cowboys. It was one of the fire-eaters who pointed out the City Aldermen, those men with such favours to dispose, and one of the midgets ran straight up the planked wooden steps in the audience and planted a kiss on to the cheek of one of them: whatever the Alderman thought of this grizzly rather un-fragrant gesture he, of course, waved to the crowd in acceptance of the honour and chuckled heartily and acrobats swung higher and higher and bright oil-lamps shone everywhere and although the dangerous gang members sat far away at the back, the light from the lamps still occasionally caught their shining earrings and the gold crosses around their necks. And sitting amongst the gang members, the tallest one of them all: wild hair, thick braces; it was only if you looked very carefully that you could see that the tall, wild figure was a woman. And it was only if you happened to be looking very, very carefully indeed that you might have

7

seen the wild-haired woman and one of the City Aldermen (a most unlikely combination) exchange an almost imperceptible nod. The midgets ran and somersaulted and the *charros* rode faster and faster round the ring, past the angry, trumpeting African elephant and past the white-faced clowns with their big red painted smiles and their false red noses and their black over-sized shoes, and the brass band with its tuba and trumpets and drums played on.

And Silas P Swift was, above all things, an incomparable, theatrical showman.

Suddenly the music stopped. Suddenly the lamps were turned low by the clowns and the *charros* and the midgets and the fire-swallowers and suddenly, now, the acrobats flew like hazy, silent birds over the audience. And then his star performer, his beautiful, scandalous, infamous Mesmerist, slowly emerged out of the shadows at the back of the Big Top and there was an intake of breath from the audience and in the half-light they saw a beautiful, older woman, draped in long, drifting scarves. And as the drums rumbled softly she lifted her arms, long glittering scarves fell from her head and they saw she had huge eyes and a pale face. And they saw that she had one extraordinary white streak of hair among the dark, as if she had once suffered some shock that had turned part of her hair ancient, or wise, or phantasmal. Then a strange husky voice, used to big spaces, called, *Whose pain can I help here?* And whether they thought she was a murderess or not, people came forward, or were brought forward by their families. For they had heard of mesmeric powers, and they were people who wanted miracles. From the shadows the Mesmerist looked up at the acrobats for a moment as if waiting for a sign. And then she pointed to a pale man in the crowd whose shoulders were hunched in pain.

8

The man approached nervously; the Mesmerist stepped forward and sat the man in a chair that had mysteriously appeared, spoke to him gently and quietly. How the audience strained to hear the words, was it *Let yourself rest in my care* or was it some humbug incantation? And then the shadowy woman, never taking her eyes from the man, began to move her arms over and over, just above him: over and over, over and over, long, strong rhythmic strokes, just above the body, never touching, breathing deeply over and over, her total concentration, her own energy going into the pain of the man and trying to move it outwards, drawing it out. Was she murmuring to him perhaps? It was not clear. The huge, hot, crowded, stinking, airless tent was silent: the audience were spell-bound, they could see that the pale man had fallen asleep, saw the strong, smooth rhythm of the arms of the woman: the arms moving over and over, never touching, over and over.

And at the end (for the Mesmerist had chosen the patient with care, and with the help of her daughter flying above the audience on a trapeze: they knew they could not cure broken limbs or cancerous growths: they could only help pain): at the end then: the man awoke, his face cleared, his body straightened; puzzlement, relief, the man looked about himself in surprise. And as, smiling slightly in disbelief, he was led away from the circus ring, suddenly there were bright shining lights again and clowns tumbled and the lion roared and acrobats flew and twirled in the suddenly bright air: *HOUP-LA! HOUP-LA!* they cried as they swung from one trapeze to another and the band played jaunty music and when the audience looked again to the centre of the ring there was no-one there.

'Was it a ghost?' One of the men with gold earrings halfstood, unsure, whispered to his companions, and his voice sounded almost like that of a child.

9

'Sit down, Charlie, you stupid bugger,' said the tall, wild woman with the trouser braces holding up her skirt, and she leant across and clouted him, 'it's only a trick!' But Charlie's face was pale in the lamplight. Under the sound of the brass band she whispered maliciously in his ear:

The devil damn thee black, thou cream-faced loon!
Where got'st thou that goose look?

but he angrily shrugged her away and spat tobacco.

The *charros* now rode in human pyramids, dangerous and clever, faster and faster around the ring, calling to each other in Spanish. 'Cunting foreigners,' said Charlie, spitting tobacco again, on to the canvas wall of the tent now. His eyes strayed to where the ghost had been, but the beautiful, shadowy figure had disappeared.

The *New York Tribune* wrote:

Newspaper reports reaching us from London have described Cordelia Preston, Mesmerist, as a scandalous and deeply immoral woman who had – it was alleged – killed the father of her children, Lord Morgan Ellis, heir to the Duke of Llannefydd – who owns, it would seem, most of Wales. (We do wonder how the Welshmen feel about that.) It is now known that the real murderess was the wife of Lord Ellis, cousin to Queen Victoria. But as we in our dear and democratic Republic know only too well, those close to the Monarchy are protected by the Monarchy (in this case until it was impossible to hide the truth when Lady Ellis tried to kill Cordelia Preston also).

*Not all the facts of this matter have come to light – and no doubt Cordelia Preston, acquitted of murder as she has been, is indeed immoral; scandalous, certainly: it is known that she is now working as a Mesmerist in **MR SILAS P SWIFT'S AMAZING CIRCUS** here in New York, which speaks for itself. But by chance this newspaper has also ascertained that both Cordelia Preston and her daughter, Gwenlliam Preston, an acrobat, regularly give their mesmeric services free, with no publicity, to one of the hospitals in New York which use mesmerism as an anaesthetic during painful operations. They work alongside the world-renowned Mesmerist Monsieur Alexander Roland, who was trained by Dr Mesmer himself and we have found that they have much success in helping patients.*

Whatever the full story let us re-iterate, as we do very often, God Bless America, the land of the free, and at least let us be grateful to Cordelia Preston and her daughter for their good works.

Mr Silas P Swift (who had made it his personal business to bring the above-mentioned good works to the attention of the *Tribune*) rubbed his hands in glee as circus audience figures soared even higher: he had taken a gamble bringing the scandalous Misses Preston to America and it had paid off beyond his wildest dreams. He was well aware that it had worked so well, at least partly, because Miss Cordelia Preston (having worked for so many years as an actress) and Miss Gwenlliam Preston (having been brought up as the daughter of a nobleman) both had a grace and dignity in their bearing that was at odds with the lurid stories surrounding them. The daughter was very pretty and turning into a most excellent acrobat and tightrope-walker but her mesmeric mother (that startling streak of white in her dark hair), was hauntingly beautiful: something almost translucent about her face and her cheekbones and her dark, mysterious eyes.

So twice daily the New York crowds poured in, hundreds and hundreds: thousands, all breathing in the thrilling smells of sawdust and elephant dung and canvas and wild animals and oil-lamps and mud and excitement. And, twice daily, in a small circus wagon among the circle of circus wagons at the back of the Big Top, Miss Cordelia Preston, immoral acquitted murderess, put on her flowing, drifting costume, pulled her long, wafting scarves about her pale face. Occasionally, startling, painful memory clutched at her and she had to bend over, gasping in shock, and her daughter Gwenlliam would quickly push past the costumes and the scarves and the shoes and the long balancing poles to reach her mother. For a moment the two would rock gently, holding each other for comfort. Once, Cordelia found her daughter, always so calm and so sensible, in uncontrollable tears in her shining, sparkling acrobatic costume in the small, cluttered caravan; quickly she held her tightly, they breathed together, thought they heard a faraway sound: *shshshshshshshshshsh*: they thought they heard the sea on a long, long shore and they thought they heard high children's voices calling: *Manon! Morgan!*

Manon.

Morgan.

Cordelia's children, Gwenlliam's sister and brother.

And then they would finish dressing and leave the little wagon and stand very straight and smile and smile and tease and talk as they crowded near the African elephant with his big ears and his small, crafty eyes; they crowded together with the clowns and the *charros* and the fire-eaters and the midgets and the other acrobats at the back of the Big Top as the dangerous lion roared and the unpredictable elephant suddenly trumpeted loudly and the Mexicans called in Spanish to their horses; and instead of the sound of the sea Cordelia Preston and her daughter Gwenlliam heard once more the sound of the raucous, excited shouting of the big, boisterous New York crowds inside, all waiting for the magic of the circus.

3

The Experimenter was late although actually, at this very moment, he was running as fast as his thin dentist's legs could carry him along Cambridge Street towards the Massachusetts General Hospital, clasping an odd-shaped bottle to his chest.

In the amphitheatre there was a loud buzz of impatience in the air: nobody ever kept the eminent and respected Surgeon Dr John C Warren waiting, so the other eminent surgeons of Boston in the audience tapped their fingers on their canes, while the medical students whispered excitedly (but reverentially quietly) amongst themselves. Perhaps it was all humbug and they'd been called here for nothing.

Two impassive figures with dark, paint-cracked eyes observed the proceedings silently. These figures were painted on the outside of two rather battered Egyptian coffins which stood upright at the back of the stage in the amphitheatre. Whether the ancient coffins so displayed contained the remnants of dead bodies from long ago and far away was not advertised.

Some of the surgeons nodded to an old Frenchman who sat amongst them: dignified, upright and still: the distinguished Medical Mesmerist, Monsieur Alexander Roland – a foreigner, sure, but at least French not English, and a much respected practitioner in some of the hospitals in Boston and New York. Monsieur Roland elicited great interest among some of the medical men: for many years in many countries he had had much success in making painful medical operations bearable to patients using mesmerism as anaesthesia. Mesmerism as anaesthesia, although many doctors refused to have anything to do with it, was not scorned outright in these big, new cities; Monsieur Roland had sometimes worked with Dr John C Warren himself, here in Boston. Many of the surgeons here today, and some of the students with special permissions, had come to watch the Mesmerist more than once – observing the total concentration of the old Frenchman on the patient. *Let yourself rest in my care*, he would say gently and then, without taking his eyes from the patient, he would begin the movements with his arms and his hands: the long, strong, repetitive mesmeric passes just above the patient's body, never touching, over and over, over and over, his breathing and the patient's breathing gradually matching, until the patient – *Believe it or not!* the observers recounted later – fell into some sort of trance. Then the operation would begin. If the patient stirred as the operation proceeded, Monsieur Roland would begin again the long, rhythmic passes, over and over, and the patient would calm, and sleep again. And yet, and yet: in truth there was an uneasiness among many medical men about the whole thing: they had seen what they had seen, but mesmerism was neither scientific nor explainable. Some of them conceded at least, however, that it was better than slugs of brandy, and the screaming.

Monsieur Roland had not, today, been asked to mesmerise

the patient before the operation, but he was particularly interested in today's proceedings.

Now, on the stage of the amphitheatre, Dr John C Warren stood beside the patient who was strapped to an operating chair; a large lump was visible just underneath the patient's jaw where his shirt lay open and ready. The patient was a New York workman who was addressed, very formally in this public arena, as Mr Abbot. Mr Abbot had a blank look on his face (but Mr Abbot could feel his heart beating fast).

Dr John C Warren looked impatiently at his watch.

Along Cambridge Street still, two men ran: one short, one tall. The short man huffed and puffed in a rather alarming manner, found it difficult to keep up; the tall man, the afore-mentioned dentist, still held the strange looking bottle in his arms and his cloak streamed out behind him as he ran up the steps into the main entrance, and then up more stairs to reach the fourth floor. With the short man heroically not far behind him, the dentist burst into the hospital amphitheatre and, trying to catch his breath and remove his cloak at the same time, informed the surgeon that he was ready. Both running men had come straight from the premises of the instrument-maker who had prepared the bottle.

Then Mr Morton, the dentist, (having received a nod of permission from the imperious surgeon) introduced his short-statured, panting companion to the patient.

'Mr Abbot: this is Mr Frost,' said the dentist.

The patient was looking somewhat bewildered as he beheld the dishevelled men and the odd-looking, tube-protruding bottle, but Mr Frost pumped his hand with enthusiasm.

'Young fella! I have come along with Mr Morton because I have already had this – ah – treatment.' Mr Frost took a huge breath to calm himself from his exertions. 'Now, young fella: look! Just look!' In his excitement Mr Frost opened his own mouth wide and pointed, endeavouring to point and speak simultaneously. 'See this space? See? See? This was a tooth. The pain was killing me, I felt like killing myself. I never knew pain like it. But I had this treatment that you're going to have now and I never felt a thing and no ill effects. I've signed a paper saying so! Go for it young fella, go for it!'

'Thank you,' said Mr Abbot, swallowing.

At a sign now from the surgeon a rubber sheet was pulled up towards the patient's neck. Mr Morton placed a tube, which was attached to the bottle in his arms, to the lips of Mr Abbot and asked him to breathe in through his mouth.

'Are you afraid, Mr Abbot?' asked the surgeon.

The young man shook his head manfully. Mr Abbot trusted Dr John C Warren; things had been explained to him carefully. He breathed in through his mouth as instructed.

Mr Morton the dentist was afraid, certainly. He had experimented for many months, including upon himself; he knew that if he failed (which he nevertheless believed he would not) he would be arrested right here in this medical amphitheatre, for manslaughter. There was perspiration on his forehead as he adjusted the tube and the bottle.

And in the silent, watchful audience Monsieur Alexander Roland understood very well what was being attempted. He had met many medical students in New York and Boston who indulged in what they merrily called 'ether frolics' – inhaling just enough of the gas to *go high!* as they told him, *like drinking champagne!* they told him. Monsieur Roland had met a young man who inhaled another gas, nitrous oxide, who said ecstatically, *I laughed and laughed! I felt like the sound of a harp!* Monsieur Roland knew experiments had been taking place for years. 'Take care there,' was all the old Frenchman ever said, and they assured him they always took care only to inhale enough of any gas to go high or to feel like a musical sound perhaps, but never enough to let themselves become unconscious. For fear they would never wake again.

The patient breathed in through the tube that was attached to the bottle, Mr Morton beside him. The painted figures on the Egyptian coffins remained impassive. After a few minutes had passed (the audience watching so intently, so quietly), the patient seemed to have fallen asleep. Mr Morton, not taking his eyes from the patient, nodded to the surgeon. The surgeon held his knife over the rubber sheet.

He spoke to his audience only once, and very briefly. 'Gentlemen. As you know this is an experiment and we do not exactly know what the results will be. I am removing this large growth that you see has grown under the patient's jaw. It is not a dangerous operation but it is an extremely painful one.' And then he plunged his knife, but carefully, knowing exactly where he could cut and where he could not, into the flesh of the man's neck. Blood spurted out immediately; every person in the amphitheatre expected a scream. They had all heard, a hundred times, the screams: screams were part of hospital operations.

There was no screaming.

The patient was sewn, the last blood was wiped away and the surgeon had washed his hands in a special bowl. Mr Abbot had mumbled, he had become agitated at one moment, but he had not woken; now he did not move, and it was difficult from the audience to see if he was even breathing. The silence in the amphitheatre was now like a shout: *Is he dead?* Not a soul stirred, not a cough. Perspiration poured now from the forehead of Mr Morton the dentist; finally he took a handkerchief from his jacket pocket to wipe it away, still without taking his eyes off the man in the operating chair for a single second. He had understood how long the operation would take; he had measured the dose exactly; it was the purest ether that could be obtained. He put his handkerchief away again, never taking his eyes from the sleeping man.

'Mr Abbot,' said Mr Morton softly to the patient. 'Mr Abbot.'

An arm moved.

And then, at last, Mr Abbot opened his eyes. (Mr Morton said later that he almost expired at this moment, from relief.)

The surgeon bent down.

'Are you all right, Mr Abbot?' There was a slight nod.

'Did you feel pain, Mr Abbot?'

They saw the patient moving his lips, wetting them with his tongue, trying to speak. An assistant brought a small glass of water. 'No, sir. No pain.'

Dr John C Warren, nearly seventy years old, piercing eyes and shaggy eyebrows, one of the most respected surgeons in Boston, bent again towards his patient, stared at the large wound and at the face of Mr Abbot. 'Did you feel anything at all?'

'I guess – I think – I'm not exactly sure – I don't quite remember. Maybe a scraping feeling? Along my jaw.'

'Nothing else?'

'Nothing else.'

The old surgeon stood upright from the patient, to speak at last to the other prestigious surgeons, and to the students gathered behind them: all those who had sat so quiet while

19

he had carried out his experiment. He bowed to Mr Morton. And then he gave his verdict. 'Gentlemen,' said Dr Warren, 'this is the first ever use of ether as anaesthetic in a hospital. We have seen what we have seen. Certainly, this is no humbug!' And the amphitheatre at last erupted with excited voices and shouts, people moving, people talking, gesticulating, shaking the dentist's hand, pumping it up and down in delight. And Monsieur Alexander Roland still sat, very quietly, in his own silence amid the echoing, triumphant voices all over the amphitheatre.

Arrangements were made for the patient to go back to the wards, the surgeon was leaving surrounded by others, but he saw the old Mesmerist, deep in thought, leaning his chin on his walking stick. The surgeon stopped.

'Ah. Monsieur Roland.' The Frenchman looked up, and nodded impassively.

'Indeed, Dr Warren.'

'But of course, we shall no doubt still call on your services in the meantime. These are early days. We shall use the new telegraph, as usual.'

'Indeed, Dr Warren.'

But they were both wise men, and they both understood. This day – not in the old world from where all science and knowledge had once come, but here in Boston, in the new America – medicine had changed for ever.

Deep in thought, Monsieur Roland remained where he was as the medical men departed, until he was alone with the painted Egyptian figures in the empty amphitheatre.

But Dr Warren had not, after all, left. He had waved his colleagues away saying he would join them presently, and he had come back: he sat down beside the old Frenchman. For a moment neither of them spoke, and then Dr Warren said abruptly, 'Well? What do you believe we have seen this day?' Monsieur Roland looked up from his contemplation. When he answered at last he spoke slowly, but forcefully.

'The more I have practised mesmerism, *Monsieur*, the more I have marvelled at the infinite importance of – and the absolute mystery of – the human brain.' Dr Warren nodded, but remained silent. 'I had hoped that this newer practice we call *hypnotism* which gives importance not just to the strength of the energy that emanates from the practitioner, as Dr Mesmer taught me, but to the energy that emanates *from the patient also*, would be a stronger and more effective way for the – the philosophy, if you like – the philosophy of understanding that we can *make the brain let go of pain*. But: you ask me what we have seen this day. We saw today that the brain can also be clinically, with a gas, artificially shut down altogether for a specified period of time. So that pain cannot be felt.'

'Do you think this is a good thing?'

Monsieur Roland was silent only for a moment. 'Yes,' he said. 'For the agony that practitioners like you and I, of all people, know patients have had to endure for so long – for as long as the world has existed almost – yes. I think it is a good thing. Dr Mesmer only had such success because there have been so few other ways of dealing with pain. But I do fear that – although they still can work in exactly the same way as they worked before this morning – from now on mesmerism and hypnotism will become,' he paused again for a moment and shook his head slowly '– pure entertainment.'

'What do you mean by that?'

'Certainly Dr Mesmer himself was a showman – when I worked with him he wore bright purple suits at his public appearances for instance, anything to get attention for his

21

work. But he was deadly serious and full of his own integrity about the actual practice of mesmerism and what it could do. After this morning I must of course accept that ether, carefully administered, will succeed as an anaesthetic and therefore,' and Monsieur Roland allowed himself a small sigh, 'the serious and most useful application of mesmerism is probably over.' He shook his head again slightly. 'I am afraid, Dr Warren, that mesmerism is already being put to many more alluring and theatrical uses than you can imagine in your wildest dreams! These days there are charlatans and wild impostors who charge large sums to thrill people with mock demonstrations of what they call mesmerism with smoke and shadows in dark rooms. Or ridiculous frauds who claim they can talk to the dead, or who give dubious demonstrations of what they call mesmerism to bored society ladies which excite emotions that it would shame me to be connected with!'

'I believe this is the first time I have ever seen you angry, Monsieur Roland!'

'Forgive me. It is almost the only thing in the world that can make me angry. To make a living, two of the people I am most fond of in the world have to demonstrate mesmerism – of which they are fine, genuine practitioners – in *circuses*. And all the time circus proprietors and music hall managers are looking for even further ways to enhance mesmerism – to vulgarise it even further to please their ever-hungry, thrill-seeking audiences: more lights, more shadows, more trapezes, more lions, more brass bands! If that is to be the future of something I respect so much, you will forgive my anger.'

'Are you angry perhaps at what you have seen this morning? That it brings to an end perhaps, your life's work?'

But Monsieur Roland smiled slightly. 'No, Doctor Warren. I have seen too much pain in my long life not to be glad if there is further – remedy.'

'There may be risks, of course.'

'Mr Morton has obviously worked very, very hard to get this experiment exactly right, for it to be more than what the students call an *ether frolic*.' At last the Frenchman's eyes twinkled slightly. 'I salute your Mr Morton, and I hope he will make his fortune! It was brave of him, and brave of the patient – and brave of you, my friend.' He stood at last. 'I congratulate you, Dr Warren.' The surgeon stood also and the two men shook hands.

A figure burst into the amphitheatre. It was Mr Morton the dentist: tall, young: twenty-seven years old and almost overcome with his excitement. 'I wanted to thank you again, Dr Warren, for your confidence in me. Not many eminent men would have taken such a risk with their reputation, I know that! It worked well, did it not? The sulphuric ether *worked!* As I knew it would. How many times have I experimented on myself, on my dog – I even sent my assistant down to the docks to see if I could *pay* a sailor to be experimented upon! Mr Frost was my first successful patient, as you know – his tooth was giving him such terrible pain he did not care what experiment he was involved in. But you have allowed me to show, in public, what I can do, Dr Warren, and I shall patent my discovery! Ether as anaesthesia! Mr Frost has adjourned to a nearby saloon and I shall join him now that I have seen you.'

Monsieur Roland put out his hand. 'Your name will go down in history, Monsieur Morton. You have changed the practice of medicine for ever, for which I most warmly congratulate you. I believe you have also changed the history of mesmerism, about which permit me to have mixed feelings,'

23

but Monsieur Roland was smiling at the young man as they all went out into the autumn morning, so immersed in what had been discovered that they did not even see two ladies in blue gowns walking two matching-blue poodles, the latest Boston fashion.

In the amphitheatre only the Egyptian mummies were left, to ponder on what had passed that day.

On the long journey back to New York where he lived, Monsieur Roland, wrapped in his dark cloak, was silent, still deep in thought; a most courteous man he nevertheless, by heroic effort, today very firmly deflected the eternal conversations that occurred when fellow passengers, realising he was a foreigner, began questioning him most intimately in a friendly manner, as Americans so frequently and insistently were wont to do.

The articulate, noisy, fast machine, the railway train, passed farmers' fields or small settlements or forests of trees, all the time clattering and chattering; a setting gold-cold sun shone on bright autumn leaves, light flickered in and out of the train windows as the trees, it seemed, rushed past. Occasionally at deserted crossroads a small mysterious group of people waved: a child with its mother, a farmer. At one crossroads a lone negro stood, unsmiling. Where had they come from, these people? There were now no houses or lights as far as the eye could see. As the afternoon sun drew downwards still, the train stopped sometimes as if it was not being fed fast enough for its own rushing speed: the passengers heard the hissing, steaming engine complaining; wood was fed into its belly; sparks flew out; railway men called to each other in the falling dusk light, and lit large lamps. Sometimes passengers got out to observe the engine, or this vast nowhere place, stamping their feet on cold hard ground, wanting to get on, wanting to be home, their breath becoming steam also, in the chilly darkness.

But Monsieur Roland did not move. He knew: what he had seen today altered everything. It would not take long in these modern times for the news to spread. Always, always, since the very beginning, he had had to fight for respect for his profession. Mesmerism had always had to travel with controversy and disapproval, because people believed that mesmerism was scientifically unexplainable – they saw it, but they did not believe it: it had to be a trick. And moreover mesmerism involved what many saw as an intimate relationship between two people who might not otherwise know one another. Many people and institutions thought that relationships of *any* kind between two people should not, quite frankly, be permitted in public: and certainly not a mesmeric one. There would undoubtedly be much jubilation at mesmerism's demise.

Monsieur Roland was correct. It did not take many weeks for the news of the ether experiment to reach Great Britain, and for an identical experiment with ether to be carried out in Scotland. A Scottish newspaper commented immediately:

> **A remarkable discovery has been made. Unlike the Trickery and Force of Mesmerism this is based on Scientific Principles, and is solely in the hands of Gentlemen, who make no secret of the matter or manner. To prevent it being abused or falling into the power of low, evil-minded irresponsible Persons, we we are informed that the Discoverer has secured a Patent.**

So Monsieur Roland understood: ether, inexpertly administered, might perhaps kill a patient, but even so it would not cause such controversy as the philosophy he had devoted his life to. It pained him very much that the final fate of the once amazing discovery of Doctor Franz Mesmer would, very likely, be the circus.

4

'I'll get straight to the point,' said Mr Silas P Swift.

It was not just the discovery of ether that affected the fate of mesmerism. This new America was abuzz, all the time, with new discoveries, new inventions, new sensations. Mr Morse's new telegraph system proved anything was possible. People talked of the Occult, of looking into the future, of Psychic Readings and tapping tables and conversations with the Dear Departed: why not? If messages could be sent along electrical wires in life, why should they not be sent along psychic wires in death? Mesmerism by itself was no longer enough, it was not new any more, not alluring enough nor exciting enough or exotic enough and Cordelia Preston's scandalous past was so soon forgotten, overtaken by other, newer dramas: audiences to the Big Top began to dwindle.

Then worse: in New York as in London, the Church, alarmed at many of the new ideas, denounced not only theatres (immoral and decadent behaviour in public places) and circuses (indecently clad ladies and gentlemen falling into each other's arms in the air): these disapprovals were old. Now they thundered against the supposed miracles that mesmerism and hypnotism and occultism and psychic dreams were purporting to carry out: miracles, said the Church firmly, came only from God. The no-nonsense American churches not only sent preachers to stand outside the big theatres in the big cities; they also arranged for them to be standing on boxes beside circus ticket-booths, fixing queuing audiences with a beady eye, denouncing naked acrobats and, in particular, mesmerism, as an affront to the Lord. All female performers including Cordelia and her daughter began to be considered not only immoral and vulgar (they had been that, always), but dangerous. The Misses Cordelia and Gwenlliam Preston because of their history received extra opprobrium and, in the new moral air, had *poisonous quackery* rather than *good works* attached to their names; Silas P Swift saw to it that Cordelia's name was quickly changed to **MRS** Preston on the posters, to at least be more respectable, but it was too late.

Newspapers now thundered: *so long as the lives of those who seek to entertain us are marked, with few exceptions, by a state of morals humiliating to human nature, we will shun them.*

Cordelia and Gwenlliam had only laughed. They were earning a lot of money and they were used to newspapers: after all it was newspapers' stories that helped fill the Big Top.

But the Big Top was not nearly as full as it once had been.

One day Silas P Swift came to the American Hotel, where they were living so sumptuously, to see his Star and her daughter. He hoped none of her mad family were present: old ladies and police officers were not his cup of tea; was relieved to see only one, although he was a tricky fellow: the Mesmerist Monsieur Alexander Roland, their friend and teacher. Tea was brought.

'I'll get straight to the point,' said Silas P Swift, disdaining tea. 'Respectability and the Church have suddenly settled like a damn great cloud over New York. Theatres and Circuses are closing all over town, all over America too, so I hear. If Phineas Barnum is running scared, and respectablising and changing his American Museum and closing all the drinking bars in the building and presenting – Good God above I can't believe it, we've been the most successful Impresarios in America! – if Phineas Barnum is presenting "Temperance Melodramas" in his American Museum, then Mr Silas P Swift's Amazing Circus will have to change also. I've already made plans. We are gonna have to travel further afield, and present ourselves quite differently. I never thought I would see the day when adventures in London and involvement in murder were no longer suitable for the American circus poster, but that day has come. The posters will have to be changed, we will travel wherever we can get work, and wages will have to be halved or worse. I've had to fire some of the clowns, and some of the acrobats too – not you Gwen, I've got plans for you. And for you, Cordelia.' He looked sourly at the old Frenchman; he was a stickler, as Silas P Swift had found in the past. But Silas P Swift was never, ever, without new plans, new enthusiasms.

'I've already arranged some bookings, and I've got some cut-price new acts from circuses that have already closed. And that African elephant was getting more dangerous and more unpredictable – it tried to attack me, elephants are damn tricky things – so I've shot it and sold it to a taxidermist. I've acquired another one that's just arrived in a boatload of stuff from India – they're smaller the Indian elephants, smaller ears and smaller tusks, I'm a bit sorry about that, but they're more easily trained I'm told – I've kept the old trainer and told him to get on with it. And I've purchased a Red Indian Chief with all his paraphernalia, he'll be a quaint extra, and they say he's a miracle with horses. And I've got a dancing bear. A white one. Cut-price.'

'I thought only brown bears could dance,' said Cordelia. It was her first comment since he had begun talking.

'Well, this is a white one, and it danced. And the lion-trainer is now gonna wear a toga and Roman sandals.'

Gwenlliam laughed. The lion-trainer had only one arm: she tried to picture him in a toga. '*Why*, Silas?'

'So's I can say he's from the Colosseum, of course!' said Silas. 'A remnant from the Roman Empire! And Gwen, you're about to become the main lady acrobat and tightrope walker, you're doing great stuff for a newcomer; you'll need new tricks and I'm gonna get you a little crown and call you a princess, that'll get them going here, we want a bit of controversy, they hate royalty but they'll love you if I get the right costume. Now. Cordelia. You're good, you're always good but mesmerism isn't enough by itself any more. Your act will still be the Star Act of course but it's gonna have to be – *enhanced*.'

'Enhanced,' she repeated.

'Let's put it like this: other circuses are going broke, well, we're just gonna change, that's all. What you're gonna need in your act is more *extravaganza*. You can't just appear from the shadows like that, that's not exciting enough, I've decided you can mysteriously appear and disappear on the acrobatic bars and wires.'

'*Silas!* For God's sake don't be ridiculous! I am not an acrobat! It's Gwenlliam who is the acrobat, as well as being a mesmerist!'

'But I'm not you, Mama,' murmured Gwenlliam, and Silas nodded.

'Trust me, Cordelia, I'm gonna make you an acrobat too! I

can do it mostly with lighting, don't you worry, just a bit of climbing and swinging. And big drumming, that'll help.' Cordelia looked at him incredulously. 'And I thought a bit of sweet music like "Home, Sweet Home" when the person goes into a trance, just to heighten things. And a new name: MESMERIST has lost its glamour. So now that you're gonna be swinging on trapezes out of the dark to do your act I reckon we'll call you THE ACROBATIC GHOST, that'll give you more powers, knowing things that only ghosts know, looking into the past, looking into the future, that sort of stuff.' He was very pleased with the new name and repeated it proudly: 'THE ACROBATIC GHOST. Nice ring to it. And you'll appear mysteriously from the heavens. We'll make it like magic.'

Monsieur Roland, who endeavoured always to remain very much in the background in conversations with Silas P Swift although both Cordelia and Gwenlliam were his pupils, stood suddenly, but he confronted the Impresario in his polite and gentlemanly manner.

'Monsieur Swift. *Pardonnez-moi*. You have already plenty of acrobats in your esteemed circus. I must advise you that Cordelia Preston is – as you of course know – a worldrenowned Mesmerist of great skill and you are very, very lucky to have her in your circus. However, mesmerism is *not* magic and it is *not* a matter of ghostly powers: mesmerism is a matter of transference of energy from a practitioner to another person for the power of good. That is all. Magic does not exist, Mr Swift. And there is nothing *ghostly* about mesmerism: no-one is pretending to look into the future or look into the past or be from the underworld, and the name you propose to use is totally misleading.'

Mr Silas P Swift actually took off his hat and threw it on to the floor of the American Hotel lounge in front of them all. 'Listen Mister – uh – Roland. *I do magic!* Cordelia here is the Star of my Circus, I brought her here from England when she was a scandal, as you of course know, with my own money, as you of course know. And have paid her handsomely and treated her – and you all – handsomely!' and he indicated the sumptuous surroundings. 'And she speaks very respectfully of you, Mister, as her teacher and one of her family etcetera etcetera. However, tastes change, memories fade – she ain't the drawcard she was, everyone's forgotten her story, there have been a hundred murders since, and mesmerism ain't the new thing it was – everyone's bored with mesmerism now, what's mesmerism when you can send electrical telegraphs and breathe in ether? People do mesmerism all over the place for pennies.' Silas P Swift paused. 'I know that Cordelia has – there's something about her – yes, there is, why, she makes the hairs stand up on my own neck, and people never quite forget her when they've seen her, I'm not denying that. However – most importantly of all, Mister Roland – my Circus has started losing money, a lot of money. We have no choice but to tour and I cannot pay anything like I have been paying. We can do a week here, a week there, some of the larger settlements – Buffalo, Rochester, Syracuse – see if we can keep ahead of respectability and the Lord. And if we run out of those places – well – we'll have to go further into the heartlands and do one-night-stands! And a smaller Big Top – it breaks my heart! But that's how it is, Mister Roland. And we have to make Cordelia seem something else. And calling her THE ACROBATIC GHOST and getting her up on the trapezes and using the lights to make her look ghostly is how we are gonna do it and we're gonna pretend that magic does exist, because *I make magic*, that's my job!'

Cordelia touched the arm of Monsieur Roland very gently. He bowed politely and turned and left: when he came back later he indicated that he was not angry and understood the requirements of the Entertainment Business but he did not want to discuss it further.

So as preparations were made for their departure from New York and as Gwenlliam perfected more and more sophisticated acrobatic tricks, Cordelia stoically rehearsed basic acrobatic manoeuvres also: *I'm not really old*, she told herself over and over, rehearsing for hours, sliding down the pole, tying small cushions to her knees, to protect them. Several of the clowns were older also; the ones who hadn't – yet – been fired took big wage cuts, frantically painted the big red smiles on their old faces night after night for the last performances in New York, terrified of losing their jobs. They drank even more heavily than they used to do, and Cordelia saw their fear. *No wonder they drink.* She ordered large glasses of red-port in the American Hotel. *No wonder we all drink.* She learnt to hitch on to a rope and half-climb, half-pull herself upwards. She balanced on a trapeze, swung on it backwards and forwards (but not too far): much of the new effects were done by Silas's clever lighting. She managed to stand on the end of a horizontal bar in the shadows as long as she had something to hold on to. She had perfected her act in the end but sometimes now she was so tired at the end of a night she thought her legs would simply fall off. She had dispensed with her corset after it had cut into her flesh (but the multitude of floating scarves hid many things). And she was now known on the new circus posters most respectfully as Mrs Cordelia Preston: THE ACROBATIC GHOST and nothing about murder at all.

Nevertheless Mr Silas P Swift was a clever businessman;

33

without his Star his circus would very likely collapse, be just like all the others. So although the wages were smaller now and although he himself was happy to travel through the night with his circus, he decreed that his Star, and her daughter, must always stay in a local hotel to sleep comfortably for a few hours and then, if they were moving on, travel before dawn next morning.

'Thank you,' said Cordelia ruefully – staying the last nights in the glamorous American Hotel in New York with its running water and all appurtenances – but she and Gwenlliam were grateful to still be earning a living and helping to support their family and to Monsieur Roland she said, and he knew it was true, 'You know we will always treat mesmerism with respect.'

On the last night before the circus left New York Cordelia and Gwenlliam sat with the people they called their family in their large pleasant sitting-room in the American Hotel: Detective-Inspector Rivers, Cordelia's husband; Monsieur Alexander Roland; two old ladies; and Cordelia's closest, oldest friend, Rillie Spoons, who held them all together and managed the money. They all drank red-port, Cordelia and Rillie filled the glasses. They discussed future accommodation.

'I am sorry we shall have to move from here,' said Cordelia ruefully.

'We will arrange all that, don't worry about all that,' said Rillie Spoons. 'We will send messages to follow the circus – and things might change again and you'll be back in no time! We all know what Silas is like!' While they were still all sitting there together a jubilant message arrived: *We've got a baby Indian elephant!* Nobody had known that the elephant was pregnant, neither the buyer nor the seller: Silas P Swift had merely laughed in amazement and said good fortune was always with him: his circus would be enhanced further by such an addition and the baby elephant was at once named 'Lucky'.

Detective-Inspector Arthur Rivers held his wife tightly in the night: whether they were lucky or not was not discussed; nor did they discuss how long or how far she might be away from him; these things remained unspoken between them, like many things.

5

'Father, I have made many enquiries regarding the task in hand and frankly I believe I still need more information. And possibly more money.'

The Mr Doveribbons, senior and junior, had had a farewell dinner at the father's club on the Strand and were now sitting in armchairs in the lounge, drinking after-dinner port and smoking cigars. Their voices were quiet under the loud bray of other gentlemen's after-dinner conversation. Mr Doveribbon was not of course a member of one of the exclusive gentlemen's clubs in London; however this respectable establishment of well-connected lawyers and doctors had its own exclusivity, and would not have dreamed of bestowing membership upon businessmen, say, or actors. Mrs Doveribbon had regrettably passed on so father and son ate here often, although they employed a cook and a maid in their house off Wigmore Street who provided much, if not all, of the ministrations once contributed by Mrs Doveribbon.

'I have given you all the information available, James – harlot, whore, actress etcetera. You have read the newspapers of the time; she didn't do it, very well, but she was obviously a whore and what's more she claimed to be a Mesmerist with all the hocus-pocus that entails.' Mr Doveribbon senior had a rather large posterior; he moved it in the leather armchair now, to make himself more comfortable; there was a squashed sound as the chair complained slightly. 'I have also given you more money than a prosperous man could earn in two years, and Boston is hardly more than two weeks from here! And when you find Cordelia Preston she will lead us to the *jewel* that will make us extremely rich men!' And for a moment both men thought again of the magic words: *ten thousand pounds*.

'You are sure the Duke will keep his side of the bargain?'

Mr Doveribbon smiled, laid his finger to the side of his nose. 'I am not a lawyer for nothing. I drew up the papers myself. We present him with the girl, and the disposal information – he insisted upon both – and he pays us the money.'

'And if we fail?'

'How can you fail? You are leaving for Liverpool tomorrow, you travel from thence direct to Boston first-class on a reliable and well-known steamer. In Boston you enquire of circuses. At each circus you enquire of Cordelia Preston – and it is very likely, my boy, that circus people know of each other. If she is not in Boston you travel to New York, it is not a long journey. If she is not in New York you travel to Washington, it is not a long journey. This is not, after all, a mountainous task, we could be sitting here with port again in a month or so!'

Mr Doveribbon junior may have been a foolish man with his *penchant* for fashionable boots and fashionable parties and dubious financial transactions supported by his respectable position as his father's successor, but as aforementioned, he was not stupid. He had prepared himself for his mission, including leaving to a trusted acquaintance the details of the on-going land deals. He had visited several circuses in the environs of London. He was a most presentable and attractive gentleman and he had had no trouble speaking kindly to the circus folk he met and eliciting information from them; he was sure he could talk man to man to circus folk in America also: he was a very confident young man. He believed he had already seen enough acrobats and clowns and performing monkeys to know what he was in for; already the strange, strong acrid smell of the dung of wild and exotic animals stayed with him. But despite his belief in himself he was still anxious.

'Father, we need to discuss further – the – erm – *disposal*.' This was the word they always used when speaking of Cordelia Preston, even if they were speaking in private: it made their activities sound less harsh, although what, after all, was a whore-harlot-actress with black and white hair to them?

The leather armchair squeaked and squelched again. 'You *of course* do not attempt anything yourself – or indeed have anything *at all* to do with it. That is nothing to do with us: we merely set the wheels in motion. But you will find people enough in America who will be happy to help you – it is a wild, untrammelled place, we know that. Mr Charles Dickens, I believe it was, said anything can be bought and sold in America if the price is right. In each place you will accommodate yourself in a good hotel and begin your investigations, and once you have found the subject of your search – and the jewel – your investigations must at once include looking about for likely disposers. Each of these three cities has a port. I have been told that you can find all sorts of fellows where ships dock.' Mr Doveribbon senior had a rather hazy view of both America and ports in general, but his son was not so unwise.

'In my opinion, Father, you perhaps underestimate the difficulties. Even a sea journey is fraught with danger as far as I am concerned, never mind searching for suitable disposers in a strange city.' Young James Doveribbon lowered his voice, even in the raucous lounge. 'I believe I need a weapon.'

Mr Doveribbon senior looked askance at the vulgarity of his son. 'You are *not*, I repeat it again, *not* to be involved in the disposal yourself!'

'It was *protection* for myself I was considering, not disposal duties.'

Mr Doveribbon senior, as has been said, never involved himself in murky physical details; he felt distinctly uneasy. 'James, you are, after all, a respectable lawyer. It is your pleasant manner, and indeed your charm, that will stand you in good stead, not weapons.'

'I am also of the new generation, Father. You are sending me off to a barbarous country and I am wise enough and experienced enough to know that one does not just walk around the docks asking people to do disposal work. I should be in some way armed. I have found an excellent, unobtrusive, well-made and rather prestigious, easily-carried knife.'

'You must not harm the girl!'

'It is not the girl I am thinking of. She is no use to us if I do not bring her safely back to these shores, I know that.'

Mr Doveribbon senior considered. 'How much?'

James Doveribbon thought quickly. He needed money still for business details in the Edgware Road. 'It is an extraordinary knife. Twenty guineas.'

His father's armchair squelched in alarm. 'Twenty guineas!'

'It is a most handsome dagger, and can be secreted easily about my person.'

Mr Doveribbon senior did not believe any dagger in the

world could be worth twenty guineas. However, James was his son and heir and about to embark on an important and valuable journey. He bowed his head in acquiescence.

His son smiled. 'I will do my utmost to fulfil our obligations in this matter,' he said, and again the magic words hovered: *ten thousand pounds*.

'And, James.' Mr Doveribbon senior looked at his son. 'Never – how can I put this exactly – never underestimate your *attractiveness* to the female sex. You may get – how can I put this exactly – even further than we hope with an heiress to a large part of Wales . . . In fact I think perhaps our plans call for champagne!' And he signalled a waiter.

Mr Doveribbon junior looked suitably modest, there in his father's club on his last evening in London, but he had a slightly smug smile on his face as the waiter brought the sparkling, celebratory, gold-tinted liquid and his father's leather armchair squelched and settled and sighed.

6

Celine Rimbaud, **LA GRANDE CELINE**, as she had been described on circus posters, was a flame-haired flame-swallower (strange but true) who had unfortunately burnt one of her eyes and part of her face one night in Cincinnati: it was said a possessive lover had tampered with her fire-eating equipment, but this was never, legally, proven. Yet it cannot be said, despite this jealous *amour*, that she was unlucky in love (unless many lovers is a sign of misfortune): Celine had been loved from Paris to New York via London and many of her lovers had been men of fortune and generosity and therefore despite her accident La Grande Celine was not, as they said in America, short of a dollar.

After the accident she wore (of course she did, being La Grande Celine) a large black eye-patch with a small pearl attached (like a wealthy pirate), which covered most of the damage and indeed gave her an exotic, jaunty look. She could no longer risk swallowing fire because her sight was no longer reliable enough for the precision needed, but La Grande Celine was a woman of great energy and enterprise: before many months had passed she had become the owner of one of the many dining saloons that had sprung up around Broadway and the adjoining streets. Her dining saloon soon acquired just the right combination of sociability, good food and relaxation. Not that many New Yorkers relaxed when they were eating: they wished to get on, back to business, and often ate in complete, hurried silence, even with friends; just the clattering of knives and forks and the chomping of food. Nevertheless Celine made her establishment as attractive to diners as possible. She paid her cooks well, oversaw the buying of produce herself, was always there at CELINE'S HOUSE OF REFRESHMENT as she named it proudly, smiling, welcoming, firmly in charge of the money that was soon flowing in. The menu was always at the window:

BOILED SALMON
SIRLOIN STEAK
OYSTERS: PICKLED, ROASTED, FRIED or RAW
APPLE PIE
CUSTARD PIE

and she made sure (checking other refreshment saloons) that her prices were always keen and competitive.

Exciting, expanding, bustling, prosperous, wild, thrilling, new-world New York had to accommodate and feed more and more people by the month. There were huge numbers of eating places and many hotels, ranging from the American Hotel and Astor House (for the wealthier visitors) to the Tremont Temperance Hotel (which was self-explanatory) and Florence's (which only welcomed visitors from New Orleans and the South). In 1845 a census had been published in the city: 371,223 souls lived on Manhattan – of which 128,492 were foreigners. They had to live somewhere so more and more hotels, and in particular 'boarding houses' appeared; now in 1849 it was estimated that at least 170,000 hopeful immigrants had landed in New York, looking for life and fortune: more disembarked every single week.

The boarding houses, either big existing houses converted, or sometimes premises specially built, were where many, many of the people arriving daily made their homes; some boarding houses offered simply rooms, some added a communal drawing-room: with luck there was a fireplace for the cold, cold New York winters. There was much criticism from some Americans, from many of their newspapers, and from many visiting commentators, about this phenomenon of 'boarding houses'; they were described as 'a threat to the American home and way of life'. The Church in America further thundered about the 'indisposition of young ladies to undertake the responsibilities and trouble of attending to domestic arrangements'. But still more immigrants arrived daily, and still more boarding houses sprang up. Some offered suites of rooms, kitchens, even baths; many still offered just a room with a coat-hook. As more and more immigrants disembarked, living accommodation became more and more crowded: now some boarding houses had already fallen into fetid slums; by the time unlucky immigrants had settled for (and even been born into) accommodation in wild, unsalubrious places like Five Points, or in the once-elegant Cherry Street near the East River, 'boarding house' was too fine a word by far.

But La Grande Celine certainly was not to be found round Cherry Street or Five Points. Her establishment was in Maiden Lane, near the corner of Broadway. And La Grande Celine soon saw what she should do next. She acquired the lease to the whole house above her eating establishment.

She employed an old friend, Jeremiah, an ex-strongman from the Circus, as her manager and bartender. Finally the following advertisement appeared in all the respectable newspapers:

CELINE'S HOUSE OF REFRESHMENT,
MAIDEN LANE,
cnr BROADWAY

The new owner wishes to advise that the extensively improved Establishment above now has a dining saloon of SUCH HIGH QUALITY AND COMFORT that it cannot be surpassed in the city. Both the food and the decoration will appeal to discerning persons, and gentle Musical Entertainment is offered with your repast on certain evenings.

A special table is screened off for Women Diners, should they prefer.

NB: Persuaded by many friends and visitors, the owner now also offers Tasteful Rooms for lodgers at excellent tariff. Why pay more? Call to View.

PROFESSIONAL WOMEN WELCOME
PROFESSIONAL WOMAN PROPRIETOR.

CELINE'S HOUSE.
MAIDEN LANE

---

*

La Grande Celine opened the big door one sweet April morning in answer to the knocker, and when she understood her visitor was a Frenchman she was (for her reactions were

44

always large) in a paroxysm of delight. No matter Celine had left France with her also flame-haired mother when she was eight, no matter she did not even remember her French father, no matter she could only manage a smattering of French phrases. She was a proud and loyal American citizen, but she had French antecedents and was proud of them: had not the French come to the aid of the American revolution? (And indeed Frenchmen were her weakness: the most passionate, the not-to-be-forgotten, love of her life had been a large, graceful, clever French acrobat with a huge black moustache called *Pierre l'Oiseau*: Pierre-the-bird, and she thought of him still.)

'*Bonjour*, Monsieur Roland!' she exclaimed when he had given his name. 'You are surely welcome. I am Celine Rimbaud, born in France also.'

The elderly French gentleman stepped into the large, picture-covered dining saloon: cheerful paintings of bright flowers, a large rendition of the Niagara Falls, and to his surprise several gaily-coloured posters. A big fireplace, not in use on this pleasant day, lay ready; armchairs and two big sofas were placed nearby, inviting guests. A friendly clock ticked on the marble mantelpiece. Two negro maids were laying thick cutlery and big white serviettes on several large communal tables, and in the corner a surprising sight: a harmonium with pedals – more expected in a chapel perhaps than a dining saloon. A staircase led upwards from this large welcoming room to the rest of the large house. '*Bonjour*, Madame Celine,' he said, noting her most interesting appearance and looking about him gravely, 'this is an agreeable room indeed. You are the proprietor of this establishment, with whom I can make enquiries?'

'I am indeed the sole proprietor. This house was the home of an early Yankee businessman,' she explained proudly, 'and of course it has plumbing, for you know New York has running water since the opening of the reservoir. If you are a new visitor to New York you *must* visit our reservoir for we call it the eighth wonder of the world!'

'I have now been here for quite some time, Madame. And we did indeed walk up to 42nd Street to view with great interest the famous Croton Reservoir soon after we arrived. We are very grateful, always, for plumbing.'

'I myself,' said Celine, 'have eaten in eateries and boarded in boarding houses that would make a strong man weep, and I try to do better,' and then nothing would please her – as they were fellow countrymen – but that they sit in the armchairs and drink a nip of brandy with coffee as they introduced themselves further before they settled to business; she apologised for not speaking to him in their native tongue. They discussed Paris with a sigh (although neither of them had been there for many years), and Madame Celine was even further delighted to find that Monsieur Roland had been born near to the beautiful *Institut de France,* not so very far from the Rue de Conde, where Celine had lived as a young child.

'Ah Monsieur Roland!' she sighed, 'I do not suppose I will ever see my beloved River Seine again – I must make do with the East River and the Hudson!' And then she laughed, loud infectious laughter – 'I am talking rubbish, I haven't laid eyes on France for over thirty-five years!' – so that he too smiled. And they went on to discuss New York with amazement: its growth, its wealth, its varied inhabitants, its own two crowded, exciting, bustling rivers.

'And now what can I do for you, Monsieur Roland?' said Madame Celine coming to business at last, looking at him with much interest from her one bright eye.

'I am, Madame, looking for a suite of rooms to rent, long-term, for seven persons.'

'Seven persons you say!'

'Seven. Five of the persons are females and were most appreciative of your advertisement.' Two women appeared just then, down the staircase, chattering together. They crossed round the side of the tables to the big front door, their skirts rustling pleasantly as they greeted and bowed to Madame Celine and her visitor most cheerfully before going out into the bright morning. One of the women was carrying a violin in a case.

'Five women!' said Celine. 'Your wife, of course. And daughters perhaps?'

'I regret to say I have neither wife nor daughters,' said the dignified old gentleman and Madame Celine's heart paid attention with some interest: Madame Celine's heart always went straight to the point and he was a Frenchman. Younger men, with all their passion and problems, no longer interested her except as fascinating specimens of the human race; she also knew a man not interested in women from twenty paces and Monsieur Roland was not one of them. Madame Celine may not have known it but she gave a very tiny sigh. To be, finally, settled with a handsome, dignified (albeit elderly) French consort here in America would be her dream, he would give class to CELINE'S HOUSE OF REFRESHMENT, he would give class to herself. 'My – companions, Madame,' continued Monsieur Roland, 'are all from England.'

'Ah.' She was sorry to hear that, it was clear.

'The reason we were so taken with your advertisement is that two of them are professional women also.'

'My, I am glad to hear that. Do tell me, what is their profession?'

He glanced at the posters. 'They are a mother and a daughter, and they work in a circus.'

Celine's mouth opened in surprise. Was this strange group of seven to be a *circus troupe?* 'Why, Monsieur Roland, can that be true? This is surely meant to be! Which circus? For I myself am from the circus! Once upon a time the circus was my life!' And the black, jewelled eye-patch itself flashed with delight and she indicated the posters. 'Mind you, the time for circuses is not so propitious as it once was. Look! *Look* at this announcement, it is trying to promote a new circus here in New York. I was reading it and ready to spit when I heard the knocker.' And she passed a newspaper to him and pointed with her very ringed finger to the bottom of a large advertisement.

> **The Manager pledges himself that this Circus shall be of a strictly moral character and free from the many Objections frequently made to Entertainments of this description.**
>
> **No females attached to this company, to assure Absolute Propriety in the performance and among the Performers. Also no Negro variety acts.**

'Is that any way, Monsieur, to advertise a *circus!*'

'Indeed, Madame Celine.'

'And look here!' She pointed again. '**This circus does not cater to deprived tastes!** Good God above! The circus is an honourable profession as I am sure you know, stretching back to the Romans and the ancient Egyptians and beyond! And we all laugh at what that Phineas Barnum has done to his

American Museum just along Broadway!' In her exuberance she jabbed her finger in the uptown direction. 'He has – I thought I was dreaming when I first heard – *removed liquor from the Museum Premises* – everybody knows there used to be a dozen bars (not to mention available women) and – because of the new "respectability" which unfortunately has emerged in this city, aping the defeated English as far as I am concerned – he is now presenting nightly *Temperance Melodramas* alongside his man-lion and his mermaid and his midgets! Have you heard of such a thing? He puts them on in what he now calls his "lecture room" so that respectable people can say to themselves they are attending a lecture – when what they are really doing is going to the theatre of course, of which they have now decided to disapprove. Temperance Melodramas indeed!'

'Indeed, Madame Celine! I remember being informed many months ago of his Temperance Melodramas.' Again he was smiling at her exuberance.

'Forgive my passion!' And she laughed again her loud friendly laugh.

'I myself understand very well your *fureur*, Madame. I believe my friends are very much of your mind. It is interesting always how soon "respectability" inserts itself into even modern and democratic societies.'

And Madame Celine nodded. They were in perfect agreement, she and this Frenchman.

'What circus is it, Monsieur?' she asked again. She wondered if some of them would be acrobats or midgets; and what might he have been himself in his day, this wonderful old gentleman? A fortune-teller perhaps?

'You have heard perhaps of Monsieur Silas P Swift?' he asked.

'Ah, Silas.' She nodded. 'He is a madman, but a showman. He was once very successful here in New York, with many exotic acts – he even tried to employ me in my glory days! His circus at least is still going, has not had to close. But I understand he has had to go touring across the country doing one-night stands to make his money these days.'

'That is true, I am afraid. They had some success in some other cities for a time but now they travel nightly, we understand. However, now Mr Swift has yet another plan afoot – he is a man of many plans I have noticed – he has last week arrived back in New York and now we are informed that he has called the circus back also. We are glad of course for we have missed our friends. We are presuming that perhaps a circus venue here has become vacant at short notice.'

'Heavens! Is he going to take a leaf out of Phineas Barnum's book and call his circus a Temperance Meeting?'

Monsieur Roland smiled. 'Who knows? We are all used to Mr Silas P Swift and his changes of plan, I and my companions. We were indeed prosperous when the circus thrived in New York as it did for many months. Since Mr Swift began touring we have tried various smaller hotels but I am afraid we are still living beyond our means. So whatever Mr Silas P Swift's newest plans we feel now that our own rooms in a boarding house would be a more sensible idea.'

Celine could not hide her delight. 'You have been a circus performer yourself, Monsieur Roland? And the others too? There are seven of you, you said?'

He understood the American way. They asked many questions: they of course wanted to know if you had money to pay but, always, they were also curious in a way that was different from the more contained English people he had been used to for so long. It had startled him at first: *how old are you? how much money do you earn?* but now he was used to it. Madame Celine may have been of French extraction but she was certainly an American. 'I am what is known as a Mesmerist, Madame.'

She clasped her hands to her heart in excitement. The rings sparkled in the bright light of the fine, spring morning. 'You put people into trances? You – why, what is that modern word I have heard – *hypnotise* people? In the circus?'

'My work has been mostly in hospitals over the years. I was able to help surgeons with operations. I can mesmerise many patients so that they do not feel pain under the knife.'

'Ah, Monsieur Roland.' Madame Celine, who had known much pain, sighed and nodded. 'That I had known you earlier in my life!'

Monsieur Roland smiled wryly. 'I am afraid that the discovery first of ether and now of other gases as anaesthetics has meant I work in hospitals very seldom these days, so I now have my own small mesmeric practice in Nassau Street. I can still assist people to deal with pain of various kinds.'

For a moment Madame Celine simply looked at this man. She saw his white hair, his wise, kind eyes and his upright back as he sat opposite her. *And is he not French? How well he would suit me!* It was at that exact moment that Madame Celine Rimbaud, who fell in love very often, fell in love (in her way) with Monsieur Alexander Roland.

'And – your other friends, Monsieur Roland?' Her heart was beating. *Is there a mistress? He is French! There is bound to be a mistress.*

'We are a group of people who have, through chance, been together for many years. As well as the two circus performers there are two elderly ladies' (her eyes shone with relief) 'and the daughter of one of these old ladies, Miss Amaryllis

Spoons,' (she heard his voice soften, it was almost painful to her) 'manages our household most admirably.'

'I see.'

'Our unusual family,' – the word *family* stabbed at her expectations – 'also includes a Police Detective from London, Inspector Arthur Rivers.'

Her eyes hardened, or rather the one eye he could see looked suddenly very stern. *Definitely not a circus troupe then.* 'Celine's House is not an establishment for a police officer, Monsieur Roland. Other people in the boarding house may feel uneasy. Members of the police in New York are not its most popular citizens. Monsieur, you are a foreigner, you perhaps do not understand, do you know they don't even wear a uniform, not even a police cap? Only a small copper star as identification – only a star, because they know they are not popular!'

Monsieur Roland stood regretfully. 'Then I am so sorry to have wasted your valuable time, Madame, but it has been a great pleasure to meet you. Although he has often, because of his work, to stay in the police department near City Hall, this police officer is part of our family.'

That word again. Family. Almost she let him go, despite her romantic heart. She disliked the New York police intensely. But then she saw again his – she could hardly articulate the word to herself – *beauty*. Who could have thought that La Grande Celine with all her life's adventures would one day find an old man beautiful?

'Monsieur Roland.' And she stood also.

'Madame Celine.'

'I do remember that there were kind policemen in London, in their uniforms, guarding the peace.'

'Inspector Rivers is one of the kindest men it has been my fortune to meet.'

52

'Perhaps he could help to guard the peace in this city! There have been several uncontained riots.'

'I believe they ask his opinion on such things, among other matters.'

'I see.' She was considering. 'Seven of you, you say.' Her arms were folded, she tapped her fingers. 'So that is, let me understand you: two gentlemen: that is you and the police officer. Two old ladies and the daughter of one. And just the two circus performers: a mother and her daughter.' He nodded, did not elucidate the relationships further, or explain how such a disparate grouping might have come together, though La Grande Celine immediately resolved to investigate these matters at a later date. For now she only said: 'Could your old ladies climb to the top?'

'Of this fine house?'

'Yes. It is five flights of stairs, I regret to say.'

'I believe they could. Their physical faculties are still in working order.' He did not mention mental faculties.

'You, of course, could do so?' But now she was smiling, teasing him, tossing her somehow-still-flame-coloured hair; the pearl on her eye-patch flashed as it caught the spring sunlight shining in through the windows.

'I think I could manage stairs.' He smiled gently back.

'It was a foolish question. I see that you could. The top of this house is a large attic, there are four small bedrooms and a sitting-room, and it is about to come free. There are even cooking facilities although I do assure you that the food here in my own dining saloon is unparalleled in both quality and value and many of my guests eat here on a regular basis at special terms. And your own water closet!' and she opened her arms wide as if she was offering paradise. 'As fate would have it the top floor will become free because in three or four days the whole family who have lived there – including two young children – are setting out overland for California! Two young children! This is the mad world of the Gold Rush, Monsieur! Of course we would have to agree terms.'

'Of course we must discuss terms and stairs, but I assure you we are an intrepid group. I would bring Miss Amaryllis Spoons to consider the rooms with you.'

Madame Celine was quite certain she would not care for Miss Amaryllis Spoons. On the other hand she did not want to let her countryman go from her.

'Very well, Monsieur Roland. Let us see if we can come to some accommodation.' She walked with him to the big front door. 'You are, if I may say so, a strange group, this – family of yours. But of course there are very many strange groups in New York.'

Monsieur Roland said nothing more but he smiled gravely at her once again and La Grande Celine suddenly wanted to seize his hand and kiss it – but restrained herself from doing any such thing.

La Grande Celine and Miss Amaryllis Spoons got on like a house on fire as the expression went (especially in New York where there were very many fires indeed – the fire bell at the top of City Hall, where there was always a watchman, rang at all times of the night and day and volunteer firemen pulled competing fire engines and fought each other to get to the street water pump first).

'Call me Rillie,' said Miss Spoons at once. 'Everybody calls me Rillie.'

'Call me Celine,' said La Grande Celine.

It was impossible not to like Rillie – small, round, warm, bustling and so loving to her poor elderly mother who (it was

54

clear to Celine almost at once) was quite mad. The other old lady was named Regina (which was rather inappropriate for democratic America, Celine thought). Regina was rather loud and odd-looking but not obviously mad in the ordinary sense of the word. Rillie, and Monsieur Roland, and these two old ladies moved into the attic of the boarding house in Maiden Lane as soon as the Californian-bound family left. The new boarders were assisted up the stairs with their belongings, including a bright yellow singing canary in a cage, by the manager-bartender Jeremiah and by the English policeman, Inspector Arthur Rivers, who was kind just as Monsieur Roland had described and (Celine noted) a very fine-looking man indeed, and as for some reason he did not even wear his police star most of the time the other residents need not be alarmed. He courteously explained to Madame Celine that he often worked at night and would be coming and going at odd hours. Madame Celine decided at once that he was not like ordinary New York policemen, but trustworthy rather. So (even though he was English) she gave him a copy of the long iron front door key. The two other ladies would be on their way back to New York next week with the circus, as instructed by Mr Silas P Swift, and now, in Maiden Lane, their new home awaited them. As Celine took up a welcoming plate of corn-cakes to the attic she observed that Monsieur Roland took the tiny corner room that was in truth more like a cupboard or a cell: a narrow bed, a coat-stand and a window in the roof. He said it suited him admirably. Celine's heart half-rose: *no mistress perhaps?* They were still unpacking: there were no further clues that Celine could ponder over.

As for Rillie Spoons (who delighted in most things about America), she was captivated by La Grande Celine: her passions, her French pretensions, her rings, her flashing eye-patch, her loud laugh and her kindness. Rillie saw at once what effect Monsieur Roland had on their landlady, and although she was perhaps not entirely forthcoming (for Rillie knew Monsieur Roland had had one great love in his long life) she was able to assure Celine truthfully that although she had known Monsieur Roland for many years and knew a great deal about his work, she believed he had never been married.

Celine sang old French songs she had forgotten she knew as she oversaw the negro maids.

Frère Jacques
Dormez-vous?

she sang as she shucked oysters with the cooks for oyster pies.

7

Celine's House, Maiden Lane

Dear Brother Alfie,
Well Alfie this will be a surprise for you. It's
me! Regina Tyrone, your sister, late of the
Cleveland Street Workhouse!! Now I suppose
you will faint!

As I have not been able to find you here in
New York all this long time, and as I have now
got a real, proper home address in New York
and not a hotel, I have today decided at last to
write to the big New York Post Office, in the
hope that you might collect mail there, and
will remember yours truly and come and find
me where I now live, Celine's House, Maiden
Lane. I been down the docks and quays many
many times since I come to New York, but
can't ever find news of you, Alfie-boy, maybe
you aint a sailor anymore but a rich farmer
hundreds of miles away maybe! You always
said you was going to make your Fortune.

Alfie you will be very surprised to find that I am in America as well as you, for the last time you seen me I was in my glory days all those years ago in London, when I was writing them street songs and paper poems about Murder down Drury Lane and Seven Dials and that. I made a fair living there, I remember you was surprised to see me, a girl, earning good money! See, all that psalm-reading and hymn-singing and bible-study our Father whacked into us done me good after all Alfie, ha! I never told anyone our father was a Keeper in the Workhouse and that's where we lived, and how he treated us.

You will not imagine I got to New York too. The ladies I was with, good-hearted they are whatever the papers said when we had our trouble, they got an Offer. I'm thinking Alfie, when I used to write those murder poems for the penny papers I never considered the actual people I was writing about, course not – here – remember the one you liked? You said it conjured a great picture in your head.

SHE TOOK A BAR AND SMASHED HIS HEAD
THE BRAINS TURNED INTO SOUP
WHAT A WITCH, SHE LEFT HIM DEAD
NOW SHE WILL FACE THE LOOP.

but maybe he done bad things to her, well I never thought of that in them days, I got two shillings for that from the Printer, he said he could use it for more than one murder if he changed the words ever so slightly!

Alfie, you heard of this new Poet Mr Poe? He writes such amazing poems that I got my fingers really itching again to take up a pen myself. I found this one called "The Raven" in a paper, in case you don't know it – but I remember you loved a good piece of poetry, you might've seen it too – a bit of it goes, I learnt it by heart, couldn't help myself it's so musical:

> And the raven, never flitting, still is sitting,
> Still is sitting
> On the pallid bust of Pallas just above my Chamber door
> And his eyes have all the seeming of a demon
> That's been dreaming,
> And the lamp-light o'er him streaming throws
> His shadow on the floor. . . .

dont know who Pallas is but it don't matter really, "pallid bust of Pallas" aint that poetic and aint the poem good and scary Alfie? "a demon that's been dreaming . . ."

My two ladies got involved in something scary in London Alfie, luckily the truth came out but they were ruined in their fine work, and we were ruined of our fine house with an inside toilet Alfie, ha! Cordelia, she was a Mesmerist and kind to sick people. Rillie she was the manager. Gwenlliam, such a nice girl, she is Cordelia's daughter, and that was part of the Scandal, now the mother and the daughter work in the circus. Rillie's mother, Mrs Spoons, she's demented, but no trouble really, I've looked after her more or less for more years than I can think, they can leave her with me and I can manage her even though now she don't know me even with a little flash of memory. Sometimes I used to see it, that flash, and she'd know it was her old friend, but not now, poor thing. Also long ago I gave Cordelia and Rillie some money to start their business but they've repaid me a hundredfold, or An Hundredfold as it says in the Bible! and they got rich, but after the scandal they got poor. Then they got the Offer, then we all came to New York.

And also we live with two gentlemen in our boarding house! One is an old Frenchy man but he's kind. He was a very famous Mesmerist and he was like their teacher when we was all younger. The other man is a Police Detective – there! bet that's startled you Alfie! But kind mind – the thing is, he is actually married to Cordelia but he works and lives partly at the police department and she tours with the circus. But he comes to us when he can, and soon Cordelia and

Gwenlliam will be back from the circus again and we'll all be together in this new boarding house we've found, it's nice, it's like a little home. He's a good man, our policeman, but sometimes something in his eyes is sad, I never say anything mind.

New York is a bustling place indeed, lots of Murders here too I see, no wonder Mr Poe writes so good, I still read them penny papers of course just like I used to, they're much ruder in America, the papers, aint they? but all the same: now I know what I know Alfie, about what they put in the papers, I don't believe everything I read even if I enjoy reading it! and anyway now that I've read Mr Poe I wish I could write better and more thrilling.

Yes it is very fine, life is very fine. But Alfie, I'm thinking, the old lady is becoming frailer and frailer, what say she dies? They might not need me I wonder? They think I'm old of course, my hair is grey now Alfie ha! I wonder what you look like? But I aint old, I still got all my faculties and facilities and I'm much sharper than they all give me credit for. I did have money under the mattress too, I brought it to America in me big hat, I made a lot of money Alfie when I was doing the poems, I aint got much now though Alfie, to be honest, but a tiny bit still under me mattress here. I aint asking you for money. But I would like to find you Alfie. Just in case. I been really looking for you., and for so long. I hope you aint in trouble, but you was always a good boy I'm thinking.

Yours truly,
Your Sister,
Regina.

Course I'm thinking a lot could have happened because I just worked it out, it's fifty years aint it Alfie, since we was young and seen each other last, it's hard to think that is so, oh Alfie wouldn't it be good to have a sing-song like we used to, after all these years . . .

8

GREEN-GROCER the signs always said outside.

Cauliflowers. Lettuce. Celery. Spinach. Beans. And cabbages, piles of large, green cabbages. Green vegetables at the Green-Grocer: good and firm at the top perhaps, soggy and stinking at the bottom perhaps, all piled up in large baskets next to tubs of big carrots and onions, outside the shops on the corners: the Green-Grocer shops. These particular establishments with their green vegetables on display outside were dotted about certain areas of Lower Manhattan; inside the Green-Grocers, among dry goods and lard, somewhat more liquid refreshments were available, especially to certain, special visitors. And people living in these particular areas of New York came in, picked over the cabbages and beans and spinach, acquired lard and the cheapest flour and the imported salt and sugar. They did not comment, the customers, the mostly female customers (except perhaps with a flick of their knowing eyes, or even a toss of the head), at the whisky fumes that seeped out from behind a dark curtain at the back of the shop, at the pungent smell of cigar smoke. They did not comment, say, at the sound of men's voices – mostly murmurs, occasionally raised, that came from behind dark curtains: that was not the customers' business. Buying groceries from the Green-Grocer, that was the customers' business.

GREEN-GROCER the signs always said outside.

Mention had begun to be made, behind the curtains of the Green-Grocer shops on the Lower East Side among the whisky fumes and the cigar smoke, of an abomination that should raise the hackles of all true Americans: of an *English* policeman, working on the docks in New York – and causing trouble. He would have to be dealt with.

It is a strange price that is exacted, sometimes, by love. It is not clear perhaps, at first, what the price will be.

Detective-Inspector Arthur Rivers, late of Scotland Yard, had begun working for the New York Municipal Police Force because he had fallen in love with a woman who had become so notorious that it was not safe for her to be seen in public in London, but who had, because the Impresario Silas P Swift certainly knew great publicity when he saw it, been quickly offered work in MR SILAS P SWIFT'S AMAZING CIRCUS in America. Cordelia Preston, mesmerist and now circus performer, had been acquitted of a murder she did not commit by a jury in London, in a case that Arthur Rivers had been involved in for the prosecution. During the few weeks of that terrible trial he had been made aware of her courage and her strength and her wild, unwise passion and her unimaginable pain. The trial was a travesty, much inflamed by a prurient press, in particular because the murdered nobleman was married to a cousin of Queen Victoria. When Arthur Rivers had asked Cordelia Preston to marry him he had feared for her safety: he had been putting in a new pane of glass in her house in Bloomsbury, London, because outside this house people who had read of this scarlet, abominable woman in the newspapers came and stood and pointed and shouted and threw turds and cabbages and rocks at her windows and one man walked up and down outside the house with a large painted board that said: **REPENT!** When he had asked her to marry him, as the crowds shouted abuse outside, she looked at him as if he was a madman.

Perhaps, indeed, he had been mad.

Arthur Rivers' first wife had died. He had two daughters, Milly and Faith, and he and his somewhat tight-lipped (he tried not to mind about this when he was so grateful for her assistance) unmarried sister-in-law, Agnes, had looked after the two girls as best they could. Arthur Rivers loved his daughters, but when he was appointed as one of the first detectives in the new police division of Scotland Yard much was left to Aunt Agnes. It was not the girls' fault that their mother had died and that their aunt had come to have such an influence over them in their most formative years. Agnes had taught them to play hymns on the new pianoforte he had optimistically bought: he had rather hoped for more popular airs, but that was her temperament. However when Agnes had encouraged the girls to skewer beautiful butterflies from their small garden in Marylebone with a sharp pin and frame them on the wall of their parlour for decoration (this being a suitable activity, she assured him, for respectable young ladies), their father knew he was lost. In time both daughters met and married perfectly pleasant-seeming young men and left the house in Marylebone; he had become a proud grandfather – they called the boy Arthur also. And the sister-in-law presumed she would go on looking after the police detective. Perhaps (although he had not thought of this), she hoped for more. Whatever her innermost desires, the sister-in-law's tight lips became more pursed still when she understood that Arthur was not to continue living in Marylebone either: *he was about to travel to America with a scandalous murderess!*

'Cordelia Preston was not, ever, charged with murder, Agnes.'

'The newspapers were full of it!'

'The newspapers are not necessarily a guide to the truth, Agnes. I have told you that many times. You and the girls shall meet her, you will see her for yourself. And whatever happens, Agnes, you know my home here is always your home also.'

The meeting however did not go well: both daughters and their aunt were, understandably perhaps, implacably opposed to Arthur going anywhere at all but their home in Marylebone; they had read so many defamatory, disgraceful, embarrassing headlines about this shameful, alluring woman (for at least a week the whole of London read of nothing else) that to have her in their respectable house was unbearable, and they were terrified that their neighbours might catch a glimpse of her. To make it more embarrassing still, none of the three women had been able to take their eyes from this anti-heroine because she had deep, black eyes and a limpid paleness that unsettled them; and one startling white streak of hair shone amongst the dark. They had not been able to take their eyes from her because although she was no longer young, and although she was of course so shameful, she was beautiful.

Since Arthur Rivers had sailed away to his new life, Agnes wrote regular, plaintive letters to her brother-in-law. He was a grandfather, his place was in London, Agnes was unwell: he owed it to her to be in London, he was a grandfather again, and again: were these poor children to grow up without knowing him, did he owe them nothing? He replied regularly, enclosing money regularly, and sometimes drawings of sailing ships for his grandson, little Arthur. And he told his London family about this great, new city: this New York.

66

Arthur Rivers and Cordelia Preston had been quietly married when they arrived; Cordelia's daughter, Gwenlliam (an old Welsh name) was glad witness (though for publicity requirements the bride had remained 'Miss Cordelia Preston'). But Arthur knew (all the odd, second family he now belonged to knew, except perhaps Cordelia Preston herself) that his love gave her strength in dark times when memories of her past threatened to overwhelm her. No-one knew how she felt about Arthur Rivers exactly, not Arthur Rivers either. Love had brought such damage in her life, he sometimes thought, that she could not consider such a thing again. He loved Cordelia Preston: he saw yet again her strength and stoicism when she joined Silas P Swift's Circus. But very occasionally, she and her closest friend Rillie Spoons would laugh now about something in their rather chancy past: it was then that Arthur glimpsed the exuberance and the joy and the wild, jaunty, confident freedom that must also have been part of her character. Sometimes she wept silently in the night in his arms; always he held her tightly: he knew all that had happened to her: he could only hold her and she did not speak. So Arthur did not speak of some things either. He did not speak of his own past life. He did not speak of the letters from Agnes in London; he collected them from the big Post Office, and kept them locked in his office.

But sometimes he felt as if a hundred tiny shards of broken glass lay there, in the space between them.

He had part of her heart only. He loved Cordelia Preston but there were lonely frays and shadows now, in his own heart, in this strange land.

When Detective-Inspector Arthur Rivers had first arrived in New York and was asked the inevitable question: 'What do you think of our wonderful country, our America?' he always answered, 'Unbelievable!' People always took it as a compliment, and so he let it lie. And it was true that he was filled with amazement and wonder by much of the big, new, exciting city with its tall telegraph poles and its glorious water reservoir and its glittering, raucous Broadway with the milling crowds and shining new stores and the hurrying, hurrying, hustling, bustling loud New Yorkers, the enthusiasm and the noise, the ebullience and the building sites, the selling, the laughing, the shouting, the headlines.

However. In London, the English policeman had understood things. He understood the social structure of his country, and he had recognised how things worked. Especially in the Police Force. He knew – of course he knew – of the small dishonours and misdemeanours of the London Constabulary back across the Atlantic Ocean, and indeed those misdemeanours in his own small world of Scotland Yard. There were always bad policemen but he worked, on the whole, with good trustworthy men. And there were, on the whole, good trustworthy masters. But here, in this wild exciting dangerous city, this New York, his mooring was much more slippery, because he never quite understood the underlying labyrinths of the policing of New York and he never quite knew for certain who was being paid, by whom, for which particular services rendered.

One of the Police Captains, a pleasant, straight-forward man who was himself very pleased when messages came from London that one of their new detectives would be arriving in New York (for news of Scotland Yard and its activities had reached America), was nevertheless blunt when Arthur raised (as delicately as possible) the subject of corruption.

'I cannot halt it,' said the Captain. 'It is the nature of a new democracy.'

The Englishman shook his head, as if to clear it. He had been a policeman for many years, and understood that things were different in New York, both in the police force and in the populace, but he had never before seen such open civic corruption – and he had never before seen one man bite another's nose off, and spit it back in his face.

And he had never seen anything like the port of New York.

At the bottom of the island of Manhattan, with the Hudson River on one side and the East River on the other, New York operated what was probably the most prosperous, and the wildest, seaport in the world. Ship-yards, breweries, iron-works, factories, slaughter-houses all stood on the shore of the East River; hundreds upon hundreds of large and small vessels importing goods and people into the new world clamoured and battled for space on the river piers; hundreds of other ships left for the old world packed with raw cotton and grain. Shantymen whistled 'Blow the Man Down' as they stepped ashore jingling their wages and looking for entertainment. South American ships jostled African ships, carrying strange fruits and spices; Mexicans and Arabians fought with sailors from Europe over portage, occasional knives flashed in the sunlight – and all that hectic, chaotic, continuous maritime activity meant that there was a huge, ever-growing, spiralling income pouring into downtown New York: money money *money* – in the last year alone the port taxes were known to have reached twenty million dollars, an inconceivable sum.

It did not take a detective long to understand that very much of these taxes poured straight into the hands of the City officials: the Aldermen: the men who had been voted to office in this new democracy. And it did not take a detective long to observe that the Aldermen, *above all else*, intended to stay in office, once they had got there. It was clear, to put it bluntly, that the city was wild with unorthodox (let us say) financial transactions.

He saw these wealthy, democratic 'Fathers of the City', the Aldermen, proudly marching in Civic Parades up Broadway with brass bands, waving red and white and blue American flags and singing lustily:

> *Hail Colombia, happy land!*
> *Hail ye heroes, heav'n-born band*
> *Who fought and bled in freedom's cause*
> *Who fought and bled in freedom's cause . . .*

And then it did not take a detective long to see those same City Fathers requiring to be paid in plain paper parcels for building contracts and ferry franchises and liquor permits and saloon licences and leases and land. They also expected to be paid by the city employees to whom they gave jobs – including policemen. Inspector Rivers therefore found to his amazement that in New York many policemen *paid* to become policemen – because they knew they would soon receive very much money other than their salaries: every brothel and flophouse and shady saloon and illegal premise and hopeful entrepreneur in New York paid money in plain paper parcels to policemen, in order to trade.

These City Fathers were nevertheless known to give as well as to receive: large sums of money were also paid out by them in secret parcels to the people whom they needed to keep themselves in power. All sorts of people received parcels of money from the City Fathers, right down to the Immigrant Runners (those deeply sympathetic meeters and greeters with Irish accents waiting on the docks).

'Welcome!' cried the Runners who met the hopeful, often

ill, bewildered, new immigrants as they came ashore. 'Welcome to America! Follow me, friend, the Holy Mother smiles upon you!' and they led the new arrivals so kindly, so very welcomingly, to food and shelter. But Arthur soon understood that these smiling welcomers were paid money for each of the number of disembarking, often desperate people they brought to the ward's feeding kitchens and doss-houses – and the names of the new arrivals were very carefully written in big notebooks. Grateful, exhausted travellers, so many of them Irish, who had travelled so far from famine and wretchedness for a new life in a new country, *of course* promised to vote for their benefactors when the vote was required. And that's why their names were written very carefully in the big notebooks – just in case they forgot their promises.

'This is how our American way of life works, Art,' repeated the police captain when the Englishman questioned him again. 'Just look at our prosperity! Look at the port! Look at Broadway – one of the most beautiful, flourishing streets in the world! All part of our democracy.'

'Democracy? Surely, sir, in *any* civilised society the police, of all people, should be impartially appointed to uphold the laws of a city with a salary from that city.'

'America is a new society, Art,' the American said, 'we are trying new ways. Remember: every man in New York has the vote, every one of them,' (he did not mean black men of course) 'and every immigrant man can register to vote also. And if they don't like what is happening they can vote the city bosses out and the city bosses know that. It's not like that in your country I think! Your Mr Charles Dickens came here some years ago and worried, as I see you do too, Art, about rule by everybody, not just by the intelligent people of a certain

71

class. That argument depends, it seems to me, on your definition of intelligent.'

The Englishman had bowed his head. He was in New York now, not London. 'I understand what you are saying, sir.'

'Art, please don't call me "sir". How many times do I have to remind you!' (Another thing Arthur Rivers had to get used to: the immediate casual usage of people's first names as soon as they met: nobody had ever called Arthur Rivers *Art* in his life.) 'My name is Washington Jackson. Everyone calls me Wash.'

Arthur Rivers had stumbled as he tried the new way. 'Well, sir – Wash' (*Wash?*) '– I do understand this is a new country with new ways. But I am a policeman, which I have always thought of as an honourable profession. Apart from money being accepted as bribes, I see here vicious, violent clashes taking place night after night between rival gangs of the wildest of men – I have seen violence here worse than in the most violent parts of London – and the police, the supposed guardians of the peace, if they do show any interest at all, are not in any way impartial! In my country the police are expected to be an impersonal authority. Here they *take sides!*'

'But Art, our policemen are members of their own communities. That is how the job of police officer works here. They are appointed in their own communities, they live there, and sometimes use their fists there, in their own communities. Is it surprising if they protect their own families first, and their own people?' Washington Jackson was very pleasant; he spoke quite kindly, but also firmly. 'Listen, Arthur, on some days at least forty boats are disgorging passengers on to our shores at the same time. There are *hundreds of thousands of immigrants arrived here*, especially Irish immigrants, and more by the day, nobody is refused entry, America needs people, but this unhindered arrival of so many foreigners leads to huge problems in our city – which you may consider are dealt with in an unorthodox manner. And yet, one day, some of today's arriving immigrants – the smart ones, the industrious ones, the lucky ones – will inevitably get the chance to run the police force and the city too! Do you think that chance exists for every man in London? I think you need to know a little more about the different problems of our city before you criticise it, Art. Balance up all these freedoms and hopes with the odd unattended riot!

'Now, let's get down to business. I hope you are going to stay in New York. I badly want you to work for us.' Arthur understood some answer was required.

'I am – interested to understand how other police forces operate.'

'Well then! Let us teach you!' And he repeated again: 'I want you to agree to work for us, Art, but you need to know something of the underbelly of New York before you decide – though I hope you will not go running home to London again in terror!'

'I try never to run from any situation, Wash,' said Arthur Rivers dryly.

'Then we are lucky to know you.' Washington Jackson studied the honourable Englishman. 'I could take you to Five Points, the place of no hope, the end of the line where Irish scum live in buildings that are sinking back into a filled-in swamp that has seeped out again. The vicious gangs there, the Plug Uglies, the Dead Rabbits – they're all very experienced at stomping on people's faces with their hobnailed boots, or gouging people's eyes out. But – I think we'll give Five Points a miss, I've got other plans for you and you can see all the

73

stomping and gouging you like down on the docks. That's where I want you, Art, down on the docks.' The detective's face showed no emotion at his fate.

'I'll take you through the Bowery first though,' said Wash, 'because that's just as wild as Five Points but there's still hope and singing and a bit of laughter in the Bowery – they don't like the British, mind, but we'll protect you! Unlike in Five Points, many of the gang members in the Bowery have got jobs – no-hope jobs, sweeps and butchers' boys, but jobs nevertheless – and they might stamp on your face and knife you in the back and throw pepper in your eyes but they still know how to enjoy themselves. Let's go.'

He sent out an order; a large group of disparate men congregated in the yard below. Inspector Rivers looked puzzled as he stared out of the window.

'We do not wear uniforms here, Art, as you observe.'

'Why is that, sir?'

'Wash! Call me Wash! Uniforms remind people of things they want to forget. Like people giving orders; forgive me Art if I am frank: uniforms remind them still of the British. It's not just the public, the men themselves don't want it either. We did indeed once try uniforms but people, I'm afraid,' the Captain smiled wryly, 'jeered and laughed in the street and after that the police men were adamant: they refused to wear them. We wear a copper star on our jackets. For identification purposes only. So: we shall not be wearing uniforms on this little jaunt of ours, but we shall, I do assure you – it would not be safe otherwise where we are intending to take you – we shall be armed with our nightsticks.' He produced his own, a sturdy club made – he told Arthur – of locust wood. 'Look at it, Art: hard, long-lasting, and' – he brought it down with a ringing thud against the wall beside them – 'it makes a loud and unmistakable sound, especially against stone, so it's a good weapon to have in the street, bang it on the cobbles or street walls and other police will come running.' And indeed at that moment an officer did come running into the room from further along the hall; Wash explained he had been giving a demonstration and they all laughed and the policeman went away again. 'And we shall not stay long at any of these places, for which you will probably be grateful. *Pigs*, I believe your Mr Charles Dickens called the people who live in these areas. He went to Five Points and described it as human pigs living in squalor with real pigs – mind you, I am led to understand that his nose was out of joint because he felt he didn't receive "due deference" in America. We don't do deference here.' Captain Washington Jackson was reaching under his desk for something. 'Actually Arthur, I have a gun also. I carry this quietly for it is not officially sanctioned, but because we're going to end up on the docks, where hatchets and spiked clubs are the norm, I'll be happier with a gun. Let's go!'

The un-uniformed police contingent with their nightsticks set out in broad daylight towards the Bowery area, which they heard, loud and wild, before they actually arrived: yelling, fighting, music, screams, rattling clattering carts, eruptions, shouts of laughter, shouts of rage.

Much entertainment was obviously available in the Bowery: Arthur saw grand theatres that had seen better days, smaller halls advertising melodramas and musicals and dancing. **MACBETH!** cried one hoarding illustrated with a crude drawing of a woman partially undressed and clutching a dagger. **NIGGER MINSTRELS! (no Blacks)** cried another. **BEER GARDEN!** cried a third hoarding, offering as much beer as a person could consume straight from the hose for three cents. And above so many of the buildings, large or small, the flag of America fluttered proudly, the red and white stripes and a blue square of white stars: the flag of the new democracy.

In all the loud, noisy alleys there were filthy basement clubs and saloons at the bottom of rotting tenements, full of vociferous voices and violins. Dangerous-looking women congregated by a pawn-shop; some seemed (to Inspector Rivers' surprised observation) to be casually filing their nails into sharp points as they called out obscene invitations to the police officers who called back good-naturedly. A band was playing in some wild, overgrown gardens, drums and trumpets, people singing anti-British songs with gusto:

> *I met with Napoleon Bonaparte and he took me by the*
> *   hand*
> *And he said 'How's Poor olde Ireland, and how does she*
> *   stand?'*
> *'She's the most distressful country that ever yet was seen*
> *For they're hanging men and women for the Wearing of*
> *   the Green.'*

In the Bowery then, there was music, as Wash had promised. And energy – a large group of young, rather oddly dressed men – roistering dandies almost – swaggered past full of life and cheek: striped trousers, bright shirts, slicked down hair; some of them tipped extraordinary, rather battered, stove-pipe hats to the police contingent: 'Wearing your little copper badges, gentlemen?' they called and laughter echoed after them.

'That's some of the Bowery Boys,' said Washington Jackson quietly. 'One of the biggest gangs, stompers and knifers and pepper-throwers all of them, tough as guts and wild and young – muggers, thieves, counterfeit money-carriers. They're usually volunteer firemen as well, many groups have their own fire-engine – and they've been known to kill each other to get to the street pump first! They send a runner to sit on the pump and fight off the others, while they pull their own particular fire engines along to the blaze! In the Bowery they'd far rather the houses burnt down than that they should lose the race, in fact they probably often start the fires themselves for the hell of it!'

'Are they all Irish in the Bowery?'

'No – although we often call them all together the *b'hoys*, the Bowery B'hoys – but there are, as in many of the gangs, all sorts of other immigrants: French, Italian, German, a few black men sometimes, all mixed in with the Irish – *and* in the Bowery gangs in particular, nativists: Native Americans.' Inspector Rivers looked startled.

'Natives?'

'By Native Americans,' explained Washington Jackson, and he laughed, 'you as an Englishman may think I mean the original Indians, who are all but disappeared, but no – the term is used here proudly by those who were born in America. They see themselves as the real Americans and they call themselves, with none of the sense of superiority that no doubt you as an Englishman see in the usage of the word "native", *Native Americans*. I myself am proud to call myself a Native American.'

Arthur Rivers digested this. 'So what ties all these different boys from the Bowery together without them killing each other?'

The captain shrugged. 'Youth, energy: who can drink the most beer, shout the loudest, bite the heads off rats, never say die, all that heroic stuff! They have all the knives and the bludgeons and the big boots – and guns too, some of them – but here in the Bowery they like best to fight with their fists. And then on Saturday nights – like all young men with energy and a little bit of money – they put on their best clothes and meet the girls and dance the new dances in the Bowery dance-halls – the waltz may even still be disapproved of in Astor Place, all that holding-girls-tight business and gliding about with them in an immoral manner, but the waltz is hot stuff in the Bowery!' In a crowd by one of the theatres, where gaily-dressed young women with baskets mingled with the top-hatted *b'hoys*, somebody suddenly screamed wildly, but whether it was excitement or terror it was hard to tell.

'That's the Bowery, Art: rough and tough and full of life. Now: the real point of this excursion: we're going down to the dock area.' The police captain gave orders to his men and they set off again, this time towards the East River, some of them winking at the Bowery women as if they perhaps knew them intimately, and the policemen themselves whistling 'The Wearing of the Green' as they marched. Arthur Rivers had worked in many of the wild streets in London but he felt that he was indeed in a strange land as the noise of the Bowery echoed still behind them.

'Good God!' was all he said when they got to Cherry Street.

'This was once one of the most elegant parts of New York,' observed the captain mildly. 'But now Water Street, Cherry Street, Pearl Street, all the streets here round the docks on the East River – these are, perhaps, the most dangerous streets of all. Yet this very street, Cherry Street, was named after its beautiful cherry blossom trees, and this very street is where George Washington was living when he became President of America.'

Arthur's face, seeing dark tenements and darker saloons, his nose assailed by horrific smells, his ears assailed by different noise, showed doubt. 'I assure you, Art, there were mansions here not so long ago, beautiful mansions and cherry blossom – then more and more immigrants pour in, and the old New Yorkers mostly move further North.' And then the American's half-jaunty tone changed slightly. 'This area too houses the jetsam of the city,' he said, 'like Five Points. But – a different breed.' And then he added something else: slowly, as if in warning:

'Listen, Art, listen: beware this hazardous place most of all, for there is some dark, dangerous energy here as well as decay. Allow me to introduce you to the territory of New York dominated now not by George Washington, but by the river pirates: the Swamp Angels, the Short Tails but – most of all – beware the Daybreak Boys: in my opinion the most vicious gang in the city. The Daybreak Boys,' he repeated. 'Not much more than kids some of them. Out prowling the river long before dawn, muffled oars, greased silent rowlocks, quiet as murdering ghosts.' And perhaps the police captain sighed. 'At least in the Bowery they fight in the open and laugh outside the music halls. At least in Five Points there is nothing to hope for. But in this area by the docks, black vicious business is carried out day and night somewhere beneath the big tenement buildings, with hidden underground passages leading to the river. We will avoid today the basement gambling dens where huge starving rats are pitted against starving dogs, but we know many imported goods stolen from the docks are held by fences, right here, in this area. And sailors who come ashore might find rooms and girls here – but often never get back to their ships ever again.'

The large contingent of now patently uneasy policemen

walked warily now, their hands on their nightsticks, no whistling now, further along Cherry Street, past basement dives and brothels and pawn-shops and Green-Grocer stores, keeping an eye out for pots of hot ash which Wash told Arthur were often hurled from higher windows on to interlopers.

Almost in disbelief Arthur read a broken sign: PARADISE BUILDINGS. Its doors and broken windows fell open and hung like caught, battered kites; inside he could see rotting corridors and staircases, a glimpse of crowded, dark rooms; outside broken steps led to vaults below. And everywhere wild, uncontained, continual, disturbing noise, cries and shouts and children screaming and something like mad, angry laughter.

'Now: a brief visit to the vaults of Paradise Buildings, Art,' Wash suggested, 'never to be forgotten! A sewer runs some-where under these buildings.' Arthur felt deeply uneasy: thought of starving dogs and starving rats. They went down wet steps covered with slime, now a police lamp shone on stinking, mud-running cellars. And suddenly in the lamp-light rows and rows of water closets stood before them in the gloom; several were being used and the occupants were not happy at a police contingent arriving uninvited: obscenities echoed, a turd landed at Wash's feet. Shadowy walls oozed with unknown liquid, an overpowering smell everywhere enough to turn the stomach. What else lay here in these cellars, Arthur wondered, peering into the foul darkness: trapdoors, secret passageways, secret cupboards full of vicious rats? Tunnels? Dead bodies? Live bodies? As they climbed back out of that hell-hole a huge number of people had suddenly con-gregated in groups at the front of Paradise Buildings: women with blank faces, dirty children, many young vicious-looking men wearing earrings: the dangerous and the damned stared sullenly and silently at the police.

Arthur Rivers stared also. 'And these too have the vote?'

'Every man who registers has the vote. As I explained. In a democracy you cannot pick and choose who might have the vote and who might not.'

There was no suggestion of going inside; the captain gave a sign and the police contingent was on its way again. 'As I say, we suspect many a foreign sailor has met his end in sewers below here, robbed and killed and then washed out into the East River. Oh – and one of your countrywomen is particularly well-known in this area.'

'As a Lady of the Night?'

The captain gave a brief, half-shout of laughter. 'You might say that. She works in a notorious bar. She must be six feet tall at least, with a fashion that is noted: her skirt is held up by men's braces and she carries more knives than a butcher. Gallus Mag they call her. Someone told me *gallus* is from an old Scottish word for trouser braces, but for all I know it means mad old witch. Take your pick.'

It was as if he had, by his words, conjured up an apparition. Round a corner a crowd suddenly erupted with shouts outside a saloon at the end of an alley; vicious fighting ensued, even from several hundred yards away a tall wild woman with flying hair in the middle of the crowd could clearly be seen – and heard – to fall upon a man with a scream of oaths. Perhaps, in a thin ray of sunlight between buildings, a knife flashed as it fell. By the time the reluctant police contingent – their hands very tightly on their nightsticks now – had reached the saloon, the crowd had dispersed. But on the pavement a stream of blood led to a dark narrow alley: the alley led back to Paradise Buildings.

The police approached the bloody passageway carefully: it appeared to be empty.

The police captain held his gun, motioned to every one of his men to raise their nightsticks, and they entered the dark, forbidding doorway of the saloon: HOLE IN THE WALL said a faded sign. When the English policeman's eyes got accustomed to the gloom there was no sign of any tall English woman with a skirt held up by men's braces. But he would have sworn that he saw, standing on a shelf behind the bar, a glass jar full of human ears.

What they did not see, none of the police officers, was a lone, tall figure laconically watching their departing backs from a small, dirty window, high up in Paradise Buildings. She saw that there was a new man among them, and she thought she had heard an English accent: *what is a buggering English buggering copper doing here?*

That then was the Englishman's educational, escorted tour when he first arrived in New York, for love. The captain's office, in the Halls of Justice behind City Hall, had windows looking out on to sycamore trees, which, after what they had seen, seemed like a mirage; on their way back they had walked through City Park where well-dressed children played beside a civic fountain. In his office, after their excursion, Washington Jackson had offered Arthur Rivers a cigar, and he had offered him a job. 'Now you have seen something other of our democratic city,' he said wryly, lighting the cigars for both of them. 'But I had a good reason for our small outing. I would indeed be grateful for your help and advice about something. We know that Paradise Buildings and Cherry Street and Water Street and places like the Hole in the Wall Saloon are where the river pirates and the fencers and the crimpers around the port operate from.'

'Did I see a glass bottle full of human ears?'

'You did. Your country-woman is renowned for keeping them in alcohol, the way men make notches on their guns – it is said she *bites* them off with her teeth but whether that is true or not I have not ascertained. Gallus Mag is a force to be reckoned with: mad as a hatter, often communicates by quoting Shakespeare,' and, despite the bottle of ears, Arthur actually laughed disbelievingly. 'But –' and Wash sighed, 'it is not a matter for mirth nevertheless. She may pop up saying *Hubbly bubbly, toil and troubly* or whatever it is those witches chant from *Macbeth* – and maybe she is just a violent mad-woman: we don't know but we do suspect that that old witch wields very much more power than is immediately obvious, down there by the docks.'

'Why not take her in? One woman.'

'We went in to that bar once, forty men, after a particularly violent affair, ears lost, dead bodies. No sign of a tall British woman whose skirt was held up by Scottish suspenders. And it was after that excursion that we realised that, although some of us have caught glimpses of her, she is never there when we are.'

'Perhaps she is one of these mythical figures people feed on – a wild woman who bites off men's ears – who doesn't really exist at all!'

'You saw her today clear enough, Art, right in the middle of that melee. And heard her too. And all that was left by the time we got there was what? A trail of blood leading down an alley: as usual, no Gallus Mag.' Washington Jackson drew long on his cigar before he continued. 'However. What I want to say about Water Street and Cherry Street is this. Even the Fathers of the City, who as you have understood countenance much, *cannot* countenance the extreme violence and loss of income from the night raids on the ships in the docks before they have unloaded. We have huge valuable imports – tobacco, alcohol, bullion, drugs, bales of woven cottons back from your English mills. There's salt, spices, antique pictures, jewellery, sugar, silk, opium and much more. The Daybreak Boys in particular are becoming too arrogant; too much of this valuable stuff is being stolen. And the crimpers round the docks kidnap too many visiting sailors and dump them on to other ships – if they don't thieve from them and murder them first. Such news travels fast, even as the port acquires more and more fame. We cannot have a bad reputation interfering further with New York port business.'

'Can the police do nothing?'

'Have you ever tried to police sailors, Art, out for a good time in a new port with a pocket full of money? We are interested in the wholesale pillaging of the ships when they dock, not the drunken sailors. We have to find a way of dealing with that.'

'I am a detective, Wash. I cannot think there would be any use of my particular skills on the East River.'

'But you could observe the patterns of the pillaging. That is detective work perhaps?'

Arthur Rivers sighed deeply: he saw how it would be. 'There is no kind of river police?'

'No there is not. But,' – the American tapped his cigar into an enormous brass ashtray in the shape of George Washington – 'I would like to give you half a dozen men. And see what you can do.'

Arthur actually laughed. 'Half a dozen men on the East River and police the docks day and night?' he said in disbelief. 'There are – what? – fifty wharves on the East River! There are hundreds of ships there!'

'But as I said, you could observe the patterns. Is it organised?

Is it random? Those things for a start. And the *b'hoys* won't know you for a while, which will protect you. But we must have results. The gangs – all the gangs round Five Points and the Bowery and Paradise Buildings and the Hole in the Wall – will have to realise that even their friends in City Hall cannot countenance the violence on the river and on the public docks. This is where the financial living of the city comes from. It must not be interfered with.'

Arthur shook his head. He wanted to say: *this will all explode one day.* What he actually said was, 'Your chief, the man in charge of all this. What is his opinion?'

The captain pulled on his cigar. At first Arthur thought he was not going to answer. Cigar smoke drifted. Outside in the distance they could hear the high children's voices as they played in the water that flowed so freely from the fountain, piped from the new reservoir. A glass bottle containing human ears not far away from here seemed like a terrible dream.

It was true, as the American had explained, that early New Yorkers had danced elegantly on Cherry Street with George Washington himself in the beautiful houses, in the days before the windows and doors hung and swayed so dangerous and desperate. But now, as Washington Jackson knew, behind the curtains in the notorious Green-Grocery stores in these same, darker now, areas, there was another dance: a different dance: money changed hands between various partners of this dance, for various services rendered in this still-new, ever-thriving, prosperous city: this New York.

'Democracy is – a messy business, Arthur Rivers.' The Police Captain sighed, pulled again on his cigar, heavy blue smoke swirled. For there were powerful movers in this dance of graft and corruption. The City Aldermen – and yes, the high-up policemen – *partnered* some of the men who lived in the dark, polluted, sinking alleys outside the Green-Grocer shops, or in filthy, fetid tenements by the river. The gang leaders could call up an army of men if required, if there was certain business to be done, certain protests to make. The gang leaders were paid for these services, and so helped to keep the immense, and growing, income of this wild port city in the hands of the democratically elected Aldermen, those men with so many favours at their fingertips.

Therefore when he finally answered, as the children in the nearby park played with the cool, clean water, the captain chose his words, it might have seemed, with care. 'The New York Chief of Police does want a river police. He will be glad of your assistance. But – do not rely too heavily on his actual support.' Washington Jackson pulled on his cigar. 'Let us say that there is much going on that you, as an outsider, will never understand, among the different – the different power-groups in New York. To be the Chief of Police in this great city a man must answer to many disparate factions. Let us just say for now that he has been described by some as a degraded and pitiful lump of blubber and meanness.' Captain Washington Jackson of the New York Municipal Police Force then stubbed out his cigar on George Washington.

Through the days and nights and weeks and months that the English detective worked on the East River Docks he had scarcely any – reliable – back-up. He worked long hours with only his detective's instinct and a couple of true, loyal men he could be certain he could rely on: many members of the police force, including members of his own small team, resented him and his English ways and – in particular – his refusal to take money on the side. (Arthur Rivers could well have done with extra money: he had many people who relied upon him, but he would no more have thought of taking this 'hush-money' than of flying in the sky.) For a long time he seemed to make no difference in the huge, wild, unwieldy, dangerous place where night fogs came down – which was also a thrilling trove of wonderfully valuable and marketable treasures, of great interest to many people, for many reasons.

And yet, slowly, over many, many months there was some success. With only the knowledge of his most trusted officers, Arthur arranged a system where the most valuable ship cargoes could send some warning ahead so that there could be proper guard put on them till they were unloaded and on their way, into the prosperous city itself or out west across the ever-expanding America. He understood that the Daybreak Boys used an old gin mill at Slaughterhouse Point as their headquarters. He found Water Street inhabitants with grievances, who could be persuaded to give information. It became clear that the junk-men of Rag-Pickers Row, who rattled their tin cans and rang their bells as they pulled their carts full of second-hand goods to sell along the streets of New York, were often the fences for the goods stolen from the docks. Lately several of the silent bands of night villains that worked the river had been apprehended. Goods had even occasionally been returned to their owners. Rogues' bodies fell into the river rather than watchmen's. The City Fathers were pleased (so long as certain of their 'business associates' were not found guilty if matters came to a head); seemed to see no irony in their divided loyalties.

But the City Fathers' 'business associates' were not pleased.

And that is why there was mention made, especially lately, among the cabbages and celery and lettuces, behind the curtains in the Green-Grocer shops. Mention of an *English* policeman.

'What's an Englishman doing working in the New York police? Who sanctioned that?' Nobody could give an answer.

'Has the guy been offered a parcel?'

'He doesn't take money.'

'Whaddya mean he doesn't take money?'

'He doesn't take money.'

'Well he's becoming a big liability. Get him.' And in the shadows a tall, wild woman smiled slightly as she silently went out again through the curtain of the Green-Grocer shop, in Cherry Street (that street where George Washington had once, so proudly, danced).

9

Marylebone

London

Dear Arthur,
I hope this finds you well, as this leaves me. The time
missives take, from London to New York, is long and so
uncertain that, as always, this letter leaves my hand in
trepidation and anxiety: such is the life you have put upon
your family left here in England.

I am writing to you at this moment in particular to
advise you that your daughter Millie has been delivered of
her fourth child, a daughter at last, whom we have of
course named Elizabeth after Millie and Faith's beloved
mother, that is my beloved sister, and your beloved wife.
Once more a child born is without a maternal grandfather
present, and the loss is keenly felt by us all, and I the only
parent for Millie and Faith!

I could wish that you would find it in your heart to give
up that fateful woman and return to Great Britain for
your support is needed here. Fred, that rather dissolute

husband of Faith if I may be so bold as to say so, was injured slightly this week when alighting from one of the omnibuses that crowd our streets. We are lucky that it was not worse and glad that his position in the school was not affected. It is not for me to say if he had been imbibing, but I have noticed he has a partiality to alcohol. Does this not haunt you Arthur Rivers? And Faith has four children also who must somehow be supported. How you can gallivant still around that disloyal country with your scarlet strumpet while your daughter suffers is not to be understood. I believe, and take comfort from the fact, that the Lord does judge us all, when our day is done.

I have been told that Prince Albert has championed the idea that your Mr Morse's new telegraph should be placed under the Atlantic Ocean in a tube and pulled along by a steamship over the miles and so reach England. He – the Prince – is a man of many ideas, some of which are perhaps a little vulgar and modern for this old and historical country – but as a German what can you expect! Our dear Queen must tolerate much.

If I was well I would write perhaps longer, but time takes toll of us all and so I will close.

Your dutiful sister-in-law

Agnes Spark (Miss)

PS we are in receipt of your financial contribution of the 7th inst.

10

The circus: dream-time for one night only in a small, small town called Hamford, many miles west of New York.

The lamps inside the Big Top cast soft warm light and odd exciting shadows, beckoning the crowds as they streamed in the falling dusk across the farmer's fields towards the magic, enchanting place: the circus. In the gloom at the back, unseen by the audience crowding into the tent, an Indian elephant stood. Small ears, ivory tusks, half-melancholy half-crafty eyes: the elephant waited, immensely patient: its trunk was curled about the handle of a very large basket on wheels which turned out to be Silas P Swift's version of one of those new machines called a *perambulator*. Inside the perambulator a small baby elephant sat: its ears poked through the specially-knitted bonnet it was wearing, and it was calmly swinging its own small trunk very gently from side to side.

The crowd inside the tent breathed in the smell of canvas and sawdust and exotic animals and lamps, shouting across to each other: eager, restless; men spat great wads of chewed tobacco which landed on the tent sides and then slid down-wards, leaving dark stains. Women in coloured bonnets called to friends in high, eager voices, laughing and waving; children played on the ground; none were concerned with the mud on their boots or their gowns or their faces as they sat or stood or pushed or settled, waiting: their excitement was barely contained as they looked at the sawdust ring brightly lit by all the oil-lamps, and at the high roof where the trapezes hung so quietly, shadowed and strange.

The coming of the circus was the most exciting thing that happened here in Hamford; how they waited, the farmers and the shop-owners and the rope-makers and the blacksmiths and the tanners and the timber merchants and their wives and their children; how they waited for the day they could ride into town, or walk down their lonely roads into Main Street where the shopkeepers would be closing their shutters or wheeling away their carts of goods and all, all of them, hurrying then towards the large tent that had miraculously appeared that afternoon in a field – the tent erected soon after the exotic, shining circus procession had ridden through Main Street with the band playing loudly. The people of Hamford queued up to pay while the Red-Coated Circus-Master shouted through his megaphone as he took the money (in lieu of Mr Silas P Swift who had returned hurriedly to New York).

ALL THE WAY FROM THE WILDS OF INDIA! he called, or ALL THE WAY FROM THE ARCTIC COAST! or ALL THE WAY FROM ARABIA! or ALL THE WAY FROM THE COLOSSEUM IN ROME! ROLL UP! ROLL UP LADIES AND GENTLEMEN! NEW CUTE LITTLE BABY ELEPHANT! ROLL UP! ROLL UP! THIS WAY FOR THE ACROBATIC GHOST FROM LONDON, ENGLAND, WHO WILL APPEAR FROM THE HEAVENS TO HELP YOU TONIGHT! ROLL UP, ROLL UP LADIES AND GENTLEMEN! ONLY FORTY CENTS, CHILDREN TWENTY CENTS! ROLL UP TO MR SILAS P SWIFT'S AMAZING CIRCUS!

Now in the tent the noise of the waiting crowd rose and rose: then suddenly the brass band marched in. Men in bright blue uniforms (bandsmen's uniforms possibly being the only uniforms tolerated in America) struck up a jaunty tune then almost at once the red-coated circus master, now wearing a top hat and carrying a large whip (the takings locked away in a big safe in one of the caravans), strode into the centre of the tent and leapt upon the brightly-lit dais. The crowd applauded from their banked, plank seats, the circus master lifted his top hat and bowed. And then the whip: *CRACK! CRACK!* and the loud sound echoed round the Big Top and then half-echoed again. And always, somehow, in small towns and large cities all over the country, always the same thing happened: people held their breath because it was there now, all around them like a dream: the magic of the circus.

The white-faced clowns with their huge red painted smiles and rubber noses and oversized shoes bounced in from the shadowy background, shouting above the band and laughing, calling to the people of Hamford, who immediately called back: *Hi there! Hello!* The clowns somersaulted, and tripped over their shoes and hit one another, and juggled coloured balls which they occasionally threw into the crowd, who fought noisily amongst themselves to possess such a treasure. The clowns carried amongst them a big net, like a fishing net: sometimes they threw one another into the net to the delight of the audience, especially the children, and the clowns bounced the victim up and down so that he seemed to fly in a most ungainly and protesting manner: *HOUP-LA! HURRAH!*

At another double whip-crack a tall, highly-decorated Indian Chief rode into the ring in his big feathered headdress and with a paint-daubed face and ringed ears and necklaces: he shepherded before him about twelve horses wearing coloured blankets: all the horses went round the ring: cantered faster and faster, their hooves throwing up mud and sawdust, then at a command from the Indian all the horses suddenly lifted their hooves gracefully in time to the band: *dancing horses!* Men in the audience, whatever they felt about Red Indians, were impressed. Then, just as the horses bowed – *look the horses are bowing!* – the aforementioned lugubrious Indian elephant with its ears flapping appeared out of the darkness, pushing with its trunk the large basket on wheels. The baby elephant was spied at once: the audience cried out in delight, *Oooooh!* they cried, *it's from the wilds of India! Aaaaaah, look, look at the little one! Look, look at the knitted bonnet! Oh isn't it so sweet!* The circus master in his bright red coat moved: *CRACK!* went the whip and the elephant pushing her baby in its moving basket stopped, stood briefly on her hind legs as the horses had done and waved her trunk, then she delicately came down to the ground, wound her trunk around the handle of the perambulator and moved on stolidly round the ring: her knowing eyes looked the audience over; they could see the wrinkled, bristly, grey elephant's flesh. The horses, held in a group now by the Indian Chief who spoke to them in some kind of soothing incantation of his own, rattled the bells on their harnesses, and the band played on.

'Queen Victoria of England has ordered three of those new baby machines, the Perambulator!' cried the circus master triumphantly through a red horn that amplified his voice, and the crowd shouted again: mentioning the Queen of England was always an adventure, you could never tell; tonight the crowd's shouting turned in some quarters to jeering: *She must have mighty big babies ha ha!* But the circus master (encouraged by Silas P Swift) liked to stir things up, whip up excitement and noise to the highest possible levels.

Now fire-eaters ran on out of the darkness; midgets appeared behind them, jumping on to each other's shoulders, cleverly juggling small wooden clubs; an exotic, humped camel was led blinking into the lights. And always, through the cries of *HURRAH!* and *HOUP-LA!* and *STEADY!* the performers were all the time talking to each other, sending each other messages, about the acts, about the audience, telling each other jokes, timing things carefully all the while – the steady, secret, on-going conversation of the circus. The exotic camel swayed from side to side as it walked so delicately, covered in rich luxurious, priceless tapestries (well, actually very shiny beads sewn by the wardrobe mistress on to blankets). *HURRAH!* The beads sparkled like jewels in the light of the oil lamps hanging all around. *STEADY!* The elegant camel with its strange humped back slowly turned its long neck from side to side, as if in disbelief at its fate, and then at another whip-crack climbed disdainfully on its thin, thin legs on to the circus master's dais, and teetered, yet gracefully, down the other side as the exciting flame-swallowers ran past, swallowing big flames and blowing them out into the air again, the drums played louder, the people shouted back *hurrah! hurrah!*

Now bright waist-coated men ran into the ring: the Mexican cowboys, the *charros*, followed by a pack of dogs; they grabbed the waiting horses, rode briefly on one, jumped to another, then to another, urged the horses into a gallop again round the ring, the barking, excited dogs followed; Mexicans jumped on to the shoulders of other Mexicans, forming their human pyramid, the audience clapped and shouted and swayed in time to the music and the men in the audience spat tobacco in delight even if the riders were Mexicans; more gobs of spit landed on the sides of the tent leaving further dark, dripping stains; and all the time: sawdust and mud flying, the Spanish cries, the now-sweating horses, the barking dogs, the sweating men, the music, the smell of the animals, the noise, the excitement: *O! the Circus!*

CRACK! CRACK! The whip flew through the air: the crowd hushed as two cages rattled into the ring, drawn by two separate horses and each accompanied by a trainer with a whip. In one cage a lion roared and every time it roared the trainer, who had only one arm and was dressed in a Roman toga, hit the side of the cage-bars with the whip and the lion roared again and bared his teeth and the audience screamed, and sometimes a horse, startled, reared upwards and was then calmed by a strange sound from the Indian Chief. When the audience turned their attention to an even bigger cage and saw a large, dirty-white bear who took no notice of a slashing whip on the bars they asked each other *Why cage a bear? Look at him! He's no trouble!* (This was the bear that had been sold cut-price to Silas P Swift, perfidiously, as a dancing bear: it had danced once it was true, and never again.) The audience could not see clearly enough the small blank eyes; they did not know perhaps that white bears ate human flesh.

The drums rolled and the one-armed lion-tamer stepped up to the side of the lion's cage. The drums stopped: the audience held their breath. Just before the door to the cage was opened the circus master spoke through his loud-hailer: 'LADIES AND GENTLEMEN AND CHILDREN. WE MUST ASK FOR ABSOLUTE SILENCE WHILE THE LION-TAMER, WHO HAS COME ALL THE WAY FROM THE COLOSSEUM IN ROME TO BE WITH YOU TONIGHT,

GOES INTO THE CAGE WITH THIS DANGEROUS WILD ANIMAL. ANY NOISE FROM YOU COULD PUT THE MAN'S LIFE IN GREAT DANGER!' There was a whispering noise as people spoke to their children; another whip-lash this time from the lion-trainer: silence: and then the trainer unlocked the cage door with his one hand and entered inside. The lion bared its teeth but did not make a sound: in that crowded tent you could have heard a pin drop. The man and the lion stared at each other. Then the trainer very gently put his whip on to the floor of the cage, put his one hand on to the mouth of the lion, opened the lion's mouth and very slowly, very gently, rested his head between the lion's teeth, his hand still holding the upper jaw of the animal. There was an audible gasp from the audience, the circus master put up a warning hand. But there was always one, night after night, town after town: *Bite his head off!* cried a young lad. In a split second the lion-tamer was on the other side of the cage with the whip in his hand (he had left the door unlocked: this was how it went, like clockwork, in every town); the lion that had been so still roared, but in a moment the trainer was outside the cage with the door locked again. (He had actually lost his arm, not when attacked by a lion but when a heavy cart ran him over, but this was never told.) He struck the side of the cage with the whip and the lion roared and charged at the bars.

How the people cheered! How they shouted and stamped in relief! *He was nearly eaten!* And the heavy smell of dung and canvas and sweat and animals got stronger and stronger and the lion roared and the whips lashed and the clowns shouted and threw more sawdust on the mud that had been churned up, from bright coloured buckets. The enclosed air was now so heavy and so hot and it had all been so thrilling that one poor lady fainted and had to be carried out, handed over the heads of crowds like a parcel, her small-booted foot falling from her petticoats in such an unfortunate manner that a cheer went up from the gentlemen in the audience.

But the lady and her naked leg were soon forgotten as the drums rolled again: two acrobats emerged: a huge muscular man with an extremely large moustache and a pretty girl wearing a tiara: *HOUP-LA!* They ran into the brightly-lit circle, waving and glittering in their shiny coloured costumes, they jumped up lightly on to the tent poles, pulled themselves upwards to grab at trapezes that hung there: *HOUP-LA!* They somersaulted between bars with consummate ease, faster and faster, the big acrobat, who called out in French to the girl, was particularly gymnastic and adventurous: he was known as *Pierre l'Oiseau:* Pierre-the-bird. The girl wearing the tiara jumped downwards towards him: *Look at her with her crown, thinks she's a princess! but she's pretty and clever, ain't she!* The Frenchman caught the young woman, seemed to throw her back again to a far trapeze: *HOUP-LA! HOUP-LA!* The crowd was wildly excited, and there was the thrill: *what if they fall?* Only the sawdust of the ring below. Gasps as he seemed to miss her with one hand, caught her with the other: *she could so easily have fallen!* Many of them, strict church-goers, forgot for a moment that this was the disreputable, un-dressed behaviour that their church ministers criticised, so entranced were they as their faces turned upwards, by the courage and the skill. Now a long pole was passed up from the ground and handed to the girl with the shining tiara: she left the safety of her partner and began walking across an almost invisible long horizontal wire, using the thin pole to balance, her feet in pink flat dancing shoes; the audience gasped: *will she fall?* Perhaps they even wanted her to fall, to add to the excitement – a trapeze artist had fallen in Hamford once, years ago; the doctor in the audience could do nothing for him: he died here in Hamford, and it was talked of for many months, added to the *frisson* now, as they watched the princess but, one foot placed, then another, breathless silence in the tent, she reached right over to the other side of the wire – and then turned and began the perilous journey back. But then: she stopped suddenly, seemed to teeter; she dropped her balancing pole to the ground, and then ran, actually ran across the wire, to the waiting arms of Pierre-the-bird, leapt lightly on to his shoulders: *HOUP-LA!* and waved prettily at the crowd. How they waved back, how they cheered her, how they shouted in delight! And then, just as lightly, the two acrobats separated and hung there above the audience, upside down, waving and swaying slightly as the crowd clapped and shouted and stamped in time to the band.

But then the band stopped playing suddenly, except for the drum which rolled again but this time it sounded slightly menacing. And somehow (the crowd looked uneasily about), the lights had dimmed, many of the oil-lamps must have been removed, or turned down. The applause of the audience faltered, the lion turned suddenly to the different sound. The other animals were all halted where they stood in the ring.

And somehow (it was not at all clear how) another shadowy acrobat altogether could just be seen above them: a figure that had definitely not been there before *at the far end of the acrobats' wire*. That was almost impossible: *how did it get there?* The other two still swayed gently on their trapezes; the shadowy figure half in the darkness further away stood poised there, aloft, motionless. The crowd were struck dumb: *how did it get there?* Then whatever it was seemed to completely disappear back into the shadows where there were – surely? – no trapezes at all. And in the spell-bound silence the drums suddenly rolled – and now at the bottom of a far tent pole where the lamps cast only a murky light, the same figure stood. It looked like a ghost. The crowd became eerily silent. The ghost moved slowly, floated almost it seemed, into more light: it was a figure swathed in scarves. The circus master had disappeared and the figure stepped up onto the red dais in the middle of the circus ring. Even the lion was quiet now: just the smell of the animals and the crowd and the mud all mixed up with the sawdust and the canvas and the ropes. Something: something about the figure standing there made everybody in the hot sweating tent hold their breath, bewitched.

And then the ghost spoke.

She (for it was, indeed, a woman) spoke in a voice that was used to filling large spaces: somehow she spoke without shouting, low-toned but clearly heard.

Whose pain can I help here? said the ghost.

This, in particular, was what the crowd had been waiting for: they had heard about this: there was a mad scrambling, men were shouting, people pushed to the front, or were pushed or carried by other people; *Here!* voices called. *Here!*

At this point the lion began roaring so loudly, and hitting its head so angrily against the bars, that his keeper had to flick his whip now at the horse that pulled the cage, making it move towards the darkness at the back (these were his strict instructions from the manager if the lion tried to disrupt proceedings) and the roar became more distant as the cage disappeared but still it could be heard, so odd out in the evening, the roar of a lion echoing through the small new town in the big new America.

The bear who ate human beings and did not dance did not make a sound in its cage where it had been placed in the circus ring. The mother elephant flapped her ears very slightly. Just sometimes one of the horses beside the Indian Chief shook its bridle and little silver bells shone and tinkled in the shadows.

The ghostly figure now made a slow, graceful gesture upwards, her draped scarves shimmered as she turned in the direction of the princess who was now standing upright on the trapeze.

And *something*: something happened, something passed between the ghost and the princess. Nothing was said: yet something had happened, almost as if the crowd had seen it, but they had seen nothing. Several people shivered uncomfortably, leaned into the warmth of their friends and family. Something silent, unspoken, and the low, low sound of the drums. Then, from her high vantage point, the princess indicated something to the ghost. She pointed, just once, towards someone who had been brought to the front of the audience.

Now: this may have seemed the most dubious part for those who were not believers in Ghosts or Magic Powers, perhaps someone could have been planted in the audience specially. But this was not New York, this was Hamford, many miles west of New York; a small, corn-growing town of less than eight hundred souls and most of them were here tonight, the tent held six hundred and it was full and overflowing. Here people knew each other, or knew someone who knew: you could not trick Hamford, 'Nothing bogus gets past the people of Hamford!' they always said to each other; no person could have been put amongst the audience as a trick, for the wild and sensible Hamford audience would have known at once, and caused a riot.

So when the lady acrobat pointed to someone in the crowd, the crowd turned to stare at a small pale woman who was being held upright by two other women and a man.

'Why it's Emily,' they whispered to one another. 'Why it's poor Emily.' The news was whispered through the crowd. Everyone knew poor Emily; her two young children had been burned, burned to death in their pretty, newly-built, newly-painted, white wooden house, and Emily had become mad in consequence; her head hurt so that she could not stand the pain and she shook her head over and over and walked the streets of Hamford wailing and tearing and was of much trouble to her family. But she would never talk about her children so that the wailing had become incoherent and – they said to each other – she had gone mad. *She needs to be taken away*, the people of Hamford said to each other, although where she could be taken was not known.

'Bring her to me,' said the ghostly figure on the dais in the middle of the circus ring, the dark, strange voice.

The pale distraught woman, obviously in pain, was brought, half-carried in fact, to the centre of the ring, the drums suddenly stopped their rolling undertone. In silence a chair was placed on the dais also and the accompanying family helped the woman up, the man tried to sit her on the chair but she lunged desperately at the figure in the scarves.

'My head aches!' she cried, shaking her head. 'My head aches over and over!' and quite clearly the hushed crowd heard the ghost say: *Let yourself rest in my care*. Perhaps something about the voice, or the words: Emily allowed herself to be placed in the chair although she still shook her head from side to side. The family, at a sign from the ethereal figure, moved back from the dais and stood motionless in the sawdust. In the shadows a horse stamped and stretched its neck, there was the tinkling of bridle bells out of the silence. The figure in all the scarves slowly unwound the ones that were around her face: the nearest people could see a fine-looking,

102

dark-haired, pale-faced woman with one odd lock of white hair in the front. The scarves dropped to the dais, the ghost moved nearer to Emily who stared even as her head still turned automatically from side to side. The figure, bending slightly, began to move her hands just above the woman's moving head and upper body, long sweeps of her hands and arms, over and over, near but not touching, over and over, moving her hands rhythmically over and over, over and over, her eyes locked with Emily's eyes. She seemed perhaps to be also murmuring to Emily as she worked – the crowd could not hear words. Emily's head still moved, the crowd saw, but she was calmer now.

And then the pale woman, poor sad Emily, had somehow fallen asleep. Her arms hung loosely beside the chair, her head fell back slightly. Nevertheless the figure above her did not stop the movement of her hands, over and over, for some minutes, sometimes murmuring to Emily still. The crowd was quiet: just excited breathing, a little coughing, a child's high questioning voice; once the elephant trumpeted and caused the crowd to stir a little, but still they watched the centre of the ring. Finally the draped, mysterious figure slowed the movements down, stood motionless watching the pale young woman, watching poor Emily who everybody knew.

As if receiving a signal (which perhaps they had: this was, after all, entertainment) the band started to play again. Sometimes Silas P Swift required a hymn at this point, that is if there had been any interruption to the circus proceedings by a religious person in disapproval at the entire proceedings (and this part was the thing they disapproved of most of all, for miracles and putative laying on of hands – it could not be stressed enough – was entirely unacceptable if performed by anyone but our Lord). But tonight there had been no such interruption so the band struck up, but very quietly, a rather sugary version of 'Home, Sweet Home'. Again the elephant trumpeted – perhaps in answer to the trumpet in the band – and the crowd laughed, half-nervously, one eye on the sleeping woman. She did not stir.

And then oddly – but it wasn't odd to the circus performers for this happened every night in every small town – the crowd recognised the tune and began at first to hum with the band, and then sing, very quietly:

> *Mid pleasures and palaces,*
> *Wherever we may roam*
> *Be it ever so humble*
> *There's no-o place like home.*

Hamford, singing softly.

And then the woman, poor Emily whose children had burned, woke.

The band tailed off quietly at the end of the verse, the singing voices died away.

Not jerkily, or frightened, or at once – but as if from a deep, deep sleep – poor Emily awoke: they saw her move; the man who stood so near, the father of the children who had burned, saw colour in the pale face of his wife. His wife looked at the ghost – that is at the figure that was swathed in scarves once more – and the audience actually heard Emily sigh, as if from deep inside her. Her head was still. And then, very tremulously, she smiled at the lady in the scarves.

'Yes,' she said, as if in answer to some faintly puzzling question, turning then to her husband. And in quiet procession, the audience stunned, the husband holding her arm – but she

104

walking herself, not carried, not led, not head-shaking – Emily and her family walked out of the tent into the darkness. And when the crowd (the crowd who knew Emily and her burned-to-death babies and her trouble and who had watched this whole scene in great amazement) looked back at the red dais, it was empty. The ghost was gone – no, there she was, by God, *up on one of the swaying bars with the other two acrobats, see! see that shadowy figure!* The shadowy figure, that ghost, was standing on a trapeze way above them, backwards and forwards in shadow and light, backwards and forwards; light somehow dimmed further and then there was an enormous crash of drums that made the audience scream with shock and then they looked back. The swinging trapeze bar was empty. In fascinated silence they watched as the empty trapeze moved, slower and slower, until it was still.

The audience roared its approval, the band broke out into a hearty Yankee march, and the whole circus: the animals, the trainers, the flame-swallowers, the midgets, the clowns, the horses and the Indian Chief were all circling the ring. The Mexican riders were carrying some of the lamps, waving them now across the audience: the tent was full of strange shadows and magic. The elephant with her baby in the new-fangled perambulator had joined the circle; all, all moved and danced, galloped or lumbered – all of them so glittering and glamorous – round the magic ring of Mr Silas P Swift's touring circus and suddenly, there above them, the princess and the big Frenchman Pierre-the-Bird, stood again on the trapezes, waving goodbye to Hamford. But the ghost was gone.

The audience, their voices still buzzing with excitement, streamed out of the tent, milled together, there in the balmy spring air. The moon, almost full, showed them their path and several blazing torches had also been placed to light their way out of the field. And at the sight of the road to send them away and back to their unending lives, a sigh seemed to drift through the crowd – *no, no, not yet* – and many of them turned back just once more, towards the circus. Torches now lit up the animal cages and the wagons and the outside of the big tent; inside the tent circus people were moving about throwing long shadows on the canvas; bundles of acrobatic bars were lifted, tent pegs and rings were pulled out of the ground: already they were packing to move to the next town and the people of Hamford felt a kind of magic melancholy: they had seen the circus, and now the circus was leaving.

And still many of the drifting audience did not leave the field, *not yet, not just yet*, wandered towards the back of the big tent, pulled by the strange exciting goings-on, the lion roaring, dogs barking, circus people calling to one another. Someone was cooking over a small fire, the smell of sausages and onions rose on the air with the smell of dung and mud and people.

'Was it a real ghost?' a child's high voice said. 'Was it a real ghost?'

'That ghost!' said one woman as they lifted their skirts high to avoid the thickest of the mud and the dirt. 'She done do good with Emily, poor Emily. I think I read somewhere years ago that she is Queen Victoria's cousin.'

'Who?'

'The ghost of course!'

'Fancy!' said her friend.

'Excuse me!' remarked another lady, 'You read that wrong! I read she tried to murder the Queen herself, that's why she's a ghost!' And the men laughed.

'Good for her!' they shouted. 'Down with Royalty!' and they started to sing an old song their fathers had sung:

> *Poor Britannia!*
> *Britannia waves the rules;*
> *Britons ever ever ever*
> *Will be fools!*

And everyone applauded and joined in, rough, ready voices, and the lion roared somewhere, much closer now, and the women screeched, pushed onwards to the bear cage. And still they said to each other: *was it a real ghost?* and wives pressed nearer to their husbands. The bear stared blankly at the human beings, not far from the bars of his prison. They could smell it, a deep, strong, off-putting scent, even though many of them were farmers and knew the scents of animals. The bear had little piggy blank eyes and, close to, the human beings could see it had lumps of fur missing; it scratched at the flesh, still watching them, and they felt uneasy.

'Well, I'd like to take that bear home,' a shop-keeper declaimed loudly and bravely. 'It don't roar, it don't move much, it's not much use to the circus but it could eat all the garbage in the gutters here and kill the rats and chase the pigs!' One of the trainers was passing.

'That bear, Mister, could eat you in thirty seconds if it was so minded,' but they didn't believe him, look how quietly the white bear stared, and just then, slowly, like a great balloon, the tent began to fall.

'That ghost, she fixed poor Emily good,' said someone again. 'Did you catch sight of Emily?'

'I did. I saw poor Emily.'

'I thought it might all be some fool trick, but how can it be bunkum if it was poor Emily?'

'And that dangerous lion! Mind you, in New York in that Museum, they say there's a lion who is a man!'

'We'll go to New York one day.'

'But we had a real lion tonight. I ain't never seen one till this night, only pictures. Look! Look, here it is.' A large group approached the cage in the shadows but the lion was in the far corner, his back towards them, pulling at a huge lump of some sort of meat.

Cautiously one of the women knocked at the bar: the lion, blood and meat dripping from his mouth, turned angrily and snarled and the woman hurled herself into her husband's arms, gasping and giggling. Then the lion turned back to its dinner. The elephant trumpeted again very near as people crowded about her cage to see the dear little baby; dogs barked, the camel stood motionless, there were warning shouts in the shadows as the last of the ropes and the pegs were pulled and the last section of the circus tent sank downwards, men catching at it before it fell to the muddy ground, rolling the canvas in an expert way. Clowns pushed past, thin lips under their big red painted smiles and the men ushered their womenfolk away at last, away from the stench and the mud and the air of disreputable danger, and the April moon shone down over Hamford.

In one of the wagons, Cordelia Preston wearily unbound the small cushions where they were hidden under her gown to protect her knees when she climbed up a big circus pole in the darkness to the shadowy heavens, where, nightly, she first mysteriously appeared, so ghostly. Standing or sitting on the swinging trapeze she had learned to cope with, but climbing up and down greased poles with ropes taxed her to her limits though she would not have admitted it to anybody. *I'm still only fifty-one*, she said to herself every night, *I'm only fifty-one*, and she unbound the cushions.

Now she could hear the laughter of her daughter, Gwenlliam, as she called to one of the *charros*.

'Hola Manuel!'

'Hola Inglesa, que tal?'

'Bien, gracias!'

Gwenlliam Preston loved the circus. She loved flying through the air: she had taken to it like a bird, she was good at it, she knew the rules, she had no sense of danger. Flying filled her soul with bright open light (so she described it to herself). Gwenlliam Preston was frightened of absolutely nothing. Tonight the small, pretty head appeared round the door of the wagon where her mother was rolling up the floaty scarves, wrapping them together with her knee cushions.

'Mama, I'm going on the telegraph wagon!' And Cordelia smiled at her daughter, blew her a kiss as she packed. She made herself, always, let Gwenlliam go even when she wanted to cry, *No! Not out of my sight! What if something happens to you?* But she understood long ago she must not hold on to Gwenlliam just because she was so precious. Cordelia too would have, once, wanted to travel through the night with the telegraph wagon. The Mexican cowboys, wild and violent in many situations, always looked after the girl carefully: they admired her light, bright courage. The candles in the little wagon flickered as Gwenlliam climbed in: to pack the tiara and the pink ballet shoes, to look for her travelling skirt and her petticoats; one more show tomorrow and then they would turn east, back to New York following the urgent summons from the man who paid their wages, Silas P Swift.

'Do you think Silas has really got a big New York venue again?' said Gwenlliam, taking off her narrow leggings in the darkness away from the candles. 'Maybe more money, Mama?' For they knew how much their earnings were needed: it was hard to be earning such meagre salaries again after their days of triumph when they were such a scandalous success. But then

Gwenlliam added: 'I'll be quite sorry to stop the touring all the same, I love it in the spring, it can be so beautiful and there is nearly a full moon tonight. But now only one more town.'

'And then home to the family!' And as Gwenlliam collected up her small bag of belongings the mother and the daughter laughed: an exasperated, longing, loving laugh.

Somewhere among the circus wagons a guitar played in the darkness. In the muddy field the telegraph wagon was ready and in the light of the lamp held by one of the *charros* for Gwenlliam to find them it could be seen that on the outside of the wagon was painted **MR SILAS P SWIFT'S AMAZING CIRCUS** in big colourful letters. Inside the telegraph wagon parts of the rough circus seating were already packed, quickly dismantled as the audience left. All the others had more time to eat and pack themselves and their chattels and the tent and the circus paraphernalia into all the wagons, where they would get what sleep they could as the long slow procession of animals and wagons and cages got on its lumbering way. But the telegraph wagon must set off at once with a hand-drawn map (Silas P Swift left nothing to chance): the telegraph wagon's job was to mark the route for all the others who would follow, and to look out for any danger or surprise.

Gwenlliam, wrapped in her cloak, climbed up to sit at the front beside the Mexican driver and his companion. Three dogs waited, alert, beside the horses.

'You good, *Inglesa?*'

'*Sí.*'

'We go nearly ten miles. You cold?'

'No.'

'So we go!' The horses set off through the field, they turned into the main road out of town and they were on their way to their next destination.

'Where you think we go from New York, *Inglesa?*'

'Mexico!' she said and they all laughed, and the Mexicans whooped and called, their voices echoing in the night.

The full moon showed them field after field of corn growing; they could see outlines clearly in the bright moonlight. Somewhere they heard the sound of cattle, sometimes they heard the sound of a running stream. When the farmers' fields finally dropped away the trees grew more dense, the way was narrow, and occasionally steeper.

After about an hour they came to the first big crossroads; the driver indicated, looking at his map by the light of the oil-lamp, that they must turn here; the other Mexican jumped off with his knife and tugged and hacked at a makeshift farmer's fence until he had a marker. So that it could be easily seen, he dipped his marker into a white substance of his own devising, and put it right across the road the circus was not to take: this was their job: to mark the route. Off they set again from the crossroads. Sometimes they stopped: Gwenlliam held the horses while the Mexicans with their knives attacked the most obvious difficulties on their way by the light of the moon: a broken tree branch, a fallen boulder; calling to each other in Spanish, laughing sometimes, and the dogs ran about and the horses shook at their bridles and snorted as they breathed the night air. The Mexicans knew their importance, as did Gwenlliam; they were clearing a safe route, as best as they were able. Several times in the past a circus wagon had overturned and once one of the drivers had been crushed and sometimes the rain was wild and heavy and trees fell across the roads; sometimes the big wagon wheels could be half in half out of mud and people had to get out and push, for the circus must go on. But tonight the sky was clear and the moon shone down and the roads were on the whole passable and the

Mexicans sang some song of their own and Gwenlliam sighed with the pleasure of it all as the night countryside rolled past and the telegraph wagon left its mysterious signs, for the circus.

Cordelia Preston was accompanied, most respectfully and proudly by one of the town elders (and his wife of course), to the only hotel in Hamford, where local young men, back from the circus, slurped beer either from large glasses, or straight from a hose attached to a large barrel. The young men, seeing Cordelia being ushered upstairs, removed their caps briefly as a salute of admiration and shouted praise at her disappearing figure: *She's real!* they shouted and then they wanted to know more, shouted at her to come down and talk to them (with all the politeness they could muster). It did not matter that she was a woman alone; it did not matter that she was not young: she was known now: she was the Magical Star of the Circus, they had seen her: they had been bewitched by her magic: somehow they would never forget her. *She's real!* they told one another. And in every town, if people saw her in person, they always wanted this apparition to join them downstairs, eat with them in the big friendly communal dining-rooms. They wanted to talk to her, ask her about her magical powers, ask if she knew anything about their dead mothers or lovers, ask her age; ask her (if they still remembered) about the scandal she had been embroiled in in London, about which they had all probably read in all their newspapers but of which they could no longer recall the details: was it true she had tried to kill the Queen of England? If so they would like to shake her hand and buy her a drink.

But after several of these friendly, inquisitive encounters: *How old are you? what do you think of America? don't you just love it? were you truly in a Murder? how much money do you earn a week?* Cordelia had learnt to swathe her figure in scarves and disappear. (Luckily she was a ghost: it had to be accepted that she was not quite like other people.) She had learned also though, to first, most politely, ask their forbearance: they were friendly, and curious, and American, and could give English people a hard time if they chose.

'Forgive me, my work is tiring, I must sleep soon,' (And that was most certainly true for fifty-one-year-old Cordelia Preston, climbing poles and swinging from trapezes.) and it was arranged that food be brought up to her room. But once the door of her hotel room was finally locked after a plate of supper had been delivered, she would give an enormous sigh of relief, take off her shoes, remove the port bottle from among her belongings and drink long and gratefully. And this she did tonight, using a tin mug she carried always in her luggage with the port.

These were the dangerous times, the port and the memories: her own ghosts. But she had trained herself most rigorously to think of the present: she channelled her thoughts into the circus, thought again of the young Hamford woman whose story she had been told later, whose head had ached so badly, and her pain. Sometimes in cases like these, as she smoothed her hands over and over, over and over, long sweeping strokes in strange brash American towns, Cordelia could feel that she, almost impersonally, took their pain inside herself to join the rest of the pain there, to allow the sad people in the small towns to rest. And she held Monsieur Roland's wise words to her heart as she always did: *We still know so little about the human mind and how it works: we are still learning and we must not stop . . . but, for so long as they are used properly, mesmerism and hypnotism will*

113

always be forces for good, whatever else is discovered. Cordelia knew she had helped the woman's pain tonight and given her, for the moment at least, rest. That was her work: that was what she did and got paid for whether in London or in New York or in Hamford, and the acrobatics and the shadows (and her memories) might exhaust her but they were to be borne. This was her life now.

She sat on her soft, sagging bed in the only hotel in Hamford, swirling the port around the glass and then drinking again. The sounds of the boisterous young men's voices drifted upwards, occasionally there was a shout and then laughter.

And tomorrow just at dawn, as usual, a driver with two rested horses and a partially rested acrobatic ghost would follow the marks left by the telegraph wagon all the way until they came upon a stream or river that had been found, near to the next town; there they would find the rest of the circus.

So, now Cordelia finished her port and her rabbit stew and her corn-cakes and washed her face. After tomorrow it was back to New York: who knows what would happen then, there was rumour of a big New York venue. But Cordelia Preston was an old hand: Silas was up to something. But maybe they'd be paid more, it would help if they were paid more. Nevertheless: who knows what Mr Silas P Swift would require of her next? She lay down at last in the bed and closed her eyes.

The long, deserted shore was their life: she would see the three blonde heads far out on the wet sand as the tide snaked out, bent over rocks and shells; all day their voices would echo upwards, she would hear them laughing and calling of their strange found treasures; wild sea-birds flew over them, and there was the smell of salt and seaweed. And then there would come a wild Welsh storm, and heavy rain would pound the sea and the wind would blow the children back to

the grey stone place that was their home as the ruins of the old castle
shadowed behind them, and the fires would be lit by the servants and
sometimes Cordelia would sing:

> *When that I was and a little tiny boy*
> *With a heigh ho, the wind and the rain*
> *A foolish thing was but a toy*
> *For the rain it raineth every day . . .*

Later in the night she dreamed of potassium antimony and
saw burnt internal organs; tears streamed down her face and
she turned wildly to Arthur's arms, which held her and com-
forted her and understood, but Arthur was not there.

And, as usual, the next afternoon they were indeed all met
up again: the telegraph wagon, Mrs Cordelia Preston, and
the long line of circus paraphernalia – packed wagons,
cleaned cages, horses and animals and people. It was almost
time for the town parade, everybody was awake now and
dressed once more in their circus attire. Water collected from
the nearby stream in big barrels was lifted on to a cart, to be
used when they left this town tonight for the long journey
back to New York; dogs chased each other around dark,
ancient trees.

Chief Great Rainbow, blue streaks painted on his face, sat in
the long wild grass playing cards for money with one of the
fire-eaters and two of the *charros*; Gwenlliam was sitting there
too and carefully watching them play, as she so often did. For
months Chief Great Rainbow had been teaching her to play
poker. He hardly ever spoke to her, but – in a most extraordinary concession for any poker player – allowed her to sit
beside him where she could see his cards, see how he called,
see when he bluffed, when he threw in his hand. 'Watch, girl,'

115

was all he said. She saw that his face, his strange dark face, never ever showed anything at all, tried to train herself to do the same.

Only once had she nearly lost her teacher: in a school of four he had a Royal Flush and she could not understand why he did not bet higher, faster; the pile of money grew very slowly, she bit her finger in anxiety that he was not making bigger bets and her finger actually began to bleed. It was clear to the other players that he must have a very good hand: they all threw in their cards, laughing at Gwenlliam, *Thanks girl*. Not a flicker showed on the Chief's face as he raked the small pile to him. Soon he got up and walked away. She followed wretchedly.

'But why didn't you double, treble the bet at once?' she said doggedly. 'You could have raised the stakes much higher, much quicker and won more money!'

Over his shoulder almost Chief Great Rainbow said, 'If I do that too fast, they know what I have, and stop betting in game. You bad luck. You show my hand.' And he stalked away again.

She sat further away at first after that, but came nearer and nearer over time until she was back where she used to be. 'Watch, girl,' he said again at last. Her face never revealed anything in a poker game ever again; now it was almost as if the dealing of a pack of cards changed her usually mobile face into a blank mask; this afternoon she watched Chief Great Rainbow dispassionately win a week's wages from one of the *charros* who was a very good poker player also.

The elephant was standing on the bank of the stream, pouring fresh water into its mouth with its trunk, urging the baby elephant to do the same. As usual the trainer complained that his elephant had to have so many gallons of water and so many pounds of hay, 'Every day!' he said, 'every day! I wish I had a camel instead!' But they all loved the little elephant:

Kongo the mother was called, and everybody addressed the baby elephant they all loved as Lucky-baby.

The red-coated circus master was an actor who had once known more glamorous times; nobody could stop him when he started on his earlier triumphs: today it was the lion-tamer, ready in his toga and his Roman sandals, who was entrapped by the booming voice: 'Edwin Forrest,' the circus master cried, 'He may be the hero of the Bowery now, but once he was my understudy!' One of the *charros* smiled encouragingly in a friendly manner as he brushed the horses nearby but the lion yawned with his big mouth wide. The band members yawned too and scratched their backs with twigs, re-woke their trumpet player, pulled on their blue jackets. The clowns removed alcohol from one of their more inebriate colleagues and re-painted their white faces, the big red smiles covering their small disappointed mouths. Cordelia, watching them, thought once again: *At least three of them are older than me, terrified that Silas will dismiss them also or replace them as soon as they find the tumbling and the laughing harder, and then what will happen to them?* One of them wearily dragged a bag through the grass, carrying big red false noses and big black clowns' shoes. *No wonder they drink: no wonder we all drink.*

Some of the Mexican *charros* were singing to a guitar, a Spanish love song, sometimes they clapped their hands in rhythm with the guitar, one of them danced, his arms above his head. By the river the white bear who would not dance scratched at its torn fur and stared at everybody from its horse-drawn cage with its small expressionless eyes. The women pulled at their acrobatic costumes, complaining in a cheery sort of way: 'Holy Mother it's still cold when the sun goes behind a tree. Thank heaven we're going back to New York tomorrow,

117

hope Silas is keeping us there'. The ringmaster, still talking of his past triumphs, pulled at his bright red coat; Cordelia draped her scarves.

The shoulder of Gwenlliam's acrobatic costume had come apart. 'Peggy Walker!' she called and others took up the call 'Peggy Walker wanted!' and a large woman emerged from one of the wagons, her arms full of the camel's exotic blanket. Peggy Walker was the miracle worker who was responsible for making sure that all the tired by now, tawdry costumes looked – at least from a distance, and in the deceptive lighting of the flickering, moving oil-lamps – glamorous and glittering. About her person were scissors and small knives, threads and pins and hundreds of shining beads. In the costume wagon were scrubbing brushes, strong soap, and buckets of water; she endeavoured to brush off the worst of the mud and the grass and the dirt they encountered, without there ever being time to wash costumes properly; the performers complained bitterly if they had to perform in wet clothes, said they would rather smell, and advised her with varying degrees of ferocity that when they died of the dropsy or the cough or the fever they would come back to haunt her.

'No! Lucky-baby, my angel, *no!*' Peggy said now, as the curious little elephant lolloped towards her and tried to investigate the shining blanket with her small trunk. Peggy laughed, pushed the little trunk away and dumped the blanket into the arms of the camel-trainer, who stood leaning on the doe-eyed, mournful camel. 'It's the best I can do, tell Silas you need a new one, if we were travelling on one more week it would fall apart completely!' and she went to work on Gwenlliam's costume. 'Your hands are cold!' 'Not as cold as you'll be, pal, if your costume falls off!' 'We're late!' 'Not as late as you'll be if the sheriff arrests you for indecency!' There was an unusual excitement in the air: Silas always travelled with them but first he had hurried back to New York several weeks ago, and now this message. Was it true that he had found them a New York date again at last? Would they be paid more at last? Laughter and banter and whistling to the dogs; midgets telling each other stories of doubtful decency and smoking dubious tobacco; the fire-eaters making a fuss of Lucky-baby but careful not to upset Kongo; Chief Great Rainbow, his feathered headdress in place ready now for the parade, fastening the bell-tinkling bridles back onto the horses (placing his poker winnings about his person so the Mexicans could not steal them back while the circus was playing). And Peggy Walker's shrewd eyes took in once more the Englishwomen, how they joined in and yet kept themselves apart. Circus folk never bothered about scandals, all had their scandals. Always when they congregated, afternoons by innumerable streams, before the next performance in the next town: always, all of them, all the circus folk told their often indeed scandalous stories: the French acrobat, *Pierre l'Oiseau,* and the Mexican *charros,* and the midgets and the true blue Native Americans like Peggy herself and the animal trainers and the clowns: they were all full of stories of their lives and their wild pasts, exchanging accounts of adventures and danger and laughter and pain. Peggy was a grand-daughter of one of the Sons of the Revolution, proud of her history and her hard, pioneering life and running away from the farm to the circus. But Peggy Walker noticed how when others spoke of past adventures, the Englishwomen remained silent. Always.

Gaily-coloured ribbons had been tied now to all the wagons. They fluttered alongside the painted words: **MR SILAS P SWIFT'S AMAZING CIRCUS**.

With a sign from the bandmaster the drum rolled, the band began to play its jaunty march – and the glamorous, exciting circus of Silas P Swift one more time swept triumphantly into town.

11

Marylebone
London

Dear Arthur,
I hope you are well. I cannot say that all is well here.
Have you not heard of the prediction of a cholera epidemic
in London? Do they not care about such things in that
country of republicans? Are you preparing yourself for
God's wrath: the next letter could easily say that one of
your daughters, or one of your (mostly yet unseen by you)
grand-children has been carried to their Maker. Let alone
myself.

You now have eight grand-children. They continue to
grow, innocent souls, too young yet to know that their
maternal Grandfather decided to abandon them to pursue
his own pleasures. Little Arthur's health has been worrying
since the day he was born, as if his very name carries with it
some desolation with a drunkard for a father and a deserter
for a grandfather – he has forgot you by now, of course.

Millie and Faith dutifully pursue their married lives
and perform their marital duties, but without a loving
father's support.

The other news that I must inform you of is that Faith's husband Fred is now unemployed. The school decided he should no longer teach. I shall say nothing of the reasons but I have already reminded you of his partiality to alcohol. We of course anxiously pray he will find another position.

The German Prince's latest idea is a Grand Exhibition where Britain's might can be shown. Queen Victoria is inclined, I have noticed, to give him his head so no doubt London will soon be overrun by aliens of all kinds, including, no doubt, wild black natives from the far-flung Empire.

It is nevertheless a fine Empire we lead and it grieves me and your daughters that you live in a country that did not see fit to be part of us. For you to live among such democratic savages is a burden for those you have left behind to pursue your pleasures; those who pray every day for your return.

I remain, as always

Your dutiful sister-in-law

Agnes Spark (Miss)

PS we are in receipt of the financial contribution of the 21ᵒᵗ inst.

Dearest Father,

Faith usually takes Aunt Agnes's letters to the post but she has trouble at home today and our aunt gave this one for me to post and, well I read it! and I am not ashamed that I read it Father, I am not really a letter-writer but I wish I had written sooner if this is what her letters are like! she tells us she writes for all of us but I am ashamed for what she has writ, it is very mean. Cholera is only a rumour Father, not a fact, and we will all be very careful and you are not to worry about things that may never happen! And dear Charlie says why shouldn't your Pa have his life for himself? and I realised I thought your life was

122

supposed to be for us because you are our father but dear Charlie set me thinking, and his Dad, who said one day: I'd be on the first ship to America if I was young, you remember him Father, Charlie's Dad? a gay old fellow and kind to me and the children even though he's only got one leg from that coach accident and so I thought I would write this naughty letter without Aunt Agnes over my shoulder for I have learnt a lot from dear Charlie and although I miss you dear Father I am glad you have a life too because dear Charlie makes me laugh and makes me happy. Well I better post this, with the letter from our Aunt.
with love from your own princess Millie XXXXX.

Inspector Rivers whistled 'Lavender Blue' as he walked down to the docks with the two letters in his jacket pocket.

'I like the music, Inspector, we should have some more whistling policemen!' commented his best assistant, Frankie Fields, and Arthur Rivers laughed, and they both laughed too as they watched the dock-men heave a large container of antique pictures and jewels safely ashore, safely arrived in New York, and the dealer taking personal delivery with a delighted flourish.

> *Lavender blue, dilly dilly*
> *Lavender green*
> *When I am King dilly dilly*
> *You'll be my Queen*

This was the song he had sung so often to his daughters when they were small girls; 'dilly dilly' they sang in delight, 'dilly dilly'. 'Faith can be the Queen, Father,' Millie had said firmly. 'I don't mind. I would much rather be the beautiful princess.'

12

When she was younger Amaryllis Spoons, known as Rillie, when something pleased her very much, would give little squeaks of pure joy. Now that she had turned fifty little squeaks still escaped Rillie often, because New York delighted her so.

Now, as April flowers danced, Rillie was seen early most mornings leaving their new home in Celine's House with her shopping basket, going to the corner of Maiden Lane and Broadway, where the German baker sold his fresh bread and the Italian woman sold fresh vegetables, and where fresh oysters and clams and crabs and fresh pies could be obtained. Everywhere, absolutely everywhere, money was being made in every conceivable way: women with vegetables and flowers in baskets selling on every corner; junk-men selling off-casts of every kind from their carts with tin cans rattling to announce their arrival; impromptu furniture auctions where wooden chairs were waved in the air; oyster-stalls selling oysters straight from the sea; huge advertisements everywhere: on buildings, on lamp-posts, on walls, on trees, on roofs: advertisements for teeth and false legs and hats and shoes and medicines. And everywhere new buildings being erected: hammering and shouting and digging and lifting and the hauling of planks. New York was a new city: new energy, new buildings; mud and dust, yes, but a cleaner, brighter hope and everywhere, waving above everything else, so proud and republican, the red and white stripes, the white stars on the blue, of the American flag.

And amid all the noise Rillie could hear the new words, *slang* it was called, she collected the words, hoarded them with delight: *high-falutin', bogus, loafer, humbug, pal, so long!*

The streets were clogged almost to a standstill with the horse-drawn carts and carriages; most people rushed past on foot: even the children rushed past with books and satchels – free education for New York children, boys and girls both – running, calling, waving, bumping into Rillie: already moving fast, like their parents. And the parents were hurrying past Rillie too, to make money: Americans, Irish, Scots, Germans, Italians, Swedes, Negroes, men, women, all rushing about: Rillie imagined their work: counting, packing, writing, eating, banking, catching fire, drinking, sawing, fishing, sewing, chopping, shouting orders, receiving orders: wharves, jetties, warehouses, ironworks, ships' chandlers, offices, workshops, factories, small shops, big department stores. Young boys ran past Rillie and thrust papers into her hands – more advertisements: dining menus, more false limbs and teeth, daguerreotypes, coffins, ice-cream; a *hum* Rillie called it all, all this energy: the hum of New York: the hum, most of all, of money. And nobody was more realistic than Rillie about the importance of the hum of money as she looked carefully at the prices on that warm, spring day, and made her purchases.

Just a few doors further down Broadway she passed the sign saying **MR L PRINCE: DAGUERREOTYPIST** and lingered for a moment just to look at the magical, real images of real people in the window. In the very first week after they had first arrived from England, as she had walked in this same delight along Broadway, Rillie's attention had been caught by a dead child in a basket: something about the waxy colour of the child's face, the sad-faced parents in dark clothes. But the small group were, oddly, entering one of the new daguerreotype studios: the parents and the dead child were greeted gravely at the door and ushered inside, out of the bright summer sunshine. Rillie, curious, had studied the big advertisement:

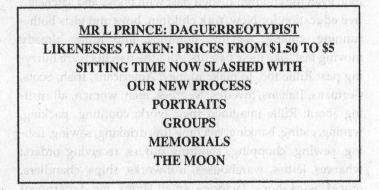

**MR L PRINCE: DAGUERREOTYPIST
LIKENESSES TAKEN: PRICES FROM $1.50 TO $5
SITTING TIME NOW SLASHED WITH
OUR NEW PROCESS
PORTRAITS
GROUPS
MEMORIALS
THE MOON**

It seemed to Rillie an odd, extraordinary list: 'portraits, groups, memorials, the moon.' She understood then that the parents were going to have a memorial portrait taken, of their dead child; saw again the sad faces. Then she hurried home at once and told the others and at her insistence the odd, newly-arrived family were indeed 'grouped', that very first week in America.

In Mr Prince's downstairs reception gallery they had all observed the soft carpets, and figures of note stared with grand importance from their places on the walls. They were called upwards and Mr L Prince placed them closely together to his satisfaction in his studio where daylight shone through a large skylight. He sat two old ladies in the middle of the composition, one robust and rather loud, the other frail: both with their heads clamped into stillness by iron headrests; he explained that despite the promise of 'sitting time slashed' the process required stillness and concentration and headrests and composition and light. Standing close behind the old ladies were two other women of very uncertain age in gay gowns and hats of the day, his eyes kept going back to one of the women, oddly beautiful and unsettling. At the feet of the old women sat a pretty young girl of seventeen perhaps: *Gwenlliam* he heard them say, when she laughed, delighted with this new experience of daguerreotyping, *you are supposed not to even smile, Gwenlliam!*

'That's a funny name,' the daguerreotypist had said, '*Gwenlliam.*'

'It's Welsh, Mr Prince,' said the girl.

And at each side of the composition a gentleman. One old and upright, white hair, obviously foreign (something about his clothes even before he spoke); and a stern gentleman on the other side, who had been introduced as Detective-Inspector Rivers. Mr L Prince had little time for the New York Police but this policeman was obviously English (not that he had much time for the English either) and was showing much more interest in the actual process than the others: asking about time, and copper plates, and silver nitrate.

'These kinds of images were at first thought likely to be of great interest to the Police Department in London,' he observed. 'But I understand copies cannot be made of a daguerreotype, and copies are what would be most useful; you should perhaps cross the Atlantic, Mr Prince. I believe a new photographic process is now being experimented with in England.'

'Why of course, pal!' Mr L Prince was almost indignant. 'I am aware of that, *of course* I am! I'm a businessman! We don't miss much here, my friend! And my passage to London is booked for next month, for that very reason! Copies are required: copies shall be made. Now look, I shall be happy to advise you coppers of my new skills when I have acquired them, here is my advertisement, keep it and I'll be in touch, pal. Larry's the name, Larry Prince. I'm an American!'

(And Inspector Rivers had caught Monsieur Roland's eye: they were taken aback on their arrival by the energy and enterprise of these Americans who thought nothing of travelling long distances, experimenting with new ideas, speaking to new acquaintances as old friends: nothing in the world was too much trouble when money was to be made.)

Mr Prince moved his reflecting mirror carefully, from side to side; eventually the mirror caught the light as he wanted it. 'That's it!' he cried. 'Now Ladies and Gentlemen, fifteen to twenty seconds are now required. I ask you now to look towards me, and hold this exact position, to remain quite still, and please, I beg of you, do not blink and please do not smile as a smile does not last well for twenty seconds.' His box-shaped apparatus was on a stand, he peered through a glass. But the frail old lady with her head in the head-rest, looked more and more distressed; she began pleating her skirt anxiously and trying to move her clamped head. Mr Prince excused himself, disappeared briefly into the next room, re-appeared almost at once with a fine, brightly-coloured bird on his shoulder, as if the old lady was a child.

'Now see here, my dear lady, watch this little bird, as still as you can. Does she understand?' he asked Rillie Spoons anxiously and rather loudly; it was clear this old lady was Rillie's mother. But he need not have worried: Mrs Spoons stared in fascinated attention and wonder at the bird that remained on his shoulder.

'Now then one and all,' said the daguerreotypist.

The daguerreotype was now in pride of place in their new home in Maiden Lane and that same day, in their first week in New York, Monsieur Roland had bought Mrs Spoons a bright yellow canary in a birdcage that had travelled from hotel to hotel and now to Maiden Lane, as part of the family.

So Rillie waved to Mr L Prince now, on this sunny April day, as he was ushering some clients inside, and then, her shopping completed, she collected up the two old ladies of their family, Mrs Spoons and Regina, from their new attic home, and took them on their daily walk. Today they walked down Broadway to the Battery Park and the Castle Garden, where weeping willows drooped beside the piers on the Hudson River. All New Yorkers liked the fresh open space of Battery Park and the old fort-castle where concerts were sometimes held; at night lovers walked amongst sycamore trees while moonlight caught the white sails on the water.

At one of the piers they saw groups of men pushing and shoving to board an old ship that looked as if it had seen better days; the men talked very loudly and confidently of gold. A native Indian wrapped in a red blanket, with strange markings on his face, stared impassively at a sailing ship already leaving, the wind filled its sails as it turned towards the open sea. A steam ship was disembarking: immigrants touching at last (just as Cordelia and Rillie and the family had themselves) the dreamed-of soil of this promised land, this Eldorado: this America. Grey, thin Irish faces looked bewildered, all the way from Liverpool; cold-eyed, welcoming, calculating Immigration Runners guided them to food and shelter; confidence men crowded and jostled and tried to swindle the naive.

Suddenly the old lady Regina called out angrily and very loudly, 'Blooming cheek!' One of the pale immigrants, having got this far, just collapsed on the pier with a tiny, shabby bag and everybody else simply rushed over him to go about their business. Regina had not a slither of sentimentality in her heart but she was nevertheless offended; she was not in the least religious either, but she had a strong historic relationship with Christian tomes. So while Rillie knelt to the man Regina stood there beside him, like a sentry and began to sing:

> *The Lord's my Shepherd, I'll not want*
> *He makes me down to lie*
> *In pastures green he feedeth me*
> *The quiet waters by.*

And although she was grey-haired and wrinkled and dressed in a baggy black gown, she had a fine voice and a respectable hat and she was upright yet and people stopped to listen to her and saw the man lying on the pier and soon one of the Immigration Runners appeared again and took the poor Irishman away.

Two dockmen wheeling huge carts of luggage had stopped briefly, resting from their heavy load, and at the end of the third verse Regina stopped singing and asked them the inevitable question: 'Do youse by any chance know my brother, Alfie Tyrone? He came from London as a sailor on one of the sailing ships, years ago.' Always she hoped someone would recognise the name eventually: 'Alfie Tyrone,' she said again.

'Not known to me,' said the dockmen today, as they picked up their load of luggage and went on their way.

Many of the sailors and the dockmen knew the old lady by sight now; 'Regina!' they would call whenever they saw her, amid the loading and the unloading and the seagulls and the crowds and the garbage, 'Give us a song!' Regina was her own person, and sometimes she would and sometimes she wouldn't; today, no news as usual of the brother she always hoped to find, she sang no more, hummed only in the spring sunshine.

The old lady on Rillie's other arm, Mrs Spoons, Rillie's sweet-faced, elderly mother, said very little but smiled often at all she saw and at Regina's singing and it was only up close that passing persons might observe the vacant look in her eyes which informed that she was perhaps not – quite – in the present. Today on the pier she spied a yellow glove: she picked it up from the wooden slats although people had been trampling upon it, and would not let it go. But then, clutching the glove, she began to show new signs of anxiety that Rillie had begun to notice: the whimpering was new, the staring about her in distress was new, a kind of panic which pierced Rillie's loving heart as she saw her mother's pale face. Her mother had been demented for a very long time but until recently it had not seemed to make her so anxious and unhappy. Rillie gave her a small, tight hug. 'Never mind, Ma,' Rillie said, 'I'm here, Regina's here, we're going home now,' and the trio turned back from the river. They walked slowly through the hustle and the bustle, still arm-in-arm, back to Celine's House in Maiden Lane making way all the time for carriers and farriers and dockmen and businessmen and shop-women, and ale-carts and wagons of cotton bales that banged and rattled past them over the cobbles. On their way home they purchased two of the newspapers that small boys sold everywhere: they always purchased a more serious one to know the news, but in deference to Regina's long-ago literary career they bought one of the scandalous penny papers as well.

In the attic Rillie settled her charges back into the rocking chairs that had been acquired for them which were placed beside the windows that looked over busy, noisy, clanging, crowded Maiden Lane. She gave them each a cup of tea and sat with her own tea at a small bureau.

Regina smoothed out the newspapers, the scandalous one first, looked for interesting information. For as long as any of them could remember Regina had been their newspaper reader; she read aloud to them every day. 'Listen to this!' she would say. She had always remained fascinated with newspapers since the days in her youth when she had worked for one of the penny papers sold on the London streets. She had shown such a particular delight in words that the editors had often let her write the loud headlines, **BLOODY BODY BURIED IN BUTCHER'S BASKET**, and she still very occasionally rendered to the others one of her short poems or songs that had been sung or shouted with great enthusiasm by the paper-sellers as they hawked their wares:

> O then he seized those lovely twins
> Whilst sleeping on the bed,
> Now with your mother you shall die
> The wretched father said:
> He seized them by their little legs
> And dashed them to the floor
> And soon their tender lives were gone
> Alas to be no more.

'Ah, those were me glory days!' Regina would say, half-regretful, half-proud, if she recited poems from the past.

Today she read aloud of a New York scandal with her usual fine poetic flourish although these days she had to hold the newspaper close to her eyes as she read. **MURDER IN CANAL STREET, HEART CUT OUT WITH SAW**. Mrs Spoons smiled vaguely, safely home, still clutching the dirty yellow glove which she refused to relinquish. Rillie bent over their accounts, adding and subtracting from a pile of money from a drawer: the money that Cordelia and Gwenlliam earned at the circus; and the money Arthur Rivers deposited with her; and the small but meticulous earnings of Monsieur Roland. What was left each month, if anything, when she had counted out what the household needed, would be taken later to the new Bank of America on Wall Street. A woman was not allowed to operate a bank account on her own, not even in the new America (although there were often letters to the papers about this) so it was Arthur Rivers who always accompanied her to Wall Street, and signed the papers. But it was Rillie who was in charge. She frowned over the money. Never did she feel that they were secure, never. The circus paid so very much less than it had on their arrival. Now, adding and subtracting figures, she carefully counted out the rent money for La Grande Celine and the money required for their daily lives.

'Listen to this!' said Regina:

A HUSKING FROLIC IN KENTUCKY.

A fight came off at Maysville, Kentucky on the 20th in which a Mr Coulster was stabbed in the side, and is <u>dead</u>; a Mr Gibson was <u>well-hacked</u> with a knife; a Mr Faro was dangerously wounded in the head and another of the same name in the hip; a Mr Shoemaker was

> *severely beaten and several others hurt in various ways.*
> *This entertainment was the winding up of a <u>corn husking</u>*
> *<u>frolic</u> when all doubtless were <u>right merry</u> with <u>good</u>*
> *<u>whisky</u>.*

'Listen,' she said again: **'GLITTERING GOLD FOR ALL NOW IN CALIFORNIA: MORE GOLD-FIELDS OPENED.'** And then she turned to the serious newspaper but it too said: **'SHIPS NOW LEAVING FOR CALIFORNIA EVERY DAY: MORE GOLD-FIELDS OPENED.'**

And above all Regina's headlines and the traffic outside Rillie could hear the bells ringing, not quite simultaneously, from Trinity Church and St Paul's Chapel, and then a fire-engine clanged past ringing its own bell, and in its cage the yellow canary suddenly joined in with all the other noise, singing cheerfully.

Rillie thought of Monsieur Roland, practising his delicate art with all the New York noise as a background, for Monsieur Roland's working rooms were only two streets away. A small notice in the window of his rooms said simply: *Monsieur Roland: Mesmerist*. Although he almost never worked in the hospitals these days, somehow he was known in the area as someone who could heal certain kinds of physical illness, or quieten tormented souls: those souls who, in this great exciting crowded city, could not deal with the new life, or their personal pain. Before he came with them to America he had been used to living alone in his small, meticulously neat room in London, at the Elephant and Castle: this communal living was hard for him, Rillie knew. But every week he deposited with her almost all his small earnings; also, with infinite forbearance, he would look up from the books he was reading and listen to, and converse with, the old ladies. Occasionally he played poker with Regina; sometimes he would talk with great patience for a long time to old Mrs Spoons, to see if it was possible to find some sign of Mrs Spoons herself left inside the anxious, kind little body, for he and Rillie and Regina and Arthur all saw the change. Mrs Spoons often had this new lost look, for she did not remember anything now: not herself, nor anyone else she had ever known.

Rillie locked up all their finances and stared out across Maiden Lane to the rooms on the other side of the street where no doubt other people were counting out money too. Rillie loved the spring, the air was different and now, at last, they were living somewhere that felt like a home. And by the end of the week Cordelia and Gwenlliam would be back in New York, and Arthur, who was working (somewhat unhappily they feared) such long hours with the New York Police, would be with them as much as he could, and their small, enclosed family in their new rooms in the boarding house, complete. These were the best times.

She looked up at the daguerreotype of their unusual family, hanging on the wall. She looked carefully at her dearest friend, Cordelia Preston. She and Cordelia had known each other and worked together for so long that they understood each other without the need of words. Once Rillie had said to Cordelia: *I'm your mirror*, and Cordelia had said: *What do you mean?* And Rillie had answered: *Everyone has to have a mirror. Someone who knows them better than anyone else. If you don't have a mirror you don't see yourself, and that's bad for people.* Rillie saw Cordelia, and loved her dearly – and saw the difference now. How jaunty they once were: how they laughed at their unexpected success with the chancy, cheeky mesmerism business they had thought of setting up; how they drank red-port and marvelled that they had been so near the workhouse and had escaped;

how glad and exuberant they were. Rillie wished so much that *that* Cordelia might – after all that had happened to her – come back. (That was the only way Rillie could explain it to herself: *Come back, Cordelia.*) But Rillie had been there, in those few fateful, terrible weeks of the murder trial when two of Cordelia's children had gone, and so had her work, and so had her reputation.

Perhaps from that, no-one came back, not quite.

13

Mr James Doveribbon should have been most comfortable at the American Hotel on Broadway: plumbing and plentitude. But it was also full of *Americans* who engaged him in conversation and questions from morning to night, and called him *Jimmy*. He was appalled. In Boston even acrobats and animal trainers had called him Jimmy and had behaved with a familiarity he found deeply distasteful.

And he was forever being asked: 'What do you think of our beautiful country?' And the truth was he found it loud, vulgar and completely lacking in proper deference to an English gentleman.

He had acquainted himself with five circuses in and around Boston and none of them had any knowledge of Cordelia Preston until finally an annoying clown who had been hanging about had tapped the side of his big red false nose above his big red painted mouth and said 'What do you want *her* for Jimmy?' in a most unpleasant and insinuating way. (As Mr Doveribbon's plans for Cordelia Preston were much more sinister than the clown's insinuations, his reaction of distaste was perhaps unwarranted.) Then the clown added: 'If you can find Mr Silas P Swift's Amazing Circus you might find Cordelia Preston,' and Mr Doveribbon's heart leapt, until he understood that Mr Swift's circus was touring the wilds of America to whence he had no intention of transporting himself: the 'needle in a haystack' analogy was only too apt as he had heard there was nothing but grain in the wilds of America. He did however transport himself as far as New York and the American Hotel where he ordered expensive champagne, for comfort.

He heard that a man called Phineas Barnum was also an Impresario. He took himself to Mr Phineas Barnum's American Museum on Broadway and saw a man-lion and a human mermaid and an interesting midget. He also sat through a Temperance Melodrama which made him long for alcohol immediately but there were no bars in the Museum, although there were about twenty saloons outside in the same block. He tried to find Mr Phineas Barnum to question him but he was nowhere to be found. He finally had a long and patronising conversation with General Tom Thumb, the interesting midget, who (interested himself in studying the manners of an Englishman) invited Mr Doveribbon to a nearby bar and bought him oysters and ale and called him Mr Doveribbon at all times. (James Doveribbon felt slightly odd in the company of a midget, thought people might be looking at him, but no-one was looking at the Englishman: they were only interested in his companion.) But of Silas P Swift General Tom knew nothing more than Mr Doveribbon had already been apprised of: Mr Swift's Circus was touring America.

Another day Mr Doveribbon emerged from the American Hotel and walked (in a foul mood because he couldn't find a free cab in this pushing, jostling, hurrying city) down to the East River dock area, where bowsprits of sailing ships reached right across the streets and ropes tangled in wheels of carts and the noise of traffic and factories and iron-mongers and ships' bells and the shouts of Irishmen unloading cargo was hardly to be endured. As Mr Doveribbon observed the raucous docks he himself was observed also. A gentleman came to his side, lifted his hat. 'Good morning, sir,' said the gentleman in a most respectable manner.

'Good morning,' said Mr Doveribbon, but warily, lest the next sentence was: 'What is your name? how old are you? are you married? what work do you do? how much do you earn? where are you staying? and what do you think of our beautiful country?'

But the polite man at his side merely engaged in pleasantries and was presently joined by another gentleman, and they even gently moved Mr Doveribbon out of the way of a huge cart. And soon afterwards they shook his hand jovially and went on their way and it was some time later that the Englishman found he had been somehow relieved of his pocket time-piece.

He was so angry he roamed the docks looking for them with his new knife in his hand – *how dare they make a fool of me!* – but the pleasant gentlemen had completely disappeared and he was instead unpleasantly surrounded by sailors and dockmen of all hues and accents who pushed against him rudely. He held his knife tightly, keen and ready to use it. He went to the watch-house outside the main police station but they only laughed and told him to mind himself. 'Not a chance in hell of finding that again, pal,' they said, 'been sold to a Jew already!'

However at last his luck changed, and the very same day.

On a public notice-board he read: WHITE POLAR BEAR FOR SALE. ALL OFFERS CONSIDERED. ALSO PERFORMING MONKEYS REQUIRED. SILAS P SWIFT. PEARL STREET NEAR PINE.

14

It was early evening when Cordelia and Gwenlliam arrived back in New York. CELINE'S HOUSE OF REFRESHMENT was as busy as always; Celine was there behind her tall desk, overlooking everything and taking the money; the pearl on her black eye-patch glinted sometimes in the first lamplight. The long tables held a German family, businessmen, workers from the counting houses (lonely young men come to the city to make their fortunes), shipmen from the docks: everybody was pleasantly welcomed by Celine as long as they did not disturb other patrons. Usually they did not: this was New York: they were here to eat, they ate quickly, wanting to get back to their busy-ness. But if they did disturb other patrons the large man called Jeremiah, who sold his drinks behind a counter in one corner, moved amazingly fast considering his bulk: people soon heard he had been a strongman in the circus.

'This is not a bar, Mister!' Jeremiah would say, and would see any trouble well off the premises before he went back to his little shelves of ale and whisky and port and sarsaparilla and root beer.

And tonight there were several ladies behind the large, prettily-decorated screen in the special part of the dining saloon that Celine always kept for women only: one of the ladies who lived upstairs, and two ladies from a nearby boarding house who were unaccompanied by gentlemen, but perfectly comfortable here. The two waitresses, who were said to be Celine's nieces, were neat, efficient girls well-trained by Celine; they took orders and rudeness and cheer with the same pleasant attention. The service was quick also: from the kitchen below there was a continual clatter of footsteps and calls of orders as the girls, or the negro maids who cleared the plates, ran up and down the stairs. Perhaps unusually for an eating establishment of this kind, a young fellow pedalled on the harmonium and played songs of the day. Sometimes he sang as well; as the new boarders walked in he was singing the latest song, 'O Susanna!', but if the customers heard they gave no sign, and if they did talk as they ate, they talked of business, or of chasing gold in California: *they say there are gold nuggets as big as eggs!* The young man pedalled furiously on the harmonium.

> *O, Susanna!*
> *O don't you cry for me!*
> *I am come from Alabama*
> *With my banjo on my knee.*

La Grande Celine, presiding over money, could only give a quick wave as the two women from the circus arrived at last, looking about them with great interest. But Celine missed nothing: saw clearly at once the excitement as her boarders all met again, embraced one another so warmly by the big front door. They were indeed a family, Celine saw, a strangely assorted family. She saw Monsieur Roland bend his head, smiling to hear Gwenlliam's excited chatter. She saw how Rillie and Cordelia greeted each other with such warmth and delight: it was as if they were sisters – perhaps they were sisters? – that had not occurred to her. And then she saw Inspector Rivers bend to kiss Cordelia's cheek, and then he took her arm as they talked and she put her hand over his and smiled up at him, and at once Celine understood, and her heart sang. And then she felt a pang of some completely unexpected loneliness as they all disappeared so quickly up the stairs to the top floor, immersed in one another.

However La Grande Celine was an American, and apart from the hopeful, somewhat romantic feelings she carried for dear Monsieur Roland in her heart she felt it only right that she should, eventually, in whatever way was required, get to know her interesting boarders and their story. With this in mind, she quickly sent an invitation upstairs, so worded that it was almost impossible to refuse: La Grande Celine had reserved the table behind the screen for perhaps an hour later. By that time the usual single ladies would have finished dining; the attic party were all invited, including the old ladies, down to supper, as her guests, and the large oysters from Staten Island, the best oysters in New York, had just arrived.

And Celine, presiding still like an exotic pirate over her dining-room and over the money, saw them all come downstairs again, all seven of her new boarders; the old lady Regina had a bright, celebratory feather stuck in her usual hat. Smiling at all her customers Celine nevertheless carefully studied the little party and the two newcomers. Cordelia Preston was startlingly attractive, and the daughter, Gwenlliam, was very pretty and somehow confident. And Celine saw at once how all of them nevertheless, even perhaps including the mad old lady who carried a yellow glove, somehow formed a loving aura around the younger girl. Sheltered from the other guests by the screen there was much quiet talk and laughter among

143

them as they ate the oysters. Regina immediately heard the music: Celine saw how she peered round the screen at the harmonium, tapped her feet. Celine saw too how everybody deferred slightly to Monsieur Roland, although he himself did not speak much but listened intently to stories the two women told of the circus. La Grande Celine looked at him – she perhaps did not realise – with great longing, as if he might provide some sort of answer to whatever it was she was looking for; then she had to turn away quickly, shake her flame-coloured hair over her shoulders with great nonchalance as she saw that Inspector Rivers had observed her. Inspector Rivers was, she saw, instinctively the protector of this strange group.

Finally, most of the customers had gone and Celine saw that her small special party was stirring also. Mrs Spoons yawned, looking vaguely about her, and Rillie turned to her at once. 'We're going back upstairs in a moment, Ma,' she said, so lovingly. Cordelia and Gwenlliam, exhausted now, looked pale. Cordelia rested her shoulder very slightly against Inspector Rivers which made Celine very happy. The harmonium player had got on to the last song of the night, it was time for love, but he was a young and robust young man so the tune was jaunty, not languid.

> O whistle and I'll come to you, my lad,
> O whistle and I'll come to you, my lad,
> Though father and mother and all should go mad
> Thy Jeannie will venture with thee, my lad.

And it was, of all people, the mad old lady, Mrs Spoons, who joined in when he came to the chorus; Mrs Spoons in her shaky little high voice had remembered something and sang very sweetly, the true Scottish version: *o whistle and I'll come to ye, my lad, though father and mother and a' should gae mad*, smiling and nodding her head as she sang. Celine saw that Monsieur Roland's attention was struck completely by this, he leaned forward with great interest. And Celine also saw that Rillie, listening in surprise to her little mother, had unshed tears glittering in her eyes.

At dawn Inspector Rivers left for the docks. He saw the small group of men on the corner of Water Street, perhaps just watching the world, perhaps watching him, for he very seldom missed such things: he was a detective after all and two nights ago he had foiled one of the gangs as they slid silently through the water with their muffled oars towards one of the ships carrying jewellery. One foreign sailor had been shot: but the detective had facilitated four arrests. They would be watching him, certainly.

Later that same morning, in the big dining-room, with sun pouring in through the windows, La Grande Celine properly met Cordelia Preston and her daughter Gwenlliam, who both delighted, as the others had done, in their flamboyant, kind landlady with the eye-patch like a pirate. They thanked her for their enjoyable supper, sat in the big downstairs room with its bright circus posters and Niagara Falls on the walls, accepted coffee which they insisted on paying for. Around them the two negro maids swept and polished the floor.

'Maybelle and Blossom,' said Celine, and the girls smiled shyly with white teeth, and polished harder. Celine lowered her voice. 'You can now get Irish maids for less,' she said, 'and Irish cabmen and Irish dock-workers and Irish shoe-shiners. All of them so desperate they'll work for less than the blacks.

But where will that all end I ask myself, if the entire Negro population of New York is priced out of work? They're killing each other already, gangs of them! I pay these girls little enough as it is, and they're good workers.'

The three women exchanged more and more animated tales about life in the circus, and Celine sighed and said: 'I say I don't miss it, but indeed, to be honest, I do sometimes still. What is Silas planning now?'

'We're waiting to hear. We were suddenly told to cut short our tour and return to New York. All will be clear in a few days, he told us. But the rumour is that we are to play in New York again for a while.'

'You'll be lucky! There is great disapproval of circuses now, you know.'

'We know very well! But Silas will have arranged something.'

And La Grande Celine laughed, her attractive open laugh. 'That madman Silas, yes he will!' she said.

When Gwenlliam understood that Celine had burnt her eye while eating fire, she looked outraged. 'But that should not be,' she said. 'The fire-eaters are so careful in their preparation, the paraffin and the fire sticks. I have watched them often.'

'Indeed,' said Celine. 'I, of course, was meticulous.'

'Then how could it happen?'

Cordelia guessed at once. 'Someone else?'

'Someone else.'

'But why?'

Celine took an instinctive wild guess. 'I expect you know as well as I do that this thing called love is not always as it says in the songs – *whistle and I'll come to you*, indeed! It can be a very – negative energy also, and takes strange forms and can do great damage.'

She would have given anything to take the words back, the expression on the faces of both women was suddenly so unprotected, their faces so suddenly pale. It was as if she had struck them. They recovered, but it was too late for her not to have seen what she had seen and she was ashamed: tried at once to offer her own life, almost as an apology. 'An acrobat was in love with me. Or thought he was in love with me, poor boy. He was German, they are usually much more contained, the Germans. Why, I have known German gentlemen who never removed their hat from their head no matter what they were doing, let alone any other piece of clothing from any other part of their anatomy.' She saw she had made them smile. 'He begged me to give up the circus and go and marry him and live on a farm – and a pig farm at that! Can you imagine! He said there was a lot of money in pigs. I tried to be very kind, but obviously not kind enough.' She sighed very slightly, just a tiny breath of something like regret. 'My flame-stick had been bent. And there was so much paraffin and therefore so much flame that I mis-timed my swallowing of it and my hair immediately caught fire and I was so terrified I somehow poked my eye with the burning stick. My colleagues leapt to help me, I was very lucky that my whole face was not burnt much more badly than it was. It took many months for my hair to grow back to what it had been and I lost the sight in the burnt eye.' She shook the flame-coloured hair that swirled so gaily about her face, and her good eye shone bright. 'I try to think it was a blessing in disguise. An aging flame-thrower is undignified – here I am in charge of my own world,' and indeed at that very moment the nieces appeared and had to be introduced. 'Actually they're not my nieces, I don't have any family, but I call them so, in order that I can pretend to have relations!' She laughed. 'Ruby and Pearl from Cincinnati,' and the girls smiled, 'and without them I could not manage,' and then the three of them bustled away because the butcher had arrived with his cart and was calling from the big front door.

'She is in love with Monsieur Roland,' Rillie told them when they came back up the stairs. Both women looked at her, astounded.

'But he's ours!' said Gwenlliam firmly, and then caught herself and said in some embarrassment, 'No, he is not *ours*, of course he isn't. But we love him.'

'Then you should not be surprised if someone else does too,' said Rillie.

'But that's different!' said Cordelia, but she too heard herself, and smiled.

'I've never been "in love" but I've seen "in love",' said Gwenlliam mysteriously and although she and her daughter were now washing all their clothes in big bowls, Cordelia slowed her scrubbing, looked at Gwenlliam uncertainly. *But what can I tell her about love?* For she understood that Gwenlliam knew – and remembered – many things. Cordelia scrubbed wildly, as if she could scrub away the past. And now Gwenlliam mixed with wild, unconventional people. Once Gwenlliam had said to her: 'I kissed a sailor on the wharf today.' Cordelia tried never to show surprise or shock at her steady, strong daughter. 'Was he a friend?' 'No, but he was lonely, there was no-one to wave him off. He was handsome, mind!' and Gwenlliam had laughed kindly.

'Celine really does want to marry Monsieur Roland,' Rillie said now. She was wringing out the water from the clean clothes into a pot.

Cordelia and Gwenlliam digested this, banging and scrubbing. The smell of soap filled the attic pleasantly. Regina was reading the newspaper but she listened carefully to the conversation, enjoyed the discussion and the clean, soapy smell.

'What does the old man say himself?' ventured Cordelia at last.

'I don't think he quite realises yet,' Rillie answered, 'but now that you've met La Grande Celine you would surely agree: it is only a matter of time before he does!'

The subject of their romantic discussion, Monsieur Roland, took Cordelia and Gwenlliam to see a medical operation at one of the New York hospitals: both women were used to attending operations. In the beginning they had thought that Gwenlliam might find it disturbing or frightening but on the contrary, she spoke to her first patient gently, a young American girl, and mesmerised her and stayed with her without blanching, keeping the girl mesmerised as they opened her stomach. Now they knew, of course, about the advent of ether as anaesthetic.

Today, Monsieur Roland told them, he wanted them to see something else.

'Ether has already been perhaps surpassed,' he told them. 'I have ascertained from the surgeon that today they are using chloroform. It is much more efficient, an inhaler bottle is no longer required. It needs however even more care than ether, for it can be more easily fatal if it is used wrongly.'

The surgeon greeted Monsieur Roland and his guests courteously: he knew Monsieur Roland and respected him greatly; he also remembered the women, placed the guests where they would be able to see. The patient was having a gangrenous foot amputated and was deeply agitated. And yet they saw how easily a sponge covered with the colourless liquid, the chloroform, put over the face of the terrified patient induced unconsciousness: it was almost instantaneous. When the man showed signs of waking, or unease, the sponge was simply placed again over his face and mouth as the surgeon sawed the foot.

Afterwards, when the patient was wheeled away, the visitors were allowed, because of the esteem in which Monsieur Roland was held at the hospital, to very gently inhale just a tiny whiff of the chloroform from the sponge themselves. 'Be careful,' said the surgeon.

'Mmmm. Yes, I know this one,' said Gwenlliam calmly, giving the sponge back to him. 'But I didn't really try it properly. I've inhaled ether a few times, that's different. This one's – sweeter, more pleasant, isn't it?' The surgeon looked astounded; Monsieur Roland and Cordelia looked somewhat bemused also.

'How do you know it?' they all asked simultaneously. She laughed.

'The midgets,' she said. 'They try everything to get a thrill. They let me try too. Everyone knows about "ether frolics"! – a great deal of falling over. The midgets like nitrous oxide best; laughing gas feels the best of all, they say to me, laughter and champagne mixed!'

Monsieur Roland spoke severely – for him – to Gwenlliam. 'It is dangerous, my dear,' he said. 'All these things: chloroform, ether, nitrous oxide can be dangerous when they are not understood.'

The surgeon had listened to this conversation with interest. *Midgets?* but remembered the women worked in a circus. But he added his own warning. 'Yes indeed, chloroform in particular should be handled with great care. It is known,' he said to Gwenlliam, 'that chloroform, improperly used, or used too much, can stop the heart beating – there have been a number of fatalities. It can be as Monsieur Roland has said: dangerous.'

'The midgets live dangerous lives,' said Gwenlliam matter-of-factly, 'and I don't usually join them for I find some of them difficult somehow – they get angry and quite violent. But I do feel sorry for them. They feel they have been somehow cheated because of their size – they know they are in the circus only because of their size, yet several of them are quite excellent jugglers. Anyway, I didn't pursue the chloroform; the midgets told me that they didn't like it.' The surgeon was fascinated.

'Did they say why?'

Gwenlliam laughed again. 'Well – they want to improve life! They said chloroform made them feel unconscious, instead of feeling like champagne.'

15

Dear Arthur,

We continue to worry that there will be cholera. Your eight grand-children — yes Arthur I will tell you again in case you have forgotten the number is eight now — are still, and I thank the Lord for his mercy in this disease-filled city, growing daily. They have many requirements. But I write again so soon because I need to make you understand that your daughter Faith's marriage is very troubled, she has a cross to bear and needs the guidance of a father for she will not be guided by me. It is with great difficulty that I have to tell you that Fred has more or less disappeared (for which we should offer thanks) but your daughter Faith has taken paid work! There! That is what it has come to with a father across the seas. And not even as a governess or some genteel work with embroidery. She is working — I cannot believe that I am writing these words — in a pickle factory in Paddington. Onions are made into

152

relish. Millie looks after her nieces and nephews. I will say no more but hope that this piece of news will at last bring you to your senses.

The German Prince has had his way – all sorts of plans are being offered and judged for an Edifice that is to be built in Hyde Park for the Great Exhibition which I believe is to be held in less than two years' time. The newspapers are full of nothing else. I do not know how the dear Queen manages with such goings-on, although such an Exhibition will be, so the newspapers inform us, a way of making the "Great" in Britain even greater. We shall see, if the Lord spares us.

> I remain
> Your dutiful sister-in-law
> Agnes Spark (Miss)

We are in receipt of your financial assistance of the 6th inst.

Dearest Father, none of us show signs of the cholera and we are looking after Faith. Fred has had trouble with the bottle for years. Dear Charlie says going out to work has made a change in Faith for the better but you know what a tease he is, she does get tired but its all right Father, Fred is hopeless, coming and going, we can never rely on him, but I look after all the children, we are managing still and if Fred disappears for good Charlie says we will have Faith and the children with us (only we hope that family group will not include Aunt Agnes.) O dear another naughty note and love from your princess Millie. PS We all send love, one day you will see all the children mine and Faith's and I am sure you will be proud of them and dear Charlie says always to me that you will find me a better daughter than when you left. And Faith's little Arthur has not forgotten you whatever Aunt Agnes says, he has kept all your drawings, he drew me a picture *of you the other day, on a ship! He copied the ship from one of your drawings and was most proud! But Father do not in the meantime feel worried, I do promise I will advise you at once if we are in real difficulty XXXXX.*

Inspector Rivers read both letters twice. He valiantly whistled 'Lavender Blue' as he walked from the Post Office back to the East River in the sunshine; his Cordelia was back, but although May flowers shone from railings and gardens and even from the holes in the broken cobblestones in the streets leading to the docks, he did not see them. There was even more talk of a proper river police department now being set up: he could travel then, perhaps, to London, where he was so obviously needed also.

> *Lavender blue, dilly dilly*
> *Lavender green*

he whistled.

And then it was a long time before he whistled again, either valiantly or cheerfully: that night his face was smashed with a broken cobblestone; his collarbone and arm were also broken.

When people talked of it afterwards they could hardly believe the cause of the riot: crowds of men gathered inside and outside the Astor Place Opera House fighting viciously over whether an English actor or an American actor gave a better performance in the Shakespeare play *Macbeth*. Inside, jeering, violent members of the audience stopped the performance; outside the police could not contain the crowds who ripped up paving stones and hurled them at the Opera House: the army was called in with guns and twenty-three people were killed, many more injured by bullets. Houses and buildings in this most respectable part of town were damaged. Newsboys shouted **RIOTS ON BROADWAY**.

Cordelia, so recently returned from the circus, did not see her husband for nearly two days, no boy came with a message; she and Gwenlliam could find nobody to answer their questions in the police headquarters which were being guarded by soldiers; the public was cordoned off from Astor Place. Cordelia stared at the huge newspaper headlines: **TWENTY-THREE KILLED** which Regina for once did not read out. Cordelia scrubbed and scrubbed at the floor of the passage outside their entrance door. 'Where is he?' she said to the floor over and over.

'Cordie, listen to this! Come and listen to this!' Cordelia kept scrubbing. 'Cordie, it is William Macready!' Rillie called out again in disbelief, 'It's all about him!' William Macready was an actor from London they had both worked with long ago: 'They were actually killing people over *William Macready*: whether he is better than an American actor called Edwin Forrest!' She kept staring at the reports in amazement.

Cordelia grabbed the newspaper, discarded it quickly. 'Where is Arthur? He always sends a message if he is not coming home and we are expecting him. Does he still do that?'

'Of course he does,' said Rillie.

'Then where is he? Why are they killing each other over William Macready?'

When, finally, Arthur Rivers returned to Maiden Lane with his arms and his hands and his head bandaged, and blood congealed on his face, Cordelia stared at him. And then she wept with relief, surprising everybody, including herself. As they all settled at last in the attic parlour, as Celine appeared with pies and beer, Mrs Spoons got up suddenly from her rocking-chair, making little sounds of distress. Perhaps she only saw a pale man with bandages, but she smoothed the policeman's bandaged arm with her small yellow glove, and he smiled at her, and held her hand with his one good one, and said that he was a lucky man to know her. Monsieur Roland, so relieved also at the re-appearance of his friend, nevertheless watched Mrs Spoons, wondering how it was that she did not at all know Inspector Rivers, who lived with them, yet showed him kindness.

The police were castigated; letters in all the newspapers spoke of 'respectable New Yorkers unable to sleep safe in their own beds'.

'The crowds were *organised*,' said Arthur again and again. 'I tell you it was not really about actors, there must have been at least ten thousand people there,' and Gwenlliam, sitting close to him now, had to stop herself from weeping: her loved stepfather so battered and bandaged and pale. 'I *recognised* so many of them,' he continued, 'there were gangs there: there were hundreds from the Bowery in their hats and their bright trousers – Edwin Forrest is a Bowery hero – they were fighting like wild animals with knives and nails and boots and cobblestones, and gangs from Five Points too, pulling up the paving.' He did not say that he had also seen members of the Daybreak Boys from down by the river only too well; he did not say that he believed he and Frankie Fields, his most trusted sergeant, had been specially targeted by some of the wild men: that they only escaped further injury when the army arrived with guns. He especially did not say: he was not sure if it was real or if he had been hallucinating: as the armed soldiers dragged him away to safety he thought he saw a tall, wild-haired woman screaming abuse at him in the crowd of fighting men; he remembered he had instinctively felt for his ear as he lost consciousness.

'Here's port,' said Cordelia, and he took it clumsily but kept on talking.

'Someone – or some persons, I don't understand America's ins and outs – but there were obviously people behind this, stirring other troubles and using Forrest and Macready as an excuse!'

Monsieur Roland looked carefully at the bandages on his friend, and then gently unwound and rewound the one across the shoulder.

'I once played Macready's maid,' said Rillie wonderingly. 'Goldsmith.'

'I once played his beloved,' added Cordelia. 'Sheridan.'

'Is he safe himself?' asked Rillie.

'He got out a back way, and if he has any sense he will have left New York. He will have been helped to get away – he has many powerful friends in "New York Society" as they begin to call themselves I notice, or "Old New Yorkers" – it was they who insisted he perform when it was already clear trouble was brewing. They simply do not understand the energy that hides in streets not far from where they think they are so safe. The Bowery and Broadway *meet* at Astor Place for God's sake! What is the matter with them that they don't see? Thousands of dissatisfied, desperate young men with too much energy living like animals – that can't go on without real trouble! Does "New York Society" not read its own newspapers, don't they know of all the rage that has erupted in France and Germany and England? The docks are full of arriving, angry people from all over the world! New York will explode worse than this one day!'

'Listen to this,' said Regina and she read out from the newspaper:

*The riot leaves behind it a feeling to which this community
has hitherto been a stranger – an opposition of classes – the
rich and the poor; in fact to speak right out, a feeling that
there is now in this country, in New York City, which every
good patriot has hitherto felt it his duty to deny: a high class
and a low class.*

'That's what I mean!' said Arthur.
'Here's another one,' said Regina.

*The promptness of the authorities in calling out the armed
forces and the unwavering steadiness with which the citizens
obeyed the order to fire upon the assembled mob is an excellent advertisement to the Capitalists of the Old World, that
they might send their property to New York and rely upon
the certainty that it would be safe –*

'Safe!' expostulated Arthur.

*– from the clutches of red republicans or chartists or
communionists of any description.'*

The detective from the docks listened to Regina's dramatic
rendering in disbelief. 'The Daybreak Boys will love that!' he
said. 'Though whether "communionists" means river gangs I
cannot say,' and Inspector Rivers put his bandaged head into
his bandaged hands.

16

Silas P Swift had a suspicious mind: he had not become a successful circus impresario without learning a great deal: he could be devious, as well as suspicious, if he was so inclined. Silas P Swift did not like people questioning him when he did not understand their motives. He had just, most thankfully, sold the big, white, probably-man-eating bear, no questions asked. When one of those *poncey* (Mr Swift's word: he had learnt it – and its rude meaning – from his Mexican cowboys) English gentlemen came into his office, without knocking, and grandly asked the whereabouts of Cordelia Preston without explanation, Silas stared, silent.

Mr Doveribbon looked around him. The 'office' was a confusion of cages, boxes, papers, rubbish, with a big man with a moustache sitting at an over-flowing, bizarre, box- and tin-crowded desk in the centre. Mr Doveribbon could hear some monkeys screeching but could not see them. 'Am I addressing Silas P Swift?'

'The bear's sold,' said Silas.

'I do not wish to buy a bear – and I also do not own any performing monkeys.'

'I have acquired the monkeys also.' The monkeys kept on screeching somewhere as commentary on this purchase.

'My mission is something else. I am looking for Cordelia Preston.'

'Is that so?'

'It is.'

Silence.

'I have – information. Information to her advantage.'

'If you give it to me I will try to pass it on should I find her.'

'No, no, you don't understand, Mr Swift – I presume you are Mr Swift or I am wasting the time of both of us?' Silas merely stared. 'It is urgent – I have information for her daughter – you may not know she has a daughter – wonderful news for the daughter, very much to her advantage.'

Silas Swift's hackles were raised, and in alarm. He certainly, at this stage in his plans, did not want anybody giving information to Cordelia and Gwenlliam except himself: he was planning to go this very day to explain to them their next circus appearance. This fellow could not know much about them if he didn't know Gwenlliam worked in the circus also. 'No idea where they are, pal.'

'Cordelia Preston has been touring with your circus and I notice that now you are not only selling animals but buying new ones, so I must suppose you have further plans.'

'I do not know your name, pal.'

'Doveribbon, Mr James Doveribbon,' and the Englishman gave an unexpected, *poncey* (Silas's word) bow.

'Well, Jimmy-boy, leave a message. I'll try and get it to them. If I see them. That's all I can do for you.'

'Are they in New York?'

'Nah. Nah, they went off.'

'Where to?'

'I am not their keeper, Jimmy. A bear-keeper once; an elephant-keeper still. A monkey-keeper if I can stand the vicious buggers. But not a lady-keeper.'

Mr Doveribbon understood that he was being fobbed off, but had the sense to see he would get no further at this point. But Silas P Swift would not get away from him now that he had found his headquarters. 'I had taken the precaution of writing a letter,' he said silkily. 'Perhaps you would be so good as to deliver it.' He lay a sealed letter upon Mr Silas Swift's overflowing desk with some distaste. 'Good-day to you, sir.'

As soon as he was safely gone Silas opened the letter.

Dear Miss Preston,

I bring great tidings. Your daughter's presence is required in London immediately, to her very great financial advantage, and I need to see you yourself, urgently.

I am presently residing at the American Hotel, on Broadway.

I remain, Madam,

Your respectful servant,

James Doveribbon, esq.

'Over my dead body,' said Silas, tearing the letter up into little pieces and scattering it over the cases and the cages and the boxes. A briefly-escaped monkey shat over the envelope: when Silas caught the angry monkey, it tried to bite his face.

17

Each day they expected to hear what was happening to the circus.

'I wonder if Silas has run away with all the money?' said Gwenlliam.

'Then you and I shall become popular Lady Daguerreo-typists,' said Cordelia. '*Portraits, groups, memorials, the moon.*'

'Mr Swift may have decided to become the Acrobatic Ghost himself,' said Monsieur Roland, without looking up from his place in the book he was reading.

'I wonder if the lion ate him,' said Rillie, stirring something in a large cauldron.

'We know very well that lion is all bark, and no bite,' said Cordelia. 'I saw him the other day cuddled up to Kongo, fast asleep!' She was cutting potatoes and had a big pile of peas beside her waiting to be shelled. 'But I hope Silas's circus isn't closing like all the others!'

'Ouch!' said Arthur, as Gwenlliam bathed his so badly-bruised face before they started playing poker. They were all together so seldom, this Maiden Lane attic family: late after-noon, the air soft and warm with spring, all seven of them sat crowded together in the room with the daguerreotype of them all on the wall. The canary was skulking silently in a corner of his cage but they could hear the carts and the horses and the people on the cobbles below. Rillie was making a steak and oyster pie. Regina with her newspapers and Mrs Spoons with her yellow glove, rocked in their rocking chairs.

'Listen to this!' said Regina; she was holding the newspaper even closer to her face than usual because she couldn't understand what she was reading.

ARE THE DEAD ALIVE AFTER ALL?

First tiny rumblings of the story had already reached New York, but now the news was given more coverage on many days: a small paragraph had become longer. Two young girls, the Fox sisters, in a small place called Hydesville in New York State, had apparently been hearing tapping sounds in their bedroom. Somehow it was believed they were receiving messages from departed souls: strange tapping sounds that perhaps brought words from another galaxy, or from heaven. There were numerous articles in which comparisons were made with the new telegraph: if electrical signs could be received across states and counties surely it was possible perhaps that spiritual signs could be received across worlds? People were now flocking to the little town of Hydesville from far and near: **ARE THE DEAD ALIVE AFTER ALL?** read Regina.

'Well, that's blooming unbelievable,' she commented loudly.

To Monsieur Roland, it was *definitely* blooming unbelievable and he suddenly stood violently in their little parlour, walked to the window as if he could not breathe: everyone in the room watched him anxiously. Monsieur Roland was a deeply spiritual man, and he was not foolish enough to pontificate on what happened after a person died; when he turned from the window, he had controlled himself and spoke very quietly. 'In my work I have been present enough times when life has left the body. I have seen the very energy that is the essential ingredient of mesmerism and hypnotism, *that very thing*, disappear from a person when they die. I have seen it: it leaves the body, sometimes wildly, sometimes gently. That is all I know. To say that this energy, or spirit, can be recovered by knocking three times for yes and two times for maybe, in answer to mundane questions, offends everything that I hold dear in my life.' Monsieur Roland spoke quietly still, but with as much fervour as a man of the cloth. 'All this is cruel, as well as being ridiculous, un-informed, and dangerous. Such promises raise hopes in grieving, ignorant people, people whose grief *makes* them ignorant, *mon Dieu*, grief makes otherwise sensible people lose their common sense – of course they are hanging on to any hope of contact with a loved one! But I think it is immoral to suggest that we will soon be meeting again in some kind of merry tapping-gathering in small-town America.' Gwenlliam went to the old man for a moment, and he nodded at her loving face, came to sit down again.

'Never mind Monsweer,' said Regina, 'there's plenty that agrees with you, here's a rude poem about it – not as good as my poems used to be, mind,' but she read with gusto.

> *Upon the bed, some children lay*
> *They heard big knocks they boldly say,*
> *And being filled with dread and fear*
> *Relate this to their parents dear.*
>
> *The parents first the tale denied*
> *But they at length were satisfied*

> *That bed-cord, head-board, bars and post*
> *Was surely haunted by the ghost!*
>
> *Now to conclude and end my song*
> *Although I've not been very long*
> *And never have I been at school,*
> *Yet I will venture APRIL FOOL!*

By now Arthur and Gwenlliam were dealing cards at the table, the policeman putting down cards and cents with his left hand. Cordelia sat close to them, shelling the peas now into a large bowl.

'Ha!' said Regina, 'listen to this: *It is reported that a reverend gentleman is seeking to arrest the Fox sisters for blasphemy against the Holy Scriptures.*'

'Oh, Holy Heavens Above!' said Cordelia. 'How often have we heard this? It's exactly what they say about us as well!'

'Do you remember, Cordie,' said Rillie, 'in London, how we were visited by that clergyman from the church just across the road? He was wearing purple garments, remember?' She had turned from her bench and was holding oysters in both hands. 'And he sat down in the basement and said we were to cease mesmerism *at once!* "It is *blasphemous!*" he cried as you handed him a glass of port – and then he finished off the whole bottle!'

Cordelia, watching Rillie waving oysters about and laughing, began to laugh herself. 'We didn't like to drink in front of a clergyman, remember? so he drank it *all*, the whole bottle and he kept saying "you must re-consider yourselves! It is the work of the LORD only, to alleviate pain!" and then he fell over!'

'He was besotted as well as inebriated!' cried Rillie. 'Even as he imbibed the port with such alacrity and criticised us roundly, he couldn't take his eyes off you!'

'And he accused me of suggesting that Jesus was a Mesmerist while he was draining the last dregs into his glass, and – remember Rillie? – we literally couldn't afford more port till we got another customer – and it was just after we started and we didn't get another customer for about two days, so we couldn't have a *drink* for two days either!'

'You should've come to me,' said Regina in a droll voice, 'and explained your trouble, I would've helped youse,' and in the end they were laughing so infectiously that everyone, even Monsieur Roland, joined in. And Gwenlliam thought: *this is how our mother used to laugh with us when we were very young children, she hardly ever looks like this now* and she looked across the poker game at Arthur Rivers and saw how he too, bandaged and bruised, observed the laughing women. He was smiling at his wife and at Rillie, but it seemed to Gwenlliam that his eyes were bruised also.

'What's this?' said Regina. She had moved the newspaper even closer to her eyes and then pushed it away further, to make sure she wasn't making a mistake.

'Where are the magnifying spectacles we purchased?' said Rillie.

'I don't *like* them,' said Regina firmly, still trying to understand the words. 'What does this headline mean: **JERKED TO JESUS?**'

'It's a hanging,' said Arthur dryly.

'What sort of hanging?'

Arthur explained that sometimes in America a man – a black man – was hanged, not legally by the hangman as in England, but by ordinary citizens taking law unto themselves, and that is how they described their own deed.

Regina looked disbelieving. 'Are you sure?'

'I'm afraid I am, Regina.'

'What about we hold these truths to be self-evident that all men are created equal and that they are endowed by their Creator with certain unalienable rights and that among these are life, liberty and the pursuit of happiness?'

'Ah,' said Arthur.

Regina turned the pages ferociously, and muttered, 'Jerked to Jesus! I wouldn't have wrote that, even in me glory days.' She rattled the pages. 'All the rest of the head-lines on all the newspapers are about blooming gold. Anyone can go, so they say, for the price of a fare. Gold. Well, why doesn't everyone go then and it'd be a lot quieter; gold, gold, nothing but gold.'

'But it would take so long to actually *get* to the gold!' said Gwenlliam. 'It's such a vast country, I hadn't even realised how big it was before we set out to cross even a little piece of it, do you know on the telegraph wagon we had to hack little paths, even between towns sometimes, and there are not even any tracks at all over huge parts of America, and there are huge mountains between here and California.'

Regina now read out to them advertisements for mail ships leaving to sail down the coast of South America and round Cape Horn and up the other side to, eventually, California – an extremely long journey that took many, many months. But this was America: people had of course already found quicker ways.

CUT THE JOURNEY TIME TO THE GOLD-FIELDS! PASSAGES AVAILABLE THIS WEEK TO CHAGRES!

---

read Regina. 'Where's this Chagres?'

'It's on this side of the Panama isthmus,' said Arthur. 'It only takes a few weeks to sail there from New York, but then people have to then find their own way across – I think it's about sixty miles – across rivers and rainforests to Panama City, on the Pacific coast. And then from Panama City they have to try and pick up a ship to sail up the Pacific coast to San Francisco.'

'Well, listen to this then,' said Regina. 'It might be quicker but it don't sound too salubrious to me!' and she read out a letter from a would-be miner in suitable dramatic tones.

> *After sailing from New York down to the Panama isthmus in an unseaworthy boat, and being taken from Chagres by cunning, unreliable Indians up the river where crocodiles lurked in shadows not making a sound, we found ourselves making an unbelievable journey through a humid, stinking, snake-infested rain-forest where cholera is everywhere. Rains came, the route was impassable, several men got ill and were immediately abandoned in that hell of vegetation and death. I immediately turned back when the route became again passable, intending to see my loved ones again in this world.*

and then as they digested that information Regina found a large advertisement:

CALIFORNIA GOLD GREASE.
If The Purchaser smears himself all over
with this amazing Product and then will roll
himself down any gold-spangled hill in
California, gold and nothing else will adhere
to the skin ONLY $10 per box.

They were still laughing when Silas P Swift arrived at their rooms to advise them of his further plans for his circus; as he spoke, both Cordelia and Gwenlliam, knowing Silas well, breathed, *of course:* wondered how it was they hadn't guessed what his next plan would be, before he told them.

The Impresario was bustling with business, breathing heavily from the stairs to the top floor (he was also aware that he had just torn up a letter that would ruin his plans completely). He began talking almost before he had entered the room. 'Ladies, I have it on most excellent authority that the miners in California have money to burn! Gold nuggets in their pockets! Nuggets as big as an apple! And nothing to spend it on and no entertainment! I wish I had thought of this earlier – we will make more money than we made in New York in the early days, more money than we can imagine in our wildest dreams and **MR SILAS P SWIFT'S AMAZING CIRCUS** is now on its way!' He placed himself in the nearest chair to continue. 'The wagons and the large animals left two days ago, to make the whole journey by sea – not the bear, I've disposed of the damned bear who never danced. Those arrangements have taken up all my time until now, but that journey can take a hundred and fifty days or more if the weather is bad, so I had to get them on their way. Now: *we* don't want to take a hundred and fifty days to get to the miners! So we humans, we will leave in a week with the horses and the smaller animals, by sea also down the Atlantic coast as far as a place called Chagres, and from there we will cross the Panama isthmus – easy.' And he clicked his fingers, as if it was already done. 'My investigations show they are now clipping time off that journey, organising the Indians properly so that they can take people – and animals – safely up river and on to Panama City. Indeed I had intended to take the elephants that way – did not

Hannibal, did not Alexander the Great, cross continents with elephants? But I have been advised that the Panama isthmus is not the Swiss Alps. However we must hope that our wagons with the Big Top and the big animals will not be too far behind us now that they are on their way – and the isthmus route can probably be done, with luck of course, in half the time! And you, Cordelia – you must, it is absolutely *imperative* that you *must*, become a Clairvoyant at once, as well as a ghost and an acrobat. You can describe to them (in the vaguest, ghostliest terms, of course) where gold will be found; I will find a misty glass globe for you to peer into – and all done on the trapeze in mysterious ghostly shadows! I can picture it now: **THE CLAIRVOYANT GHOST!** You swing from nowhere, holding the misty globe aloft, crying: "I SEE GOLD!" You can describe a hill, a river, a bend in a path – anything, and then – pouf! – the misty globe and the Clairvoyant Ghost dissolves, simply dissolves into nothingness – and the trapeze is left empty like usual – only more exciting – we'll get smoke and mirrors and you will dissolve – into nothingness!'

'And where have I actually gone, Silas?'

'Oh, you can jump, disappear into the smoke, we'll get a special invisible wire for you to hang on to, or we'll do something with the lamps. We can charge as much as ten dollars per ticket for such an act – we shall make thousands! – and we can start with all this stuff before the big animals arrive even!'

He was so excited, so caught up in his dreams, and also so anxious now to get his ladies on the ship and away from New York, that he had hardly acknowledged that Monsieur Roland and a bandaged Inspector Rivers and Rillie and the old ladies were in the room also. Because Monsieur Roland was such a courteous gentleman poor Silas P Swift was greatly taken by surprise at what happened next: everyone else in the room was shocked beyond belief.

The old man hauled the circus proprietor to his feet by his cravat.

'Monsieur Swift. I will not even begin to discuss with you the foolhardy danger of your plan to put so many lives in real danger! I will be most interested to hear if your lion and your elephants that you have sent off to their fate arrive safely to the other side of America without losing their minds! But I *will* discuss mesmerism with you just once more. I have stood by for years to see you push Cordelia Preston from her original role as a Mesmerist of note, further and further away from integrity and further and further down your circus path of quackery and dishonour. If she was not a woman of great moral fibre she would have been lost long ago!' Silas P Swift, who was bigger and stronger than the Frenchman was nevertheless unable to move, although Monsieur Roland no longer held him by the throat. He felt Monsieur Roland's eyes burning into him. 'How many times do I have to explain it to you Monsieur Swift? *Mesmerism is a philosophy of honour. It is not fortune-telling. It does not see into the future or talk to the dead or see gold.* It is the harnessing of human energy for the power of good, especially for the relief of pain both physical and emotional. *That is what it is!* However, Monsieur Swift, I have just the performers for you. There is talk of two sisters who tap tables and talk to dead souls and I am sure they could be persuaded to see gold as well – the Fox Sisters, I believe they are called – employ *them* to see gold in crystal balls on trapezes in your circus!'

Monsieur Roland who was usually so observant did not see the worried face of Rillie, the open mouths of the old ladies, the shocked face of Gwenlliam nearby, he did not even look at Cordelia. But he controlled himself at last: Silas P Swift could see the extraordinary inner strength of the old man as he made himself speak in a quieter voice. 'You will forgive me, Monsieur Swift. I speak of my life's work. I cannot, of course I cannot, speak for my dear friends and pupils. They are in charge of their own lives and they have my respect and love whatever they do. But I am unable to stay in the same room as someone who speaks with such ignorance. *Excusez-moi.*'

And Monsieur Roland left the little sitting-room and all the beating hearts. They heard his footsteps going heavily down the stairs.

For some moments nobody spoke. Mrs Spoons let out a tremulous little sigh at the cessation of such drama which she certainly understood to be drama even if she did not understand its content, and the canary, as if to cheer her, did begin singing at last, its cheerful little song was the only sound now in the attic room. At last Cordelia motioned for the circus owner to sit down again. She had seen Gwenlliam's face: Gwenlliam loved the circus with all her heart. She had also caught the odd look on Regina's face: Regina would wonder if old ladies would really have to cross cholera-drenched rain-forests, where silent crocodiles lay. She had not looked at her husband.

'Silas,' said Cordelia in a calm voice, 'you always have brave dreams. But – animals as well as people along almost impass-able tracks in the rainforest? Apart from all of us what about the horses? They are not pack-horses, they are circus horses: highly-trained, highly-strung – how many of them will arrive alive? I have heard that the Panama peninsula is sixty miles wide. From what we have read it will mean many months' journey, and it is quite clearly extremely dangerous.'

Silas P Swift was not a man ever to acknowledge danger. 'Sixty miles! Have we not travelled so very much further than sixty miles with neurotic horses? What are the Mexican *charros* and the Indian Chief for? What do you think I have been doing in New York these last weeks? Looking into all these matters with my usual careful planning! Already the wagons and the larger animals are steaming down the coast! Do you not understand what I have been arranging while you have been having a little holiday? Within a week my circus will be aboard one of the daily vessels now leaving for Chagres, with or without you, frankly. With my good planning, and luck on our side, I intend that we shall arrive in San Francisco and get to the gold fields before the rainy season begins. I have planned everything.' He spoke with great authority and self-assurance – but in fact he knew that he needed both women, and in particular Cordelia: her act was still the one that made his circus different from all the others.

'With *great* luck on our side as I understand it,' said Cordelia dryly. 'Very well. But you must give us *some* time to make up our minds about coming with you.'

'What do you mean? You must come! I brought you from England! We absolutely must leave as soon as possible!'

'Then let us say tomorrow afternoon, Silas, we will let you know. It is a very big decision. It would mean leaving New York for a very long time.' She looked briefly now at her husband; his face was quite blank as he listened.

'There will be more money of course, Cordelia, much more money once we get there.'

'We know better than many the importance of money, Silas. But we have a family, as you know, with whom we must discuss all this.' Silas bowed politely towards the police inspector in his bandages, to Rillie, to the two old ladies in their rocking chairs: this strange collection was no business of his. He trusted Cordelia implicitly: if she said tomorrow then tomorrow he would have his answer. He had had such a vision of gold and glory he had for a moment forgotten her odd intransigence even when she needed money, and now there were huge fortunes to be made. But he needed Cordelia, by God he was lost if she said no, or the poncey fellow found her.

'Of course if you simply cannot be a fortune-teller for the gold, we will still have the acrobatic ghost, as usual,' he said in a placating manner. 'For the sake of the old man.'

'Tomorrow, Silas,' was all Cordelia said.

On his way out, Silas P Swift passed a tall young man who was obviously also a policeman, all bandaged up like the one inside: Silas observed the copper star with distaste.

Before any of them could make any comment at all about Silas and his plans, the tall, bandaged policeman appeared at the attic door.

'Ah, this is my good and faithful colleague, Frankie Fields,' said Arthur. 'He was punched too, as you can observe! How are you, Frankie?'

'I'm fine, sir, it was only my left side, and my knuckles are the worst, and I'm pleased to say someone's face will be showing their work! I was wondering how you are, sir? And I've brought you all the reports of the riot, and the boss wants your own report. There was a big fuss in the papers.'

'I saw,' said the inspector dryly. 'I better come and see the boss. I can't write a report like this.'

'I'll do it!' said Gwenlliam and Frankie Fields simultaneously, and then they both laughed and Gwenlliam, although her mind was on California, looked at the tall good-looking policeman with interest and Frankie Fields, although his mind was on the riot, looked at the very pretty young lady with interest. This did not go unobserved by the police detective.

'Take over my poker hand with Gwenlliam,' he said to Frankie, 'while I read all this stuff. And then I'll write my report with your help.' He looked at Cordelia as he heaved himself up stiffly from her side: his expression was unreadable. *Are you going to California?* perhaps he was asking.

'The pie won't be ready for about an hour,' said Rillie.

'We'll go for a walk, Arthur, while you write your report,' said Cordelia. And she gave a small helpless shrug by which she meant: *I don't know*, but perhaps to Arthur it seemed she meant: *I don't care.*

Mr Doveribbon (who had discreetly followed Mr Swift) – all this brisk *walking* they did in New York exasperated and exhausted him – of course expected policemen to wear uniforms, did not know that one policeman had just gone into CELINE'S HOUSE OF REFRESHMENT and another was already ensconced in the attic upstairs. (Mr Doveribbon did not know either that a New York HOUSE OF REFRESHMENT could also let rooms and that this was the home of Cordelia and Gwenlliam Preston.) He turned away as Silas P Swift reappeared, then followed him again; this time past great filthy stinking piles of rubbish on the East River docks to something that was signposted as the Brooklyn Ferry Terminus, where crowds jostled and pushed as they boarded. Silas P Swift boarded amongst the crowd and foolish Mr Doveribbon did the same. It was not a long journey across the river; just as the ferry was pulling in to the other side with people pushing and shoving to get ashore first, Silas took advantage of the unruly crowds, stepped back, seemingly slipped – and simply knocked Mr Doveribbon over the side railing of the ferry and into the shallows of the insalubrious East River.

People turned briefly at the splash and the yell of Mr Doveribbon; one of the crew sighed and turned to find his boat-hook, leant down in to the water.

Silas P Swift meanwhile went about his business.

18

Celine's House
Maiden Lane

Dear Brother Alfie
I'm wondering if you got my letter. Nah,
course not, or you'd find me, Alfie-boy, I know
you, I know you'd find me. I can't think of any
other way for <u>me</u> to find <u>you</u> after so long so
I'll keep writing.

I'm wondering too if you've maybe gone
after gold Alfie? You would've as a young
man but I've been thinking a lot and I reckon
you're 70-ish now. Bit of a journey for a 70
year old, Alfie! Though I know you would have
done it once.

We're just now talking about gold in our
place too. The circusman wants the circus to
go to California. Well Alfie I'm older than you
and I'm about 70 years old too and I think I'm
probably too old to go chasing gold, not that I
feel old mind, but I feel something bad when I
hear about journeys across an isthmus and

crocodiles and snakes and that. And the old lady, Mrs Spoons, she's completely gone in her head absolutely now, she could never make it. She made that trip across the Atlantic a few years ago now and I think that's it for her, for travelling.

After the circusman left, a policeman came, with reports for our Inspector who got hurt in a riot, and it is a very small attic so our ladies have gone walking, 'just for a walk' they said to me, as if I was mad as the mother, 'while the policemen work.' But I know they'll be chattering away about this California business, I wish they'd talk in front of me so's I'd know what they were deciding. 'Look after Ma,' said Rillie – which is what I've always done since years and years ago in London when I rented a room from them, stopped her falling into the fireplace many a time! Anyway they have gone for this "walk" and given me peace, and the old lady is fast asleep in her rocking chair, and our policeman and his man, they're murmuring and writing at the table, so now I can write to you again Alfie, he is a kind man, Alfie, this Inspector Rivers, even though he is one of them, I think he got quite badly hurt in this riot thing– beaten up it looks to me. And this Cordelia I told you about who works in the circus, Cordelia needs him, whether she thinks she does or not. She was a belter once, that one! Ah –

she's quieter than she used to be. But her
daughter, Gwenlliam, she'll go to California
I bet! I tell her stories at night when she's
going to sleep, we share a room, she
snuggles up in her bed and says 'tell me a
story Regina,' and I do and she falls asleep.
I shall miss her if she goes.

Anyway. Why I been wanting to write again
Alfie, was I wrote a new poem the other day, I
sort of wrote it for us, you and me, well, for
you really, after I been reading that Mr Poe.
So here goes. You'll know what I mean
anyway.

> Sometimes when I am sleeping,
> I wake and my heart is beating,
>   Beating, beating in the night.
> I remember days of long ago
> The Workhouse where the lights were
> low
> And Father punished with a blow
> For everything we did not know
>   Beating, beating in the night.
>
> He beat us for doing nothing wrong
> But I and Alfie held our song,
> For he taught us also the love of words
> That words could roll, and sound like
> birds
> And in our heads we held those words
> When there was
>   Beating, beating in the night.

179

So there you are Alfie. For you.

Anyway Alfie, I am still looking for you. I don't really think I could manage California. I asked for you down at the docks again only yesterday, I ask all the older sailors specially, surely some of them know you, Alfie Tyrone I say and they shake their heads. I do wish I could find you. This is like sending a letter into the sky.

Well, I hope this finds you well Alfie boy, if it finds you.

Your sister
Regina.

19

Leaving the policemen to their business they walked slowly down busy-as-usual Broadway, not speaking much, and then in the dusk, like other New Yorkers, they sat amongst the trees in Battery Park: Cordelia, Rillie and Gwenlliam. The sun was low and glittering, seeming to set fire to the white sails on the Hudson. Weeping willows drooped beside the river, some thin men fished with string. It was cooler now and the women held their cloaks about them as they sat close together on the grass. Gwenlliam stared up into the shadowy branches of the sycamore trees but did not say anything.

'Well?' said Rillie, finally.

'Indeed,' said Cordelia. Again they were silent, and then Cordelia burst out: 'He's *mad!* The whole idea, *California!* – it sounds so preposterous: Kongo and Lucky already in the hold of some ship on its way down the Atlantic coast and the poor old camel on its thin spindly long legs and the lion in its cage, and painted wagons rolling about!' Cordelia half-laughed, but it sounded like rage. Gwenlliam still said nothing, but now looked at them carefully.

And then another silence, broken at last by Rillie.

'Cordie, Ma and Regina could never go to California! In the end we can't drag them along, over and over, moving on to the next place. It could take anything up to half a year to get there, whatever Silas says.' And Rillie took a deep, deep breath. 'This time, I can't go.' And she smiled wryly at her old friend. 'One of us has to say it.'

Cordelia sighed in exasperation, and anger still, and a kind of resignation. 'I know you're right, Rillie, course you are. Insane old Silas Swift! I can't think why we didn't guess what his next plan might be, with GOLD! in every newspaper,' and Cordelia shook her head in the half-dark and said:

> Gold? Yellow, glittering, precious gold?
> This yellow slave
> Will knit and break religions; bless th'accursed;
> Make the hoar leprosy adored; place thieves
> And give them title, knee, approbation
> With Senators on the bench.

'Shakespeare. *Titus Andronicus*,' said Rillie, and they all laughed.

'And would much of the *yellow, glittering, precious gold* come to us I wonder?' continued Cordelia. 'I'm not that keen to dissolve in a puff of Silas's smoke up on an invisible wire on the other side of the continent – yet what shall we do to earn money, otherwise? Oh god, *oh god*, here we go again, why does it always, in the end, come back to the same old story, no matter how we think we have moved on? *Money money money*. How long can we live, Rillie, with what we still have, without the glittering gold?'

'You know we've always survived somehow, Cordie. I've saved everything I could from the good times in the circus;

Arthur and Monsieur Roland give me money. We would have to move somewhere cheaper than Celine's House before long, but we'd survive, with their help.'

'I'll go to California,' said Gwenlliam quickly. 'I'll earn the money. I'll send money. I'd like to go.'

Cordelia leaned into her daughter's shoulder, sitting beside her there in the dusk in the park. Regret and pain and the difficulty of decisions sat beside her also. 'It would be the most marvellous adventure, Gwennie, of course it would.' She sighed. 'And the truth is, you would be a much better acrobatic blooming ghost than me! My knees are damned!'

'Except – I'm not you, Mama,' said Gwenlliam.

'You would be better than me,' said Cordelia again. 'You are a kinder person. Monsieur Roland always said kindness is important, in a Mesmerist.' She mused on this for a moment. 'I am many things but I am not, I think, particularly kind,' but Rillie nudged her on the darkening grass as if to say, *don't be silly.* For a long moment the cooler night closed in around them; Cordelia could feel her heart beating and the old clutching feeling in her stomach: *Do I go across America? Or is this where I lose Gwenlliam too?*

'The handsome policeman said he was sure he could beat me at poker!' Gwenlliam said suddenly, indignantly. 'Not many people can beat me now after my lessons with Chief Great Rainbow.'

'If you look into that handsome policeman's eyes as you were,' said Rillie, 'instead of at the cards, you will lose, young lady!'

'I am a good poker player!' the girl re-iterated, 'as long as I do not get distracted,' and they laughed at her and Gwenlliam's cheeks were quite pink, and Cordelia leaned again, just for one more moment, against her beloved, beloved daughter.

'I must go and find the old man, and bring him back home,' she said at last, sitting upright. 'I don't think I have ever seen him so angry. Silas is so – undiplomatic.'

'Not to say tactless and rash and rude,' said Rillie dryly. 'And preposterous and, as you say, mad!'

'But he is a showman!' protested Gwenlliam. 'They have to be like that!' and they half-laughed again, the three women sitting on the grass in the park.

'We have to talk about it all together,' said Cordelia briskly. 'Arthur too. We'll have to give Silas an answer.' But she was thinking, *o god o god what do I do now?* She shook herself slightly. 'I'll find the old man,' she said again. 'We cannot have him wandering New York at night, he hasn't even got a thick cloak.' She scrambled up off the grass. 'Poor old fellow, he has probably gone to Nassau Street to get some peace – ah, it is truly amazing that he who lived alone for so long now somehow lives in a small attic with six other people.'

'Tell him that pie will be nearly ready,' said Rillie. 'That's an advantage of communal living, tell him!' They moved to accompany Cordelia but she was already gone in the half-light, moving quickly as she always did, damned knees or no, and as Rillie and Gwenlliam stood themselves and then moved in the direction of Maiden Lane, they saw Cordelia's light-coloured cloak ahead of them, catching the misty gentle light of the gas lamps sometimes, among the trees and the busy, bustling people of the city.

Neither Gwenlliam nor Rillie spoke of Arthur Rivers but both of them were thinking of him: Cordelia had not been back two weeks.

As Cordelia turned towards Nassau Street she stopped for a moment outside the Daguerreotype Studio of Mr L Prince.

She stared at the photographs in the window, beside the sign that said PORTRAITS, GROUPS, MEMORIALS, THE MOON. Now in the dusk, and in the soft light thrown by the gas lamps along Broadway, the faces captured there were like dark paintings: haunted, mysterious; *each one a life*, she thought. At the bottom of the sign in small writing it said, and this was not the first time she had observed it: LESSONS GIVEN IN DAGUERREOTYPE.

Where the small sign in Nassau Street said: *Monsieur Roland: Mesmerist* there was a light in the window. She knocked on the door and he answered most courteously, as he always did, and ushered her into the second, larger room. If he was still angry he gave no sign. 'Rillie says, come home for the pie,' said Cordelia.

'Thank you,' he said, and slowly he pushed his spread-out papers into a pile on one side of his table. 'But – sit here, my dear, just for a moment.' He offered her his own chair. Light from one of his lamps spilled out over the table and the papers and the books. Monsieur Roland sat on the client's chair, across the table from her and then he spoke again before she did.

'Gwenlliam will go, of course, to California.'

Monsieur Roland seldom spoke of love. But Monsieur Roland had loved Cordelia's Aunt Hester, and he had loved and protected Cordelia, and most of all he had loved and protected Gwenlliam – who carried sweet drifts and reminders of Hester in her face and her nature. He was her teacher, as he had been Cordelia's. *She has the gift*, he had told Cordelia. *And she has something else. She has the presence of kindness. She will always make people feel better. As Hester did.*

If Gwenlliam went to California Monsieur Roland would miss her most painfully.

'She wants to go very much,' said Cordelia, trying to sound

positive and cheerful. 'I curse Mr Silas P Swift and his insane plans but, of course, it is a shining adventure.'

He nodded. 'Of course it is an adventure. But this will be a hard decision for you, my dear.' He did not make it clear whether he meant Gwenlliam's decision, or her own, and she did not answer.

They heard the tiny beat of the flame in the lamp. People hurried past the small window, voices and footsteps and carts rattling and horses trotting. *So long, pal!* a voice called from the street. *So long! So long, pal!*

But he asked the question again. 'And you, Cordelia. What will you do?'

She looked at him despairingly for just a moment. And then she shrugged. 'Silas – to give the devil his due, as Mr Shakespeare would put it – has always paid us well. I have to work – we are too many for you and Arthur to support, and of course I know – though he thinks I do not – that Arthur needs to send money back to England to his family there. I know he feels they must have support of some kind from him when he is so far away.'

'He does not often speak of his family.'

'No,' said Cordelia, 'he does not.' A tiny pause: neither of them speaking. 'I put it down to the fact that he has a sister-in-law who is in charge of his house who is –' she gave a small resigned grimace, remembering the unhappy meeting in Marylebone, 'difficult.'

Monsieur Roland regarded her. She said no more.

'I think,' he said, 'that there are other things we must talk about at this – this turning point, as well as California.' An expression of alarm crossed Cordelia's face: *surely he is not going to ask questions about Arthur and me? about my marriage? I do not want to talk about that.* Monsieur Roland's long, thin fingers rested on the papers beside the lamp; she saw notes in his small, neat handwriting, and when he began to talk it was not her marriage he spoke of.

'Cordelia, the great days of mesmerism are now – irrevocably – over.' She made to speak: he put up his hand gently. 'Listen for a moment, I am not changing the subject of our future although it may appear that I am: if my words are somewhat chaotic it is only because my thoughts are not yet perfectly ordered.' She saw that his eyes took in all the books in the room and on his desk. He took a breath, like a deep sigh, and then he began to speak.

'It is of course not easy for me to think that my life's study and work has been, after all, superseded by new discoveries – I speak of course of ether and chloroform, not all the excruciating rubbish that fills the newspapers about psychics and spiritualists and the tapping of tables. However.' His fingers drummed now on the papers. 'However my study and my work may lead me, even now, down new paths myself. Perhaps lead to new ways of healing. Physical pain is not the only pain in the world.'

There was a knock just then at the street door and Monsieur Roland left the room; she heard murmuring voices, appointments discussed. People did still look then, for this healer. *That's what he is above all other things*, she suddenly thought. *As there have been since time immemorial. He is a wise man and he is a healer.* The soft light from the oil lamp tried to reach out across the sparse, dark room.

When he came back, bowing in apology at the interruption, Monsieur Roland walked to the small window, looked out at the busy evening street. 'Over and over again I am impressed by all the hopeful *energy* here. It is amazing to observe. Therefore do not ever think, Cordelia, that I regret that we came to New York. What an extraordinary city it is, and how, somehow, optimistic,' and she could hear the smile in his voice.

'All my life I have studied human energy, that very thing we see so clearly in these streets, and my belief is that the energy comes from the human mind. You and I close down pain, only instead of using some chemical means we use our own energy to unblock our patients' energy, for the same ends. I think that is miraculous, in its way.' He turned back to her. 'And I have always thought, in studying people, that *the strength of their mental energy* made them into who they were. That mental energy is somehow the basis of personality.

'But then –' and he came back to sit with Cordelia at the table. 'Then I started to live in the same room, so very often, as Mrs Spoons.'

Cordelia was so startled that she repeated his words: *Mrs Spoons?*

'These last few years,' he continued, 'living so closely to Mrs Spoons, I think I have learned something so important yet I am only just now recognising it, and putting it into coherent thought. All I thought of was energy, the uses of energy. I had never fully understood the importance of memory.'

'Memory?' He could not have surprised her more.

'But think of it, Cordelia.' He leaned across the table. 'Think of it. What are we? What makes us know who we are? We *are* our memories. Our memories are what we are made of. What use is all the mental energy in the world if we do not know who we are? We know who we are, because we *remember*, for what else makes us ourselves, gives us knowledge of ourselves, our life?' He patted at one of the books on the table. 'I, of course, am not the first person to think this; for a long time philosophers have thought about memory. John

Locke here says *the memory is the self*. Mrs Spoons still functions as a living body, yes, she still breathes and eats and sleeps – but she has no self, because she has no memories. And yet she was a young girl who grew up in London, who married Mr Spoons, who had children, who had Rillie, who lived with Rillie and Regina and you in London, who boarded a ship and came to live in New York. She, most tragically I have now begun to see, remembers none of this – no wonder she has become so anxious and disturbed – I cannot believe I had not thought of this before. *Mrs Spoons has an illness*. She is stranded in a world of nothing.' He heard Cordelia's intake of breath.

'That sounds so – so lonely!'

'Indeed. What a terrible, lonely illness it must be. And yet – of course – it is not so simple. You and Rillie always talk of how very kind she was when she was a younger woman. We see that in her odd way she is *still* kind – think of her with Arthur and his bandages, she somehow saw that something was wrong, wanted to comfort him: even though she does not remember who he is. Does that mean kindness is not a memory? And lately – you were there – she joined in that song: *whistle and I'll come to you*, she sang, she knew the words – she knew them in the old Scots version even – something there inside her still. Do music and kindness stay perhaps, when everything else is taken away by this cruel illness?' He was speaking very slowly, as if nothing he said was certain; he saw her confused face. 'Just a little more patience,' he said smiling a little. 'I am not, as I said, exactly changing the subject of California.

'Because I have been thinking a great deal of Mrs Spoons and her lost memories, I began to think of people who – something I have noticed in my work and not given due importance

189

to – people who do not *lose* their memories, as Mrs Spoons has done, but who – how can I phrase this correctly? who put memory away – block out, as it were, memories. Because they are perhaps too difficult to bear.' He saw her face and spoke quickly, 'I live with you also, Cordelia. I see in your face every-day that you remember.' She nodded briefly; for a moment they sat together in silence. 'Although you very seldom speak of the past,' he added.

'No,' she said at last. 'I do not speak of the past. But I live with people who know what happened; you were all there, Arthur was there. I do not have to *discuss* things. I think it is undignified to go on and on and weep and wail – I literally cannot imagine any situation where I would tell my story to anyone else ever, ever again.' She looked at him firmly. 'It does not mean that I block it out. But I live a new life now. The old one is over.'

He simply took her hand in his, held it across the table; if he thought differently he did not, at that moment, say. They sat in silence. Then gently he released her hand, turned the lamp up slightly. 'But, my dear, some people, and I now – belatedly – recognise this from years and years of work – some people per-haps block their memories *without perhaps knowing they are doing so.* And here we get to my real point at last: just as we use mesmeric passes to unblock the flow of energy in another person – listen, here is my exact thought – I wonder whether it would be possible to *unblock memory* – for perhaps it is blocked memories that give people some at least of the – the emotional pain that we as mesmerists sometimes try to deal with, which – as you know – often shows itself as physical pain.'

Cordelia suddenly saw the circus tent in Hamford: the young woman, Emily, the blinding headaches making her turn

190

her head backwards and forwards, the burnt children of whom she could not speak. 'Yes,' she said slowly. 'I am certain that can be true.'

'And you know, Cordelia, here, in this new country, people are not bound to the past, to old ways of thinking. I think it is no coincidence that these modern inventions – the invention of the telegraph say, and indeed Mr Morton's work with sulphuric ether to close the brain down – were discovered here, and not in the old world. Tradition does not stifle, here.'

'Mr Daguerre's daguerreotype was invented in your own country!'

'And of course I speak in large generalisations. People will invent things in all countries. But who saw so very quickly how to make money from daguerreotypes? Where were the first studios set up, the cheap portraits taken, cheap enough for so many to have them? America! In which country was Mr Daguerre most feted and recognised and given ribbons of honour? America! America *embraces* new ideas! Well – this is *my* new idea: if people could first *speak* to us if they come for our help with pain, we ourselves might possibly observe signs of the memories that they hide, but yet that so distress them. And if we could make them see what damage they do to themselves would that make it easier for the physical pain that they bring to us to heal? By talking to us, might they understand themselves?'

'Certainly people love to talk, in America,' she said dryly.

'Of course! That is my point! In America people talk all the time to complete strangers about the most intimate things without demur – and also ask very intimate questions of oneself. La Grande Celine, for example, recently asked me without any reticence at all whether I owned another jacket, and exactly how much money I earned as a mesmerist!' but she saw that he was smiling in the lamplight and she smiled herself.

'What did you say?'

'It had not been a good day here in Nassau Street – although I do still, occasionally, have good days. I had had two patients. I had charged one dollar fifty to the first and the other offered me a half-guinea coin as all that she had, so I bowed and accepted. But I will not even pay my rent here in Nassau Street on that! I gave Celine this information as requested and she immediately insisted that I have hot chocolate mixed with *cognac*!' They both laughed now, yet he sighed and got up again from the table and the light, moved into the shadows by the window and back again, pacing as if he urgently required more space. 'Dr Mesmer recognised that energy could be blocked. I am – just to re-iterate what I am stumbling towards – I am wondering if memory gets blocked also, perhaps because it is too painful. And if it was released, would real healing follow? Would we help the process, just by listening much more? If we could help a man to see into his heart, it might just take away the pain in his head. That is all.'

'But what if people do not want to remember?'

'Then – perhaps we are inviting madness. If people will not allow themselves to remember we cannot help them. And I do not even know if this new way of helping them would give us any success at all. But we could try.'

'But – but how exactly. You have not said *how*!'

'Perhaps – just by inviting them to talk to us?'

'And still use mesmerism?'

'Yes. Perhaps. It is *that* that I still have to work out.' And he gave an odd shrug of his frail old shoulders. And then he looked down at her where she sat at his work-table. He trod so very carefully, spoke so very gently. 'Perhaps you yourself might one day find the need to talk again of all that has happened to you so that,' (carefully he spoke, gently) 'so that it does not haunt you so. You perhaps do not altogether *live* your new life yet.'

'Of course I do! I am not sick! I do not have pain! I have married Arthur!' She was shocked by his words to her; almost she was affronted, yet somehow she was never affronted by her beloved Monsieur Roland. He put up his hand, understanding.

'My dear I have talked for far too long and you and Arthur and Gwenlliam need to speak of many things. I am not – I think you know me better than that – trying to keep you in New York – but just suggesting new work here perhaps, if you do stay. And now we must go home.' And she realised that he was offering an alternative to Silas's acrobatics, if she needed it. The lamp flickered as they moved at last to leave. The extraordinary conversation was over for now, yet she could not help asking him curiously: 'You say you began these new ideas because you observed Mrs Spoons. You do not think that Mrs Spoons' memories too are somehow blocked? That we could help *her* with your new ideas?'

'I have talked to Mrs Spoons many, many times over these last months. I believe she knows us as familiar things, as her rocking chair is familiar, and she is kind to us sometimes, as she was always kind, but does not recognise herself and she does not recognise us. Neither she, nor we, are inside her head any more. I think we must assume, as much as we can assume anything about something so complicated and unknown as the human brain that, in some people, parts of the brain die, that the memories of Mrs Spoons are quite dead, and gone from her and will never return. That is her illness, and we cannot assist with that. I wish that was not so, my dear, and I would be glad to be proved wrong tomorrow, but I think it is true,' and at that very moment there was a knock at the door and they both jumped slightly. But it was Gwenlliam who burst into the small rooms, red cheeks from running fast from Maiden Lane to Nassau Street.

'Is something the matter?' Cordelia moved to her daughter at once.

'No!' Gwenlliam started to laugh at their alarmed faces. 'Of course not! But do you know what time it is? When are you coming home? We want you both home! The handsome policeman Mr Frankie Fields has taken Arthur's report – his very angry report, I must say – to the police station and now has returned to eat with us as invited by Rillie; the steak and oyster pie is ready; Rillie and Arthur and Mr Fields and Regina have all had a glass of port, and I have even had time to play that Mr Fields at poker – at the moment the score is equal! We are cosy like a royal family in our little attic, but we need you to complete it, come home! And I wish the proper summer would hurry up. It is cold in here now.' Neither of them had noticed. But Gwenlliam stood there, so young, so excited, so full of life's adventures and they knew she was really saying, *Come home and talk about California!* and suddenly Cordelia made a small sound, moved swiftly, hugged her daughter to her fiercely, held her very tightly for a long moment. And then she lifted her head, and nodded, almost imperceptibly, to Monsieur Roland. And he understood she was saying: *I will stay.*

And then she turned back to her daughter. '*Of course* we cannot all pack up together again and go to California, my darling, the way we left England! Mrs Spoons would never survive such a journey, Rillie will never leave her, and where we go, Regina goes, we would never leave her now – and my ancient knees, my damned knees! – oh god, imagine us all with canoes and crocodiles and snakes and rainforests! But you long to go, Gwennie, I know, I know – and I promise that whatever else is decided, I will not stop you. There!' And finally Cordelia released her daughter from her arms, smoothed her hair, and then pushed back her own hair from her own eyes. 'And, old man,' she said fondly to Monsieur Roland who had been listening quietly, 'without you we would have crumbled years ago and you cannot get away from us now! Over my dead body would you ever be travelling through crocodiles to California! But Gwenlliam is different, she is the only one amongst us who is really young and has a whole life waiting, and the rest of us will be waiting for her when she returns. Of course I *know* you want to go to California with the circus, Gwennie, I know how much you love that life.'

'But – you will not come?' Gwenlliam looked at her mother uncertainly. 'I love you too, Mama.'

'I know you do, my darling – but this is *not* a choice between one love and another! They are different loves. Then Cordelia took a deep, deep breath and said: 'We will talk to Peggy Walker.' She explained to Monsieur Roland in a cheerful voice: 'She is the wonderful Wardrobe Mistress you have heard us talk of, who makes us all so shiny! She will – I am sure she will – be willing to be Gwenlliam's guardian and I will stay in New York and work with you.' And Monsieur Roland understood, again, the strength of Cordelia Preston.

'I'm not sure that I am any longer young enough, Mama, to require a guardian!'

'Keep an eye on you playing poker then, and indulging in ether frolics! We know perfectly well you can be whatever ghostly acrobatic oracle Silas may require just as well as me –

and with much more agility, and I will make Silas pay you a grand, grand fee.'

Gwenlliam looked then at Monsieur Roland. He was very contained, this old man that she loved, but it was he who had found her own talent, taught her everything she knew.

'You know I will support you whatever you do,' he said gravely. 'I trust you with our craft absolutely.' But words unspoken drifted: how could they not? *We must hope that we will all be together again.*

'I do not have to decide yet,' said Gwenlliam in a sudden, small voice.

Monsieur Roland said, 'We will rely on you heavily, *ma chère.* We will rely on you to support us in our old age!' And the drifting moment was banished and he was smiling and Gwenlliam hugged him; she could feel his thin bones.

'Celine has been *devouring* the newspapers,' she told them then, 'for of course having worked in the circus herself she knows Silas, and he told her, when he left us today, of his plans and his dreams, so she has come up to the attic with all the newspapers she could find and has been reading out the bits to us that show how terrible and how dangerous California is! She and Regina, vying with each other to read of the worst disasters! Celine cannot bear that we should go – she is fond of us I think but, most importantly, she has fallen in love with you, Monsieur Roland.'

He looked embarrassed. 'People do not fall in love with old men, my dear. Though I do say she does make a very fine *chocolat chaud.*'

'She has had quite enough of young men, I believe,' said Gwenlliam teasingly. 'You remind her of her French childhood and she thinks you are beautiful and kind. She only falls in love with Frenchmen you see – why, the great love of her life –

she has only just confided this in me – was *Pierre l'Oiseau*, Pierre-the-bird – you know, you know – my French acrobatic partner with the big moustache. She had not realised he was in our circus until I mentioned him yesterday.'

'Is there then some way we could ask *Pierre l'Oiseau* to remain in New York when the circus goes to California?' asked Monsieur Roland, and he was only half-joking. Cordelia began to laugh, to see Monsieur Roland's discomforted face, and he tried to laugh also. But at last he shook his head and caught her eye.

'I loved your Aunt Hester,' he said. 'That was love, for me.' And then he added quietly, 'She was my joy and my life. That is the memory for me: the one that makes me know who I am.'

'But Celine has such high hopes!' continued Gwenlliam piteously. But he shook his head again, smiling nevertheless as he locked the little front door where it said so modestly: *Monsieur Roland, Mesmerist*, and the three walked home along Broadway to the attic, and the pie, and their family.

The leaves were green, and flowers could be seen in the strangest places: along Broadway, in Battery Park, beside the Croton Water Reservoir, even growing sometimes by the Green-Grocer shops with their cabbages outside and their curtains at the back. Arthur insisted on going back to work: he and Frankie Fields walked openly on the docks with their bruises and their bandages as if to say: *Not yet, b'hoys, not yet.*

Mr Doveribbon, rescued by a big shipping hook from the shallows of the dirty, disgusting East River, had taken to his bed at the American Hotel, expecting to have contracted a dangerous fever; he was so sorry for himself and so angry that he considered returning to London. He had to use *ten thousand pounds, ten thousand pounds* as a mantra to recover himself. He then, not having died of drowning or contamination but sneezing often, had himself measured at a Jewish tailor for another grey suit (*give me two*): was impressed despite himself by the speed at which these Americans worked, although of course the workmanship could never be as good as that of an English gentlemen's tailor.

And in the meantime Cordelia and Gwenlliam walked down Maiden Lane towards the office in Pearl Street to meet Mr Silas P Swift as promised. They had talked and planned and had decided between them how Gwenlliam might best transform herself from the tiara-wearing princess into the Star of the Circus (who actually did not tell fortunes or look into the future but would dance in the high shadows and mesmerise those who needed her). They swept into his office and Cordelia presented their plan.

'It will be even more thrilling, Silas!' said Cordelia. 'Gwenlliam is young, and a wonderful, wonderful acrobat as you well know. *And* a wonderful Mesmerist. And, incidentally, Gwenlliam will require at least double the salary that you originally paid her, and more if you are a success in California.' Cordelia Preston, born in a theatre, had nevertheless had so much practice at being a lady of class in England that she could not speak in any other way: had not forgotten how to impress, quite cold and firm.

Silas P Swift did not care about English social *mores* in the least but Cordelia nevertheless always intimidated him slightly. He was enraged and disappointed at her defection, and doubtful. 'I got you to America! It is you who have always been the Star. It is you people queue to see.' Then he spoke almost as if she was not there, addressing Gwenlliam. 'There is something about her. Something odd and powerful and it is nothing to do with youth or age. She gives me the shivers when she appears up there in the shadows, even now. Cordelia, come on pal, I will pay more money!'

But Cordelia was firm. 'Do you know how old I am, Silas?'

He blustered, embarrassed. 'That is not the point. Why, I am turned forty myself, I have grand-children.'

'Well, I am *almost*, but not quite, old enough, Silas, to be your mother, and therefore your grand-children's great-grand-mother. And I am sure you would not consent to your own mother and all your family crossing America in search of gold either!'

'A family is parents, children,' said Silas sullenly, used to having his own way, 'not old ladies and gents.' He had not forgotten Monsieur Roland's rage.

'No Silas, family is a word with many meanings. A family is the people you live with and love and depend upon, and who depend upon you also. But my dear man, you should be pleased! You should be excited! Gwenlliam is young and pretty and the miners will love her: as I keep telling you youth is such an advantage, she can do many things I am no longer capable of. She has been trained in mesmerism just as I have – she has been scandalously under-used – and you know very well she is a much finer acrobat than an old woman like me with cushions tied to her knees, can ever be. She will be stunning!'

He considered, stroking his moustache pensively.

'You'll have to be called **THE CLAIRVOYANT GHOST**,' he said to Gwenlliam at last. 'Or I won't agree.'

Neither of them answered: this was bargaining time.

'What happened to the bear, Silas?' asked Gwenlliam.

'I have no idea, great fraud that it was. Bear pie probably: I sold him. It's *brown* bears that dance, I know that perfectly well. I don't know how they got that old white one to trick me, but they did! Well, he's probably gone to Bear Heaven now, the menacing, useless old humbug. I never did feel safe with him – they eat humans, you know.' At last he looked at Gwenlliam carefully. 'Hmm. Gwenlliam as an Oracle perhaps?' he suggested slyly. 'That idea I had – showing, just more or less, where the gold is, by looking in a crystal ball? I could charge twenty dollars for that!'

Gwenlliam laughed. 'Stop it, Silas! We've been through that! I feel as Mama does, and as Monsieur Roland does, about mesmerism. But I shall appear in the shadows, as,' she flashed her mother a glance, they would have to compromise slightly, 'as The Clairvoyant Ghost if you absolutely insist, but no crystal balls, it must still be mesmerism as we know and understand it. But listen, listen, Silas, I've had some ideas, listen. What about a gold wand shining high up there? *Gold*, you understand, gold wands in gold-fields, catching the light . . .' And she began to describe to Silas her ideas for new excitement, her voice dancing and tinkling as it always did; her manner confident, as it always was. Cordelia watched her daughter, listened in silence, did not allow herself to be anything but supportive.

'And so, Silas,' Cordelia said at last, 'you see Gwenlliam's enthusiasm. With all her talents she will be even more of a success than I. And she *wants* to go with you, Silas; look at her, she can't wait to start rehearsing new ideas. You can start on the ship down to Panama – plenty of ropes on a ship! She loves the circus and we have already talked to Peggy Walker about acting as her guardian when she is not sewing beads and washing the trousers of clowns! However.' Cordelia's voice became stern. 'We know very well all the difficulties and dangers of getting to California and in exchange for what we have agreed, you must contract and agree that she will be paid in advance as soon as you make money and that in two years she will come back to us. It is only, after all, two years,' she said to Gwenlliam, but her firm voice shook slightly.

'Well,' said Silas, disappointed still, still unsure, but recognising one of them was better than none when he was planning to leave so soon and indeed could have lost both of them if that letter had been delivered. 'Well. Nobody is you, Cordelia, and when we come back you will have to join us again.'

'I give you my word I will re-join the circus on your return if you are not satisfied with my talented daughter. How's that for a bargain?'

He stroked his moustache over and over. 'Well. I agree but only because I have to – no offence, Gwen.' He thoughtfully gestured over their heads with his hands, already he was planning the new sign: **THE CLAIRVOYANT GHOST** in huge letters. 'And perhaps just a tiny crystal ball?' Again he gestured with his hands, he could see it all: **THIS WAY FOR GOLD!**

'No!' said Gwenlliam herself. 'No crystal ball, Silas. Extra somersaults, and a magical wand – but made of gold, of course – we will mesmerise all the miners with a golden wand!'

And with that Mr Silas P Swift had to be content.

20

Peggy Walker, the costume keeper, the person who made every thing and everybody in the circus seem to shine and glitter, had indeed agreed to act as Gwenlliam's guardian: she had come at once from her boarding house in Brooklyn to Maiden Lane, met everybody, been looked over and approved of. She hugged Gwenlliam as she left. 'Get packing, pal, it will be an adventure!' said Peggy. 'We will write letters full of gold!' And in the attic in Celine's House all felt the excitement, even as they dreaded the loss. Cordelia's face was pale as she smiled and smiled.

As soon as everything was arranged with Silas Cordelia said she was going to buy herself a new hat. This was so unlikely that no-one in the small sitting-room believed her, although they would never have dreamed of saying so.

'Shall I come, Cordie?' Rillie knew Cordelia so well: it was not a hat, it was something else.

'No, no, I will surprise you all!' (But Rillie had asked if she might come because she saw that Cordelia's hands were shaking as she drew on her gloves. She was battling with something. *Something*, Rillie knew.)

Trying to avoid filthy, dancing mud and shit and dust raised by the clattering horses pulling the carts and the omnibuses, Cordelia walked towards the Brooklyn Ferry Terminus. Flags of America hung proudly on buildings even as garbage lay in the streets, flies and rats everywhere and summer still not properly arrived. The smell and the piles of rubbish got even worse as she approached the docks. New York may have been a prosperous port but the docks beside the ferry were filthy and in a great state of disrepair, planks of wood dangerously loose above the murky water, and beside a particularly fetid pile of rubbish a very small black man was standing and hitting at the pile with a stick, shouting CUNTING NIGGAH! CUNTING NIGGAH!, hitting the garbage over and over as people hurried past.

They streamed aboard the ferry, Cordelia carried along in the great swarm of people; she hardly noticed that she was jostled and pushed by the crowds, albeit in a friendly manner. The East River was crowded with a hundred vessels as always: big, small, old, new, American, foreign. Rubbish and dead rats could be seen in the water below and – as the ferry churned and Cordelia stared into the dirty water – other strange things could be seen also: iron, wood, a tailor's dummy with no arms, soggy newspapers, something that looked like half a bedstead. And something that looked like bones.

Brooklyn was bustling also and Peggy Walker met her on the shore, wearing a myriad of shining scarves. She led Cordelia up a hill to the colourful room she rented in a large house which overlooked the East River and Manhattan; from Peggy's window they could see the docks and the buildings and across the water, above everything, the spire of Trinity Church. Cordelia tried to take in the room which was bright with colour, furnished with all sorts of odd and interesting objects as well as Peggy's bed: painted pictures, a moose's head, an American eagle, a mirror decorated with shells, and a clock in the shape of George Washington in his uniform, with his hands pointing to the minutes and the hours. Peggy was in the middle of packing: clothes and sewing materials and shining beads scattered everywhere.

'I got your message, Cord,' said Peggy. 'Sit here,' and she cleared an over-flowing chair and offered beer and biscuits. The cushion on Cordelia's chair was decorated with the American flag.

She held her beer, but did not yet drink. Peggy saw that there was some battle in her face, as if she wanted to speak but was unable to do so. 'I am so grateful to you, Peggy,' Cordelia said at last. 'I know you will watch over Gwenlliam as best you can,' and Peggy laughed: they both knew Gwenlliam was efficient and cheerful and clever and would very likely watch over Peggy.

'Stop worrying, Cord. I'll be there. Ain't no Indians or crocodiles going to get us!' As they talked Peggy was embroidering a bright new blanket with beads, no doubt for that exotic camel, if it should survive the journey. 'Still, you could have knocked me over with a feather when Silas arrived here with all his plans and dreams. It won't be for ever, knowing Silas, and I sure don't want to live with gold miners for ever; I heard they have spittin' competitions, ten dollars a spit, mind! I'd like a bit more culture than spittin'. Well – if we make our fortunes it'll all be worth it! Fingers crossed.' She kept on sewing but from the corner of her eye saw that Cordelia was making an enormous effort, a great deal of swallowing. 'Come on. What's on your mind, Cord?'

On the last day before they left London for good, Cordelia and Gwenlliam went back to the little churchyard at the Elephant and Castle. They had had a small headstone erected over his grave. It read only:

MORGAN
BELOVED BROTHER AND BELOVED SON

Despite the freezing cold there were small signs of spring. There were crocuses at the foot of a bare tree, irregular dashes of yellow and purple. But they felt a terrible, painful regret that this boy, who had so dreamed of going to America, was staying here. Once more they wept; they saw their old Welsh home: the gatehouse, and the castle ruins behind and the endless, endless sea and the broken hulls of ships lured on to the rocks by smugglers – ships that were once perhaps from the new country that Cordelia told the children of: America. 'It's a new country,' she had told them. 'We shall all go there.'

At last, arm in arm, dressed for the last time in the black clothes of mourning, the two women turned away from the grave and walked towards the churchyard gate. They turned back once; two black-gloved hands were raised, just for a moment, in farewell to a life that was gone.

'If – if anything should – that is if anything should happen to Gwenlliam, should she become ill for instance –'

'You're looking on the blue side.'

'I know. I do not want to but I must. You are going so far and if – if anything happened I would want you to know a little more about her, that she was not with a stranger. Not, of course, that you are a stranger at all.' Cordelia downed most of the beer, put the glass beside her; her hands shook badly, Peggy saw how she literally forced herself to speak. 'Listen, Peggy. Gwenlliam had a sister and a brother. Manon and Morgan. Perhaps she might want to talk of them.' Cordelia did not realise it but as she spoke her voice became even more English still, as if to escape emotion. 'I – I was once a well-known actress in London. I worked with Edmund Kean. I worked with William Macready, the one in the Astor Place riots.' Peggy listened stoically. She did not care for the English type of acting. 'I left the stage – I thought for good – when I –' she stumbled on the words, 'I fell in love and married. I had three children. They were taken away from me by their father.'

'Cruel bastard, was he?'

'We had lived for eight whole years, all of us, including him often, in a wonderful old gate-house beside a crumbling family castle, on the Welsh coast.'

The deserted shore was their life: she would see their blonde heads far out on the wet sand as the tide snaked out, bent over rocks and shells; all day their voices would echo upwards, she would hear them laughing and calling of their strange found treasures; wild sea-birds flew over them, and there was the smell of salt and seaweed. And then there would come a wild Welsh storm, and heavy rain would pound the sea and the wind would blow the children back to the grey stone place that was their home as the ruins of the old castle shadowed behind them, and the fires would be lit by the servants and sometimes Cordelia would sing:

> *When that I was and a little tiny boy*
> *With a heigh ho, the wind and the rain*
> *A foolish thing was but a toy*
> *For the rain it raineth every day . . .*

'I simply thought, when he left us for long periods, that my husband had much business to attend to in London. He was a member of the aristocracy and I was, as I say, an actress. So I

206

should have known better. It – it transpired that the marriage was – it was a hoax.'

'Well, well, here we would know better than to trust any English nobleman! You sure came to the right place when you came to America.' But Peggy Walker was a sensible woman and saw that her interruptions would not help Cordelia tell her story. She endeavoured to concentrate on the shining beads.

'One terrible day he sent a message for me to go to London urgently, and while I was gone he had the children taken away to be brought up as their own with his – his new, noble wife. I only found them again ten years later. By then Rillie and I had set up our mesmerism business. To survive.'

'Ten years! My, that is so terribly sad. How did you find them again?'

'Gwenlliam – Gwenlliam found me.' Peggy wondered if Cordelia was going to faint. So she spoke very cheerfully.

'Why, I might have known! Gwen's a sensible girl with spirit. The best combination of all for any girl.'

It was the voice. Absurd as it seemed after so many years, and despite the clipped words and the drawn-out vowels of the nobility, she was certain she recognised the voice in the next room, and hearing it, Cordelia actually made a small sound, a cry, as if she was choking: the room spun and beads of perspiration broke out on her forehead and her top lip and her chest and her legs.

Would Rillie know? Did Rillie think this was just a new client? **Was** *this just a new client?* **Am I mistaken?** *Any moment then, Rillie would bring the owner of that voice into the big, dark room where Cordelia carried out her mesmeric practices.*

Cordelia's panic was such that for a moment she stared about her star-decorated room frenziedly as if to find a place to hide. She finally sat down on the usual dark chair, quickly blowing out two of the nearest candles so that the darkness was more intense than usual. She pulled the flowing scarves over her head the way she always did before a customer entered: the drum that was her heart beat wildly.

The door opened and a young woman entered. Rillie indicated, as she always did, that the visitor should sit on the sofa, and then the door closed softly behind her. Cordelia saw that the girl – the pale, pale girl – was adapting her eyes to the darkness and then she understood that the girl had seen her.

Cordelia would have to speak.

'How can I help you?' she said and her voice was like a whisper.

The young woman did not answer at once. Her long fair hair was caught at her neck, she was older, and she was so pale, but it was the same face, the beloved face. Without any sound tears suddenly fell down Cordelia's face in the flickering darkness. She saw a face that she knew, yet did not know: the grey enquiring eyes, the same quirky, open face as Aunt Hester, and the eyes.

'We were told that you were dead,' said the young woman, and Cordelia heard that her voice trembled.

Very slowly, wondering if she was dreaming, or insane, Cordelia unwound the scarves from her head: they lay there, glittering, across her shoulders. Very slowly she walked towards the sofa and as she walked the words emerged: 'I did not die,' and the girl nodded and the dark flickering room spun round.

But it was an old family adage: none of the Misses Preston ever fainted.

The two women regarded each other. Rillie's flute began to play from the next room as it always did when Cordelia was working, to give the atmosphere.

'I recognised your voice, Gwenlliam,' said Cordelia.

'They said you were dead, Mama,' said Gwenlliam.

Very slowly still, as if she was ill, Cordelia sat beside her daugh-

ter. 'I looked for you in Wales so many times but the old house was locked up years ago and the castle has crumbled even more.'

'Yes.' The flute went on playing, very quietly. Still they sat quite apart, stared at each other. **Ten years gone.** For a moment the silence was so extraordinary that it was as if the room was empty. And then there was a little avalanche of words.

'Gwenlliam, where were you taken? They must have taken you all away somewhere almost at once because I returned home straight away and –'

'– and yes, that same day you were sent for to London some men and a lady came in a carriage and just took us away. I just had a moment to leave a small letter in our tree-house, I did not know where we were going but I thought –'

'– and I looked in our tree-house, it seemed the obvious –'

'– and I knew you would look there, I knew. If you were alive I knew you would look in the tree-house.' Their voices made small gasping sounds.

'But there was a storm. By the time I got home our house was locked up, and there was a terrible storm. There was no letter, I climbed up into the tree-house. There was no letter but I knew you would have left one, if you could –'

– and I wrote 'they are taking us away' but I could not tell you where we were going. They just picked us up and took us away, they took us far north, somewhere near a place called Ruthen I learned afterwards, another old stone house but nowhere near the sea. And they told us you were dead.' And all the time they sat stiffly apart, staring at each other in disbelief. 'We have lived there for years and years.'

'What – what did you do? How did you live? Who – who looked after you?'

'We had many tutors. Morgan would do nothing but read and paint pictures, even when they sent him to a proper school. But

Manon and I learnt young lady refinements.' Cordelia saw them all, with tutors far away, their birthdays passing, and herself trying to pick up a life back on stage, an older actress now, playing witches and faerie queens.

'And have they –' neither of them specified who 'they' might be '– have they –' Cordelia was trying desperately to make sense, 'have you all been looked after?'

'In a way.'

'Manon?' she said the word out loud carefully, as if it was precious china.

'Manon has just been presented at Court. She is to be married on Friday. To a Duke.'

Cordelia tried to hide her look of shock. **Manon married? To a Duke?** Manon was seven when Cordelia had waved goodbye.

She made the next word. 'Morgan?' There was no answer. 'Morgan?' she said again urgently.

'He is – as he always was.' And Cordelia again made that sound, like an odd choked cry. She looked quickly down at her own hands. She saw the anguished little boy's face when his head hurt, the anger, the smoothing of the head, the silence; heard not Rillie's flute but the sound of the sea, children's voices calling to each other across the long empty shore below the old stone house; bright blue flowers and wild red and yellow flowers bent with the wind. She looked up again and saw the young woman in front of her; above her the pretend stars caught the candlelight in the dark room.

She had to ask a thousand questions or none. Finally she said, 'How did you find me?'

'Just a few months ago Morgan was taken to Cardiff for his headaches and –'

'– he still gets headaches?'

'They are different headaches from before. In Cardiff Morgan found your advertisement in the newspaper. MOTHER IS

LOOKING FOR TREE-HOUSE CHILDREN. *Did you put an advertisement for us in newspapers every week? All those years?'*

'I put it in every year. On his birthday. But – there was never any answer.'

'He found it, and he showed me but I told him he was foolish and he got angry and tore up the newspaper,' and again Cordelia saw the small, anguished face from the past. 'I did not think Morgan could manage finding you again,' Gwenlliam said simply. 'It took him too long to recover from your going. But of course I wondered if it was you and I made up my mind to reply secretly as we were coming to London for Manon to be presented to Queen Victoria, and then to be married.'

'But – I did not get a letter.'

'Miss Spoons found it.' She heard Cordelia's gasp of shock. 'She contacted me at once. It was such luck, Mama, for my stepmother requires all my letters from me, but I was just returned this afternoon from walking in the Square, the boy was there and he gave me the letter from Miss Spoons – I just turned around and came here, I took a cabriolet by myself, I had never done that before.'

Cordelia tried with all her strength to remain coherent, to speak normally, to say something normal. Candles flickered. 'You are all then – all – in London? Manon? And Morgan? And you.'

'Yes. Morgan and I have never been before, but Manon loves London and the noble life. But Morgan and I always planned to run off to the new country. To America.'

'What do you mean?'

'We always dreamed of going to America. You told us about it, that it was a new country, that it just jumped up out of the sea – but our tutor told us that America was there all the time.'

'Oh! O, Gwenlliam, I made it up to amuse you all! I did not know anything at all about America!' And both women, remembering, actually laughed for a second in a surprised manner that

211

a part of their past was touching them on the arm like a ghost, and then their small laughter stopped, and then the silence came again.

'But London was always Manon's dream. Our grandfather – that is the Duke of Llannefydd – he is an awful, awful, cruel old man and he is always drunk and he smells of whisky and bad teeth and we have to kiss him and he runs our lives and makes the decisions – even Father is scared of him, I think. The Duke has a house in Grosvenor Square.'

'Yes,' said Cordelia finally. 'Yes. I know that house. Once I tried to look for you, in that house.' There were too many unanswered things in the air: neither of them knew how to wade through such dangerous waters. Just the sound for a moment of uneven breathing, the clearing of a throat.

The pale girl suddenly leaned forward. 'I walked up and down Little Russell Street as soon as I got here. I remembered the name, and the stories of your mother and Aunt Hester and your life in the theatre. And meeting your Aunt Hester when she came to see us in Wales. I remember I held her hand and we showed her the shells.'

And for the third time Cordelia made the same sound, the small choked cry. '**Your** Great-aunt Hester!' she whispered. 'You look so like your Great-aunt Hester,' and somehow she at last enfolded the fair-haired girl in her arms and her scarves and they became entangled as they wept.

And as they wept the pale girl kept saying: 'I do not understand anything.' At last she stared up through her tears at her mother. 'There are so many questions running around in my head. Why did my father divorce you? Why did he say you were dead? What happened when he sent for you to London?'

'Let us not speak of these things yet,' said Cordelia quickly, and she held her daughter tightly.

212

And all the time Rillie heroically played the flute in the next-door room, wanting, with all her heart, to make them live happily ever after.

Cordelia's voice came out of a dream. 'When she found me, Peggy, they were by then young people in society with their whole lives dominated by their terrible, domineering grandfather. It was not known – and could not be known, of course – that they were actually born out of wedlock. Their father had married a distant cousin of Queen Victoria.' Peggy bit cotton impatiently. 'My eldest daughter, Manon, married a duke. Rillie and I went secretly into the Church in our best clothes and watched from a corner pew. She was – beautiful.'

At last Peggy was unable to contain herself. 'Cord, listen! *My* grandfather died in the Revolution fighting those damned English with all their high-falutin' nobility, thinking they were above everyone else and their cruel class rubbish! I am an American. You surely cannot expect me to be impressed because your daughter married a duke!' The sewing needle flew in and out. 'It was so sad to lose your children for all that time but it seems to me that Gwen is much better going to California than marrying those sorts; I reckon you have saved her from a fate worse than death by bringing her to America.'

Cordelia gave a little gasp. Her face was so white that Peggy relented. 'Well, never mind. I hope the girl who became the Duchess is living happily ever after.'

'She – I could not make myself known to her, of course, it could not be known that the new Duchess of Trent was illegitimate. She was very unhappy with her noble husband and . . . she killed herself.'

The needle stopped. Peggy wished her last words had stayed in her mouth.

At the immediate post-mortem there was no doubt at all how Manon, the young Duchess of Trent, died; the newspapers soon had all the details and more. She had asked the groom for potassium antimony, saying she had a sick horse to deal with; she died by three o'clock that afternoon in great agony with burnt internal organs: she had dressed in her wedding-gown, her face was twisted in terrible pain, she lay upon her new matrimonial bed in her new Duchess-of-Trent house in Berkeley Square, in London.

'And my son' – Cordelia's voice became almost a whisper – 'died also. Gwenlliam is all I have left.' Silence in the room in Brooklyn. George Washington ticked and tocked. Peggy leant as if to touch Cordelia's arm but Cordelia moved away slightly. 'There is more. Very soon after they found me again their father was killed by their stepmother, after she had understood that he had deceived her, that I was actually still alive.' The words came now in a torrent. 'She had, of course, like the children, thought me dead and had agreed to take the children as her own when it was found she could have none.' Then Cordelia made a sound that was half an ironic gasp, half a cry of pain. 'For various reasons *I* was at first charged with the murder.' Peggy did put the sewing down then but Cordelia seemed not to see her, so great was her effort to finish her story quickly: she spoke now very, very fast. 'That was how I met Arthur, my husband, he was the detective in charge of the case. I was found not guilty but much of my life had become very public. I was by then a very prosperous and well-known Mesmerist in London; Monsieur Roland was my teacher and my mentor and Rillie was in charge of the business. Of course after all this my – reputation – was lost completely and I could never have worked again. It was –' at last a small smile lurked in Cordelia's strained voice, '– all the lurid stories in the newspapers, even over here, that made Silas offer me work in America. When his circus was at its peak. And so we came to New York and we lived at the American Hotel and were briefly very notorious – but very prosperous!'

And Cordelia stopped at last.

Peggy Walker actually whistled, sitting there with her shining camel's blanket. 'That is some story, ma'am!' But Cordelia shrugged.

'I believe now that most people have stories. It is just that they are not necessarily made so public as mine was.'

'Now don't tell me that the wicked stepmother, that cousin of Queen Victoria, Queen of England and the Empire, was hung for murder!'

'Of course not! She was a distant cousin only, I believe – finally she had attacked me as well – but she was related to royalty and the coroner made it impossible for the jury to bring any verdict but that the children's father was "murdered by person or persons unknown".'

'Very, very hard for you, Cord.' And kind Peggy Walker, who was after all an American, could not help it: she asked just one more question. She asked it kindly, but she asked it.

'And your son – how did he die?'

'I – I –' Cordelia crashed up from her chair. 'Peggy, *don't. I can't do any more.*' She moved quickly to the window, looked across again at Manhattan. The tallest point, the Trinity Church spire, pierced the sky like a knife.

Gwenlliam ran for the doctor: Cordelia stayed with him.

'Mama, it is different, it is a different pain in my head than usual,

help me Mama! I cannot even bear it, something is happening inside my head!' and he vomited again.

Cordelia took a deep breath and stood beside him. The smell of vomit came upwards: she did not notice. For a moment she held his head as she had used to so long ago when he was a small boy, now stroked his hair. Then she felt his fifteen-year-old body convulse again. She moved back slightly and swept her hands, the mesmeric passes, over his agonised little face, over and over; she must not weep, she could not help him if she wept. Sweat, not tears, poured down her face as she tried with every inch of her being to force the energy from her own body into his. Behind her, her own shadow huge on the wall moved over and over, just above him, shadows of her moving arms swept across the ceiling again and again and again. He fouled himself in the bed and cried out but it was the pain.

'We will never be apart again, Mama? Now that we are found?' The voice started deep and ended as the whisper of a child. She smiled at him and her tears fell on him and they saw the sand stretching out for ever, the secret rocks and the sea.

'Never, never,' she said, smiling at him. 'Now that you are found.' Still she tried; she passed her hands just above his head, over and over; he waited for the release she would bring him as she always had when she held his head when he was little. And so great was his trust in her that when he felt himself floating away he thought that she had saved him.

Her hands went over and over with all her strength and all her love, all the pent-up love of the years, over and over. She did not hear the others come, did not hear anything. Until Monsieur Roland gently took her shoulders.

'Mesmerism cannot bring back life, my dear. It is not magic.'

Then Cordelia looked at Monsieur Roland, and understood.

'He had always had terrible headaches. Soon after I was re-united with him he had an apoplexy caused by a haemorrhage of the brain. He could not have lived.' Still Cordelia was looking out across the river, and then suddenly she turned sharply. Tears poured down her cheeks. 'That is my story, Peggy Walker.'

'I am so sorry, Cordelia.'

'What is yours?'

'What?'

'What is your story?'

'Why, Cord, you've heard it twenty times by twenty rivers! Of my mother, proud Daughter of the Revolution, married for love and brought down by a fool. I ran away from the farm, and joined the circus and never, never went back. All those pioneering farmers' wives all over the Mid-west going about with their shocked faces,' she said scornfully. 'They were full of bogus romancing. They had no idea how hard the life would be but whatever did they think it would be like? I worked with La Grande Celine when that mad German was pursuing her to marry him and live on a pig farm and I told her – *Don't do that, Celine!* Course then her story erupted too. She's a brave woman, that Celine. See, there's another story. Mind, I suppose there's hundreds of people that don't have such stories, but then we don't meet them, not in our line of work!' And Cordelia tried very hard to smile, and then Peggy, seeing her recovered, came to the window and, very briefly, held Cordelia's hand tightly.

'I'm glad you've told me. I'll look after Gwen the very best I can, and I won't talk of any of this unless she brings it up first. There's my word on it. Now,' she said briskly, bustling back to her camel's blanket, 'we all agree Silas P Swift is insane. California is a mad, mad idea. But it is true that news is filtering back now of other entertainers who have made the journey and are now making their fortunes, so maybe – just maybe –

we'll do the same. Or maybe on the other hand we'll end up like the farmers' wives, shocked that we were such fools. But at least those of us who read the newspapers are aware of the dangers and the difficulties. Letters will be very slow at first, of course. However, the journey is now about *money* and, mark my words as an American, money means faster and faster journeys and mail deliveries *will* be found – that is the American way. And Cord, what I think is this: we are not just one, we are a circus, and we must just hope, I think, that with so many of us – who after all know each other and will help each other – we will make it.'

'Including a lion and elephants and a camel?'

'Perhaps they will travel better than mere mortals,' said Peggy dryly. Cordelia looked up at George Washington.

'Oh!' she said faintly. 'I did not realise I had stayed so long. I did not tell them I was coming to talk to you again: I told them I was going to buy a hat. I'll have to buy a hat!' But Peggy saw that Cordelia was exhausted; she did not move from beside the window.

'Ah ha!' said Peggy. 'I believe I have, exactly, the thing.' She rummaged about in one of her over-flowing cupboards: a most beautiful, stylish grey hat with a small veil appeared. Cordelia made a small sound of admiration. 'It belonged to my poor mother.'

'Oh. She has died then?'

Peggy was silent for just a moment. 'I did not, after all, tell you the whole of my story. Funny isn't it, how we do not tell all? I know you too have only told me the bones.' She sighed. 'My mother could not, in the end, bear her life. Brought down by a fool, as I told you. One day she walked into a lake. That is when I ran away and I took a few of her things with me. You have entrusted your daughter to me, so I would like to make you a present of my late mother's beautiful hat. I know I have the best of the bargain.'

Gingerly almost, Cordelia placed the exquisite hat upon her head.

'My, my, Cordelia Preston! You look like a – you look lovely! It is so odd that the hat has not dated – or maybe its time has come again. You look –' She stopped. 'I can understand why Silas is so angry with you.'

'Is he so angry with me?'

'Course he is. You're his Star. You've got something that the others ain't got, even Gwen. You've always had it, that strange ghostly look. It affects people. Look at you, specially now with your face so white.'

'Gwenlliam is equally as good as I am as a Mesmerist. Monsieur Roland taught Gwenlliam also and Silas does not know how lucky he is to have her – she will be a stunning Ghost – especially as she actually *is* an acrobat also and doesn't have to tie little cushions to her knees!' Cordelia in her hat did then try to laugh but not very successfully. 'Ah, Peggy – take good care of her.'

'We're all survivors in the circus,' said Peggy Walker briskly. She reached for a brandy bottle, just poured it neat into their beer glasses. 'Gwen loves the circus, any fool can see that.'

'I know. That is why I must not stop her, even though I can hardly bear to –' and Cordelia's voice cracked at last, 'to – to let her go.' She drank quickly.

'Silas P Swift is a madman,' said Peggy, 'but I do admire him also! There he is, running around New York making all sorts of arrangements, it can't have been easy to get those animals and all the circus paraphernalia away when there's so many people fighting to board ships, for the gold. And you know he has already sent people ahead across the isthmus, to advertise, to see the lie of the land – a sort of sea-going telegraph wagon to put signs out for us when we arrive!' And then they both did laugh, and Cordelia drank the rest of the brandy quickly and thought wryly of Monsieur Roland: she had made herself tell her story to someone else, after all.

21

Mr Doveribbon could have happily knifed Silas P Swift with his new weapon as he shuffled and sneezed around the American Hotel: in fact had briefly planned to go back to the circus office and do so. But he had the sense to know that this action, while it might mollify his hurt pride and his ruined suit, would not advance his cause. He must surely be, after all – for the circus man had behaved most suspiciously (and tried to drown him! the man was a criminal!) – very near to his prey: he only had to follow the circus.

What did advance his cause was lounging about the next day (as discreetly as possible: he did not want further violence – though if he was offered some he would, this time, give as good as he was given) in the environs of Silas P Swift's office in Pearl Street. It was such a hive of activity – a great deal of banging, a great deal of delivering and collecting of trunks and boxes and cages – that obviously something big was going on. There was a yard at the back: Mr Doveribbon had not observed this on his first visit: he saw now a cage from which the screeching monkeys he had heard previously were desperately trying to escape. In the yard horses were corralled by bright-coated, dark-skinned young men: it seemed the young men were going to ride the horses somewhere, they spoke to the horses gently. Finally Mr Doveribbon found himself an excellent vantage point. One of the hundreds of dock saloons in the area was situated on the other side of Pearl Street; from there he could not see all the activity but he could see if anything came or left the premises. First though he looked gingerly about him: New York was a wild place, certainly. But this saloon seemed not as violent and dangerous as some of the saloons he had seen in New York, it had polished wooden tables. He ordered himself oysters and ale as that was what most of the customers seemed to consume. After a while the young, flaunting, foreign men returned with the horses: obviously they had been exercising them. The circus was presumably preparing to be presented somewhere; Cordelia and Gwenlliam Preston were almost certainly near, although Mr Doveribbon wondered if the mother would allow the daughter near the environs of a circus: the Duke of Llannefydd's daughter! Surely not! Midgets came, none as handsome as General Tom; men and women arrived who could have been clowns or acrobats, sometimes there was shouting, sometimes there was laughter, once someone burst into loud tears. But Cordelia Preston must be an older lady, and the only older lady who came called out to Silas about something to do with – he may have misheard – satin trousers – in a loud American voice.

Mr Doveribbon took advantage of the friendliness and informality of his surroundings, the Broadwalk the saloon was called, for some unfathomable reason of its own. He made himself friendly also, turned on all his charm in this atmosphere of men off-duty and business *camaraderie*. That first day, and the day after, he met businessmen and sea-captains and dockmen and traders, they all mixed with each other quite freely he noticed; he sat with them in a group, inconspicuous but a generous purse. He behaved most pleasantly among his new companions, talked to them all, bought them drinks, even joked about being an Englishman; 'I'm travelling the world!' he told them. 'And I love America!'

'Good for you, pal!' they said, slapping him on the back; he saw knives and sometimes even guns, casually worn; he heard stories of fights and fists and girls and money. And all the time he watched the comings and goings of Mr Silas P Swift's Amazing Circus.

The Captain of one of the new fast clipper ships boasted of the new speeds, told them of gold in California, told them of travelling to the other side of America, of wild storms around the Cape, through the Straits of Magellan: Mr Doveribbon shuddered privately at the thought. Dockmen boasted of the wealth of the New York port. They all seemed open and friendly, nothing like his devious acquaintances in London who talked round a subject for hours. Wild Irishmen who could not hold their drink crammed together in one corner, shouting; the noise in the saloon rose and rose but it was all a cover for Mr Doveribbon who sat in the middle of the saloon, protected by his new companions while he watched all the activity across the street: Silas P Swift roaring and ordering about and almost tearing his hair and his moustache in an agony of impatience, it was clear, to get things done.

Mr Doveribbon was careful – his activities as a detective were improving – not to ever drink too much in this volatile saloon; he kept his proper drinking for the American Hotel where he felt he was at least among his own class. In the Boadwalk he did not say he was keeping an eye on the circus across the street. He told them his name was Frederick and they called him Freddie-boy immediately and teased him about his fine grey suit and he laughed and drank beer and told lies and generally behaved like a good fellow. He kept an eye out too for someone who might do a 'disposal' job – there seemed to be several likely characters: it was quite clear he was surrounded by crooks and chancers as well as (or perhaps including) sea-captains and dock-workers: he was in the right place for business of many kinds.

But on the third morning he arrived at his saloon to find that Silas P Swift's yard and office were empty and all the gates locked.

'Where are they?' he cried wildly. 'Where's the circus?' He could not believe they would travel *by night*. His usual drinking companions looked at him in surprise.

'What's the circus to you, Freddie-boy?'

'I have – a friend, a friend I was counting on seeing before they left. Where have they gone?'

'Why, California, pal. Didn't your friend tell you? They left at dawn, carting everything down to the docks!' And Mr Doveribbon was gone, running down to the East River like a man possessed, sweating, almost weeping. And as he ran, over and over in his mind the thought: *California! The other side of the world! I have to stop her and I don't even know yet what she looks like! How can I find Cordelia Preston and stop her if I don't know what she looks like?*

224

22

The family stood there in Battery Park on a fine morning in early June, all of them including Mrs Spoons, and also including of her own volition La Grande Celine who had bought Monsieur Roland a new jacket for the occasion (very slightly purple, having heard that Dr Franz Mesmer wore a purple jacket), which he was, out of kindness, wearing. Cordelia was wearing the stylish grey hat and the pain in her eyes was concealed from most under the veil. Already it was early summer: Silas P Swift was beside himself, knowing they had to get to the gold fields in time to make money before the rainy season came there.

They had all wept. Gwenlliam had wept as she packed trunks with her clothes and her scarves and her pink tightrope shoes and her boots and her candles and her wax taper matches and her DOCTOR WRIGHT'S INDIAN REMEDY and many parcels of soap, but nothing could hide her excitement at starting out on such a tremendous adventure even as tears poured down her cheeks. She begged and begged for the daguerreotype from the wall; Cordelia took her back to the studio and had the girl's portrait done, to put on the wall in its place.

'Hello again!' said Mr L Prince.

Cordelia watched very carefully: saw how Mr Prince moved light, slanted light, then how he disappeared only for ten minutes and was back with a portrait of Gwenlliam in a frame as requested; he had caught her expression – the sensible, spirited girl – exactly. While Gwenlliam packed the picture of her family into her trunk, Cordelia put the portrait of Gwenlliam on the wall in Maiden Lane.

The sailing ship *Beauty*, bound for Chagres on the Panamanian isthmus, had been loaded on the East Docks: the hold became crammed with its exotic baggage. Even though the elephants, the lion, the camel, the wagons painted **SILAS P SWIFT'S AMAZING AMERICAN CIRCUS** full of planked seating, had left for California over a week ago with the Big Top folded into a huge parcel – even so, there was still much to transport. Some of the acrobatic bars; Peggy Walker's boxes of costumes; the clowns' big bag of huge black shoes and bouncing balls and red rubber noses; horses; dogs: these were all taken aboard the *Beauty* and the new monkeys were loaded in their cages. The monkeys screeched without cease. The horses, herded by the whistling, calling Mexican *charros* skittered nervously in their own shit as they were led into their own big cages, the whites of their eyes showed as they tossed their heads while the Indian Chief, without his headdress, tried to calm them with his sing-song incantations. The dogs barked wildly, madly, locked in boxes, not to be confused with the pigs snorting in boxes which were to be food for the passengers. Great vats of water were being loaded for the passengers also; Silas P Swift was almost beside himself, shouting instructions as boxes of dogs teetered and crashed into cages of horses and water leaked from one of the big vats and poured over the deck. Finally the hold was hammered down and the ship moved away from the pier.

The wild cacophony of noise emanating from the disappearing *Beauty* made it clear to the running, sweating, grey-suited man who arrived at the East River that the circus was aboard this particular moving ship; however he understood from the shouts around him that the *Beauty* with its sails still half-furled was sailing round, with the help of a lighter, to the Battery on the Hudson to pick up the passengers; Mr Doveribbon therefore kept running, again he could not find any cab in the crowded streets, so he simply ran across Manhattan, arrived at the Battery to find the passengers had already boarded the *Beauty*, were calling their last farewells. He stood, half bent over, trying to catch his breath: he was so wildly angry and frustrated and heated by running that he actually vomited on the pier and over his boots: he felt constrictions in his chest, considered he may be having a heart attack.

The ship, the *Beauty*, was of solid build and had a solid history, which was something; the assembled family saw with horror some of the wrecks that passed for ships that were also loading passengers: people did not care how they got to the goldfields as long as they got there; there were scuffles on the wharf and the waving of tickets to board very risky-looking boats. So Cordelia and Rillie and Regina and Inspector Rivers and Monsieur Roland – and surely Mrs Spoons if she had still had her mind – thanked any gods listening that Gwenlliam was on a trimmer, finer vessel. All had been explained over and over: the circus was to disembark at Chagres and cross the Panamanian isthmus by native canoe and then on foot or on mules or on their own horses: Silas P Swift believed, or said he believed, that it was not only a quicker way but a better way to transport all the animals left. Arthur Rivers, trying to cheer himself up, for he had become so very fond of his wise and loving step-daughter, conjured up for himself a picture of Silas P Swift, sailing calmly up river in a native canoe with the screeching monkeys and mad dogs, in control of everything. He turned to share this vision with Cordelia, but she only saw the departing ship.

Earlier La Grande Celine had suddenly darted forward and tapped the shoulder of *Pierre l'Oiseau*, Pierre-the-bird, who was saying goodbye to an immense family: he stared at her first in amazement, then with pleasure: he had picked her up for a moment (and she was not a small woman) thrown her upwards, and caught her again, before he joined the other passengers as they crowded up the gangway in answer to the ship's bell. La Grande Celine's face was very red. All had straggled aboard with backward glances: the ringmaster, the clowns, the band members carrying their trumpets and their drums, the midgets, the flame-throwers, Peggy and Gwenlliam and the rest of the acrobats, Silas P Swift with his lists. Not to mention all the hopeful young men set for California who could not have known they were to be travelling with a *circus.* The noise of the terrified horses, the barking of the dogs, the screeching of the monkeys, was clearly heard, echoing from the bowels of the ship.

'O the poor things!' cried Rillie, but it was Regina who said to her: 'Usually it's human beings locked down there, Rillie, you know that yourself,' and Rillie nodded, remembering their own luck in travelling First Class from England, thanks to Mr Silas P Swift. Pierre-the-bird waved to his family and waved to Celine who was still looking heated; one of the midgets had spied Cordelia on the shore and was being lifted by one of the clowns, to wave. Cordelia's hand lifted, but automatically, as

228

if she was a dead wooden figure. And the panting, heaving Mr Doveribbon, pushing nearer to the ship, trying to see the departing passengers despite his vomited-upon boots, was nevertheless brought up short by the pale, extraordinarily beautiful face almost beside him now, although he could not clearly see her eyes.

The sails of the *Beauty* flapped wildly, they were raised slightly higher as the ship was pulled away from Battery Park by a lighter, and caught more wind. Arthur saw Cordelia's face, the little veil on the elegant hat hid nothing from him, he gently placed her arm in his, felt her icy skin. And he said, and the words were heard (with great astonishment) by the panting man in the grey suit: 'Dearest Cordelia, in only two years Gwennie will safely return.'

Rillie saw Monsieur Roland's stricken face and took his arm also; La Grande Celine, recovered, bravely took the other. Everybody waved and waved; Mrs Spoons, looking at the others and copying them, waved and waved; and the circus band had begun to play 'O Susanna!' from the deck. And now everybody knew the new words, the gold-miners' words:

> *I soon shall be in Francisco, and then I'll look around,*
> *And when I see the gold lumps there I'll pick them off the*
>   *ground,*
> *I'll scrape the mountains clean my boys, I'll drain the*
>   *rivers dry,*
> *A pocket full of rocks bring home, so brothers don't you*
>   *cry!*

O Susanna! O don't you cry for me, everybody sang then, and Regina was actually singing the *O!* of *O Susanna!* when she caught sight of an old man. He was wearing a strange hat, rather like a squashed top hat, and a bright waistcoat, and he was talking most animatedly, waving his arms, with two other men, all of them about to board another, much smaller, vessel.

So as the *Beauty* pulled away from the New York shore, and although Regina's hand was lifted in farewell, and her mouth was open – *O!* – her face was turned towards the smaller vessel, and in the direction of the top-hatted man.

O Susanna! sang Regina in astonishment. And then: 'Alfie?' said Regina, almost to herself. And then she shouted very, very loudly indeed: *'Oy! Alfie-boy!'*

23

The very moment he returned from the urgent business in New Haven that he had been embarking on that day, Alfie-boy came immediately to Celine's House in Maiden Lane. He was carrying fresh beef, two pineapples, oysters, a bunch of summer flowers, some books, and an extremely large box of English chocolates. In his pocket he also had two bottles of rum.

At the Battery Pier that day he had, briefly, turned almost as pale as the sails on the *Beauty* as the circus set off on the long journey.

'Queenie!' he had said unbelievingly over and over again at the gangway to his own small ship, unable, it seemed, to believe what he saw. 'Queenie, on my life!' he said, and to the bemused amazement of his business companions who were waiting to embark with him, he had hugged and hugged a weird-looking old lady with a feather in her hat while tears poured down his own old cheeks.

Now, in the hot attic room, all the windows were wide open as the close, humid summer evening fell; they left lighting the lamps as long as possible to keep cooler. Alfie hugged Regina again several times, smiling and smiling now, and

231

gave her the books and the English chocolates: everything else he gave to whomsoever would unload him. Now he sat at ease wherever required, in his bright waistcoat with his squashed top hat on his knee, and filled the small attic parlour with his enthusiasms while everybody ate chocolates with glee. Cordelia and Rillie had their boots off, padded about in bare feet; Alfie observing this and that Monsieur Roland had loosened his collar and removed his jacket, at once did the same. Rillie undid the top of her mother's blouse to cool her: they could see the pale wrinkled skin. Only Regina appeared not to notice the heat, entranced by her brother's appearance at last.

After all the years Alfie still sounded like a Londoner but his speech was peppered with those new American *slang* words that so delighted Rillie. Outside the last of the summer light slowly dimmed; inside Alfie told them he was involved with importing and exporting; they understood he had a lot of business with shipping.

'Then why ain't I seen you before, Alfie? That's what I want to know. There's a big mystery here – I been asking and asking for you down them docks for years now. Lately I even wrote you letters to the big Post Office.'

'Who'd you ask for, Queenie? Who'd you write to?'

'Who d'you think? I asked for you, Alfie-boy! I wrote to Alfie Tyrone. I asked and asked for Alfie Tyrone.'

'Yes. Well. That's a understandable mistake.' Alfie rubbed his nose, cleared his throat. 'You remember our mum's family was called Macmillan?'

'Well?'

'And our grandfather was called George. George Macmillan.'

'Silly old fool he was. Well?'

'And you remember, Queenie, I run away from home soon after you did, and then I found you writing them poems for them newspaper printers in Seven Dials?'

'Well?'

'Well – the thing is – our dad came looking for us.'

'*Did he?* You never told me that.'

'Well, I punched him, the old humbug.'

'You never!'

'I did. After all the years. I punched him right in his face and I smashed his nose and his teeth – I didn't know me own strength Queenie and that's a fact! And I said if he ever come back after us I'd tell the Cleveland Street Workhouse he was cheating them, taking things.'

'Alfie!'

'D'you know,' he informed the assembled, fascinated listeners in the attic, 'that man beat us till we was bruised. Me, and Queenie, and our mum. He was a rotten man and when I saw him down the Strand and found out he was trying to find us to make us go back I punched him for all the times he punched us. But I did damage him, and I wasn't sure how much, maybe I'd killed him I thought, so I vamoosed quick, that very day, but I signed on with a different name, just to be sure. That was that day I come and told you I was going to America, Queenie, only I never told you why it was so urgent. So everyone in America, excepting my family of course, calls me George Macmillan. No wonder you couldn't find me even though I'm so well-known! Everybody knows me! You ask for George Macmillan tomorrow and I bet you can find me straight, anywhere on the docks!'

It was at this point that Inspector Rivers returned from the Police Department. Alfie was briefly discomforted to know that there was an English policeman actually living in his sister's household, but it didn't take much calculation to work out that when Alfie left England, aged sixteen years having badly beaten up his father in the street, Inspector Rivers would hardly have been born. Rillie at last lit the lamps, even though it meant that moths flew in and fluttered round the flame.

Alfie Tyrone drank tea with them perfectly politely while they observed him; laughter had crinkled up his cheeks and his eyes.

'Well, well, Queenie!' he said. 'Well, well, Queenie. We're old now but you look just the same, you know! You always looked like a mad bird. I brung you some poetry books there, look! All you people know she was a poet? All them penny papers with poems about murder and that?'

'Alfie!'

'Why, Queenie, you was a poet of renown when I left you,' and he quoted immediately and proudly:

SHE TOOK A BAR AND SMASHED HIS HEAD,
THE BRAINS TURNED INTO SOUP.
WHAT A WITCH, SHE LEFT HIM DEAD,
NOW SHE WILL FACE THE **LOOP**.

'I never forgot that, I think it's clever. I tell it to all my friends, and that my own sister wrote it. You been writing more, Queenie?'

Regina thought of her poem influenced by Edgar Allan Poe which she had sent to Alfie Tyrone care of the Post Office, New York. 'I might've,' she said mysteriously.

'We knew she was a poet, Alfie,' said Rillie. 'She was probably the only poet in London who made money! She was also the only person we knew who *had* money and she lent it to

Cordelia and me when we first started our business in London. We could not have done it without her.'

'And I think, also, that Regina once saved my life,' said Cordelia.

'Well . . .' Regina began modestly, but then she laughed. 'I did an all, Alfie. There was this horrible cousin of Queen Victoria, she had a knife and she was screaming at Cordelia so I come running with the first thing I could lay me hands on. Guess what it was, Alfie! Nah, you won't guess, it was a chamber pot and I bopped the mad woman on the head, and what's more it was full!' Alfie, feeling he was missing big chunks of an interesting story, nevertheless roared with laughter, and Cordelia found herself laughing with the others, even though she sometimes woke from uneasy dreams, remembering the dark night and the screaming woman.

'There, Queenie,' said Alfie, wiping his eyes with a large handkerchief from about his person, 'a heroine. And good-hearted as ever under your cross voice – and it's not just me who says you're a poet!' He turned to Rillie politely. 'And what business was it that you two was running, my lovely?' he asked.

Rillie and Cordelia looked at each other; a wry, dry smile was exchanged. 'Well,' said Rillie, 'it's a long story, Alfie, but we were a business – ah – well, actually we were actresses who ran out of acting and so we were short of money – we had *no* money actually, – and we had to work to survive so with Regina's help we set up a business. Cordelia was known as a Phreno-Mesmerist at the time. I was her – ah – manager.' Alfie looked most admiring.

'Your own business? And women too! You was brave. Was you something like them Fox Sisters that I been hearing about?'

'Are they still continuing with their rapping and tapping, Monsieur Alfie?' asked Monsieur Roland in surprise. 'I had not heard that.'

'Ah Monsweer, I have my uses. Because of all my business, I sometimes go down and use the telegraph. I see all sorts of things coming through.'

'Alfie, you never!'

'Course I do, Queenie! I'm a businessman.' He turned to Monsieur Roland. 'Sometimes news stuff comes through on the telegraph, sir,' he said. 'They're certainly news, these Fox sisters. I think they might have started touring about and tapping at tables in other places. They say that Mr Phineas Barnum has shown his interest, so I guess they'll arrive in New York one of these days!'

Monsieur Roland did not want to spoil this fascinating evening by getting angry all over again. 'Those frauds,' was all he said.

'Alfie-boy, when you say you're a businessman, do you mean really and truly? Like – like businessmen in England?'

'You mean, doncha, like those high-falutin' business *gentlemen* in England! It's different here, Queenie! Anyone can make their luck if they work hard and don't loaf about. That's me! And we have to thank the old humbug for making us read and write, I guess.'

'I know. I say so myself.'

'I'm still glad I punched him.'

'Well, come on then, Alfie-boy, you mentioned a family – any wives?'

'Course!'

'Well – am I an auntie then, for instance?'

'An auntie? You're a blooming great-auntie as well and if things take their turn, I'll be a great-grandfather and I expect that'll make you a – what? A great-great-auntie, so prepare yourself.'

'A great-great auntie!' She stared at him with her mouth open.

'We ain't chickens, you know!' Everybody laughed: none of them had ever, once, seen Regina at a loss for words.

'Do you live nearby the docks Alfie?' asked Inspector Rivers.

'I got a few places, sir, actually, I do so much travelling with the work. By the docks I've got a place to lay me head, yes, and me and Maria – that's the wife now – we got a house by Washington Square but she's away just now visiting two of our daughters who have settled in Tarrytown up the Hudson; she tries to get out of the city in the summer. Some of my boys – that's your nephews, Queenie! – they work for me, they live all over the place, where we need organisation: New Jersey, New Orleans. I'm quite well-off you know, sir,' he ended modestly.

'Indeed you must be,' said Arthur, impressed. 'What kind of merchanting is it Alfie, that you do?'

'I'm a facilitator, sir: that's what I call it, a *facilitator*. What it really means is I do the wheeling and dealing, I'm a price-negotiator, I put the pig-iron in touch with the machines, you might say. Or the corn in touch with the bread, the cotton in touch with the gowns. Everything – fruit, spices, you name it. I been here in New York, up and down, even right through the long lousy depression after '37 I never lost me nerve. I *organise*, see? I love it, I've always loved it and I'm good at it, been doing it for years. Do you know, sir, I once had a job in them counting-houses for the port, to help collect the taxes. Do you know what they do in there? They count beans! They count corn! They count cotton! What a lot of humbug! I'm surprised they're not all in a lunatic asylum!' Cordelia and

Rillie and Mrs Spoons were spell-bound; Monsieur Roland marvelled at the energy of the man who could not be much younger than himself; Inspector Rivers listened intently and Regina looked round proudly, as if to say: *I told you I had a little brother.*

'Anyway, I got out of there quick and got into the real action. I've driven all over – huge carts of rye and huge carts of cotton and huge carts of oysters too. Now I pay people to drive huge carts for me. You know them ironworks down by the river? Me, I helped get them really going. Organised them. Delivered iron from New Jersey for machines and ship-hulls, always on time, always reliable. Cotton? I went south and got it back up to the docks – but I don't like that slavery business, there'll be trouble, I reckon. You can't make men animals and take away their freeness, whatever the colour. Our father – eh, Queenie? – who certainly art not in heaven, he taught us to read and write like kings. Shame he had to beat us black and blue at the same time. You people know what his job was? He was a Keeper in the Cleveland Street Workhouse – he had too much power over other people's lives and what little they had, he took it as well, the bastard. So I don't like people not having freeness. We soon got out anyway, eh, Queenie? But, man, was we educated!' And he was laughing as he spoke and the others couldn't help but laugh too although they were shocked by his story and looked at Regina in great surprise – all these years she had never once mentioned her father, or the workhouse.

'Alfie,' said Inspector Rivers, 'do you know anything about the gangs that work down at the docks?'

'You mean thieving the ships?'

'Yes.'

'Them Irish bastards – now, all right, all right, they're not all

238

Irish, and I know we are, me and Queenie, from Irish stock – Tyrone, well, you can't get much more Irish than that can you? Our rotten old father was Irish. But we got a lot of other mixtures as well, eh, Queenie – our grandmother was Scottish and our mother was born in Glasgow before she came to live in London and our rotten father might have been called Tyrone and called himself Irish but he was a blooming Londoner, so we've had lots of other things knocked into us as well as our name. Well, after all, can you imagine a real Irishman calling his daughter Regina! I feel sorry sometimes, for the *b'hoys*, some with nothing but their own shit – o, I do beg your pardon ladies, excuse me – but they are as poor as louses some of them, and still arriving in New York every day thinking it's the promised land. And even the gang *b'hoys*, with their fighting fists and their stomping boots, lost souls with fancy shirts sometimes, born in America a lot of them, but not feeling part of everything. But you're talking about the river gangs, ain't you, sir?'

'I am, yes.'

'They're a mixture of everything, those ones. There's a lot of Irish, of course, as I say, but plenty that call themselves true blue Americans – and Germans and Italians and God knows what else. They do more damage to everybody's prosperity, those waterside gangs do, than a tornado might; well, that's my opinion on the matter.'

'Alfie,' said Arthur Rivers, 'I think the Lord sent you! You are a man after my own heart. I am pleased indeed to make your acquaintance.'

'And yours, Inspector – although I don't usually like New York policemen, I do have to say.'

'Nor do I, on the whole,' said Arthur and although there was sadness here in the attic room for Gwenlliam gone, the

239

room echoed with laughter, and stories too, and Rillie passed cake and Cordelia, although her hand shook slightly from weariness for she had lain awake so many nights since her daughter had left, poured Alfie's rum for everyone, and made the others guess where Gwenlliam might be now. (And Gwenlliam Preston sailed on down the Atlantic coast to make her fortune; at last they could see the isthmus in the distance, and although there was sadness at what she had left behind she was excited, and laughing also, with Peggy Walker and the acrobats and the flame swallowers and the *charros* and the Indian Chief and the clowns.)

'Hey, Queenie, you still sing?'

'Course. Sometimes.'

'Oh, we did sing in that workhouse!' said Alfie. 'When our dad came rolling in drunk it was Irish songs of course, eh Queenie?' And to the surprise of everybody, Alfie and Regina who had not seen each other for fifty years, broke into the same song, at the same time, both with good voices still.

> *Tis the last rose of summer*
> *Left blooming alone*
> *All her lovely companions*
> *Are faded and gone.*
> *No flower of her kindred*
> *No rosebud is nigh*
> *To reflect back her blushes*
> *To give sigh for sigh.*

Everybody in the little attic had been too taken aback by the sight and sound of these two old people singing to join in; at the end they applauded at the pleasure of it, Rillie wiped a tear from her eye.

'And remember our dear old mum singing, Queenie – her own songs from Scotland, when dad wasn't there? Come on everyone, don't leave us high and dry this time!' And before they knew it all the inhabitants of the attic room, including Mrs Spoons who tapped her feet and smiled and sang, had broken into jaunty song and their voices echoed down the stairs of Celine's House and out into Maiden Lane, off Broadway.

> *O whistle and I'll come to ye, my lad,*
> *O whistle and I'll come to ye, my lad,*
> *Though father and mother and a' should gae mad*
> *Thy Jeannie will venture wi' thee, my lad.*

24

Marylebone
London

Dear Arthur

Newspapers say that the epidemic is here, is everywhere, and

that people die all around us, they say <u>near</u> to us, Arthur, I assure you. Millie has surrounded me with chloride of lime, a dreadful thing. Can you leave your family to the mercies of a rampaging epidemic? Is it to be left to me, to carry the responsibility of your own – I repeat – your own family while you live in a godforsaken country with your fancy woman? Do you think at this time that we are interested in pepper and quinine arriving safely on the New York docks? I do not care if the Lord takes me, so great is my burden. Your place is here and you do not fill that place and <u>I</u> am left to be the head of <u>your</u> family instead of a peaceful old age. Eight wild grand-children and seven of them never knowing their grandfather and the eighth forgot him long ago.

Faith's husband Fred apparently appeared again recently in want of <u>money</u>. Millie's husband Charlie hit him. That is what I hear from my lonely life – I would not have heard that either, only little Arthur told me.

> I remain
> Your dutiful sister-in-law
> Agnes Spark (Miss)

PS we are in receipt of the financial contribution of the 9th inst.

Dearest Father, the cholera epidemic is not in all areas, we did have two deaths in Marylebone but it is a safer area than many, and we are none of us hurt and we take very great care with soap and with chloride of lime. You remember my dear Charlie works for the local water? and they think it may be water causing the epidemic and are hoping to present their ideas. And Father, ignore Aunt Agnes, me and Charlie <u>are</u> interested in your work on the New York docks, it sounds very exciting, I just hope that no-one ever takes a fist to you!

O Father, Fred with his drinking has been a terrible worry, it is true he came to Faith and tried to get money, it was so lucky I was there at the time, I ran home to get Charlie and Charlie was so mad that he did punch Fred right on his teeth and told him to go away only in rude words and Faith was crying, and the children – well Faith must come and live with us now that is certain, Aunt Agnes will not have them in Marylebone, she says she is too ill, poor old trout. Though I do not mean to be disrespectful. O dear, o Father, I could do with your advice! Charlie's father tells us his terrible old jokes and tries to make us laugh, he is a cheery old fellow. and I will write a more cheery letter next time XXXXX

25

Having followed, to Celine's House, Cordelia Preston and her strange party of old women and lady pirates and foreign gentleman (again not understanding that New York policemen did not wear uniforms) where could Mr Doveribbon go (having of course changed his de-spoiled boots in the American Hotel and handed them to a servant) but back to his only friends in America: to the dockmen and the chancers and the sea-captain in the Boadwalk, near to which Silas P Swift's locked gates mocked and taunted him: GONE TO CALIFORNIA.

He drank heavily and angrily – his pals thought he had a broken heart; he bought drinks, he mumbled obscenities: he behaved more and more like one of them, not like a gentleman lawyer from London.

'My heart is broken,' he admitted.

'Go after her to California, lad! Get yourself some gold while you're about it!' And Mr Doveribbon spluttered over his drink and actually laughed.

'I'll be after gold all right!' he said.

The sea-captain's clipper, *Sea Bullet*, was in dock, having some repairs done to the hull. The captain himself was a dark, brooding, unpleasant-mannered man in many ways but he was Mr Doveribbon's best friend at the moment. 'You'd have to wait a while for me,' said the sea-captain. 'Get a steamer, not as fast as me and my *Sea Bullet*, but the next best thing, and I'll see you there!' Mr Doveribbon suddenly became very alert.

'Do you stay long?'

'Just to unload, and reload,' and the sea-captain gave a crafty look from under his big, dark eyebrows. 'Mail. And passengers. And this and that.'

'How long is the journey to San Francisco?'

'A steamship: a hundred and twenty days or more.'

'*Good Lord above!*' Mr Doveribbon blanched.

'Me and my beauty: ninety if I'm lucky and smart.'

'Could you bring us back? Me and my girl?' Their heads leaned closer and closer together till the June moon was full over their heads outside, but they did not notice. Mr Doveribbon told more truths than he was usually wont to do. So did the sea-captain. To their great surprise they found that they could be mutually beneficial, one to the other.

Mr Doveribbon booked a first-class berth to California on a steamer – with some difficulty and passing of money in all the gold-rushing: he had two days to wait. Again the sea-captain and he sat together drinking heavily in a corner of the Broadwalk, their heads almost touching.

For Mr Doveribbon had one more job to attend to.

By now he and the sea-captain knew a great deal about one another. 'I can help, pal,' said the sea-captain.

The following afternoon the two men were to be seen in a notorious edifice in Five Points: The Old Brewery. It was once a brewery certainly; now it was a tenement that had sunk sideways into the rising mud of the filled-in swamp on which it had been built: a dark, stinking, crooked building of dark corridors and hopelessness and Mr Doveribbon thought he had entered hell. He had, however, only entered one of the premises housing some of the members of the Dead Rabbits Gang; down the two visiting men went (only safe because they were escorted by one of their drinking companions from the Boadwalk), down and down into basements of purgatory and there Mr Doveribbon, conferring with the sea-captain, gave instructions to some Irishmen and parted with twenty-five dollars, one third of the payment: the rest to be paid by the sea-captain on acceptance of proof of success, should Mr Doveribbon have already departed for San Francisco. The sea-captain would bring the proof with him.

Sometimes, on these hot summer evenings, having spent the day planning and conversing with Monsieur Roland for their new venture, Cordelia walked alone down to the Battery Gardens, near to the last place she had seen her last child: it was against all the emotional rules she had set for herself: these were her lowest hours.

This evening she watched the last ships pulling away from the piers. The waving crowds dispersed, all going about their New York business again; Cordelia could not possibly have known or cared that a disappearing steamship held a man called Mr Doveribbon. A summer night breeze blew in off the river, the moon was hidden now behind clouds, lovers strolled away, she walked quite alone in the darkness. She watched the shadows and the lights of the departing ships and did not see the men who walked near until – (and no Regina to sing loudly:

The Lord's my Shepherd, I'll not want
He makes me down to lie

and draw attention) – until the two men had bundled her away silently to the edge of the river, something immediately stuffed into her mouth to stop her screaming and something else: *scissors to her hair?*

She heard them whispering together, heard their Irish accents. 'Can you see? Where's the knife?'

Cordelia struggled wildly, tried to scream.

'Hellcat!' He hit her across the face, again she fought them. 'Jasus, I've dropped it now. Here, use this.'

'Not scissors, you nincompoop! This can't cut fingers! They want a finger.'

'Oh ferkin' Jasus.' Still they whispered. 'I've dropped the knife somewhere in the dark.' They felt about with their feet, holding the struggling, gagged woman. Something slipped into the water beside them with a small splash. 'Ferkin' hell, it's gone!'

'Jasus, you great lolloping id'jut!'

'Well, here, there's a fine lot of hair here, this Welsh Duke those two were murmurin' of will just have to do with ferkin' hair, hurry!' and they quickly pulled at and tore and chopped and cut her long hair and then they threw her into the dark water. They had a long stick and when she surfaced, gasping, her clothes first floating and then filling with water, they pushed her down.

'Right, that's it, go! There's people comin', look there!' and they were gone in a hurry, back to the Boadwalk with their proof, for the rest of their money. The whole incident had taken only a few moments.

'What's that?' cried a small boy, walking with his father who was lighting their way with a lamp. 'Is it a big fish?'

The father stared intently, then told the boy to hold the lamp and shine it on the water: the father quickly threw off his jacket and dived into the Hudson, pulled the unconscious woman on to the shore. They turned her upside-down, all proprieties forgotten, water poured from her hair (the remains of her hair) and her mouth and her body and her clothes.

They lay her on the grass, nothing about her person to say who she was, a strange compelling face – *was she breathing?* – something odd about her hair, her clothes torn. People who had gathered now at the commotion stood helplessly, some left shrugging, *another suicide*, but suddenly there was Rillie: Rillie had come to look for her dearest friend, worried at the way she quietly disappeared again, guessing she might have come down to Gwennie's pier again. And never, ever, *ever* would Rillie have believed for a single second that Cordelia had jumped into the Hudson no matter how she felt: she knew her friend too well.

She pushed past, knelt to the body. 'Cordelia,' she said briskly, 'Cordelia,' and she slapped her face gently as in the darkness people stopped, curious, or moved on. 'Cordelia!' said Rillie, urgently now. One woman who had been quickly moving through the dark Battery Gardens intent on business quite different, nevertheless stopped at the sound of the name: *Cordelia.* The passing woman was very tall with wild, wild hair; if you had been able to see her clearly in the night you would have seen that her skirt was held up with men's suspenders; she glanced at the wet figure in the darkness on the grass.

'Looks pretty dead to me,' a man said.

The heroic father, still dripping with water, not wanting his son upset further, picked up his lamp and his jacket and his boy and disappeared; the curious tall, wild woman went on her busy way also, pondering nevertheless that she had never before heard of someone called *Cordelia*; nor *Shylock* for that matter; nor *Lady Macbeth* nor *Titus Andronicus* and she laughed to herself in the night on her way back to the Hole in the Wall near Paradise Buildings and a passing person could have heard her muttering:

> *but long it could not be*
> *Till that her garments, heavy with their drink,*
> *Pull'd the poor wretch from her melodious lay*
> *To muddy death.*

But Rillie Spoons had no such acceptance of that fate for her friend. She had immediately sat Cordelia up and pushed her head forward; she hit her on the back, so that Cordelia spewed forth more water from the Hudson; Rillie then wrapped her own cloak tightly about the shivering, half-conscious, half-choking woman, asked a man still watching to quickly help them to a cab, and took her home. Luckily Arthur was there: white-faced he ran downstairs, quickly he took the bellows from the fire-place in Celine's dining-room and ran up all five lots of stairs again to the attic; he applied the bellows to Cordelia's mouth to Regina's alarm and the distressed incomprehension of Mrs Spoons; Cordelia breathed and coughed and spluttered more water. Arthur nodded to a devastated Monsieur Roland who helped to lift her and turn her gently, pushed her now extraordinary-looking head forward over a bowl, put many blankets over her to warm her. Arthur warmed her hands and her feet over and over. He had at once assumed it was some river-gang-related attack from his friends down at the docks, but as Cordelia came and went from them she murmured once: 'the Welsh Duke will have to do with ferkin' hair.' It seemed so *unlikely* that they could not understand. They looked in bewilderment at the remains of her hair as sometimes she still vomited up more water. And all Cordelia said was, again: 'the Welsh duke will have to do with ferkin' hair.' At last, after several hours, she breathed more easily, fell asleep, they lay her gently back in her bed.

The next day she was clearer, stronger. 'It was two Irishmen,' she said matter-of-factly. 'They tried to drown me for some reason connected with the Duke of Llannefydd.'

'But why would that fat, drunken pig cut off your hair?' said Regina. So much of the hair was gone, much of the white streak as well as the long dark tresses. She looked strange and fragile and violated and she had a black eye and marks on her face.

'You must never, *never* go out in the evening alone again,' said Arthur.

'Who saved you?' said Rillie suddenly. 'I've just realised: someone must have pulled you out of the water.' But Cordelia had no recollection of being saved by the heroic father.

And then she gasped. 'Oh! Thank the heavens that Gwenlliam is on her way to California! None of you must tell her anything about this if you write, she is not to be worried. At least she is safely out of the way.'

Slowly she began to recover. Rillie had to cut off most of the straggly bits left of the hair; in fact it had been so attacked that there was not so very much hair left. Rillie tried to shape it somehow, hoping it would grow again. 'It doesn't matter,' said Cordelia blankly. Then she got very, very angry and her anger exhausted her again.

'Cordelia,' said Monsieur Roland gently. 'Cordelia.'

Arthur Rivers smoothed his wife's hair, or the remains of it, with something like very loving exasperation. Very quietly and kindly he tried to get more information from her: did she see them? where was she walking exactly? what exactly happened?

'I am not in need of a police-detective!' she said to him and everyone heard the anger in her voice to her husband. 'I cannot tell you anything more, Arthur, so stop asking me: it was dark, it was quick, they had Irish accents but so does half of New York. They said the Welsh duke would have to do with ferkin' hair.' And then suddenly she did remember something, paled further. 'Oh God. They said he wanted a finger.' The memory made her even angrier. '*I do not want to talk any more about it!*'

'But I need you to talk about it, dearest Cordelia,' he said gently, 'so that we can find who it was who attacked you.'

'Go away, Arthur! I do not need your detection skills, I know what this is: it is the past, and the past cannot be "solved" by a detective. The Duke of Llannefydd may think he can destroy me still, but of course he will never destroy me. I shall walk wherever I like, but I *will* endeavour not to walk deep in painful thoughts by a riverbank in the dark. That evil old bastard will never get the better of me and my daughter, thank God she is gone to California!'

'You know what, Cordelia?' said Regina. 'Now that Rillie has cut your hair you look like a daisy.'

'*What?*'

'A black and white daisy, spiky and short. With a cross face by the way, just like daisies have.' And Cordelia laughed shortly.

'I don't *care*,' she said.

Monsieur Roland looked at her, looked then at Arthur's pale face, quite blank now. Cordelia Preston was the strongest, most courageous woman Monsieur Roland had ever met and he loved her dearly. But she was not *easy*.

26

Sticky, humid, summer city nights, open windows in the small, hot attic; noise and smells and insects and heat all floated in.

Alfie became a regular visitor to Maiden Lane when his work brought him to New York. He always sat talking first to his sister, but then could often be found deep in discussion with Arthur, their heads together in a corner of the small parlour as they discussed the troubles on the East River. Or he would tell Rillie where to buy the best – but the cheapest – meat and vegetables. Or he would calculate distances and count days and give Cordelia comfort while her mind conjured up wild pictures of shipwrecks, savages, cholera, death.

Obviously Alfie saw Cordelia's different hair: they told him something of what had happened. 'Someone was paid to do that,' he said in alarm. 'Have you any idea why?'

'It doesn't matter, Alfie,' said Cordelia quickly and there was something in her tone that stopped Alfie asking further questions at this point. He said instead, most sensibly: 'Well, you must walk with a big stick now, my lovely, like the policemen do.'

But Cordelia said: 'When I was a girl I was sent to play in Bloomsbury Square in the night sometimes, because my Aunt Hester, who was a Mesmerist' – she looked at Monsieur

Roland for a moment – 'had customers and my mother had –' (she paused only for a second) 'customers also. So I was sent to Bloomsbury Square with a penny for the muffin man and our old flat-iron to carry in a pocket in my cloak to hit people with! It used to weigh me down when I tried to climb trees when I was young – and I have found it, I brought it with me to New York, look!' and she showed them the old flat-iron from long, long ago. 'Isn't it funny and heavy! I'm glad we have more modern ones now.'

'I remember that old thing!' said Rillie.

'Oy, Queenie!' said Alfie. 'Our mum had one of these! Look!'

'And I'll carry it in my pocket again,' said Cordelia and somehow they all laughed even as they worried for her safety.

But she was true to her word: she was alert, and ready, but no-one came near. Her hair grew very slowly and unevenly, Rillie had to keep cutting it; Cordelia hid everything under her beautiful hat. She had finally controlled her wild, flailing anger; she smiled at Arthur in apology. Mostly one of the others contrived to walk with her always: she understood their kindness but longed to stride about alone as she used to do. She carried her old flat-iron but she absolutely refused to be intimidated: she believed the men had what they wanted and thought she was dead. (She did not know that not only did her assailants think they had done their job and had been paid accordingly, but also that the captain of a clipper called the *Sea Bullet* had all her hair neatly packed in a small satchel: proof for the Duke of Llannefydd that she was drowned and no more to be thought about.)

But sometimes she could not eat or sleep, so strong was her fear that she would lose Gwenlliam to the wilds of Panama, or the Pacific ocean, or California: *did I make the wrong decision? should I have gone with her? thank God she is out of the way:*

thoughts tumbled around her head as the weeks and months passed and she had no news or information. It was as if Gwenlliam had vanished into the sky. 'This is Gwenlliam,' Cordelia would say to Alfie again, showing him again the new daguerreotype on the attic wall. 'I write often,' she said, 'so there are a large number of letters following her across America!' And on the next visit Alfie would calculate again, occasionally bringing Cordelia maps he had acquired from his multifarious contacts; together they would pore over them, marking possible dates and distances.

'But it will still be a long time, my lovely, till she gets to San Francisco, and a long time before a letter can get back to you. It's no use expecting letters yet.'

Alfie was particularly fascinated with the ideas of Monsieur Roland, often asked him questions about mesmerism. 'When these Fox Sisters that make you so mad come table-tapping to New York, Monsweer, as I'm sure they will one day, we'll go and see them, you and I, we'll make a good pair to check them over.'

'*Oui*, Monsieur Alfie. I would like that, if I can contain myself! You said you use, in your work, the new telegraph, which involves tappings also, and I would assume these young ladies have read about that and turned it into something else in their young and fertile imaginations. Do you know how it actually transmits, this telegraph? The electrical one I mean, not the table-tapping!'

'Well, I ain't a scientist, Monsweer, and it's all to do with this electrical business, but, as I understand it, the sound made by the taps whizzes like mad along overhead wires – Mr Morse had to get wires put in between Washington and Baltimore before he could send his first message, so that was forty miles of wire for a start.'

'What was the message?' asked Regina.

'WHAT HATH GOD WROUGHT?' said Alfie and he and Regina both laughed, and then said simultaneously: 'Numbers, Chapter Twenty-three,' to the amazement of all present. 'Our father made us learn the Bible, like I told you!' said Alfie. 'We can quote like this for hours!'

'Did Mr Morse just put wires along railway lines and tap out the words?' asked Monsieur Roland.

'Nah! Right palaver it was, but that Mr Morse was determined – and you know he's really a painter, not a scientist – I thought artists were supposed to be dreamy fellows, well not this Mr Samuel Morse! At first he put copper wires inside pipes under the ground, but something went wrong in the pipes, I think they hadn't been insulated, anyway, so next they tried putting the wires overhead. And then trees damaged the wires and they fell down. But now they've got it organised, like you say, and you can see them, wires on telegraph poles along railway lines wherever they can, and these days you can send news from New Orleans to Washington! There are short taps and long taps and the combination of taps spells out words. Everyone who transmits and receives has Mr Morse's alphabet in front of them – like, if I remember, one short tap is E. Two taps, one short one long, is A. Three short taps is R, etcetera etcetera, and the taps are sent buzzing along the wires.'

'That's blooming amazing, Alfie!' said Regina.

'And very, very useful for my business, Queenie: *COTTON WAGON LEFT WED 10am*. And one day I reckon they'll lay a wire right under the Atlantic Ocean, Monsweer. Imagine if we could tap a quick message to London!'

'Imagine if we could tap a quick message to California!' said Cordelia.

'Now that I consider it, so much in the world is about

energy, ain't it?' said Alfie, and Monsieur Roland nodded, smiling at this energetic man. 'Human energy for your mesmerism, electrical energy for the telegraph, and I suppose you might say coal energy to drive them steamboats! What else new will they invent, I wonder.'

'Well, Monsieur Alfie,' and Monsieur Roland cleared his throat in a most uncharacteristic nervous manner, 'I am myself trying to invent something new. And I would be most grateful for advice from a businessman like yourself.'

Alfie looked very interested. Monsieur Roland was silent. 'Well, go on then, Monsweer.' Monsieur Roland looked embarrassed.

'Well – ah, *mon Dieu* – it is about advertisement. It is a new field for me, this American way. My rooms in Nassau Street are surrounded by advertisements painted on posters and walls and doors and windows and trees – and even roofs – in extremely bright colours: I have counted Wooden Legs and Arms for sale, Oliver's Oyster Pies, Song Birds, Paperworks, Female Medicines, Cheap Teeth Extractions, Gentlemen's Medicines, Hair Restorer, Daguerreotypes now Coloured – I could go on and on and on, Alfie. My rooms are small and my notice is small and Cordelia and I are about to begin a new, slightly different business. How do I advertise it without –'

'You mean without being vulgar, doncha?'

'I know I am lost in Nassau Street,' said the Frenchman. 'But it is somehow offensive to me, the idea of painting **MESMERISTS** in huge letters and coloured paint, on the door – and yet I see this is my own foolish fastidiousness. This loudness is how everything is done in New York, and here I am at last wanting to offer some new ideas, and somehow I have to – to use that word I find so difficult – publicise it. And call it something else. Something new.'

'You've always told us Dr Mesmer wore purple suits to draw attention to himself,' said Rillie. 'He was not averse to publicity!'

'Are you suggesting I wear a purple suit and call my new ideas *Rolandism* and distribute bright announcements by hand?' he said mildly and everybody laughed; La Grande Celine's slightly purple jacket had gone quietly back into a cupboard: Monsieur Roland was inordinately fond of his meticulously looked-after old black jacket and would not change it, Rillie had always lovingly sewed the cuffs when they got too threadbare. 'I keep thinking that this idea needs another way,' he said, 'and it needs another word altogether. There is a Greek word for healing: THERAPEIA. I feel I want to describe where I am going as Mesmeric Therapeia. Or Hypnotic Therapeia. But not too garishly,' he added hurriedly.

Regina said: 'Well – *that* kind of language ain't going to call people in exactly, is it! And also, if you don't mind me saying so, you could do with a few pictures to jolly that place up!'

'What about: Mesmeric Healing?' suggested Rillie.

Now Cordelia grimaced. 'It sounds like those new advertisements the churches are using: JESUS HEALS: ENTER NOW. Who would have thought that religion would start advertising itself!'

But Monsieur Roland and Alfie both laughed.

'The Church *invented* advertising,' said Alfie.

'The Church has always advertised itself most brilliantly, my dear Cordelia!' said Monsieur Roland. 'What do you think those great cathedrals all over Europe are about? But – ah, *mon Dieu* – it is no wonder I cannot decide how to advertise these new ideas when I hardly understand them myself. Perhaps Monsieur Alfie you can help me, being a businessman.'

'But what's this new thing you've invented, Monsweer? You

haven't given me the guts! What are we supposed to be advertising?'

Monsieur Roland explained that he and Cordelia had now planned for many hours about how to move their work in another direction; they wanted patients to perhaps talk more, if they could, about themselves and what was ailing them. And now they wanted to begin this new experiment. Alfie listened carefully, asked a question or two as he always did when he was listening to other people, and then he stood, addressed the room as he might a meeting; he stroked his whiskers and then stood there with his hands tucked under his bright waistcoat.

'Now, here we are on my territory. Here I can help. You want customers, right?'

Monsieur Roland nodded.

'Right. Now: you and Cordelia want more talking to help people before you heal them – and quite right too, that makes sense. I mean who better to explain, I imagine, than the person who is ailing? Them doctors think they are gods and hardly let you blooming speak!' He brushed one of the flapping moths, seduced by the lamplight, from his face. 'Right. You know what, Monsweer Roland? I'm glad you are starting to understand New York! I seen your little sign in Nassau Street. I've walked past there twenty times and never even noticed it till Queenie told me. Sure we use words here that stand out and colours to draw attention, that's America. Now, I don't see why you can't advertise this new way without the vulgarity – or, anyway, what you see as vulgarity cos you're not an American. I'm lucky – I was a Londoner before: me and Queenie, we was a bit vulgar to start with! Now. You have to, I'm thinking, make a sort of compromise. I agree with Queenie, you don't want to sound too high-falutin' or people will be put off, but you *do* want to draw attention to yourselves, doncha,

259

so you can't be too bloody *English* about this, pardon my French, or you won't get customers, cos they are in the end customers, ain't they? Customers with problems, you might say.' Monsieur Roland bowed his head in agreement.

'You want them to talk, right? So you gotta tell them that – and just by the by, you be careful, because someone like me could come along and talk your blooming head off!' and everyone laughed and he put up his hand. 'Nah, what I'm leading to is, why not just *say* it, instead of messing around? Why not just put up a much, much bigger sign on the door – big, so that it attracts, but not vulgar colours, not for a gentleman of your refinement – and make it really, really simple: it could say, like,' and he drew lines of writing in the air with his hands, 'PROBLEMS? TALK TO A MESMERIST.'

They heard Arthur coming up the stairs, so when he entered the room Alfie said with the same flourish: 'PROBLEMS? TALK TO THE MESMERIST!'

'Problems causing pain?' said Arthur. There was something in his voice, some tone, that made Cordelia suddenly look at him sharply, but he was addressing Alfie and Monsieur Roland.

And so it came about that a very different sign was seen on the here-to-fore unnoticeable door in Nassau Street, though without bright colouring: a very large white sign with black lettering, arranged by Alfie from a Printworks.

PROBLEMS CAUSING PAIN?
TALK TO THE MESMERIST.
Monsieur Roland
Mrs Preston.

Alfie wanted **TALK TO THE MESMERIST** to be followed by several very large exclamation marks; Monsieur Roland was not to be persuaded.

'And yet – I don't know what it is exactly that will happen,' said Cordelia to him nervously the day the sign went up.

'Nor do I,' said the old man. 'But if you get any unexpected visitors who want to cut your hair again, bang immediately and loudly on the wall!'

'No, no I am not nervous about *that*,' said Cordelia. 'I mean I am nervous because – it is something new and we don't know how it will transpire.'

'Well, I am nervous too,' he said to her gently. 'But we must be brave enough to begin. It is an experiment. It is mesmerism with talking.'

27

Alfie's wife, Maria, returned from Tarrytown to Washington Square as the hot, humid weather burned itself out at last, and Regina immediately began to be bombarded with invitations: she must go and visit her large family. But Regina refused to go to Washington Square: in truth she was nervous, although she did not quite put it like that. 'He might ask lots of them to come to meet me, all those new people I'm auntie to, and I might not like them,' she said firmly. 'And this Maria – she's a Southern lady so he says. What am I to say to her? And then how would I get home again – I ain't staying there!'

La Grande Celine, as usual involved in her boarders' dilemmas, had the answer. 'Why, I can solve it!' she said at once. 'They shall come to my dining saloon.' So it was Celine who made all the arrangements for Alfie's family to visit Maiden Lane: Regina got more and more nervous and uneasy as the day approached. The smiling waitresses, Ruby and Pearl, moved the screen that protected lady diners from the rest of the dining-room so that a larger table could also be brought in and a measure of privacy still maintained.

'I'll only bring half a dozen,' protested Alfie when the plan was made known to him, he understood his sister's nervousness. 'We don't want to frighten Queenie off!'

'A table for twelve-ish to sixteen-ish then!' said Celine.

'Monsieur Roland smiled at her. 'You are very kind, my dear,' he said. 'We are very lucky to have found you.'

'Perhaps you would wear your new purple jacket,' she said.

'I shall,' said Monsieur Roland and Celine sang 'Frère Jacques' in the basement kitchen, smiling and singing as she helped to prepare the feast.

Alfie had offered money for this large celebratory meal but Rillie and Cordelia, despite knowing that their finances were becoming less and less secure, would not hear of it. 'Regina has lived with us and helped us for more years than I can remember,' said Rillie firmly to Alfie. 'This meal in celebration of her new-found family will be paid for by us with great pleasure.' She went with Inspector Rivers to the Bank of America and withdrew extra money. Inspector Rivers knew very well she was anxious about their financial security as the weeks went by: he was becoming uneasy himself; although they still had some savings he knew TALK TO THE MESMERIST was not yet bringing in money: at the moment his was the only financial support coming in to their family. He could not even begin to consider that Charlie, Millie's husband at one of the Water Boards in London, was the only other person involved at the moment in supporting some of the nineteen people Arthur Rivers felt responsible for. But he had taught himself to never interfere with Rillie's bank account: he was the signatory that was all. So he made no mention of financial difficulties, signed the form.

Rillie and Cordelia bought flowers and they set them out on the long table before they went upstairs to put on their best clothes; Blossom and Maybelle giggled as they polished and polished the chairs and the mirrors; Ruby and Pearl laid best cutlery.

Regina meanwhile nervously sang several psalms upstairs and read aloud headlines from the newspaper: **GIRLS STAB OVER LOVE OF BANKER** elicited great interest until she realised she had mis-read it: it was actually **GIRLS STAB OVER LOVE OF BAKER** which was somehow different. When she then came across a story about a group of would-be gold-miners who had left New York over a year ago to try to make their way overland to California, whose bodies had now been found in the Rocky Mountains, she turned the page quickly and read out more advertisements instead. She told them all it was just another day after all: she put her celebratory feather in her hat nevertheless. Mrs Spoons, uncertain as she was led slowly downstairs where she was going, or indeed who she was, clung to the small yellow glove: earlier she had displayed great anxiety when Rillie had insisted on washing it in a bucket of water.

Two buxom matrons with much style and charm were introduced as two of Alfie's daughters. One of the husbands worked for Alfie, the other worked on a newspaper: they both wore bright waistcoats, as Alfie did. Only two of Alfie's innumerable grand-children had been allowed to come on this momentous visit: they looked about them with great interest, studied the circus posters when they weren't studying their new Auntie Queenie and her funny hat.

And then Alfie proudly presented his wife: they had understood, from his visits to Maiden Lane, that there had been several: this one, Maria, was a widow he had met while arranging cotton sales in the South.

Maria had a fan which she idly fluttered, more as if it was part of her clothing than there for weather, for the days were cooler now. She had very many curls under a large hat and she was about the same size as her buxom step-daughters. She spoke in a languid Southern tone when she asked where she might be seated; she bowed to Regina most graciously as they were introduced. But then she spoiled the Southern lady picture by suddenly giving Regina the most enormous hug, smothering her in sleeves and shawls and perfume. 'Ah declare, Ah haven't seen Alfie cry for years!' she said beaming, holding Regina away from her to better observe her. 'Ah am so very delighted that he has found you. How old are you?'

Everybody held their breath. Regina looked at the warm, well-meaning face in front of her and said: 'To tell you the truth, Maria, I'm not that sure. I think I'm seventy-three. How old are you then?'

Maria was not flummoxed in the least. 'Ah'm sixty,' she said, 'and do you know, Ah work for Alfie just like his sons do! When Ah met Alfie – that was about twenty years ago – and we came to New York where ladies do different things than in New Orleans, he said it would be lovely if Ah learned to read better, so Ah got myself a teacher and not only did Ah improve mah reading but Ah learned accounting. And now Ah do all his accounts books! What do y'all think of that? And look here – hand me that there parcel, Dolly – even though the summer's over Ah thought to introduce all you ladies to the Southern custom of keeping cool when required!' and she handed out pretty fans to all of them, including La Grande Celine. And then the Southern lady fanned herself (giving them a lesson, although Cordelia and Rillie, having been actresses, understood fans) and finally sat down – but not before she had charmed Arthur and greeted Monsieur Roland in French. Alfie kept looking about proudly, watching their reactions.

Ruby and Pearl served Staten Island oysters and fresh bread from the Maiden Lane German baker and beefsteak and fried potatoes and apple pie and mountains of cream. Jeremiah the barman brought beer and port and whisky, and sarsaparilla for the children. Mrs Spoons studied her fan with enormous interest, gave a little sound of pleasure as Rillie fanned the air about her mother's face for a moment.

'Of course, I'd have found him years ago,' said Regina, 'and there'd have been no need for all this palaver, if he hadn't changed his name to blooming George Macmillan who was our fool grandfather who should've joined the Temperance Society!'

'Why, *we* all call him Alfie, of course!' said Maria. 'He always said he liked his own name better but, as Ah know and you know, he had to change it for convenience long ago.'

The grand-children had rehearsed 'Pleased to meet you, Great-Auntie Queenie,' and having said it at least four times both wanted to play the harmonium. Other diners looked up briefly as odd sounds came from that instrument, but, as always, went on eating quickly so that they could return to their business. A ray of autumn afternoon sunshine glanced in, caught the polished cutlery. After a while the grand-children exhausted the possibilities of the harmonium and returned to observe their odd and interesting aunt.

'Grandpa told us you are a poet!' The young girl's voice was high with the excitement of the day. 'Did you know the late Mr Edgar Allan Poe?'

'O, I taught him all he knew,' said Regina, and as their eyes widened she said: 'Nah, just kidding, but I learned him,' and, just sitting there at the long dining table, she began:

> And the raven, never flitting, still is
> sitting,
> Still is sitting
> On the pallid bust of Pallas just above my
> Chamber door
> And his eyes have all the seeming of a
> demon
> That's been dreaming,
> And the lamp-light o'er him streaming
> throws
> His shadow on the floor. . . .

Mrs Spoons, who had heard the words many times although she did not remember, had kept time with her feet. The grandchildren – all Regina's new relations – looked at their Aunt Queenie, amazed; the little boy clung to his mother and stared and stared at this strange old lady. The husbands banged their glasses on the table and everyone joined in the applause.

And then Alfie stood to make a speech, his thumbs resting in the pockets of his waistcoat. He thanked the family for their kind hospitality and then he said: 'All my life, I told them I had a sister. My sister Queenie, I said to them, was a poet, but we lost each other. I always remembered one or two of her poems, I recited them to the kids, "that's your auntie," I used to say to them,' and the buxom daughters nodded in smiling agreement. 'Now. You might think, in fifty years, a brother and a sister would forget. But not us. I have found that my sister Queenie has been writing me letters to the New York Post Office – no, Queenie,' he said, as she half-rose in surprise, 'they don't just throw them away after a month, you know, not when there's so many people coming and going: they've got a storeroom. And I went down there and I asked if there was any letters for Mr Alfie Tyrone and I gave the boy a dollar and I said, "look carefully, lad, and I'll make it worth your while further," and back he came, Queenie, with your letters. I shall treasure those letters for ever, Queenie, they are my personal property, but now, listen: in one of them, Queenie had written me a poem. She wrote it for me, she said it was for me, and I tell you what, I cried when I read that poem, and I never even shared it with Maria but I'm going to read it you all now.' He had magnifying spectacles and he drew them from his waistcoat.

His wife looked at him in surprise; Cordelia and Rillie looked at each other in amazement and then they both looked at Regina, who they had known – and yet perhaps not known – for so long. So many emotions flitted across Regina's face that Monsieur Roland, also watching her, wondered if she might faint (although that was a most unlikely scenario). The grand-children were wide-eyed at the story.

Alfie held a paper in his hands and read:

Sometimes when I am sleeping,
I wake and my heart is beating,
          Beating, beating in the night.
I remember days of long ago
The Workhouse where the lights were low
And Father punished with a blow
For everything we did not know
          Beating, beating in the night.
He beat us for doing nothing wrong
But I and Alfie held our song,
For he taught us also the love of words
That words could roll, and sound like
birds

And in our heads we held those words
When there was
                    Beating, beating in the night.

'This is the story of our life she has told, in a poem.'

Cordelia and Rillie had surprised tears on their cheeks, the grand-children's eyes were now nearly popping out of their heads.

'Now tell me she ain't been a teacher to that Mr Poe fellow!' Alfie said, and he blew his nose on a big handkerchief. 'And Maria and I – who have talked a great deal about Queenie and me finding ourselves again,' and Maria was nodding and smiling and crying and fanning herself, '– would be very proud, if it so transpired to be suitable of course, for my sister Queenie to come and live with us in Washington Square.' He saw his sister's startled face. 'If it transpires to be suitable is all I'm saying, Queenie!'

Finally, after many weeks, with much prompting from her newly found family, Regina got up the courage to travel, at least for a visit, to Washington Square. 'Just to have a look,' she said briskly to Cordelia and Rillie. 'I ain't staying long, I don't want to leave the old lady for too long.'

Alfie came in the morning to collect her in a small carriage: he disapproved of such things and would have walked himself, but wanted his sister to be comfortable.

'Do you think I should be expecting letters yet, Alfie?' said Cordelia.

'Not yet, my lovely. I'll do some more calculations in a week or so, but not yet. Are you taking good care and carrying that flat-iron?' (Regina had recounted to him the whole story.)

'I'm seen with it everywhere!' said Cordelia. 'Just like the old days in London, Alfie!'

'Good girl!' and he laughed, and then fussed round his sister. 'Come on now, Queenie,' and he helped her and her small bag of belongings up the little steps of the vehicle as everyone waved goodbye. It was cold, he wrapped a rug about her knees. Regina Tyrone had never travelled by carriage and she looked about her in a disapproving manner.

'I ain't staying long! I'll be back soon!' she called to the others loudly. Mrs Spoons, watching the others, waved and smiled, just as they were doing.

28

But the pale face of Mrs Spoons became paler, she twisted the yellow glove round and round and round and the vacant eyes did not understand. It was Regina who sat in the other rocking chair. It was Regina whom Mrs Spoons didn't know – but missed: London, New York: it was Regina who for years had briskly hauled her from the fire when the others were out, or when Rillie was working. It was Regina who sang, in her hearty voice. It was Regina's voice too that read out the newspapers for hours on end.

So now, when Mrs Spoons woke in the morning, when Rillie had settled her mother into her rocking chair beside the window in the attic in Maiden Lane, Mrs Spoons would sit pale in her own chair, her eyes darting about the room. The empty rocking chair beside her she could not understand, the silence of the voice. She became more and more agitated as the hours passed, began to rock wildly, making strange distressed noises. Most days Rillie sat in the empty chair and tried to explain but Mrs Spoons could not understand. When Rillie said *Regina* there was no look of recognition in the eyes of the old lady, just incomprehension as the hours passed. She looked at the yellow glove with the same bewilderment and dropped it to the floor.

And then one morning she suddenly said quite clearly, 'It's all right about the cake, course it is, but Bert said I shouldn't leave,' and her voice and her rocking and her incoherent words became more and more agitated. All day Rillie bathed her mother's distressed face gently with a cool cloth, spoke to her over and over. She tried to interest her mother in the little yellow canary but Mrs Spoons' eyes wandered away even as the valiant little bird sang its heart out. When Monsieur Roland and Cordelia came back from the rooms in Nassau Street in the early evening they heard Mrs Spoons' thin, high cries of distress as they came up the stairs to the attic; they saw that Rillie had been weeping. And Monsieur Roland understood that although Mrs Spoons did not remember Regina herself, she remembered *something was not there*. He took Mrs Spoons' hand and spoke to her for a very long time. Cordelia poured Rillie a large port and put her arm around her distressed friend. Monsieur Roland explained to Mrs Spoons that her oldest friend, Regina, had gone to see Alfie's family, that they lived in another part of New York, that she would return with lots of interesting stories; as he spoke he slowly, gently, passed his hands over her face and her small distressed body, over and over, over and over. She became calm for a time: not asleep, hardly awake, but calm and still at last.

'Has she been like this all day?' he asked Rillie quietly.

Rillie tried not to weep again as she looked at her now-peaceful mother. 'This is the worst she has ever been, ever. Who would have thought she would have even known that Regina was not there? How can I help her?'

'You do help her, Rillie, my dear,' he said. 'You help her every day of her life.'

When Mrs Spoons opened her eyes and saw Rillie sitting beside her she smiled gently as if in recognition and Rillie

272

smiled back and bent and kissed her mother. But then very soon the eyes became confused again; they stared out of her pale, old, dear-to-them face, uncomprehending and lost.

'Come to bed now, Ma,' said Rillie softly, at last. The frail, pale little face looked intently at Rillie for a long time and then Mrs Spoons, who had bravely and uncomplainingly crossed the Atlantic from London probably without knowing that she did so, gave a small shudder and died in New York, as her daughter Rillie gently and lovingly held her hand.

They sent a message to Regina, and Alfie brought her back again for the funeral.

'I shouldn't have gone!' said Regina, who was very, very distressed. She had gone away against all her instincts; and of course this changed everything. But both Rillie and Cordelia hugged her and told her what a good friend she had been for so many years, and Monsieur Roland said, 'She was a very old lady.'

Rillie said sadly, 'I have been trying to work it out. I think she was nearly eighty.'

Alfie arranged everything: Mrs Spoons was buried in the graveyard of St Paul's Chapel on Broadway and Rillie, weeping during the short impersonal service, put the yellow glove on to the coffin as they lowered the small box, holding the small body, into the earth in the churchyard that looked out across the Hudson River and perhaps (Rillie wanted to believe), in the distance, to London.

'Now then,' said Alfie briskly. A friend of his owned a rather noisy stout and oyster cellar nearby and a small private room had been taken, at Alfie's request. There Cordelia and Rillie and Monsieur Roland and Regina and Arthur Rivers and Alfie Tyrone drank to the memory of Mrs Spoons and told stories to

273

Alfie of her life in London; and in her memory too, remembering how she still knew the old Scottish words and the tune when everything else was gone, they sang quietly:

> *O whistle and I'll come to ye, my lad,*
> *O whistle and I'll come to ye, my lad,*
> *Though father and mother and a' should gae mad*
> *Thy Jeannie will venture wi' thee, my lad*

They all insisted that Regina go back to Washington Square after the funeral as she had hardly been away: again they waved as the two old siblings rattled away into the night from the corner of Maiden Lane, Alfie having calculated for Cordelia, as usual, Gwenlliam's putative progress. 'She'll be well flying that trapeze by now!' he called from the carriage. 'You'll be getting a letter before too long!'

That night Rillie Spoons went to bed alone for the first time for so long that she could hardly remember how many years. Although Mrs Spoons had been a little quiet figure curled at one side of the bed, Rillie felt lonely for all the years and years they had been together, and wept; felt that this change was somehow more than she had understood, that now she had nothing left of her distant past, and wept. Cordelia crept into the room: they did not even need to speak so deep was their understanding of the other after so many years: Cordelia simply sat on the bed and held her friend in her arms until she fell asleep. She heard at last Rillie's deep even breathing but Cordelia stayed there, holding her gently, and thinking of all that had been, and how far they had come. Cordelia remembered that Rillie had once said to her: *I'm your mirror. Everyone has to have a mirror, someone who knows them better than anyone else. If you don't have a mirror you don't see yourself, and that's bad for people.* But Cordelia was Rillie's mirror also: always Rillie was reliable and loving and looked after them all but she too had a heart that needed holding. Once a fortune-hunter had pursued Rillie, under the mistaken assumption that she was wealthy: Monsieur Roland and Regina and Cordelia had foiled him just in time, but Cordelia saw then how high Rillie's hopes had been for other happinesses. Rillie was full of love; she had loved her little mother dearly, and Cordelia understood more than anybody what this loss would mean, and all night she held her dearest friend.

They had reckoned, of course, without La Grande Celine.

Several weeks after the death of Mrs Spoons she came upstairs to talk to Rillie: making sure all the others were there also. She so obviously had something of importance to say that Arthur courteously pulled out a chair for her.

'Why, thank you, Arthur. Good evening everyone.' Then she took a deep breath and tossed that flame-coloured hair, and smiled. 'Rillie, I have wanted to ask this of you for so long but thought it was too much. I have never had somebody to share my responsibilities with me in the dining-saloon. I never, ever, have a day off, an evening off. Please, *please,* will you work with me downstairs as often as you feel able? (Did they hear a small, small squeak of pleasure?) We can come to some agreement about sharing the time and I will pay you handsomely, I promise.' And the pearl on the eyepatch flashed and Celine smiled and smiled and her smile encompassed Monsieur Roland as well, as if to say: *we could stroll to the Battery Gardens one evening now, you and I.*

Rillie actually laughed: 'I *would* enjoy that!' she said and everyone was so pleased to hear that laugh again, 'and I would be so very glad to be earning some money for our family.'

'As the last person who worked with Rillie,' said Cordelia mock-portentously, 'and she was, Celine, my business partner for many years, I cannot recommend her too highly, although I must warn you that she can be somewhat imperious at times! I would also like to suggest that you ask her to play her flute when times are quiet,' and Cordelia and Rillie laughed together as they used to laugh and Monsieur Roland nodded to Celine as if to say *thank you my dear* and Celine swooned very slightly.

So, some nights now, there was Rillie at the cashier's desk: courteous, firm, kind, hospitable: all the things she was, and the sadness in her eyes lifted. Just sometimes she walked down to St Paul's Church in the morning and sat and talked to her little mother, telling her all she had been doing. Mrs Spoons could not reply but then she had not replied for many years, so perhaps things were much the same.

29

TALK TO THE MESMERIST may have been adjudged a success by some of the ones who did the talking.

But for Monsieur Roland and Cordelia it was an abject failure: a misguided and horrendous mistake of gigantic proportions. It was such a magnificent failure that as the first winter snow came Monsieur Roland persuaded Arthur to paint over Alfie's proud notice altogether, much to the disappointment of some New Yorkers who had partaken of the TALK TO THE MESMERIST service with great pleasure, for two dollars a time.

Monsieur Roland had read many books and thought a great deal and talked to Cordelia a great deal. 'The thing that really interests me, the blocked memory, will of course not be obvious at the beginning,' he had said, 'and in many cases perhaps not even relevant but I do not conceive how else to start, except by inviting people to talk to us. This will be an on-going process if we are really to assist them, and perhaps we will learn many things, but let us see what happens. At first, I am sure, they will talk to us of their immediate physical pain and perhaps their immediate problems.'

Even this wise man had not understood how right he was.

It was not that the people who came – customers, as Alfie called them – had not been forthcoming. They were forthcoming, certainly. So forthcoming indeed that they almost drowned the practitioners in a mountain of words, often loudly. Yet the practitioners had planned (they thought) so carefully: Cordelia with her short hair bound in a long, flowing scarf, and Monsieur Roland in his meticulous old jacket, would sit, one each in the two rooms in Nassau Street, an oil lamp on each table, and two chairs. Instead of the old words *Let yourself rest in my care*, which the Mesmerists used when people presented headaches or a painful back or a shaking hand, they would say instead: *There is something that might help the mesmeric passes to assist you in a more useful way. Tell me how you think this pain occurred and tell me how you feel*. And oh, they *would* tell how they felt, these Americans: at length, unstoppable, so that hours ticked by and the voice did not cease except to take another breath.

'I am so *sorry!*' Cordelia had cried despairingly to Monsieur Roland after one particularly difficult afternoon in their newly-painted rooms, but at the same moment as she despaired she started laughing helplessly at her predicament. She laughed and laughed: tears bordering on the hysterical pouring down her cheeks. 'They won't stop! *They will not stop talking!* I can't make them stop!'

It was only when he said, 'I do indeed understand,' and she looked up and saw his wry, nonplussed expression that she understood: Monsieur Roland could not make them stop talking either.

People did have, as Monsieur Roland had expected, problems: some large some small: some presenting real physical anguish, some giving a headache or a churning stomach.

Many of the problems were concerning money. Monsieur Roland and Cordelia (not without their own financial difficulties) quickly learnt that in this new country, with riches unimaginable for some, those that could afford to talk to the mesmerist in the first place probably had enough money to survive – but often the problem was not so simple: they wanted to acquire *more* money – many people, as the money came to them, wanted more. Their heads ached, or they seemed to have the rheumatism, because there was more money to be had and they were not acquiring it. And then there was love and death and children and loneliness and disappointment. If the practitioners were looking for blocked memories they were certainly not, it seemed, going to find them this way. This whole experiment was as far from Monsieur Roland's initial ideas as it was possible to be. The flow of talk, in this land of talkers – after all they had been invited to talk, had they not? and paid good money – was unstoppable: nothing was easier to these people than to tell their most intimate secrets and as Monsieur Roland and Cordelia had not thought to – had no idea to in this early stage of their experiment – make parameters or time their clients, so an afternoon would pass, the chill and dark of night would come down and still the Americans talked: all efforts at interruption were useless. Often Monsieur Roland and Cordelia would realise that they were listening not to one voice but to two: from each of the small rooms loud, unstoppable voices booming out, telling their problems on and on to the Mesmerist, just as invited. And then worse: now that talking was part of the process the clients would often ask questions of the Mesmerists. 'How do you like America? how old are you? are you married? how much money do you make?'

Sometimes, when she finally got home to Maiden Lane, Cordelia announced that she thought the whole of New York was full of mad people; Monsieur Roland with all his long experience did not fare much better. He said to Arthur Rivers: 'I need you at the door, to haul a customer out, still talking. We ourselves can hardly cut them off mid-sentence and ask for two dollars when the allotted span has come, if I could only see what an allotted span might be!' and, although they laughed because they could do no other, they could not find a solution.

Alfie said, 'I told you! I told you I could come and talk your head off!'

Rillie said sensibly, 'You should have a loud bell, and ring it when a certain amount of time has elapsed,' but Cordelia explained again: these clients had certain expectations: they were paying good money to talk, and they were un-interruptable. There were exceptions of course, but on the whole if these Americans paid two whole dollars to talk, they would indeed talk for as long as they liked and nothing would stop them.

They battled on for several months but in truth there were so many new ideas in the American air: so many signs and adver-tisements: Mormonism, Shakerism, Baptistism, Spiritualism, Occultism: mesmerism was of the past. Although the customers who did come very much enjoyed their two dollars' worth, the number of customers did not suddenly enlarge: the word *Mesmerist* no longer had power to draw. Not only had TALK-ING TO THE MESMERIST been a philosophical failure: it was also a financial disaster: they covered the rent of the rooms in Nassau Street, but almost nothing else.

'It is my fault, my dear,' said Monsieur Roland. 'I have not thought it through properly, after all. This is not the way. I am sure there is something here, something we are touching on –

of course there is, there must be, for people seem to need to talk so much. But this is not the right way.'

'How they delight in such a chance!' said Cordelia. 'And by paying two dollars they think they have paid for the right to talk until the gas lamps come on all along Broadway!' And she thought of the restrained clients she used to have in London, from whom sometimes it was hard to elicit any words at all.

'The Americans are a new breed,' he said wryly. 'Yesterday evening a man, who had very much pain in his shoulders, asked me how my two dollars I was to be earning from him was to be invested and whether he could become my financial advisor.'

Cordelia laughed. 'What did you say?'

'I said – thinking of how dear Rillie looks after our money so carefully and makes it stretch so far – that I was investing it in a woman, and he immediately – *immediately* – launched into information of a speculation in "saloons with ladies" on Pearl Street. "Can I interest you in that?" he said to me. "It will make your fortune."'

Cordelia was laughing still, but only in sympathy. 'And his shoulders?'

'He was there for more than two hours, unstoppable. I can say I now know very much about Wall Street which perhaps one day will be of use to me, but not, alas, today – and of any memories he may have had of his life I uncovered none. Finally I persuaded him that I thought I had enough information to mesmerise him and assist his painful shoulders. He sat fidgeting and still talking and it required every ounce of my concentration to make the passes over him, to calm him, and help him. He thanked me profusely afterwards and said it had been good to talk and his shoulders felt wonderful!' He sighed. 'But I could have helped his shoulders without any conversation at all! It is, as I said, my fault, Cordelia. Mesmerism and money and memory and monologues combined is a complete and utter failure. I do still believe there has to be another way to move forward from Dr Mesmer's work, and I don't mean hypnotism – I am trying to find some other healing. However, I think we must both agree that TALKING TO THE MESMERIST must be accounted a grand folly.'

Cordelia could only nod in relief.

Alfie reluctantly changed the sign, for they had a lease on the rooms and knew they must work somehow. 'In a few weeks,' he said to Cordelia, 'you'll be able to start looking for letters from California. Not yet.' He was organising the repainting. The sign remained a little bit large, but the lettering was smaller on Monsieur Roland's insistence even as Alfie pursed his lips and shook his head. It simply said:

> **MESMERISTS**
> **Monsieur Roland**
> **Mrs Cordelia Preston.**

Again Alfie pleaded for at least **MESMERISTS!!!!** Or even more likely **HYPNOTISTS!!!!!!** But Monsieur Roland thought the word hypnotist would not be properly understood. 'We *do* hypnotise, that is what a good Mesmerist has been doing for the last few years, endeavouring to join our own energy with the energy of the – to use your word, Alfie – customer. But the very word *hypnotism* has – already – become much associated with quacks and rascals. At least some sensible people know that mesmerism is a serious science, even if it has had its day.'

But his shoulders hunched. He was more devastated than they really understood, at this failure.

And they all knew that even with Rillie working now with La Grande Celine their finances were no longer at all secure and their savings were dwindling fast. Arthur Rivers' mind was much pre-occupied; he would have prayed, if he had been a religious man, that Charlie would not lose his job at the Water Board in London.

I must somehow earn some money, thought Cordelia.

So early one morning she made herself walk briskly to Mr L Prince's Daguerreotype Studio on Broadway, looked carefully in the window, the notice was still there: LESSONS GIVEN IN DAGUERREOTYPY: ENQUIRE WITHIN.

Over the final, half-nightmarish, half-comical days of TALK TO THE MESMERIST as Cordelia had watched the faces of the talking Americans, she had thought: *my work has always involved looking at faces. Even long ago, as an actress I learnt my craft from other people's faces.* She remembered the mad, wonderful face of the actor Edmund Kean, playing King Lear when she played his youngest daughter: her namesake, Cordelia. She remembered, beginning her career as a Phreno-Mesmerist, scanning the faces of her first customers for clues as to what they might want to hear. She remembered the first hospital operation she had ever worked at as a medical Mesmerist: she was terrified to see surgeons with rubber aprons and saws, but she had looked at the pale woman under the rubber sheet and suddenly Cordelia understood: the woman was looking at the surgeon also, and was very much more terrified than Cordelia – for they were to saw off a breast. And Cordelia had, from the clarity with which she understood that woman by looking at her face, found her own courage to help. *I think my work has made me understand, sometimes, people's faces. Perhaps I could learn to capture expressions permanently.*

She stepped quickly inside the daguerreotype studio; she was wearing her beautiful hat.

Mr L Prince recognised her at once: the one with the white streak of hair and the face you didn't forget. 'Good morning, Mrs Preston,' he said, bowing slightly. 'How is your pretty daughter? Have you come for a further sitting?'

'I want to take lessons,' she said.

He was extremely surprised (surely she was too old, and a woman too?). However: business was business. 'It will cost fifty dollars for ten half-day lessons. At the end of ten lessons you may make a daguerreotype.'

She had already planned this with Rillie: *I must try and earn money, I would like to try this, shall I try this Rillie?* 'I have the money here,' said Cordelia.

'In that case: call me Larry,' said Mr L Prince. Cordelia took off her hat: he may as well see her now as later. But in fact he said: 'Well well. I heard there were new hair styles.'

With Monsieur Roland's agreement Cordelia made the few mesmeric appointments that came her way in the afternoons. Every morning she presented herself to Larry Prince, daguerreotypist. There were four training students, Cordelia was both the oldest and the only woman. Every morning Larry re-iterated to them the most important principles of daguerreotypy: it was based on two vital elements – a chemical element and an optical element. 'And if you don't have a feeling for light and shade you are wasting your money and you are wasting my time. I went to England. I saw the new photography, I know they can make copies – but they can't take such beautiful portraits: I still reckon this is the best way to get a likeness.' Cordelia, not the young gentlemen, was asked to dust the portraits in the reception gallery every morning: this she did without complaint, watching everything. No wonder Larry talked of light: the first thing he did every single morning was run upstairs to his studio with its large skylight and look at the daylight coming in, study the daylight, discuss the daylight, bemoan the daylight if it was grey. She saw how patient Larry was, how meticulous, how he moved mirrors over and over until he was satisfied that he had the best possible light caught on a customer's face, before he took the picture. *He's like Silas Swift*, she thought. *Using light for effect.*

Soon she was not only dusting portraits but buffing and polishing the plates used for the daguerreotypes, thin sheets of silver-coated copper: whole plates, half plates and smaller. 'The more you polish these, the better the image,' Larry told his paying pupils. He had a dark-room where he covered the plate with 'secret' ingredients: 'We all have our secrets to enhance our images and make the plate light-sensitive,' he said. 'We are like painters of old, Michelangelo himself had his secrets,' and then he put the finished plate into a plate-holder and allowed one of the students to take it to the large camera that was waiting in the studio on its stand. In the studio ladies and gentlemen always waited nervously, patting their hair.

The actual taking of the picture – 'I can usually do it in ten seconds now,' said Larry proudly – was the thing that took the shortest time of all. While the customer, daguerreotyped, waited in the noble reception gallery downstairs where all the dusted portraits hung, Larry, or one of his students, developed the image over the vapour of heated mercury.

After ten lessons, Cordelia was permitted to make her first picture, as promised. Arthur, protesting, sat for her, his head clamped into the headrest. 'But you mustn't smile, Arthur!'

'I won't smile,' said Arthur, regarding his wife gravely. He remained quite still for seventeen seconds.

'Not bad, pal!' said Larry when Cordelia brought the finished half-plate daguerreotype in a small frame downstairs to the reception gallery and even Arthur himself saw that it was good. Something there in the face, something gentle, but something else caught, something perhaps of the dilemmas of his life. Although perhaps Cordelia did not exactly understand what it was she had captured there.

'Well, well, well,' said Rillie and Celine admiringly.

'You've caught his soul,' said Monsieur Roland.

One day Larry Prince took a daguerreotype of Cordelia.

Light caught her dark eyes and the bones of her pale face and her strange, new style. Her hair had been so damaged that it hardly grew: almost always she wore a long scarf tied around her head, the ends fell across her shoulders, a gay, jaunty look.

'They cannot frighten me', she said. 'My daughter is safely far away.'

30

Cordelia ran.

She had begun haunting the Post Office: Alfie had said it almost was time. First she allowed herself to go every second day; finally she was going daily, more and more anxious. When the parcel from California finally arrived Gwenlliam had been gone from New York for 221 days.

When Cordelia was given the parcel and saw, underneath all the stamping and stickers, her own name in Gwenlliam's lady-like handwriting, she ran and ran home, dodging the crowds, holding the precious parcel tightly with her hands in her woollen gloves. As she reached the corner of Broadway she heard a whistle, Arthur's whistle: he was coming up Maiden Lane from the opposite end, from the docks, and had seen her. 'Quickly!' she cried out to him. '*Quickly!*', hardly able to speak.

'Cordelia, whatever is the matter?' He ran towards her, looking to see if she was being followed.

'*Gwenlliam.*'

'What? What is it, Cordelia?' He felt his own heart catch suddenly.

'A letter from Gwenlliam. Well, I hope it is a letter.' She tried to calm herself. 'For she seems to have sent us a book.' In the attic Arthur took out his knife, Cordelia grabbed it from him; her fingers shook as she cut at the string and pierced at the wax, refusing help, while they sat round her: Rillie, Monsieur Roland and Arthur Rivers: this smaller family.

Quickly she tore at the last of the paper.

There was no letter. Just a quite large Holy Bible, a black-covered Holy Bible. They looked at one another, confused. HOLY BIBLE it said quite clearly. Very slowly Cordelia opened the book. The Chapter of Genesis stared at her, but looked rather odd, the pages hung strangely. She turned the first pages – and suddenly understood there were no more pristine pages in the bible, but a large hole cut in the middle of them. 'Oh,' she said faintly.

For there, placed tightly inside, gold nuggets winked back at them.

'*Oh*,' said Cordelia again, very, very faintly indeed. Most of the nuggets were the size of perhaps a large walnut, or even a small egg; one on the top was misshapen and knobbly, no bigger than a cherry. It looked like a little snail. And, underneath the nuggets, was a very thick letter.

Dearest Mama and Arthur and Monsieur Roland and Rillie and Regina and Mrs Spoons, I have your picture beside me as I write, I see you all in Maiden Lane, all the dearest people in my life.

I write from Tent City — so we call it — that is, from a place called Sacramento, up a river further inland from San Francisco — where Silas P Swift's Circus is not the only activity in a canvas-covered space! Although they are starting to build here now (and we live, Peggy and I, in a real hotel!) it is Tent City indeed, I think the whole place has only been here a few months: the miners here live in tents, the stores are in tents, grog stores too and eating houses and dance halls and gambling parlours – and canvas drinking saloons! There is even a 'Cultural Tent' where they have a club and cigars and the one piano in Sacramento is in there and rude pictures in decoration! I am quite familiar with this decoration as it was in this 'Cultural Tent' that we did our first rather odd performances because our tent and wagons and animals have only just caught up with us. Peggy and I agree we do not know how to describe everything: Sacramento is simply a canvas gold town. It has its own newspaper – filled with advertisements for stores, and rumours about gold, and notices of miners wanting to buy or sell mining equipment, and always a big notice for SILAS P SWIFT'S AMAZING CIRCUS! and it is all such an adventure to be here – but underneath there is nothing, no history, no past, just gold-digging – and very much ill-health and disappointment I think. But it is – almost – romantic in the evenings when they light the lamps in all the canvas saloons and the canvas stores, then soft light shines through and there is music and you cannot then see the mud and the dust and there is a grove of oak trees towards the river. And very many miners back from the riverbed – if they are not dying of dysentery or cholera – pile into the circus tent in the evening, evening after evening in fact, cheering and shouting and spitting tobacco on the tent walls.

Cordelia looked up uncertainly at this point. 'Cholera?' she murmured, 'Would Gwennie get cholera from miners spitting?' but Arthur touched her shoulder and indicated the letter.

We got to San Francisco in September: tied up at the wharves next to lots of – completely empty – windjammers, the crews had just walked off them all it seems, and joined the gold rush! But we found at once that another circus had _already_ appeared

289

and was putting up its paraphernalia in San Francisco. You can imagine the anger of Silas to see competitors — he whisked us off in a rage to Sacramento where parts of the mining are centred — he was smart in a way to make this mad gamble, for apart from card playing and saloons-with-ladies (where they must queue) and the aforementioned Cultural Tent with its piano, there is nothing else for the miners to do when they crawl exhausted into Sacramento town with their gold — o the gold, the gold the "yellow, glittering precious gold" Mama — so they spend a lot of it on us. In fact they don't seem to <u>save</u> money these young men — they just spend it! O it is a crazy, wild, exciting and extraordinary place! (San Francisco is more of a real place than Sacramento, with real buildings, but most things put up quickly and looking flimsy and great fogs rolling in every day from the sea.) The miners just long for some sort of entertainment — anything. In the cultural tent someone plays 'The Last Rose of Summer' and 'Whistle and I'll Come to You,' and 'O Susanna!' and hymns and the miners sing and sometimes they cry. They also have a canvas Dance Hall with a trumpet and some fiddles but hardly any women, though there are some women. If we go, Peggy and I, we are swept off our feet — and often the miners have to dance with each other, most of all they love to waltz, the naughty waltz that everyone used to disapprove of, just to hold someone I think, they are so lonesome. Perhaps it is the stores and the grog saloons and the girls and the gambling tents and the circus that are benefiting most of all from this gold rush . . .

The journey from Chagres across to Panama City was as terrible as we had heard, only worse: humid, dangerous, we travelled in Indian canoes up the river. The main problem coming up the river was the horses — the charros wanted to ride them overland but large parts were almost impassable so horses had to swim or be got into native canoes, can you imagine some of those horses? — Silas understood then he should have had them transported by ship, that his eagerness to get the circus performing, at least partially, where the actual gold was, had overcome his good sense, but being him he couldn't admit to this and he shouted a great deal, especially when two horses finally died — one broke its leg so badly it had to be shot, the other just lay down one morning and couldn't or wouldn't get up again. The charros hardly spoke for several days. There was steam rising from the river and everybody laughed at me because I thought it must be hot water in the river. Yet I have seen such amazing things — I did see crocodiles with their strange cold eyes and snakes that could poison, but also I saw flamingos and monkeys and palm trees and bananas growing and unbelievable bright flowers. Two of the new monkeys disappeared at once — of course they would rather be free — and so the rest had to be kept locked up in boxes all the way and they are sharp and angry and sullen-eyed even now as they do their antics for the miners, I find them quite scary. And, so yes, we and the horses and the dogs and some monkeys finally got to the end of the river. But two of the midgets had died by then, it was so terrible, poor things, as if they were simply not big enough, or strong enough for the difficulties, for it was indeed, difficult. It was probably cholera so it was said. We had a short funeral at Cruces, a horrible place at the head of the Chagres River, the other midgets wept and drugged and swore, and still we had many more terrible miles to travel, walking or riding through hot, wet rainforest and loathsomeness, narrow tracks and snakes and things like big bats flapping out of the dark vegetation suddenly, across our faces — I cannot believe that all the rest of us survived to the other side of the isthmus, to Panama City, and I hope we never,

<u>never</u> have to do that journey again. And when we did finally get to Panama City we thought we would never ever leave: hundreds — no, thousands — of men fighting to get on whichever ships finally arrived at the port, fighting to get to California, some people had been there for months waiting for ships that never came. We were only a small part of this huge mass of gold-seekers. When ships did arrive people paid treble or more for a ticket, screamed about foreigners on the ships, bribed Captains. Some were so despairing they set out to sail up the Pacific coast in home-made canoes, or tried to go across mountains. Silas had to bribe and barter and plead to get us and the animals to San Francisco, who knows how he finally got a circus on board — it was a kind of Silas miracle. People slept everywhere on every ship, on the decks in the lifeboats, every ship was dangerously overloaded.

So: we arrived at last in California, in one condition or another. And Silas P Swift's wagons, now they have finally arrived in Sacramento, are a battered memory of what they once so proudly were, the drivers told us they nearly got smashed to pieces sailing around the Cape, Silas is sending for paint. But at least we now have our own tent and all the proper acrobatic poles and wires and everything.

But — oh I keep putting off writing about the animals — Lucky-baby, having made it round the Cape in storms and calms, died on his second day in Sacramento, just lay down and died, everybody cried, it seemed so cruel when he had actually survived the journey. And now the mother elephant, Kongo, has become insane and hits her head on the poles and the trees and turns round and round and then shakes her head from side to side, it is very sad to see, remember that woman in Hamford, Mama, whose children were burnt? it makes me think of her. They say it is too dangerous to keep Kongo now, that she could suddenly rampage and do damage because she is mad, Silas is so angry, he was told only African elephants were dangerous, not Indian ones. And I hear she will be shot today — so all that terrible journey, for what? Ah, remember Mama, how Lucky-baby seemed to smile at us when he lifted his little trunk and flapped his big little ears? And how he gambolled along and made us laugh? And now, no elephants at all. Silas fired the trainer, said it was all his fault but the trainer didn't care, said he'd rather be a miner anyway and off he went, up the river. The lion and the camel are extremely battered also but still alive — as you remember Silas didn't even keep the white bear, one of the trainers says that bear was the most dangerous animal in the circus although people don't believe a bear can be more dangerous than a lion. The lion trainer point-blank refuses to wear his toga any more because the miners laugh and whistle.

The miners are rough (or perhaps they have become rough being here) and also very very tough I think, for the work is so hard we are told and they do not all succeed although as I say the ones who do throw their money at us. Silas cannot believe the amounts he is taking every night, he says we shall all be rich in six months but the rains come, they say, in November and it is already October so I think it may be his wild hope rather than the truth. Although he is taking very, very much money Silas does not yet have his usual sleek look back. His eyes have a rather — it is hard to describe it, a rather surprised look in them all the time now, as if even he did not quite expect it to have been as it has been. Did you know that the Native Indians here knew of the gold but never touched it because they believed it was 'bad medicine' and belongs to a Demon who lives in a lake? Sometimes, on a difficult day here when you see some of the miners, it is hard not to believe that the Indians might have been right.

Oh. I just heard the gun-shot. Kongo.

My best time is upside-down on the trapeze waiting in the shadows, there I can study the audience quietly — not that the Big Top is quiet ever! for the miners have been drinking usually and they shout and cheer and as usual spit their great wads of tobacco, I never saw such spitting as here! The sides of the tent are almost black, even though they get scrubbed every week. I continue to have no clairvoyant qualities at all (or I would be able to give you the date I will arrive home to Maiden Lane again, and hold it very close to my heart!) but Silas has made no further demands in that direction, just seems happy with the name and my acrobatics from the darkness and my gold wand! But I have had some success with the mesmerism, dear Monsieur Roland, just in case you think it is now all drum rolls and trapeze jumps! I have success with their headaches and some rheumatics, and sometimes I feel it is just disappointment and sadness and loneliness I am helping with a little. Sometimes — I hope you will still approve of this, almost it is — it is like a 'crowd-mesmerism' if I can call it that. Because of the loneliness and disappointment of so many I try and — well, I try to take them all in, all, with a wide gesture I try and — of course it is probably not exactly mesmerism but I seem to be able to hold them all, just for a moment, and wish them hope, or magic, or luck — something like that. 'All will be well,' that's all I say, but it seems to catch something in their hearts. And, just for a moment, there is not a sound. Does that make sense? Is that mesmerism? It feels like it — as if just for a moment I hold them all, and help them. For their life is so physically hard that many of them seem to be killing themselves, literally I mean, and I cannot help them with that. Thousands of men, trying to be quickly rich. Lately the miners have been bringing their sick friends to me at the hotel, to my horror — I keep saying to them 'I am not a doctor!' and they reply darkly, 'nor are the doctors.'

There _are_ eight or nine doctors here — well, the sign on their tents say so and they charge _ten dollars_ for a consultation — but I am not sure if they are doctors really — someone in the poker tent told me the other night that some of them are miners who got sick of working so hard!

I have heard very much talk of what the miners do. They are usually away from the town for about three weeks at a time, digging up the river, camping on the hillside. They scoop up water and dirt from the bottom of the river and they swirl it around and around until they can see if there is any gold colour lying at the bottom of their pans. But there is very much back-breaking digging: sometimes with rewards and sometimes there is no reward at all. Yesterday a miner returned and came to the circus but he fell ill during the performance and called for his mother and was in very great distress and I calmed him and stayed holding him, and just talking to him, till he died.

The greatest test to our health and sanity are the biting little flies, _mosquitos_, as the charros call them. Of all people, (this will interest La Grande Celine!) Pierre-the-bird suffers most — the _mosquitos_ love him, he hates them, he swears and hits and scratches, all loudly in French, he insists he will leave the circus, Silas insists his system will become immune to them and offers him tequila. The _mosquitos_ were everywhere, although now as the weather changes, not so many as before, thank heaven. Some carry disease, some just bite to eat our blood I think, and they all, all of them, screech and buzz in our ears!

295

There is a bank here (a bank in Tent City!) but some miners just pay at the ticket office in gold — flakes or nuggets. $5 Silas is charging (remember it was 40 cents in Hamford Mama?) and they pay! There is just so much money around (or gold I should say rather — they weigh it and use it for transactions all the time, everyone has scales, including Silas!) An ounce of gold which they might get in a day (though they might get very much more, and they might get nothing) is worth $16 they tell me — but a pound of coffee can you believe costs $4 here! As you remember, Mama, it was agreed that Silas was to pay me a large advance sum once we got here. When I reminded him of this, he reminded _me_ that I am therefore tied to him and the circus for the foreseeable future. But I know he is already, as I said, making enormous amounts of money and he said recently I was worth my weight in gold (and he has not paid me this but he has, as you see, paid me a great deal!) And also, the strangest thing, last night the other miners insisted on giving me the small nugget that looks a bit like a snail, it is from the miner who died in my arms — yet many of them would have benefited from having it themselves. His brother cried and gave me the little nugget and the other miners cheered — and yet they kill for gold as well . . . These miners from all over the world are such a strange mixture of greed and generosity and violence and kindness — anyway, the tiny nugget in the bible is the one they gave me. I made Silas pay me in actual gold and you will see — if it arrives as I very much pray that it does — that I have sent it to you in an interesting and safe (I hope) way with this letter. I considered long how to send it safely and hope the Lord will forgive me!

Well, it is all most interesting. Peggy and I often look at each other and say 'This is most interesting!' if we find we are morose. We have both had many proposals of marriage, even the ladies in the gambling saloons and the grog stores get proposals but they say: 'we can make better money not being married thank you!' Sometimes when Peggy and I are walking, miners pass and just stare at us, not in a frightening way, it does not feel frightening, they just look at one or other of us as if to say: "that is a woman. I have almost forgotten what a woman looks like." Poor things, they talk all the time of going home — as soon as they are rich.

You can write to me at San Francisco, care of the Silas P Swift Circus, like we said, Mama and I am sure I will get it. (I queued the very first day we landed, just in case, at the Post Office in San Francisco but it was foolish to think I would hear from you so soon.) I would be so glad to hear from you for it would remind me that life is not all tents and _mosquitos_! It _is_ wild here, it is indeed like nothing I have seen or experienced in my life, but it is exciting also and you are not to worry about me, you know very well Mama that whatever befalls I can look after myself!

Peggy Walker is with me, sewing acrobatic costumes as I write, and she sends her greetings to you all and I send my thoughts and my dreams and this bible and all my love. Let me know, dear Monsieur Roland, if it is mesmerism? Holding them all for a moment, and trying to give them hope? It does feel that it is so. Dear Mama, I hug you so tight.
    Gwenlliam.

And then silence: all of them silent, the gold nuggets shining and winking, the broken Bible, the pages from the letter, Gwenlliam looking down benignly from the attic wall.

'Yes,' said Monsieur Roland. 'That is mesmerism.'

'Yes,' said Cordelia slowly, the letter against her heart. 'Yes. On stage, just once or twice, it happens like that. You *hold the audience*, something about the energy of the actors and the energy of the audience – both coming together for a moment. You can feel it. It is like mesmerism.' And the old man nodded.

'Kind, clever Gwenlliam,' he said.

Next day Rillie, accompanied by Arthur as usual, took the gold nuggets to Wall Street. It was snowing, they bundled themselves up against the cold, sleighs passed them along Broadway and the snow laid a kind of eerie quiet in the still-bustling streets. Inside the bank Rillie took off her gloves, brought out the precious parcel from a pocket inside her cloak. She handed the nuggets over the counter. The bank clerk actually whistled. 'Wow, sir!' he said to Arthur. 'I'll have to weigh these, they'll be worth a dollar or two! But I'll need some explanation. I'll get my boss.'

'I am a police officer,' said Arthur Rivers, and showed his small copper star which he kept in a pocket of his cloak. The bank teller's face relaxed. 'Oh, a policeman,' he said. 'That's different. They deposit all sorts of things.'

31

Dear Mama and Arthur and Rillie and Monsieur Roland and
Regina and Mrs Spoons,

    I have received two letters! Oh I miss you all so much yet I
never knew how much I missed you all until I saw your writing,
Mama. It was wonderful, so wonderful to hear all your news, the
plans for TALK TO THE MESMERIST, and to think of Regina
finding her brother Alfie, <u>at last</u>! after so many years, and that his
name is George Macmillan and he is a businessman on the docks!!
She used to tell me stories of him when I was falling asleep in
Maiden Lane, remember Regina? Please tell Alfie Tyrone — or
George MacMillan if that is what you call him now — that I hope I
meet him too one day. And he uses the telegraph! Silas was always
obsessed with the telegraph — but of course no such thing in Tent
City — or anywhere on this side of America! Everyone, everyone
wants communications from the real world. We have heard that
over forty thousand letters came to San Francisco on just one mail
ship last week, they had to <u>lock</u> the Post Office while they sorted it all
because so many people were queuing and banging on the windows
and the doors! And then the Expressmen, they pick up all the
Sacramento mail from San Francisco and bring it through on a
river ferry, and mine was brought right to the circus instead of

going to the Post Office, the Expressman (who has been to the circus) said he was going out to the diggings so he brought mine too, so I paid the man two dollars and he gave me the letters. (I would have paid ten!) He told me that there is always a lookout waiting at the top of Telegraph Hill in San Francisco and as soon as they see a ship in the distance they wave flags and everybody rushes and starts queuing at the Post Office!! I will try to write more often now that I realise the joy of receiving. I do hope my parcel came safely to Celine's House, it is a long time round Cape Horn, but not so long as it was, and they say it is safe, and soon it will be even quicker for there are, we hear, new clipper ships that almost fly . . . the rumour is that one did that long journey in eighty-nine days! Six months ago they were saying more like double that . . .

And on these ships that arrive come more and more men still, wanting their share of gold, anxious that they are too late, that El Dorado will be empty. And they are indeed almost too late for this year. Everyone talks daily now of the rainy season and looks at the sky even though there is no sign — they say it will come to Sacramento any time now but Silas says we will stay till the last moment before we move back to San Francisco as we will probably never make this much money again. The talk now is that surely the gold will 'run out' round Sacramento. The hills are covered with hundreds of tracks as miners take different digging routes to and from the river, to try to find more gold, and more gold, always following one rumour or another and one cannot help but think it must indeed therefore be all gone before too long. In the meantime the circus is still packed nightly and I still have some success with the things we know we can heal; and with that moment with all of them that I told you of.

Still Sacramento grows by the week, wooden houses especially — the place has changed even since I wrote to you first, already not quite the tent city I described. And there are *now real Theatre Performances even here! I managed to see a performance of a rather brief run of "The Bandit Chief or: the Forest Spectre", starring a lady called (on the poster) <u>Mrs Ray from the Royal Theatre in New Zealand</u>. 'Just call me Colleen,' she said to me afterwards, for we were so glad of a bit more female company, and she and I both enjoyed playing poker in the gambling tent, we were both quite lucky. But I only play poker, I keep away from the roulette wheel and the <u>monte</u> games! This "Bandit Chief" was a truly terrible play with an incomprehensible plot (though Peggy Walker and I did not say so to Colleen of course); very much fighting with swords although the reasons were not clear; then Colleen ran on stage looking very distressed and waving her (bare) arms to heaven and tearing at her (flimsy) garments. The miners loved it! absolutely loved it! Colleen was a bit older than me but she was great fun to be with, looks a bit like Celine, the same red hair, only Colleen has a large bosom which she used to great advantage. But the run of the play finished and they were to go elsewhere — or she met — I don't know — a sailor or a sea-captain, anyway off she went with a cheery wave to who knows where, and our female companionship sadly dwindled.*

La Grande Celine, who had been invited to hear the letter, laughed. 'I have always wanted to meet someone who looks like me!' she said. 'May "The Bandit Chief" come to New York and perhaps you and I could attend, Monsieur Roland!'

'Delighted,' he murmured kindly.

Still so many different races here, (apart from all the Americans arriving now every day from every route): Chinese, Peruvians, Chileans, Sandwich Islanders, French, English, Italians. And of course lots of Mexicans from across the new border between

America and Mexico, as well as our own charros. At first our charros were so happy — so many _amigos_, so much Spanish talking and music and laughter. Often when I first arrived I fell asleep to the most wonderful Spanish guitar music from somewhere in the night, like when we used to tour, Mama, but much, much more. But I have seen a very horrible thing and it has caused unrest in the circus also and the guitars have stopped. There has been some thieving, I do not know the truth of it but last week a group of miners took a Mexican (not one of ours thank God) and tied a rope around his neck and hung him to death, just on a tree, and _no-one stopped it_. Like 'Jerked to Jesus' Regina, remember? Our charros are angry and resentful and there has been more fighting. In fact the place is more violent, it feels, as each new group of hopeful men arrive. At the beginning it was so exciting that I did not altogether understand all the underlying tensions. There is no governance here of any kind, only the military, and they are left over from the Mexican war when America won this place, this California, from the Mexicans. But the miners don't like to be given rules or orders by soldiers — or by anyone for that matter — and anyway so many of the soldiers (like the sailors from the ships) have deserted and are now miners themselves! (one told me a soldier's pay is $7 per week, so who can blame them exactly). So if there is some trouble the miners take the law into their own hands. I wish very much, dear Arthur, that you were here, a proper policeman (with your handsome tall assistant, Mr Frankie Fields, please give him my greetings and say I have won much money at poker and will play him again when I return, probably with more success!) Sacramento does, sometimes, feel a very dangerous place but you must not worry because we in the circus look out for each all the time, especially the women are cared for carefully, I promise.

It is all so very exciting and so very terrible and I am fine, I am fine, I am earning so much money, I will send another bible soon, and I am learning many things and I do love the circus still. But I miss you all most terribly and as I have been writing this I can see you all in Maiden Lane, the canary singing perhaps and Mrs Spoons and Regina rocking in their rocking chairs just as always, and that is so comforting to me. I send love to you all.

Gwenlliam

32

Dear Mama and Arthur and Rillie and Monsieur Roland and
Regina and Mrs Spoons and La Grande Celine and Alfie Tyrone,
(that is George Macmillan), if he is passing, and Frankie Fields
if he is passing from the police force also,

More letters have arrived. Now I know that you are planning
with Celine a dinner for Alfie and his family, oh Regina I wish I
was there to meet them all. Well, I will one day. And I long to
know how TALK TO THE MESMERIST is going, maybe you will
change the world! You cannot imagine what the letters mean to
me, all of you, everything, and yours so often, dearest mama.

I am in San Francisco now and writing just a quick note
tonight because one of the new clippers is leaving, and I want
to send a letter on it with another Holy Bible! They say these
ships can get round Cape Horn to New York in less than a
hundred days if the winds are right! faster than the steamers!
What a beautiful ship it is, the <u>Greyhound</u>, it looks like a bird
with all its sails, I have just been standing on the wharf
looking at it, part of me wishes to fly on it to all of you with
this letter . . . "Silas," I say – many of us say, especially

Pierre-the-bird who hates it here — "let us go home now, we have all made money and everything is changing here," but Silas says: soon, soon, not yet . . . I have already told you how many people arrive every month, and still they arrive in their thousands, called by the gold. Five hundred 'saloon ladies' arrived yesterday, from Australia.

'Pierre-the-bird? He wants to come back?' and Celine's voice actually trembled slightly as she interrupted. She looked to Cordelia for confirmation; Cordelia nodded quickly, 'That's what she says,' and went on reading.

And here again is my gold. I hope the Lord wont mind me sending gold this way — it is well known that thousands, probably millions, of dollars worth of gold are being shipped out of California — (we still say to each other it is the money of the grog-shop owners and the store owners and the gambling saloon owners! — we hope the miners have sent lots to their families too as they are doing the hard and dangerous work.) The bank buildings have become so huge even in the time we've been here.

The rains did come, as expected, and when they came they did not stop but Silas was ready and we were all, animals and humans and the Big Top, on the river ferry down from Sacramento to San Francisco before we had time to think about it. Apparently our circus is superior to the other one so we are doing well in San Francisco also! But it is very cold here now and we are glad of the proper big hotel, Peggy and I, San Francisco has changed so much even in the few months since we arrived: more streets, more houses, more hotels, — and saloons and grog-shops of course! And lots of the big windjammers — and the coal lighters and the fishing boats —

which lay deserted at the wharves when we first arrived because the crews all wanted to join the gold rush — have now been bought by people with sense — who use them to take passengers and goods up and down to Panama — not only because there are still so many people and cargo waiting at Panama, but because some of the early miners are leaving here now, they are going home with the gold they have, they don't like what it has become here and who can blame them. Many many Americans have arrived by now from all over this huge country and there is much bad feeling now against 'foreigners' — even though California was Mexican not so long ago — I understand they are putting a foreigners' tax on foreign miners saying all the gold belongs to Americans only, but half the miners are Mexicans and Chileans and Peruvians and Brazilians and Englishmen and Frenchmen and many other . . . Our charros are very uneasy, two of them have left the circus. And the new arrivals kill Indians (who used to help with the panning in the beginning) as if they were animals. Chief Great Rainbow hardly speaks now, he doesn't even play poker much. I often see him after the show, sitting by himself in the darkness, smoking tobacco, and I think what he has seen here has almost broken his heart. And there are fights and very much violence and to be truthful I do not find it as exciting as I did when we first came — but more dangerous and hard, not so much laughter as there was. Even when <u>we</u> came they said to us "oh you have missed the best days" — even though there was still much gold to be had, and now <u>we</u> shake our heads like old-timers and say "ah the best days are over" — even though there is <u>still</u> gold! Remember when those miners made me take that little nugget I sent shaped like a funny snail? — that is what I mean, I cannot imagine anything like that happening now, there is no longer that kind of atmosphere.

Although we still get lots of people coming to the circus Silas has had to put the entrance fee down to $2.50 ($2.50 for a *ticket! that is still a fortune is it not!) because now miners aren't earning and the wealth of the town was based on them rushing in with gold. Several times some of them have tried to go back up to Sacramento but the town has been flooded out by the winter rain, little boats go up the main street they tell us. All everybody is doing is looking at the sky again and waiting for the spring.*

But he – Silas – has paid me again and so there are nuggets in this bible also, and I am sure I will soon hear from you that this 'holy gold' is arriving safely – especially on the beautiful clipper that awaits this letter from me, sent on a foggy, windy day.

I send my love and my thoughts to you all and, Mama, I hold you tightly.

Gwenlliam.

33

The gold nuggets. It was a most peculiar feeling for the inhabitants of the attic in Maiden Lane. Once the contents of the second gold-filled Holy Bible which had arrived on the *Greyhound* had been deposited at the Bank of America in Wall Street, their bank account was extraordinary. Even at the height of their success Cordelia and Rillie had never felt secure, knew how very quickly life could change. But unless the bank fell down they were almost wealthy: riches coming out of the ground, sent insouciantly by Gwenlliam inside Holy Bibles: a casual fortune almost as if to prove that it was true: America *was* the land of fortune and dreams.

For some weeks now the usual letters from Agnes Spark (Miss) had ceased arriving. Arthur did not know whether to be pleased or sorry but he worried about his family in London as he stalked the docks.

Spring had arrived in New York and Regina had not returned to Maiden Lane. How they missed her dramatic renditions of the headlines and news reports: other people reading out the newspapers was not the same. Cordelia and

Rillie took turns to read out the headlines and the advertisements but somehow:

GAY'S CANCHALAGUA:
Californian Plant of Rare Medical Virtue
For all ailments: Instant success guaranteed!

---

did not sound the same; nor the headline: **FOX SISTERS TO VISIT NEW YORK: MAKE AN APPOINTMENT TO SPEAK TO YOUR LOVED ONES** which Monsieur Roland threw out with the rubbish. Rillie observed the worn cuffs on his old jacket (for the new purple jacket was still at the back of the cupboard) and made devious plans to acquire the jacket from him briefly, to attend to it.

Alfie informed them that, actually, Regina was seventy-five years old: 'I'm seventy-three!' he said, 'So I know she's seventy-five!' and he insisted that they all attend a party in her honour that her family were arranging for her in Washington Square. So Arthur Rivers found himself ushering his little party aboard an omnibus one Sunday and although hats were knocked sideways and skirts caught under other people's feet they all arrived safely at the big front door on one side of elegant Washington Square, where tall trees blossomed. Rillie and Celine between them carried a huge bunch of spring flowers; Cordelia carried Gwenlliam's letters.

They all knew that Alfie was – as he had indeed told them – 'quite well-off'. They had not quite understood that he was positively, hugely rich. Although Maria herself opened the door, 'Ah have been waiting by this door for an *hour*, Ah do declare!', it was clear that they had many black servants and five floors of luxury. Regina did not just have her own room (only one floor up so that she did not have to climb too many stairs), she had *her own water cistern*. There were so many nieces and nephews and cousins visiting from other parts to meet this extraordinary newly-found relation that Regina had solved her dilemma of remembering their names by calling everybody *ducky*.

'What d'you think of that, ducky?' she said to all and sundry. 'Me own water cistern! Now there's a blooming miracle!'

They may have lived in a grand and noble house but it was a very loud birthday party; at one point a chilly gentleman from a nearby house in Washington Square knocked on the door to complain; somehow Alfie enticed him in and gave him a large glass of Irish whisky. At the end of a feast of soup and fish and joints of beef and pork and chicken and pies and oysters that made even Celine's eyes widen, a birthday cake was brought in. The children actually screamed with delight: it was the biggest cake they had ever seen, and it actually had seventy-five candles lit upon it (which Regina insisted on blowing out without the help of anyone else although she was quite red-faced at the end of it).

Then they sat in the very large parlour and Cordelia handed the letters from California for Regina to read out to everyone: there was a hushed silence, even from the children: getting a real letter about real gold was different from reading the headlines, everybody enjoyed hearing of gold nuggets worth many hundreds of dollars sailing round Cape Horn inside the Holy Bible. 'This is America!' they all said.

'Can I hold one?' said one of the grand-children. 'The gold?'

'Oh, I'm so sorry,' said Rillie kindly. 'We had to put them in a bank.'

'No,' said Cordelia, 'here is the little funny-shaped one,

from the miner who died, his brother gave it to her, remember? I carry it around for good luck, just till Gwenlliam comes home again. Here,' and she produced the small nugget. The children crowded round, looking at it with big eyes, touching it, throwing it gently up into the air. 'It looks like a little snail,' they cried to each other and Cordelia thought, *so this is the journey of this nugget of gold: the young man took it from the river bed in Sacramento and died from getting it, and here are children playing ball with it in Washington Square.*

Then Alfie asked Maria to sing. Without any false modesty she went to the piano. 'Ah come from the South,' she said. 'We have different songs there, but Alfie has always liked them, and the servants like them,' and she began to sing.

> *Nobody knows the trouble I've seen*
> *Nobody knows, but Jesus*
> *Nobody knows the trouble I've seen*
> *Glory Hallelujah.*

As she sang, the room became so quiet that you could almost have heard a heart beat. Servants joined in from wherever they happened to be: a soft low accompaniment. The visitors, including the man who had come to complain and had stayed to drink Irish whisky (sitting in some delight next to La Grande Celine with her eye-patch), were stunned. Maria had the most beautiful voice, as if she was a trained singer. 'Ah *was* trained,' she said modestly later. 'Ah sang in public. But that was long ago. Really, Ah sing for Alfie and the family now,' and Alfie looked proud and pleased.

'Imagine hearing that when you wake up in the morning!' he said. 'I'm a lucky man!' and he smiled at Maria and she smiled back.

Then he announced to his visitors that the now ever-more-famous Fox Sisters were this very moment on their way to New York. 'And I seen a telegraph – they're staying at the Howard Hotel. And where is the Howard Hotel – owned, I do believe, by a cousin of Phineas Barnum? Four doors away from youse all, in Maiden Lane, on the corner of Broadway; now, who could have arranged it better! They are to do their stuff in one of the parlours of the hotel – four of these things they do – they call them a *séance* – every day. The *séances* take thirty people a time. So let's go and see. We can all go. Not just you and me, Monsweer Roland, but Cordelia and Rillie and the Inspector. And Maria refuses to attend –'

'Ah find it an affront to mah Lord,' said Maria firmly.

' – but Queenie of course absolutely insists on coming also. And when I made me enquiries I asked them how much and they said, very shockedly – ha! – that there was no fee, but people might perhaps care to make a donation to their expenses.'

'Ha!' repeated Monsieur Roland. Regina, knowing the old man's views, had several newspaper articles on the subject ready for them which she now read aloud with great relish:

> *No respectable person, we trust, will countenance what is a*
> *rank insult to God. These blasphemous knockings, which*
> *they pretend are caused by the Deity, should be put an end*
> *to, the parties arrested, and sent to a lunatic asylum.*

'Amen to that,' said Maria.

'And why do you think it is,' said Monsieur Roland, '– after all the history of all the world, after all the knowledge of the Ancient Greeks and the other respected philosophers through the ages who have always grappled with these age-old questions – why do you think it is that an answer to the mystery of the afterlife has been found in *America*, where pursuit of ancient philosophies is very low on the list of priorities? To make money, of course!'

But Regina had not quite finished. 'What's the Styx, Monsweer?' she asked.

'It is said to be the river between the living and the dead.'

'I thought so. Listen to this: "*An electrical telegraph across the Styx – before they can get one across the Atlantic – would make Death less of a separation from friends than a voyage to Europe!*"'

'There Monsweer!' said Alfie. 'You can't fool New Yorkers! We'll find out for ourselves now!'

'They're very kind but I'm glad I've got me own room,' Regina confided gruffly to Cordelia and Rillie later, showing them the aforementioned water closet and the big clothes closets and the big bed, and all the spring flowers they had brought that had, magically, appeared in her room, filling it with the scent of freesias and hyacinths. 'I have to come away here sometimes and rest and read some poetry and that. Or the newspaper.' She looked at them. 'I do miss you,' she said in embarrassment. And then she embarked on the longest speech they had ever heard her make in all the years they had known her. 'And ain't it odd, I do miss the old lady, we'd been together for so many years, I often think of her, funny old thing. And I miss young Gwennie though I never told you. She never complained about sharing an attic room with an old lady, and I bet I snore too! But she's gone to make her own life, think of those letters! And I'm glad, and good luck to her. But – the thing is, I do like being around Alfie when he's here, and that's a fact. I ain't talked about me childhood for fifty years and now it seems we start talking about it every week, I dunno why, not as if it was a bed of roses. And one thing I'm helpful with: I do reading with the grand-children, make them learn a poem or two. Bright little things, some of them.' She became gruff again. 'But look at these cupboards!' She twiddled with the fancy door-knobs. 'They keep wanting to buy me clothes, and I keep saying I ain't interested in clothes! Too late to make me interested in clothes!' She twiddled and banged but it was clear she wanted to say something else. 'I miss you,' she repeated at last, 'after – after everything, like, all we been through. But – Alfie really wants me to make my home with him and – well, I think I might stay, if it's all right with you. I know I wouldn't be here at all if it wasn't for youse.' And Cordelia and Rillie both felt a pang of surprise and regret but they could only give Regina a hug and say *of course* it was all right, and they missed her too, and they would never lose touch with her, ever.

The small and crowded rooms in Maiden Lane where they had made their home seemed quiet and empty. Seven people had become four; the yellow canary sang as usual, but the rocking chairs were still, and Regina and Gwenlliam's room was empty. Rillie wanted Monsieur Roland to move into it but he said he was happy where he was. Another summer was beginning. But although Cordelia went to the Post Office every single day, there were no more letters from Gwenlliam.

There were no letters for Arthur Rivers from London either. He wrote and asked if all was well, enclosing the usual remittances.

'Why has she stopped writing?' said Cordelia. It was weeks now, unease drifted, stronger and stronger as the days passed.

'She shouldn't be *gambling*,' said Cordelia.

'She said it was getting wild and more *dangerous*,' said Cordelia.

'Perhaps California has run out of gold and she's on her way home!' said Cordelia. She stared at the daguerreotype on the wall.

The others spoke optimistically; it was well-known that everyone complained about how irregular the mails from California could still be.

'They will be moving back to Sacramento, Cordelia,' said Arthur, 'for the rainy season is surely long gone. There are lots of reasons for a letter to be delayed.'

Although the daguerreotypy lessons were over, Larry Prince asked Cordelia to still come in to his studio to assist him three mornings a week. He would pay her, of course.

'You're not bad at this, pal,' he said. She buffed silver-coated plates and learnt about chemicals and secret ingredients and understood more and more about shadows and light and captured faces, but the only face in her mind was her daughter's.

34

It was almost evening.

Gwenlliam sat, her cloak wrapped about her, on a discarded wooden crate on one of the San Francisco piers; often in the late afternoon she sat here, to see the ships coming and going from the enclosed San Francisco harbour. She liked watching the busy port, the loading, the unloading; and always she waited for the beautiful clipper ships. The clippers gave Gwenlliam the most pleasure of all: the wind filled their sails and they seemed to fly. *One day perhaps I will fly home on such a beautiful, fast vessel.* Tonight there were no clippers, but on the deck of a small schooner near to her a shantyman sat cross-legged, sewing a sail, whistling in the darkening day. One by one lights began to come on aboard the ships along the shore as sailors lit lamps.

Almost every day big ships and little boats disappeared towards the Golden Gate and the fog. If she'd recently written a letter to her family she imagined the letter rushing out into the Pacific Ocean and on to Panama and New York and Maiden Lane. And if she saw flags waving on Telegraph Hill, which meant a mail ship was arriving, she would run and queue in the post office with everybody else in San Francisco.

All her family wrote; Regina's letters made her laugh, and her mother wrote most of all, telling the news of all the people she cared for and missed so much, sending to Gwenlliam love and security.

Gwenlliam watched the bustle all around her. Tonight there were barks and brigs, and the schooner, and several steamboats. And even if there had been a clipper she would not have been able to board it: Silas would not think of leaving California, they were still earning too much money to leave. And although they all knew this to be true there was a feeling among the circus troupe that things had changed; it was harder and harsher and they had seen things that disturbed them, and Chief Great Rainbow's silence spoke to them most of all. They wished they could go home.

Gwenlliam breathed in the chill, fresh air, turned to go back to the circus.

And as she turned she almost collided with an extraordinarily handsome gentleman who must have been standing very close behind her.

'Good evening, Miss Preston,' he said gravely. 'A busy place indeed!' And he bowed in the dusk in a way that only Englishmen bowed, and removed his hat.

Gwenlliam was used to people knowing her name: most people in San Francisco had been at least once to Mr Silas P Swift's Amazing Circus. She smiled at the good-looking Englishman. 'The ships often take letters to my family,' she said, 'I love to imagine them speeding down the Californian coast.'

'Where are your family?' asked the gentleman politely.

'New York – they say the journey can be done now in less than a hundred days by clipper ship! Almost they fly!'

'You fly yourself in my opinion, like some beautiful bird!

You must forgive me for addressing you so familiarly, Miss Preston,' (and almost she laughed: did he not know he now dwelt in the land of familiarity?) 'but I have been several times to the circus and admired your skills. You do look so wonderful as you fly through the air. Please allow me to introduce myself: I am Mr James Doveribbon and I am recently arrived in San Francisco.'

'Have you come for gold, Mr Doveribbon?'

Mr Doveribbon smiled his very attractive smile. 'In a way I have come for gold,' he said. 'But, Miss Preston, I do not yet have many acquaintances in San Francisco and I had thought to visit Mr Silas P Swift's Circus again this evening. May I accompany you to your destination?'

'Of course,' said Gwenlliam.

And so the pretty Miss Preston and the extremely good-looking Mr Doveribbon turned from the harbour, a handsome couple, and made their way to where evening lamps glowed and the soft light made San Francisco look less like a muddy, clapboard gold town, and more like a city of fortune and dreams, as advertised.

35

Cordelia and Rillie walked to the Howard Hotel where crowds had gathered. At this moment the Fox Sisters were some of the most famous people in New York.

FOX SISTERS SPIRITUAL SÉANCE said a notice. Several men held large boards which read DO NOT INSULT OUR LORD and other like quotations.

'But don't you think, Cordie,' said Rillie, observing the interest shown by passers-by, 'that those sisters are just like we used to be, trying to make a living? How can we, of all people, judge them? Of course it will be a fraud, we know that better than anyone, and they will know quite well what they're doing. They are trying to make a living, just as we were.'

'Just what I was thinking,' said Cordelia wryly. 'This whole thing reminds me of us in London, all those years ago, but on a much bigger scale with lots of American publicity! Look at all the newspaper headlines!' For small boys thrust newspapers at them at every opportunity.

The others were waiting for them near the *séance* room, upstairs: Monsieur Roland, Arthur, Alfie and Regina. Regina had obviously had some *haute couture* discussions with her sister-in-law or her nieces for she was dressed as Cordelia and Rillie had never seen her before, in rather monumental fashion. 'They made me do it,' she said to them, very off-hand, 'but I told them: just this once. Look how big this blooming hat is!' and she actually pulled it off, immediately looking more like herself, but in fancy dress.

Alfie was talking to Inspector Rivers and Monsieur Roland. Regina lowered her voice conspiratorially. 'They're really really kind,' she said. 'They've even got me a rocking chair! But, just sometimes still, it feels not *quite* right. I still miss your ma, Rillie, funny old bat though she was. And I miss youse all, chatting away in one room. I'm used to one room. Any more letters from our girl?'

'No letters,' said Cordelia shortly.

'Come along then, ladies!' called Alfie, for they had been requested to enter a dimly-lit hotel parlour where they placed themselves, as invited, around a long mahogany table in the latest style. Dim lighting indeed: one candle on a shelf behind them; curtains tightly shut.

But it was not as any of them had expected.

The first thing that shocked Cordelia and Rillie, and even the sceptical Monsieur Roland, was that the sisters who were ushered in and introduced, the Fox Sisters, Kate and Margaret, were so terribly young – the youngest one, Kate, was probably only about eleven or twelve; even the next sister, Margaret, looked only perhaps about fifteen. There had been so many, many newspaper column inches devoted to these sisters and mysterious raps from the dead; there had been many reported examinations of the sisters (by groups of upright city women of course), to see if they hid something in their clothes or their shoes to make the strange knocks: nothing had ever been found, but accounts of the disrobing and the body-checking were often front page news and had all added to the rather *louche* publicity. So Cordelia and Rillie had imagined them as knowing young women, (knowing how they themselves had been when they set up their mesmerism business). But the Fox sisters, who were dark and exceedingly pretty, were very respectably and respectfully demeanoured – and very, very young to be taking on the whole of New York and to fool them. There was an entourage of course: a much older sister, Leah, who seemed to be in charge; a rather harassed-looking older woman who turned out to be the girls' mother; and several gentlemen who took donations quietly. One of the gentlemen made a short speech after he introduced the sisters.

'The Fox sisters are transmitters,' he said, 'for the spirits to converse with mortals. We ask you now to all place your hands flat upon the table. We must wait now for some time, as we often do, to see if the spirits are willing.' The men and the mother disappeared. The older sister stood to one side. Just the two young girls, sitting at a large table with strangers.

The second thing that surprised them was that the *séance* did not, in fact, take place.

And it seemed to be, in some way, Cordelia's fault. The youngest girl, Kate Fox, had large soulful eyes that shone very dark in the dim candlelight as she suddenly saw Cordelia at the big table, and Cordelia and Rillie, who were watching them so very, very carefully, saw that Kate made a tiny, tiny sign to her sister Margaret who was even prettier and whose eyes shone very brightly also as she saw Cordelia too. The much older sister whose name was given as Leah, who seemed to have no problem with the lady with the white streak in her hair, said, 'Sometimes we use mesmerism in our work. I will now put my sisters into a magnetic sleep, the better to speak to the spirits,' but Kate and Margaret both raised their hands slightly to stop her, did not move otherwise. In a long silence, while they did not take their eyes away from Cordelia's face, they seemed to be listening to something. Once Kate said, and her voice was almost that of a child: 'Is the spirit here?' but there was no answer. And there were no raps on the table or under the table or above the table as had been described in all the newspapers. And then in a very polite, regretful voice Kate said: 'We are so sorry. This happens sometimes. The spirits cannot come.'

There was a joint stirring round the mahogany table of disappointment or anger or scepticism (and Leah seemed to look distinctly cross). 'I've come from the *Globe*,' said a journalist in disbelief. But the young girl, Kate, simply repeated with great dignity, 'I am sorry. The spirits must have been delayed in some way. They will return at 5pm.' Despite himself, Arthur Rivers (wondering what he was doing sitting with his hands on a mahogany table with thirty other credulous people), laughed aloud at such exactitude. But the young girl seemed not to hear: she and her sister simply got up and left the room; the older sister could do nothing but follow them.

There was a great deal of apologising from the entourage, some money was returned, other appointments were made for the next session, some people left. There was a rattle of teacups from other, much more brightly-lit rooms in the hotel: a dining-room nearby, another parlour.

'Perhaps I could persuade you to take refreshments with me,' suggested Alfie. And so they sat together on wooden chairs in the other parlour to eat gingerbread and drink sarsaparilla, while next to them some rather boisterous uniformed members of a brass band ate oyster pies, their instruments poised beside them. Regina engaged the tuba player in conversation, asked him what songs he knew.

Arthur Rivers said quietly, 'They recognised you, Cordelia.'

'It seemed like that. But whyever would that stop them?'

'Did the circus go to Rochester?'

'Yes, it did.'

'They will likely have seen your performance. If they are frauds perhaps they think you will find them out.'

'But I have found them out already – of course all this is a fraud! But I would not stop the proceedings – good heavens, Rillie and I have done things exactly like this!'

'They are not to know that,' said Arthur.

'And you are not a fraud, Cordelia, my dear,' said Monsieur Roland wryly. 'And the sisters probably do know that; all will have been explained to the older sister and there will be not a mesmeric trance in sight at 5pm if you are still in the audience. And who knows, they will probably have ascertained certain facts about your past by then – if they can find old newspapers by five o'clock – and the spirits will regurgitate them!'

'I hope they will not,' said Cordelia crisply.

'Well, I just hope our rotten old father ain't coming back to haunt us,' said Alfie ruefully. 'That would be a terrible surprise I could do without! It's all a bit too dimly-lit in there for my liking.'

'I'll slap him, Alfie, and tell him to go away again,' said Regina, 'if he appears!' and then she turned back to the tuba player whose mouth was full of oyster pie and said, 'Yes, well, "Whistle and I'll Come to You" always goes down well, don't it!'

At five o'clock they were all back in the dimly-lit parlour. Some of the people from the earlier postponed *séance* had returned, some new faces, including a weeping woman in a large hat, were sat around the mahogany table. The girls were once again ushered in and introduced: the same introduction: The Fox sisters are transmitters. The two younger girls sat, composed, at the big table and this time they did not look at Cordelia in particular. The woman in the big hat continued to weep.

Cordelia was greatly surprised by the concern in the youngest girl's face as she looked at the weeping woman. Little Kate Fox got up from her seat and went and put her hand for a moment very gently on the woman's arm. Nothing more. The woman looked up, stopped weeping, and for some reason actually removed her large hat. She looked much more human and still sad, but she was no longer crying. The young girl went back to her seat. And then the group of people sat in silence in the gloom. Everybody, including the Fox Sisters, again had placed their hands flat upon the table, as instructed.

What had also not been made clear in the newspaper reports was how very long it all took, this contacting the spirits. Perhaps ten minutes passed. 'Is the spirit willing to converse?' said Kate. Five more minutes of silence. Regina was getting very restless indeed this second time around and coughed loudly several times. There was no other sound in the room except that of people breathing and a gentleman clearing his throat. Then there was a long sigh into the silence, as if somebody's patience was exhausted: Rillie was almost sure it was Monsieur Roland but dared not catch Cordelia's eye in case they laughed.

Finally Regina said loudly, '*And I meanwhile will keep thy tongue fast fixed in thy mouth; dumb shall thou be, when those wouldst fain expostulate with a rebellious brood.* Ezekiel 3,' she added, by way of explanation. This interruption was tolerated but not discussed. And then it came. Just one small sharp tap from nowhere, into the silence.

Margaret Fox said: 'Does somebody wish to speak?'

Three taps. *Yes.*

'To somebody in this room?'

Three taps. *Yes.* The hands of the Fox sisters remained quite still, flat upon the table like everybody else's. Whatever was happening they were not making tapping noises on the table with their fingers. Or their hands.

'A gentleman?' said Margaret.

Silence.

'A lady?'

Three taps. *Yes.*

'Who is it that you wish to speak to?' There was suddenly a great cacophony of taps. 'Do you wish us to use the alphabet?'

Three taps. *Yes.*

As letters of the alphabet were read out the taps that came from nowhere started to spell a name: *G. E. O.* which made Alfie Tyrone (alias George Macmillan) stiffen in his seat but suddenly, instead of continuing with that name, there was another urgent rush of taps and some more spelling *H. E. R. B.* Then there was another loud banging of many taps and *G.O. A.W.A.Y.* was spelt out. 'I do beg your patience,' said Margaret politely. 'The spirits are quarrelling about who should speak first.' There was a murmur of laughter around the table and a definite relaxation of tension. Nobody around the table claimed either Geo or Herb as their name, or the name of a person they wished to contact.

'You said a woman,' said Margaret politely into the air. There was a series of taps. It was ascertained that *E.L.I.Z. A.B.E.T.H.* had been spelt out. Cordelia felt rather than saw Arthur Rivers' reaction: he was suddenly very tense beside her: Cordelia knew Elizabeth had been the name of his first wife.

'It is he!' cried the weeping woman who was not weeping now. 'He is calling me. I am Elizabeth!' she informed the table in a great state of disarray. Arthur Rivers relaxed. 'My husband is calling me! John! John!' and she leaned forward and seemed as if she would embrace the mahogany table in her arms.

Kate said in her soft child-like voice: 'He is listening to you. What would you like to ask him?'

The woman sat up from the table, tried to pull herself together, seemed not to know what further action was required. At last she spoke, her voice was shaking. 'But – are you well, dear?'

Three taps. *Yes.*

'Has your illness gone from you?

Three taps. *Yes.*

'Has all that terrible pain gone from you dear?'

Three taps. *Yes.*

'Do you think of me?'

Three taps. *Yes.*

The weeping woman suddenly seemed very frail and very dignified as she looked intently at the table, as if it was speaking to her. 'Is this a trick, dear?' she said to the mahogany table. 'Can you prove to me, dear, that it is not?' There was no tapping. Just silence. The woman looked shocked, as if perhaps she had broken the spell, but she did not speak, just looked up at last to the young girl, who held sanity in her power. The taps began again.

I. L.O.V.E Y.O.U. R.E.M.E.M.B.R.E. M.E.

And although the deceased had not been able to spell 'remember' quite correctly, the weeping woman nevertheless looked at the table and at the mediums, with something in her face, some gratitude, or release. And then she picked up her large hat and quietly left the parlour. And Cordelia thought: *in a way, they are doing the same thing that we do. They are giving comfort.*

The tapping began again almost immediately: it seemed that *H.E.R.B.* had been waiting for a chance to speak, although nobody in the room seemed to want to claim him. But before he had finished tapping out what he wanted to say the visiting brass band struck up in the corridor outside. *H.E.R.B.* was not in the least put out. As strains of – not 'Hail Colombia' or the ubiquitous 'O Susanna!' – but a very jaunty version of 'Whistle and I'll Come to Ye My Lad' came in under the door (as if in fact old Mrs Spoons was making contact from the outside corridor), the spirit just tap-tap-tapped cheerily along in time to the music (making Rillie and Cordelia laugh) until the brass band, their oyster pies obviously consumed, had marched down the corridor, down the stairs, and out on to the street. And then Herb carried on.

I heard gold is found, was tapped out. *Is gold rush still going?*

'Tell him there's thousands still going to California,' volunteered a gentleman.

'There's thousands still going to California,' said Margaret Fox dutifully.

Thanks, pal. Good luck then! So long.

'So long,' answered Regina, as if it was the most natural thing in the world to speak to a tapping table.

Tap tap. Another message arrived immediately. *A.L.F.R.E.D.*

Alfie, who had been leaning back against his chair, did not move.

'Is anybody waiting for Alfred?' asked Margaret, but nobody answered.

'Is anybody here called Alfred?' Regina finally nudged Alfie with her elbow none too subtly but he did not look at her. Nobody answered.

A gentleman ventured, 'Could they mean Fred? My old grandpappy was called Frederick.'

A conversation ensued about the family of the gentleman with a grandpappy called Frederick, in fact the conversation was quite earthbound as the gentleman at the table informed the spirit of all the family news. Suddenly the tapping became a cacophony, rather as it had earlier when G.E.O. and H.E.R.B. were fighting for ascendancy.

'There are children here,' said Kate Fox and for the very first time she looked straight at Cordelia.

Cordelia let out a tiny gasp of surprised anger. But almost at once her face became completely blank although the taps came now in rapid succession: M.E. was tapped out and then N.O. M.E. F.I.R.S.T.

'There's two of them.' Kate and Margaret looked only at Cordelia. Cordelia looked expressionlessly back.

The spirits tapped. C.

But another woman around the table was clamouring: 'It is for me! It is Algernon,' she kept crying wildly and finally there was much contact with a dead child indeed called Algernon and the tapping got quite over-excited at one point and the bereaved mother, through her tears, said, 'He was always a trouble, bless him.' The taps were in full perform-ance now, seemingly from nowhere, most likely from underneath the table. Then Margaret said: 'A father is calling.

Has somebody lost a father recently?' and several people clamoured to speak to dead fathers and messages of love and affection and news were exchanged. And then the taps ceased. And then the *séance* was over. The Fox sisters left the parlour quietly.

But as everybody slowly made their way out to the lighter air of the hotel corridor, putting donations in a large box near to where more people waited patiently for their turn, a card was handed to Cordelia by one of the money-collecting gentlemen. On it was written, in what seemed to be hastily written childish writing: *Tomorrow. Private séance. Noon.*

Alfie pulled at his waistcoat and stroked at his whiskers as they walked back to Celine's House where La Grande Celine was waiting to hear a report (not able to leave her cash-desk in her dining-room).

'Come!' she called. 'The table behind the screen is free, there's melon and apple pie and monkey nuts, I'll join you.

'I don't believe a word of it!' said Alfie, sitting next to Regina, 'But I didn't answer to me name, Queenie, just *in case* our dad is looking for me!' and Regina chortled, and Cordelia gleefully told Celine of the spelling mistake, *remembre me,* and Rillie recounted with great merriment the local band playing and the spirit tapping in time to 'Whistle and I'll come to Ye My Lad' as if Mrs Spoons had sent a request from another place. 'Just like when I used to play Schubert on my flute!' cried Rillie, laughing still, 'To make a nice atmosphere for Cordelia when she was doing her mesmerising. Dear old Ma, I shed a little tear as well as laughing! Made me think of her.'

'There's so many quotes in the Bible I could've used!' said Regina. 'No wonder the Church ain't too keen on this, did you see all them protesting posters outside about God being the only miracle-worker? This is a blooming Miracle Competition!' and she chortled again and explained to Celine about Ezekiel 3.

Monsieur Roland looked at Cordelia.

'Well?'

She waited for a moment before she spoke. She did not mention the little card she had received. 'I don't know how they do the tapping and the rapping,' she said at last, 'I watched them very carefully, as I saw you did, and I have no idea how they make the rapping sound. Perhaps it is bones in their knees or their toes. Perhaps they have other people assisting them. Do you have an answer?'

He shook his head. The others were recounting still to Celine; Monsieur Roland and Cordelia sat at one end of the table. 'As for calling out names,' she said, 'I expect they do sometimes recognise people or gather information about their clients when they come in. But I bet they almost always use popular names, or ask very leading questions – did you notice how cleverly they *received* information from the audience? Both "Elizabeth" and "Fred", common names, elicited information from the audience, all that is easily explainable, and of course someone's father will have died. But – isn't it odd – they're not at all "knowing" as I expected them to be, they are well-mannered, pleasant, very attractive – and so young! Somehow they are in the business of comfort, don't you think? Just as we are.' He said nothing. 'I know, of course, that it's a trick,' said Cordelia.

'Of course it is a trick but I do agree there was something' – he paused for a word – '*sympathetique* about those younger girls. They genuinely wanted to please and help and comfort. I too had assumed they would have been more tricky. I mean – with tricks.'

'Yes,' said Cordelia. 'And I thought it was funny. In a good way. Young girls having fun, is what I mean. I loved it when the spirit tapped in time to the band! One of the girls was doing it, somehow, obviously – but it's just the sort of thing a young person would do and it made me laugh! We always surround death with sadness, I never expected to laugh. But I was angry when they tried to speak to me,' and her lips tightened. 'However: they have a kindly manner, sympathetic, as you say. They help people.'

'And what do you think the tapping sounds are, Monsieur Roland?' called Celine across the table. He shook his head, Cordelia answered.

'Rillie Spoons, you crack your toes sometimes, you've always cracked your toes when you take your boots off! Take your boots off and show them! It has to be a trick, but it is a very clever trick – in their leg-bones maybe? If it isn't their toes?' Rillie obliged by cracking her toes and indeed a certain tapping sound emerged and everybody laughed.

'I'd love my dear old ma to appear if I cracked my toes,' said Rillie wryly. 'Just to see her again and give her a hug.'

'I have been wondering,' said Monsieur Roland, 'I wonder if – perhaps it started off as a childish joke, to tease their parents or their neighbours and then it all got out of hand and their elder sister joined in. And I read somewhere that there are Quakers who support them – and if religious people were telling them it was real they probably did not know how to bring it to an end. And who is to say they do not now half-believe it themselves, having been believed so often by others? I know that grief and loss make people mad – some people will look for anything even if it is patently untrue, to take away their pain. But in our work we do not lie to them. We do not tell them that they do not really die, and that anyway when they do they'll be able to come back and chatter and tap on tables. These Fox children – for I see that they are children – are made dangerous by the way they are promoted by adults who should know better – and who stand to earn money from them.'

'Perhaps it doesn't matter, dear Monsieur Roland,' said Cordelia gently at last. 'If what they do helps people deal with pain. That woman with the hat. They helped her.'

'You surely did not think she was really talking to her late husband.'

'Of course not! But maybe, in her sadness, *she* thought she was. Does it matter that she was not? Do you know what I think? I think they should be left alone to do whatever it is they do, for people who pay a few dollars for comfort.'

'My dear, there is not much intellectual rigour in your argument.'

Cordelia laughed. 'My dear Monsieur Roland, I do not imagine I have a bone of intellectual rigour in my body!' From further down the table Arthur Rivers got up to leave for the docks. He called over to Alfie. 'I am glad you arranged our outing,' he said, 'thank you. I found it most amusing! And they did ask for Alfred!'

'Now listen, Arthur, nobody calls me Alfred!' said Alfie. 'I've never been Alfred. Even me own father never called me Alfred. Tell them, Queenie!' and Regina nodded. 'And if he never called me Alfred in life, he sure as hell ain't going to be allowed to call me Alfred in death! Excuse me, dear ladies, my language comes from my relief at not having to confront my father after over fifty years of getting away from him!'

As Arthur made to leave Cordelia came to the door with him and, unusually, took his arm. 'They would choose well-known names of course, Arthur. That would be the trick. There was bound to be more than one person to whom the name of Elizabeth meant something.'

He looked down at his wife for a moment. 'I know that, Cordelia,' he said to her in the doorway of Celine's House.

How lucky she is, thought La Grande Celine, seeing them standing there together, who believed she never missed anything.

'Oh!' cried Regina. 'I left me big hat!'

Next morning Cordelia showed Rillie the small card: *Private séance. Noon.*

'Shall you go?' asked Rillie curiously.

'Private séance indeed! I'd be interested to study them further but I fear they'll start saying "there are children here" like they did last night.'

'O heavens, they're so young, and they make spelling mistakes! They probably looked up your story as Monsieur Roland said, and thought to comfort you!'

'I don't want odd little girls who know nothing about me trying to comfort me!' said Cordelia with some heat and Rillie saw she had a strange, strained look on her face. 'Oh, forgive me, Rillie,' and she tried to laugh, 'I'm probably being graceless about little girls who probably mean well, because I miss my own beautiful and interesting girl so much. It is just – I have just come back from the Post Office again. It is ludicrous I know but I go to the Post Office every single day, sometimes twice a day. Why are there no letters? It's weeks and weeks and weeks. I've started to worry about her, in the wrong way, that something has happened to her. What about the duke? What say he sent Irishmen after her as well?'

333

'Cordie, listen to me carefully! I am absolutely certain we would have heard from Peggy Walker or Silas by now, if something had happened.'

'I know, I know. In my head I know. It's just that in my instincts I am frightened. And I just do not want those Fox children talking to me of *my* children, any of my children at all, although I know they will have found old information about me, and I do believe they mean to be kind. It's just instinct,' she wailed. 'Oh – I'm just as superstitious as anybody!'

'Where's your instinct, Cordie?' said Rillie, trying to make her laugh. But Cordelia Preston did not laugh. Instead she put her hand suddenly on her own stomach.

'Here,' she said.

Cordelia finally presented herself at the parlour in the Howard Hotel at noon as invited. Only the older sister, Leah, was there, lying on a *chaise longue*, and she looked distinctly unwell. 'I get bad headaches,' she said apologetically and she held one of two laudanum bottles in her hand, the other lay beside her, and her eyes were slightly blank: it was clear she was taking a great deal of opium, there in the hotel parlour.

The door opened and the two younger sisters rushed in, followed by their mother and the two gentlemen who were always there accepting 'donations'. The young girls stopped hesitantly when they saw that their visitor had already arrived. They smiled at Cordelia and, when they did speak, spoke to her with great shyness and respect. Kate, blushing slightly, brought a small posy from behind her back and presented it to Cordelia. 'We wanted to meet you,' they explained in unison.

'We saw you at the circus in Rochester,' said Margaret. 'Not very long before we heard the knocking sounds in our house.'

'We never forgot you,' said Kate. 'We had read all about you. You are very famous.'

'You are famous now,' said Cordelia, holding the little posy, smelling the flowers, smiling at these young girls because she could not help it; there was something so open and unaffected about them.

'We had to see you, the spirits have been calling you,' said Kate in her soft childish voice. 'And we wondered also if we could quickly learn to be Mesmerists if there is time afterwards.'

Quickly learn to be Mesmerists! 'I believe your sister said she is already a Mesmerist,' said Cordelia dryly.

Leah still lay with her eyes closed on the *chaise longue*. 'Well, sometimes we pretend to go into a trance,' said Margaret quite without guile. 'People seem to like it, and we want to do what-ever helps them best to be receptive. But, my, we would like to learn properly – to do it to other people! After we have called up your spirits?'

Cordelia looked at them sharply, slowly took off her gloves. 'Perhaps,' she said, 'I could help Leah with her headache.' But Leah, the bottle now empty and on the floor beside her, was asleep.

'We all get headaches,' said Margaret, simply. 'We all need laudanum. Something in the family, I guess.'

'I think it is because we concentrate very hard, very often,' said Kate. And she looked up at Cordelia with her large, dark eyes and Cordelia, so used to intuiting what other people were feeling, thought they both seemed simply too young and too artless to be lying, or concealing. She felt an odd

335

shifting, falling feeling in her head, shook herself slightly, *don't be silly.*

'Sit here, Kate,' she said at last.

'But – o no – I do not wish to be mesmerised, not at all, I wish to *learn* to mesmerise other people. Not like Leah, but properly.'

'I think nobody can be a Mesmerist who has not been mesmerised themselves, Kate. It is part of the understanding and the training.' The young girl sat reluctantly. Cordelia began the long, slow, sweeping strokes, over and over, over and over, past Kate's head and shoulders, never touching her, over and over. Kate seemed to be asleep very quickly: everybody in the room watched silently. Cordelia stopped making the long passes. Then everybody sat very quietly.

They could hear Leah's deep laudanum-filled breathing; one of the attending gentlemen coughed uneasily; they watched Kate, who after some time moved one of her arms. Then she opened her eyes. She looked at Cordelia, kept looking at Cordelia. Cordelia's face was a mask. At last Kate spoke, but she said nothing about mesmerism. 'I have a message for you,' she said. 'From your son.' Cordelia's face showed nothing. She did not speak.

After a few moments of odd silence Kate said: 'It is true, isn't it, that there is sometimes an energy between people?'

'Yes,' said Cordelia. 'I believe there is.'

'That is what we feel,' said the young girl simply. 'You will see. Thank you for mesmerising me. Now – let us talk to the spirits now, just for you.'

Cordelia turned to the others in the parlour. She observed that Leah was now, at least, partially, awake. 'I wonder,' Cordelia said, gravely, 'if you would be kind enough to allow me to have a little time with Kate and Margaret alone. There is something about mesmerism that I as a practitioner need to impart to them privately.'

'But we want to talk to the spirits who so long to speak to you!'

'I need to talk to you,' said Cordelia briskly. 'Do you have cloaks?'

'But they cannot possibly go out, there are people waiting on the hotel steps.'

'I live by here,' said Cordelia, 'and I know another way.'

'It would be nice to go for a walk,' said Margaret, 'we never go for walks now because too many people recognise us.'

'But – there is a public *séance* at three o'clock.' Mrs Fox was quite bewildered at the turn of events. 'I do not think this is a good idea.'

'I will return them well before that time,' said Cordelia firmly. 'A little air will do them good.'

And so it was that the Fox sisters and Cordelia Preston found themselves taking back alleys until they were away from Maiden Lane. They crossed Broadway, the girls looking about them with great interest and enjoyment, and also they chattered and laughed with Cordelia quite un-selfconsciously about the tap-tap-tapping they had first heard in their house, giggling now at their own fears, and how they had called for their parents, and their parents had called for the neighbours, and how far they had travelled, to be here in New York with her. And then they had arrived at Battery Park where Cordelia sat with them under a sycamore tree and the girls stared at the boats arriving and leaving. Cordelia watched them all the time as they talked: so excited and somehow heightened, yet so open and somehow guileless. They were very lovely-looking young girls: it was hard not to watch them: Cordelia wished she could catch their images. *I would like to make daguerreotypes of these faces.* No wonder they were successful, especially with gentlemen; who after all would not want to look at those attractive young faces?

'Look at all those people waving and crying!' said Margaret. 'I should not like to leave America.'

But Kate said to her, 'Oh, but Maggie, one day we will go to England and France and everywhere!'

Very gently Cordelia spoke. She held her posy of flowers, buried her nose in the scent. 'Why did you not want to be mes-merised, Kate?' The girl looked startled but Cordelia carried on. 'I am a very experienced Mesmerist. Did you think you could trick me?'

Kate was blushing. 'I – I felt something. I definitely felt something.' Her sister listened very carefully.

'But you fought what you felt, I think.'

'I – I want to help people. I – Maggie and I have a feeling for what people want. We only pretend to go into a trance to make it a bit more dramatic sometimes – but we don't want to be in a real trance ourselves, of course we don't, we couldn't help people that way!'

Margaret said simply: 'Sometimes it's as if we can feel what they want to hear. Really, it is like that.' *They are so beguiling,* thought Cordelia, and again: *no wonder people find them so intriguing.*

'Yes,' said Cordelia. 'I do believe you both have – you have an unusual empathy towards other people. I can see that.' Then very quietly she said: 'Do you often need opium?'

'Oh, yes,' they both said. 'Most days. For our headaches. We get too excited otherwise and can't do our work.'

Cordelia did not allow anything to show on her face. She did not even ask about the mysterious rapping sounds because, oddly, it was not that that puzzled her: they would make the sounds somehow, probably clicking their bones as Rillie did. She sat in silence with the sisters.

And then was alarmed to see that Kate suddenly had tears in her large dark eyes, dark eyes that looked almost purple out in the daylight. 'That wasn't why we asked you to come, so that we could be mesmerised! We thought you might quickly teach us a few useful things, but what we really wanted was to bring you messages from your children, and you won't allow us to. Why, we read about your life! We know the terrible things that happened to you, we used to save the newspapers. We came to the circus twice, just so that we could see you again! Why did you stop us? Why did you not allow us to – to give you some comfort? That's why we asked you so privately, so that your children would come and no-one would hear, only you!' Kate was weeping unrestrainedly now. Cordelia felt inside her pale cloak, passed her own handkerchief. Margaret began to weep also. 'We wanted to help you!' Some terrible perverse reaction inside Cordelia wanted to laugh at this predicament: two strange, weeping, perhaps deeply hysterical young girls under a sycamore tree in Battery Park. At 3pm and at 5pm and no doubt at 8pm they would be giving people messages from the dead. She would have given anything at this odd moment for a glass of port.

'I expect you could have given me something, some comfort, and I am very grateful to you for thinking of it.' Cordelia took a deep, deep breath. She understood these girls better than they understood themselves perhaps, but it was not her intention to hurt or harm them.

'I would never think to – damage you,' she said carefully. 'And I am very glad to have spent this time with you. But I believe I know,' she added very quietly but they heard every word, 'and I believe that you know also, that the comfort you wanted to give me would have been from you, which is very, very kind of you, but it would not have been from my – my own children.'

Neither of the girls spoke. Margaret brushed her face with her sleeve to brush away tears, an odd child-like gesture. Kate's very real crying became quieter and she looked at Cordelia but said nothing. The silence went on and on; around them New York hurried and bustled. Margaret bit her lip several times, Kate fiddled with the folds of her dress and Cordelia's handkerchief.

'Well,' said Margaret suddenly, as if the previous words had not been uttered, 'the boy Algernon got through anyway. Fancy calling a child Algernon!' and she and Kate, tears forgotten, erupted into childish laughter. Cordelia remembered the woman calling, 'It is Algernon!' The girls themselves had not spelled out the name. *How they have learned*, she thought wryly. *Asking if someone has lost a parent or a child when the answer from probably more than one person will likely be yes.* The girls were now exchanging ridiculous names that had appeared at their *séances*: St John, Marmaduke, Puss.

'Puss?' queried Cordelia. 'Was it a cat?'

'No, it was an auntie! Auntie Puss!' and both girls laughed in the warm air. *And they mean well.* She thought of the empty laudanum bottle, lying on the floor of the parlour. She knew she should disapprove but, whatever Monsieur Roland said, she and Rillie, very much older, had done something of the same thing themselves, and had sustained themselves, in the evenings (when they could hardly believe their luck at succeeding so well), with large glasses of red port. She felt a great wave of affection for these almost-children: their defiant secrets, their daring.

'Let me look into your futures,' she said. 'Give me your hands.' And like any old trickster herself she held their palms and said: 'I see that you will both become rich and famous and will make many people happy. Margaret, you will meet a tall dark stranger. Kate you will meet a tall fair stranger. And you will both live happily ever after.' And she joined their palms together and held them in hers for a moment, and then let them go. They were all smiling, as if, with the clasping of hands some wordless, private contract had been made.

'Can you tell the name of my tall dark stranger?' said Margaret eagerly. 'So that I will know when I meet him?' As if she believed every word.

'Oh – you will know,' said Cordelia. 'One always knows!' And the Fox sisters giggled together like any young girls and for a split second Cordelia allowed herself to think it was Manon and Gwenlliam, her lovely daughters, who sat with their mother, laughing and full of life under the sycamore trees. And as they walked back up Broadway the girls again chattered completely un-selfconsciously, again as if Cordelia had not spoken; they told her excitedly of the famous people who had come to their *séances*, and where they were going next.

She left them safely near the back door to the hotel. She was still holding their small posy. 'But do not play games with mesmerism.' And they nodded obediently.

'Will you come again?' asked Kate, so anxiously.

'Perhaps,' said Cordelia. But she knew she would not. 'Go now,' she said, and the young girls waved, a little regretfully perhaps, and then they looked back once more, as if they knew also that they would not see her again.

And then Kate came back.

A tiny wisp of sound on the air, almost inaudible; almost Cordelia was not sure she heard it.

'It is a trick, the tapping.' The words were gone, as if they had not been said. All Cordelia heard was the young girl's uneven breathing. 'But not the – the *feeling*. The feeling is real.' Then a little flurry of words. 'Whatever it is that is troubling you so, Miss Preston, I hope it will get better.' And again Cordelia felt the shifting, falling sensation inside her head. And Kate seemed to understand this: gave a small, puzzled shrug. 'I don't know how I know, I can just feel it,' she said quite simply. 'Here.' And she put her hands on her stomach.

And then she was gone.

36

Marylebone
London

Dear Arthur,

You write and enquire why there is no letter! Well here is
the answer: little Arthur died nearly two months ago, you
remember him? The grand-child you knew? Or have you
forgotten? His small coffin went alone into the earth, and
no husband to comfort Faith, nor no father either. Live
with that, Arthur Rivers, if you can.

I entreat you to return to your duty in London.

The Lord has seen fit to visit me with much further
tribulation, my head aches all day and night, if it were not
for Millie I do not know what would happen to me. All
doctors are useless. I am no longer able to attend properly
to your house in Marylebone, there is no money for any
servant. Millie suggests that they should ALL come and
live with me! Seven children! I am too ill and in too much
pain, each part of me aches and swells and of course I

cannot have those wild children here. As for Faith's husband, the drunkard, the less said about him the better.

Nobody cares what happens to me, yet I gave up my own life to look after your family, yours, Arthur Rivers, yours.

London is topsy-turvy, foreigners everywhere, all the preparations for Prince Albert's Exhibition, one cannot go anywhere (not that I do) without falling over foreign people, they are opening brothels all round Hyde Park, the foreigners.

I remain your dutiful sister-in-law
Agnes Spark (Miss)
PS We are in receipt of five payments.

Oh Father, I am so _sorry_ for the long silence, everything here is more and more difficult. It was so so sad about little Arthur Father. It was not the cholera, which is over, but another fever and Faith without the support of a husband, that was hard for her, drunk old Fred disappeared and has never been seen again. We are so glad of your letters, and the money, but life is so exhausting. O Father could you come home now, perhaps just for a short while and sort things out somehow, just a little? I tried to talk to Aunt Agnes as you suggested but she is so adamant. We will be much kinder to Miss Preston now that we have grown up ourselves, Father, how horrible we all were then. Nobody remembers all that scandal now, there are newer and bigger scandals every week – a man cut up two women in Islington yesterday and put the pieces in a railway carriage and the penny papers say 15,000 aliens deluged London last week, who immediately set about hiring houses to set up brothels and gambling dens to cater for the millions who will attend, they say, Prince Albert's Great Exhibition next year but Charlie says 'if you believe everything in the newspapers you would never leave your house' (like Aunt Agnes.) Shall

344

you insist that we all move to Marylebone father, despite Aunt Agnes's protestations? it would be cheaper – we all eleven of us live now on Charlie's wage from the Water Board and your kind money, (without which we would have drowned long ago Father) Perhaps – perhaps you _could_ come home for just a little while just to sort out things? I am at my wits' end trying to please everybody and manage the money, thank goodness for dear Charlie who helps and supports me always. Faith is living with us now, and I cannot dare leave any of the children with her at the moment, she lost her job at the pickle factory, she is very sad and low and weeps very much and we found little Arthur's pictures that you drew him, he had kept them always, in the larder, at the back of all the jam and pickles, I did cry when we found them, dear little boy. O dearest Father, I miss you so much – I cannot write it. But I know too that you have a life of your own now, and I am so glad you are happy. So if you cannot come home just now then – well, well when you can dear Father, it would be so lovely, but we will manage till then.

Love from Millie. XXXXXX

It was a hot, humid evening. Inspector Arthur Rivers was alone in his office so no other New York policeman (who would simply not have believed their eyes) saw their boss with tears on his face, for of course he remembered little Arthur, he had held him and had loved him and been proud: his first grandson, given his name, and he had drawn him sailing ships. And sailed away.

Perhaps the tears were for many things that he had not wept over, for men, of course, did not cry.

He sat there in the hot, humid night air, surrounded by reports about violence and robberies and murder on the New York docks: he thought of the little boy, he thought of his dear daughter Millie trying to deal with all the family problems and not enough money and yet trying even now not to put pressure on her father, he thought of his wife Elizabeth who had died too early, he thought of Cordelia: suddenly he felt he could not breathe: he saw her with her short, spiky hair and her flat iron. Cordelia had said: 'the past cannot be solved by a detective.'

He stared again at the dock reports, the words were blurred. He did not read the letters again but he put them, not in his locked office drawer, but in the pocket of his cloak. He knew he should have talked of these letters with Cordelia long ago, but there were so many things they had not talked of.

Perhaps, after all, the shards of broken glass between them were impassable.

The thought formed itself.

I will return to London.

37

Later that same hot, humid, unbearable New York evening La Grande Celine, just counting her takings at the end of the evening, just calling goodnight to the two little negro maids, Maybelle and Blossom, who always worked with Celine till she finished and then scampered off to their small room in the basement, heard knocking at her big front door.

'There's always one,' she said to the girls, 'and always the same cry: *one more drink Celine, just one more drink!*' But she nevertheless motioned them to stay a moment, took up the stick she always kept by the cash table. Jeremiah had gone; the boarding house guests, once trusted, had their own keys. She strode to the door and opened it, the stick ready.

A figure stood there in the darkness, they could smell him (they presumed it was a him) before they could really make much else out about him. 'We're closed,' said Celine firmly, moving to close the door again but before she could do so the man spoke.

'Mrs Cordelia Preston?' he said, 'is this the place?' They heard a strong Irish accent.

At once La Grande Celine took his arm, ushered him inside. 'What is it?' she said, knowing Inspector Rivers was not here, at once fearing news from the docks about his safety; no-one forgot the Astor Place riots.

The man was so thin he looked as if he might break, Celine could feel the bones. His clothes were threadbare, his long whiskers and long hair black with dirt, his shoes not much more than holes and flapping leather, and over his shoulder he had a battered bag. They saw at once he could hardly stand. Helped by Blossom he sat gingerly on a sofa near the door, and pulled his satchel round to the front as if with the last of his strength. 'Open it please, for the love of God,' he said, as if with his last breath. 'A letter.'

'Get brandy,' Celine ordered Maybelle; Blossom knelt at the man's feet and undid the buckle on the satchel. Briefly, the Irishman looked in some way offended or disgusted that a negro was anywhere so near him, but he had no strength to do or say more. Celine bent down, trying not to feel sick at the stench coming from the man, and looked inside the satchel. Inside, wrapped in a filthy, crawling garment of some kind, there was a letter addressed – the writing had half-run but it could partly be read still – MRS CORDELIA PRES and CELINE'S H. On the back she could just make out FROM SILAS P.

'Quickly,' said Celine to Maybelle as they put brandy to the lips of the man, 'get Cordelia.' They heard Maybelle's feet running up the steps above their heads, then footsteps running down. Cordelia and Rillie arrived first, both in their night-gowns, followed by Monsieur Roland still holding a book he had been reading, his magnifying spectacles still in his hand also.

Celine gave Cordelia the letter, Cordelia saw the half-illegible writing that was not her daughter's, bent at once to the man. 'Are you from California?'

'Sure an' I've come back,' he said with difficulty. 'Tis a wild bad place and she should not be there,' he suddenly got a spurt of energy or anger, 'tis like a cesspit of men crawling and dying and looking for the gold, and Panama City a vision of hell with us all going and coming and all for what?' And then, even with the help of the brandy – or possibly because of the brandy – he fell backwards, half into the arms of Blossom, who heroically paid no attention to the stink of his clothes and his body.

'Is he dead?' said Rillie fearfully.

Blossom listened. 'No, ma'am,' she said, 'Ah done can hear his heart.' The man opened his eyes briefly. 'She's an angel from heaven,' he said.

'Me?' said Blossom, almost offended: she had no more love for the Irish than the Irish did for the negroes.

'There is a place at the back,' said Celine, and she and Blossom and Monsieur Roland between them lifted the unconscious man, and everyone gasped slightly as three gold nuggets fell from his satchel. Rillie placed them back in the threadbare bag. They carried the man to a bed in a small room like a cupboard and as they lay him carefully there and placed his bag beside him he opened his eyes briefly.

'She took my brother to Heaven,' he said, 'she's an angel but now' – and some spasm shook him – 'now I've crossed that isthmus and me pals dying like me brother I don't care if I go or not,' and then his eyes closed again.

They assumed he was delirious; Rillie murmured to him: 'You are home. You are safe. You are home. You are safe,' but to Monsieur Roland she whispered urgently: *does he mean Gwennie is dead?*

'Run for the doctor next door, Blossom,' said Celine, and Blossom was gone, but Celine shook her head grimly as she looked at the man. 'Would you stay with him, Maybelle?' she asked, but almost apologetically.

'He can't be left by him alone,' said Maybelle, but she placed herself as far away from the Irishman as possible.

The others went back to the big room where Cordelia sat: brave, stoic, courageous Cordelia Preston: simply too frightened to open, alone, the envelope with the strange writing, waiting for them and staring at the big, dirty envelope. And then the front door opened, and Arthur Rivers came in, holding, this time, letters of his own in his hand. He looked extremely surprised at the people in night attire in the diningroom; he saw his wife's face.

'Someone has brought news of Gwenlliam,' whispered Cordelia. 'It is not her writing.'

Arthur had no time to ask more before he was followed in at the front door by the doctor.

'Quickly,' he said. 'They're bringing fever.'

'What do you mean: fever?' said Cordelia fearfully.

He spoke tersely. 'Cholera. Where is he?'

Celine took the doctor to the small room, the policeman went too, stuffing his own letters quickly back into his cloak. 'He brought a letter to Cordelia from California,' Celine explained to them. 'We don't know anything else about him.'

The man was now unconscious; the Doctor examined him very, very carefully. 'You are extremely lucky,' he said to them after several minutes – or perhaps he said it to the unconscious patient, it was hard to tell. But then he did turn to Celine and Arthur. 'We know they are bringing back the cholera from the Californian journey, that's why I came so quickly. He's got almost everything else wrong with him but not that, he'll probably live. Who is he?'

Arthur said, 'I've just looked in his satchel but there's no record of who he is, just some gold nuggets and some rags.'

'He'll probably live,' said the doctor again. 'But burn the rags. Lucky man to end up in Celine's House. He probably lives in Five Points! Give him food, let him sleep for a long, long time.'

The letter was from Peggy Walker. Cordelia's fingers, holding the open letter at last, trembled as she understood that. It was written two and a half months ago.

Dear Cordelia,

I do not have any idea about how to start this letter so I will just plunge in straight because it must be taken down to the docks within the hour, Silas and two of the miners' leaders have already gone to check the one ship known for certain to be leaving San Francisco today, though there may be others, and he has ordered one of the charros to wait with me for this letter and then ride fast so it can be given to someone reliable on that ship, someone who is taking the overland route from Panama City. That is the quickest way to get a letter to you.

And thank the Lord you told me what you did of Gwen's background or I could not have made head or tail.

Gwenlliam has disappeared, or rather, for we <u>think</u> we know what has happened, she has been taken away by a man from England. This man turned up in San Francisco some time ago, pretended to be a charming and pleasant Englishman – one of those ones who is actually good-looking but not in his soul, you know, who thinks he's God's Gift – you know the type Cord, to be honest they don't go down well in America, those types. Anyway we thought he had come to wait for the mining season like

351

all of them. He said he was a fan of the circus and he introduced himself about a bit in his lordly way, and complained about how long it had taken him to get here, one hundred and thirty-two days at sea he kept saying as if he was the only traveller amongst us! He kept asking if it was quicker by land, but when they told him about crossing the isthmus and all the hardships that entailed, then he said 'Catch me wading through rain-forests with snakes!' and then he shut up. And then after a few days, Gwen was quite sick of him hanging about, anyone could see. But he would not go, finally he insisted he had to speak to her alone on important matters. We all thought he'd just seen her in the circus and been taken with her, there's lots like that, she's had lots of marriage proposals I can tell you, but once we saw she was not interested, we told him to vamoose, but he was like a leech until she consented to meet with him privately – but us all watching nearby enough (she had about twenty guardians that afternoon, Cord!) to make sure he did no dastardly thing, a bumptious young Englishman if I ever saw, by the name of Mr Doveribbon (which in my opinion is in itself enough to arouse suspicion.)

And there she was, our favourite, blossoming girl, when suddenly after the 'private meeting' with this fellow she came back to our hotel room and she was so pale I suspected all sorts of stuff. "I'm all right, Peggy," she said to me but I said to her, No you're not, pal, and I'm your guardian, I promised your Mother, now what has happened? She kind of shook her head, "it's too hard to explain," she said, "it's about the past," and do you know what she did Cord, she actually vomited in a basin, that really did shock me. And I said, I know everything about

352

your past pal, your mother made sure that I did. She looked surprised then, "about my father and the sham marriage and us being kidnapped away from mama?" Yes, I said. Your mother told me everything, and then she washed her face and she did sit on the bed, come on Gwen I said.

"He knows all about me," she said and her voice was very flat, nothing like she usually is.

Who? (but I knew of course)

"Mr Doveribbon. He's been sent here by his father who is a lawyer to take me back to London. He knows about me growing up in Wales with my brother and sister, he knew Manon had married a Duke and killed herself and he knew Morgan was dead and he <u>talked about it all</u>, as if he had the right to speak of those things to me, that is my private history, not his to talk of in the way he did. He said I must come back to England immediately, that my – my grandfather (and she could hardly say the word grandfather, Cord) is old and ill and insists on my returning for he wishes to make me his heiress." She looked at me then, Cord, and her eyes were really piercing and angry, I was quite alarmed, you know how gentle and sensible she is and – after all – you might think she was telling me good news perhaps, if she was, say, to be an heiress? Easier than the circus!

But she said: "He was so smug! As if he was bringing me good news! I <u>hated</u> that old man. He was cruel, especially to my little brother, he bullied him and would never let him paint and Morgan was a wonderful painter. That old duke stank, he drank whisky and shouted and arranged our lives, our father was weak and I am sure he was too scared of his father to really marry my mother, that old Duke was a monster, and I <u>hated him</u>. He was a foul monster and my mother suffered so much, I had hoped he had died years ago, I do not want anything to do with it, and Mr Doveribbon told me that it is my solemn duty to return, that everyone is trying to find me because there is an enormous amount of land and money involved. I am to be an heiress, he said, and I must go back at once and then Peggy do you know what he said then: he said he will marry me because I would need to be <u>protected</u>! Me!"

I laughed then, I could not help it. Our Gwen, our independent spirit, she is happiest with circus people, with our life, I know you told me she was raised as an English lady and somehow she is too, an English lady, but not like any other English lady I've ever met! She's great in the circus, Cord, a great hit, she's not you of course, she doesn't have that –"thing" –Silas calls it, that thing that makes people not be able to look away from you, Cord, but you'd be proud of her, the miners love her, they do, and the French acrobats and the charros and the midgets (sadly depleted, you probably heard) who always shared their little secrets with her. And Chief Great Rainbow – "she'd begun to play poker <u>with</u> him, before he got so upset about the killing of Indians here, an Indian chief playing poker with a woman, it is unheard of! But I think he was proud of how well she'd learned.

What did you say to Mr Doveribbon Gwen? I said, still laughing but I soon stopped because you know what Cord, she cried then, dear young Gwen, why, I never saw her weep before in all the time I've known her. She was glad I knew about the past I think, so you did right Cord, when you told me, though I never mentioned it till that day. I think she would not have told me any of what happened with Mr Doveribbon, if she had had to explain. "The arrogance!" she kept saying, "he was so arrogant, so sure he was doing right – _I'm doing this for you_ – he said, _I have crossed the world for you!_" She said the idea of leaving the circus and going back to that life she was forced into when she was young, and being with the cruel old duke again, was so terrible it made her feel violently ill. Then after a while she dried her eyes. "I don't know why I cried Peggy," she said. "It is just being reminded of those bad times." You don't <u>have</u> to go Gwen, I said, you are your own boss, pal and she said "yes, I've told him I want nothing of this and I do not want him to speak to me again. And what's more I'm going to tell the charros he is bothering me, they'll keep him away!" And she suddenly actually laughed and then she said: "Fancy coming all the way from London to <u>gold mines</u> to talk about fortunes! How very inappropriate when we've got our own! I don't know why I'm crying at all!" and I laughed, and she was still laughing, in that brave way she has even when (I have seen it, Cord, since you told me her story) she has hard memories to hold. And in the end Mr Doveribbon seemed a bad dream.

She would not see him or talk to him again, he came hanging around of course but the charros stood around when they understood she did not want him, they are devoted to her those Mexicans, they just told him to vamoose – and they can be wild, those Mexicans, if they don't like somebody. And then he disappeared so of course we thought he'd gone for good, and Gwen was so glad. And we thought that was that. We just forgot about him. Though I could see it had shaken her. What had happened.

"I'm finding it hard to write to Mama," she did say to me. "About all this. It is the past and we thought it was over." And she sometimes said that same phrase again "the arrogance!"

Cord, when Gwen was coming back to the hotel from the cards tent last night – "I was only five minutes before her, I said I'd boil some water – she just disappeared, somewhere between the gambling hall and the hotel.

We can't be certain, San Francisco where we are playing now, is a wild place and there is much violence and crime here, it is full of swindlers and rogues. Yet we doubt anyone in San Francisco would do her harm, people <u>know</u> each other. She is special, she has become very, very popular, not only the acrobatics, she has had real success with the mesmerism, people are often astounded, and most people in town know who she is. The camel trainer, he's sure he saw Mr Doveribbon back hanging around the tents last night before the circus started, but nobody else saw him. But I suspected that Englishman at once anyway. So I told Silas the whole story, and about Mr Doveribbon being a lawyer's son and trying to make Gwen go back to England and as soon as I said that he went very odd. It turns out that just before we left New York Silas received a visit from this same Mr Doveribbon – "He hasn't been here?" said Silas, amazed – if only he'd been around and seen him here, but you know Silas, always rushing about, planning and counting the money, we still have huge audiences. Anyway Mr D. somehow knew you worked for the circus and had given Silas a letter to deliver to you, Cord, something to your advantage.

Well you know Silas, Cord, he's not a bad man, I mean not a bad man <u>actually</u>, by that I mean not evil. O God the charros are calling for this letter. Anyway Silas didn't tell you about the letter because he wanted you both on that boat to California. He ripped it up, he told me.

So Gwen has disappeared, Silas has ordained a great search and inquiry and as I say, is now checking any leaving ships – everyone is keeping an eye out for her. Nobody heard screaming or a struggle but we know there is no way she would have left the circus, or gone with him. But there's no proper police here, or government, or anything – I mean we can only do what we can do ourselves. Silas will find her if anybody does, the circus is nothing without her, I mean nothing special – and I know Silas, he feels guilty also.

She has only been gone since last night, and today is May 14th, and no big ships have yet left since yesterday morning. Thank God we're working in San Francisco still so we can keep a check on such things – we were to go back to Sacramento when the gold-fields opened again after the worst of winter but we are doing so well here now that there's gold again – or we were until last night. The charros will go straight to the docks with my letter which I must now close, it will get to you the quickest route we know how, and if there is any sign of her or Mr D. on that next ship leaving they will be hauled off and this letter will not come. But there are smaller private boats, even fishing boats! leaving for Panama all the time of course, people aint got patience in this place, though if this Mr Doveribbon somehow manages to get her as far as Panama without us stopping him he still has to make the rest of the journey. We have moved as fast as we could but maybe not fast enough. The one thing that keeps bothering me is that I do not believe anyone could make

Gwen do something she did not want to unless she is physically unable to get away from him. She may somehow turn up safe and sound tomorrow in which case I will write again immediately. Goodbye Cord, the charros are calling and calling, they will give this to someone bound for New York by the Panama isthmus, unless they find Gwen first.

I'm so sorry Cord.

Peggy Walker.

Cordelia did not understand that she had dropped the letter on to the floor. She did not understand that she had walked to the window that looked out on to Maiden Lane in the night, and that carts still rattled past over the cobblestones.

We are our past, Monsieur Roland had said. Memory – that elusive, tricky, sometimes catch-by-the-throat thing called memory – defines us, and makes us who we are.

Ellis sent for her. She was to come to London at once, without the children; she was to go at once to an address off the Strand. She had never been apart from them: promised she would not be gone long; she would bring Papa back with her and he would never go away again. As the carriage rolled away she saw Morgan, five years old, crying and fighting, held by his six-year-old sister: Gwenlliam's long fair hair blew across her face as she bent to him. Seven-year-old Manon stared stonily at the departing carriage: she had wanted to go to this place called London too, would not wave to her mother. Something, some instinct, made Cordelia rap on the carriage roof. She quickly jumped down, was almost blown off the narrow coast road by the wind as she stood there looking back, but she was too far away, already the children were shadows through the long, long grass; the broken stone of the ancient Welsh castle stood far above them as the wild wind blew.

On the long journey to London Cordelia went over her life, its too romantic, too unbelievable turn. The doubts she had pushed away over the years in the wilds of Wales reared up and her heart beat like a drum the nearer they got to her old home: London.

Waiting for her at the address she had been given off the Strand was not Ellis in their London house, but a solicitor in legal chambers. He had papers and a sum of money.

'Lord Morgan Ellis regrets, Miss Preston –'

She looked at him in surprise. 'Please do not address me as Miss Preston. I am Lady Ellis.'

'I am afraid you are not, Miss Preston. The – ah – marriage ceremony in the chapel all those years past was conducted by – a friend. It was a jest.'

'A jest?'

'Ah – no – perhaps that is not the word. But it was not legal nor binding.' He sniffed. 'You are not, and never have been, Lady Ellis.'

Something kept her upright. 'I would like to see my husband.'

'I am afraid that is impossible. And I must point out that Lord Morgan Ellis is not, nor never has been, your husband. You are not to return to Wales, the Estate has been closed up. And I am afraid that that is the end of the story.'

She again repeated the words in complete disbelief. 'The end of the story? **The end of the story?**' Suddenly she lunged out at the solicitor, taking him indeed by surprise for he had never been lunged at by any woman. She actually punched his head against the wall of the room off the Strand before he managed to escape her. 'What about my children?'

'You bitch!' he screamed. 'You actress whore!'

'**What about my children?**'

'They are not your children, they belong, in law, to Lord Ellis. I have here two hundred guineas for your trouble.' And then observing the incredulity in her eyes the solicitor, before she could attack

359

him again, was out of the room, dining out for some nights on the story of the harridan-whore-actress who thought she was a Lady.

Cordelia returned to Wales that moment, that same day, hiring a private coach, not even going to Aunt Hester, travelling day and night, refusing to stop except to change the horses; she arrived back to find that a spring storm raged along the Gwyr coast, rain fell across their way and the wind was wild. As she approached the stone mansion and the castle ruins on the cliffs, as she saw through the driving rain that the tide was out as far as the eye could see, as she approached the gates, she knew: the children were gone, their home was closed and locked and no fair heads played among the seaweed and the rocks on the long sand. There were sparks of lightning as she stood there in the rain and then the thunder echoed. Somehow she climbed over the iron gates by the stone walls, tearing her cloak, but the house was closed and barred. Of her children there was no sign, except for the house of branches they had built in the oak tree. The oak tree. She climbed quickly up to the small tree-house in the branches where they left their letters for each other. The slanting heavy rain and the strong wind had already caught at, torn, a piece of white paper, it had spiralled away and up into the heavens: it had disappeared long before Cordelia had come home.

A great cry echoed through the rain into the long grass and the wild flowers and the castle ruins and the empty sands below as Cordelia ran like a demented soul in torment around and around the empty stone building. **Where are my children?** What would happen to Morgan with his anger and the storms inside his head? No-one knew how long Cordelia Preston stayed outside the locked mansion in the storm, but the tide returned below her; the sea that often seemed so benign hurled itself against the jagged cliffs below, drawing back and hurling itself, again and again.

Cordelia Preston might have hurled herself against the cliffs also, but she was the niece of Miss Hester Preston: and now it seemed she *was a Miss Preston still. The Preston women did not, in the end, hurl themselves anywhere but at life.*

But here, in New York, so many years later, the pages of Peggy Walker's letter strewn over the floor, Cordelia Preston put her face in her hands, and huge, heaving sobs came from deep inside her.

And this is my fault.

38

Chloroform. Not the ether, nor the nitrous oxide that the midgets used every night after the circus to make themselves go high. *Chloroform.*

Gwenlliam knew it was chloroform.

She had smelt chloroform: the midgets had tried chloroform and discarded it; she had smelt chloroform in the hospital with Monsieur Roland: she recognised it at once: the odd, slightly sweet smell.

She had no idea where she was, or how long she had been there but felt some movement, a silent carriage perhaps, the horses trotting gently over fields of grass. She drifted with the quiet horses, did not open her eyes – indeed it was too hard to open them, they were so heavy . . . she floated rather . . . floating along these fields. Drifting, slow, she wandered ponderously back in her thoughts. The circus, the empty trapeze swinging slowly backwards and forwards as the miners called out and applauded and spat tobacco as they always did, the miners pouring out to the saloons and the saloon girls as they always did, *my turn for a waltz,* meeting up in the lamp-lit darkness with the other acrobats, wandering to the gambling tent, playing, winning? and then some elusive memory of walking, walking with footsteps, was it footsteps? but it was too much effort to think of the footsteps, she let herself float over fields of dreams drawn by the silent, graceful horses.

And then she remembered.

Some immediate instinct told her not to open her eyes. She listened carefully. A sound. A sound like a running river . . . sitting beside rivers outside small towns as she and the fire-eaters and the acrobats and the Indian Chief played cards and the baby elephant poured water over its head and the sewing needle of Peggy Walker went in and out. *Peggy Walker. Where am I?* Again she listened to the sound, the river, and then she heard it: the slap of a sail as the wind caught it full. *I am on a boat and someone put chloroform over my face.* Faintly she could smell it still, as if it lay on her skin, or in her hair.

Again the sound of a sail in the wind. *Chloroform*. There had been stories. Young girls overpowered by evil men with chloroform that their evil desires might be fulfilled. She observed herself carefully without opening her eyes to see if evil desires had been fulfilled upon her but felt as if she was as she had been and – she softly, gently, moved a limb, several limbs – was still also wearing all her clothes including her small boots.

Chloroform. What had that surgeon in the hospital said about chloroform? *Chloroform, wrongly administered, can stop the beat of the heart.* Her heart had obviously not stopped because she could feel it beating in outrage as more thoughts came to her. Again she heard the sound of a sail in the wind. *But where am I?*

Again she saw herself coming back from the gambling tent, twenty dollars' winnings in her cloak pocket. She saw herself waving goodnight to the *charros* as they rubbed down the horses, waving to one of the acrobats who had been in the dance hall and was now walking arm in arm with one of the store owners, to the midgets congregated on the street corner

363

where one of the doctors advertised medicines, she waved and she walked, she saw the lights of the hotel where Peggy Walker had gone to boil water and then footsteps, footsteps behind her and . . . nothing . . . darkness.

And now a light seemed to flash inside her head . . . if she opened her eyes now she would see: Mr Doveribbon, the lawyer's son.

She breathed in and out, smoothly and gently as if she was asleep.

Quite clearly she understood. Her fortune could not be claimed if she was not there to attend her grandfather and as she had chosen not to align herself to Mr Doveribbon he had used chloroform to ensure her attendance. *Too much chloroform could stop the heart.* Did Mr Doveribbon have that important item of information?

In and out went the slow, even breathing.

What a mistake Mr Doveribbon had made. For Gwenlliam Preston would never *never* co-operate with anybody belonging to the family of the Duke of Llannefydd, who seemed to think it was perfectly acceptable to abduct her twice, and take her away from her life.

The smooth gentle breathing continued while her deductions continued.

Peggy Walker knew everything. Would Peggy Walker guess what had happened to her? Peggy Walker would write to New York at once. But a letter surely could not get to New York any quicker than a person, and there were no telegraph poles stretching from San Francisco to New York, to take her story. Arthur. Arthur was a policeman, a proper policeman, a detective from Scotland Yard. Peggy would find a way to get a letter to New York urgently. The charros would help her. Arthur was a detective. He would find her . . .

In and out went the slow, even breathing.

Would Mr Doveribbon arrange for them to take the safer route, around the Cape, the route he knew, or would he arrange for them to take the quicker more dangerous route across the Panama isthmus? Somehow this felt like a small boat: if it was, it must be taking them from San Francisco to Panama. She had heard his interest in other routes: was he thinking of the dreaded isthmus? Or of Mexico? If she screamed in the madhouse that was Panama who would hear her? Mr Doveribbon knew she had a family in New York: did he know they would be looking for her? And if she demurred about moving one foot in front of the other would he, not knowing the dangers, continue to administer further chloroform and perhaps stop the beating of her heart? Should she demur? Or travel calmly back to New York under the auspices of Mr Doveribbon?

Gwenlliam had not been present when both Cordelia Preston and Peggy Walker had agreed that she was a sensible and spirited girl. The sensible and spirited Gwenlliam Preston, now THE CLAIRVOYANT ACROBAT (who did not alas have the clairvoyant powers to have foreseen this situation), understood she had only one option, which was to be at this point sensible (till she found out his plans), and to be later: spirited (when she tried to thwart them). *I will be sensible and pleasant as far as Panama, and then I will somehow elude him and get back to San Francisco.*

She wondered what had happened to her twenty dollars, her poker winnings, whether they were still in the deep pocket inside her cloak.

In and out went the slow, even breathing and then, as if she was only now waking, she gave several small sighs, opened her eyes at last, saw in the light of a tiny high-up window Mr Doveribbon (as she had foretold without magic powers). He was sitting on a small stool beside the bulwark, watching her. She looked around the very small cabin. She could see blue sky through the tiny window; she could feel the sea: almost certainly this was a very small boat, not a large one. She seemed to be on the bottom layer of two stacked beds. A little bag: presumably belonging to him as she had not been invited to pack a travelling bag. No visible sign of a chloroform container but she would take no risks.

'Hello, Mr Doveribbon,' said Gwenlliam Preston. 'You had better use this chloroform sparingly, or you will have a dead heiress on your hands.' She sat up. 'Are you aware that chloroform, wrongly administered, can stop the beating of the heart?'

39

Once Gwenlliam had made her decision she was perfectly amenable and seemed, to Mr Doveribbon, to accept his plans without demur, as he had assumed she would, in the end. They were dealing, after all, with so much money: he would not of course trust her absolutely, but who in the whole world would throw away the chance of an enormous fortune? (Foolish Mr Doveribbon, who knew her so little.)

'Chloroform, wrongly administered, can stop the beating of the heart,' she had said. She noted he was at once discomforted: perhaps concerning the fact of her understanding so immediately that he had used chloroform, and her unexpected knowledge of that anaesthetic. 'Tell me, Mr Doveribbon, what is' – (she hated saying the word, forced it out) – 'what is my *grandfather* proposing, that you should risk all to kidnap me and get me on this vessel to Panama?'

Again he was discomforted: he did not like the word *kidnap* and how did she so immediately know where the boat was going? She had been unconscious for some time: he had carried her in the dark along one of the smaller San Francisco wharves and into the waiting schooner (previously arranged) within fifteen minutes of putting the chloroform over her face, saying she was his cousin, and extremely ill, not that anybody he met seemed to care a tuppenny damn: San Francisco was a wild town, after all. Now that they were safely on their way he spoke in irritation rather than any stronger emotion: he was relaxed now, but she had caused him an enormous amount of trouble; he found it hard to forgive her for the long and tedious and frighteningly stormy sea journey he had had to make, because of her. Also he knew he was extremely personable: he was used to young ladies falling at his feet, not requiring kidnapping. 'If you had behaved as any sensible young girl would have behaved none of this' – he spoke the word distastefully – '*subterfuge* would have been necessary. I am doing this for you. I was simply asked to return you to Great Britain – to your great advantage.'

'I am not a parcel, Mr Doveribbon,' but she was smiling slightly. 'What great advantage exactly?'

'Most of Wales,' he said in an off-hand manner.

'He does not own "most of Wales", Mr Doveribbon,' she said calmly.

'He owns a great deal of it. As I told you quite clearly in San Francisco, he has a deep objection to a distant second cousin owning what he has owned: you have to remember you are his grand-daughter, and that blood tie has rewards – although it also has obligations.'

She looked at him. It was such a strong look it made him feel slightly uneasy. He thought he would not like her to ever know what had happened to her mother.

But his object had been achieved and they were on their way not to New York, but to London. He had found the jewel. *Ten thousand pounds.*

They were the only passengers. He had hired the small

schooner and the discretion of its crew: it was his father's money he was using until payment from the duke could be obtained, but the cost would be nothing, in the end. He smiled at the pale girl on the small bed in the small cabin. 'Despite the unfortunate facts of your birth you are nevertheless his only son's only living child and he wishes to bend the law – to your advantage. He is an old man not in robust health. He is one of the richest men in Britain and he insists on seeing you before he signs the somewhat convoluted paperwork that is required, and so this whole business became urgent and necessary.' And he smiled at her again. 'I say to your advantage, Miss Preston. Also to mine.' He knew his physical attributes: no woman he had ever met had, in the end, refused his advantages. (Foolish Mr Doveribbon: did he not know that Gwenlliam's perfidious father had been devastatingly good-looking also?)

'I presume I may walk on the deck?'

'With me by your side you may walk anywhere. The crew is four men and the captain but you will hear very little English.'

'Are they Spanish?' She tried not to sound too hopeful; he would not know that her long association with the Mexican *charros* had taught her a deal of basic Spanish.

'They are not Spanish. They are from the Sandwich Islands and have some strange language of their own. Only the captain speaks English and I have explained that my cousin has moments of insanity so that he must not adhere to anything she might say. I also have further chloroform at my disposal.' He was almost self-satisfied: no sign of discomfort now.

'You do, I hope, understand the dangers of chloroform, illused.'

'You have not been ill-used, Miss Preston.'

That was the only moment she almost lost her composure. *Not ill-used? Chloroform stuck over my face and kidnapped! Taken from my life a second time because of that monstrous, hateful old man!* She remembered how Chief Great Rainbow had taught her not to show any emotion: she took several deep breaths. The blue sky seemed to move through the tiny window above and she heard the sea, and the wind in the sails. 'Do you play poker, Mr Doveribbon?'

He was amused. 'Of course. I have seen that you too have interest in the game.'

'Perhaps we might play, to pass the time. For money.' *I will need money for my fare back, who knows how much if people are waiting for a passage in Panama, still clamouring for gold.*

'Do you have money about your person, Miss Preston?'

'Not as much as I might have had, had I been given notice of my journey. But unless' she paused, 'it has been stolen, I do have money about my person.'

He was offended. 'I am not a *thief!*'

'Also, according to you, I will soon have a great deal of money, so if I lose badly you may feel you could stake me.' Again she was smiling. 'So perhaps we might walk on deck, and later play a game or two, to while away the time.'

He could not but be impressed by her resilience and calm. He bowed. She slowly got up from the low narrow bed. She felt dizzy and sick but she gave no sign to her captor. 'May I wash my face?' He bowed again, totally at ease now. She was not to know she looked pale and frail (but looks are sometimes deceptive).

'I will leave you and wait on deck,' he said. 'Even you, I think, will not be so foolish as to jump into the sea.'

'On that, I think you may rely.'

As soon as he was gone she vomited into a bucket. After that she felt much better, but wished she had clean clothes. There was water in a bowl. She threw it at her face, over and over. There was water in a bottle. She drank it thirstily, hoping for the best. At last, still slightly unsteady, she climbed a little iron staircase into the fresh spring air of Baja California and the Pacific Ocean.

Almost, she might have enjoyed the journey. At least she had her own cabin, and the key to it; Mr Doveribbon seemed not to have any ungentlemanly plans regarding her person. The Southern Californian peninsula slipped by: the sun shone often, one of the crew members of the little schooner caught fish for them to eat, the air was fresh.

'Where are the Sandwich Islands?' she asked the captain. He pointed far to the west.

'*Hawai'i*,' he said. 'We call my home *Hawai'i*.' The schooner was called, she ascertained, the *Moe'uhane*; the brown-skinned captain who spoke to her only when Mr Doveribbon was with her, told them the word meant *dreams* and Gwenlliam smiled at him, with her own dreams of being back very soon with the circus in San Francisco.

Often other ships passed them, coming and going; once they were blown off-course and the small crew were up and down the masts, pulling in sails, letting them out again. After more than two weeks with no changes of clothing of any kind available, Gwenlliam, to put it politely, stank; she had also, so far, won fourteen dollars from Mr Doveribbon to add to her original twenty dollars that were still there in the deep pocket inside her cloak. She tried to make him play often. *I will need money.*

*

'When do we reach Panama?' she said to the Captain one day, as a beautiful clipper glided by to their west like a fast bird and to the east clouds, or land, lay like a dream.

'Leave those details to me,' said Mr Doveribbon, guiding her away from the wheel, watching the clipper carefully also. He actually raised his hand in a salute. 'Beautiful ships, aren't they?' he said. 'Like birds, as you told me when we first met.'

She looked again at the white sails in the distance and then carefully at the far coast that had come into view that day; she guessed that they were passing Mexico: the *charros* had proudly shown her Mexico on their way to California. Panama was coming nearer. For the first time she provoked him. 'I need *clothes*,' she said. 'Linen. Things that women need. I need to get them in Panama. This is disgusting.'

He was embarrassed. 'Make a list,' he said. She was at once alerted. *Make a list? For whom? Surely we will be stopping this journey in Panama?* 'Make a list,' he repeated peremptorily.

'I would like to purchase such things myself.'

'That will not be possible.'

'Are we to change vessels at Panama?'

'Leave those details to me,' said Mr Doveribbon.

'As a kidnapped person,' she said firmly, 'I need to know if I am to travel back through the isthmus. I have done that journey already and you have not: I have met the crocodiles and the Indians and the snakes and the steaming river. You would be wise to be advised by me on certain requirements. And I assure you I shall cause some damage if you do not allow me to purchase the clothes that I most urgently need. I do not think it is necessary that I should *smell*.'

'Make a list,' he said for the third time. 'But I assure you that I have a very great aversion to snakes. And there will be no crocodiles.' *No crocodiles.* That meant no isthmus. He would surely not have the courage to cross the wilds of Mexico with her, and they had left the mountain passes behind. That meant he planned to go on by ship. This little vessel would never make it round the Cape, or through the Magellan Straits that she had heard of so often in travellers' tales as they exchanged stories of their journeys on sunny mornings in the drifting dust of Sacramento. Somehow she had to get off the *Moe'uhane* with her thirty-four dollars, and away from Mr Doveribbon: *I will be ready, I will just jump off at the wharf and run.* But at once she remembered. There was a bar outside Panama City: tides and rocks meant it was too dangerous for vessels to approach near: ships had to anchor well off-shore, passengers were carried to and from the shore in small lighters. Would the *Moe'uhane* be small enough to slip through the surf and rocks to the shore, or would it anchor? What was he planning? Sometimes she would see him talking to the *Moe'uhane* captain; they would break off their conversation when she approached.

She made her own plans. She made herself remember everything about Panama: the harbour was crowded with ships and there were lighters coming to and fro from the port to the bar all the time, ferrying passengers, ferrying goods, ferrying animals. Very well. Somehow, even if she had to jump (she was an acrobat after all), she would be ferried also, if the *Moe'uhane* anchored at the bar. She was alert at all times: at night she locked the door of her cabin and also put the one little stool under the handle: he could not get in without her knowing. She was alert at all times.

But not alert enough. She felt safe up on deck, surely he would not attack her in front of the Hawaiians? She was actually leaning on the deck rail one morning in broad daylight and she could actually see in the distance some of the old Spanish buildings of Panama City coming nearer, when she caught suddenly the odd, sweet smell, and oblivion came.

40

For just one night, the first night after the Peggy Walker letter, Rillie and Monsieur Roland lay awake all night in their separate bedrooms because they could hear the terrible weeping of Cordelia. Sometimes they heard the low rumbling sound of Arthur Rivers' voice and then again the anguished, torn sound: the sound of pain. And the sound of the past.

At dawn Rillie and Monsieur Roland heard Arthur getting up and knew he would not have slept as he closed the door and walked quietly down all the stairs. Along Maiden Lane toward the docks on the East River although the morning air was already hot, the policeman nevertheless pulled his cloak tightly around him, as if for comfort.

At Celine's House they explained it to Cordelia over and over, as if she were child: if a letter had arrived, Gwenlliam may, very possibly, be on a ship arriving any day also. On some ship come round Cape Horn from California, one day soon; or on some ship from Chagres, on the Panama Isthmus, one day soon. Whichever route had been taken they told her, it was likely that Gwenlliam Preston would emerge at one of the docks with an Englishman. Her family would therefore be waiting. There was no other way to think about it. They all set to work. They refused to consider thoughts about needles in haystacks, and they had Alfie Tyrone on their side.

Each day now Cordelia felt she was in some way floating somewhere above herself, looking down at the neverending chaos that her past had wrought on the lives of those she loved most. *This is my fault.* Then she looked at the daguerreotype on the wall and the beloved face. With all the self-control she had left, she set to work also.

From the newspapers (on one of which one of Alfie Tyrone's sons-in-law worked) and from the Battery Park and East River piers (with which Alfie Tyrone and his sons were intimately familiar, as now was Police Inspector Arthur Rivers), ships were checked: anything from California. The shanty-men sang and shouted as they rolled up the last of the sails; smaller steamers bellowed black smoke; both passenger and merchant ships disgorging goods and people into New York: at the piers on the Hudson Cordelia and Rillie would ask urgently: *where have you sailed from? which ship?* as crowds disembarked.

'Oy!' they heard, and there was Regina, slightly smartened up still by her family, but dressed more like herself, and no big hat. 'I made Alfie bring me,' she said. She was carrying a small bag. 'I've come back,' she said, 'until we find her.' All day her loud voice could be heard: *where have you sailed from? which ship?*

Alfie and Monsieur Roland tried to check boats arriving at the Hudson River piers: all the riff-raff, all the leaking ships and water coffins that plied up and down the Atlantic Coast between New York and Chagres, besides the more stately sailing boats and the noisy steamers. Often there were not passenger lists of any kind on some of the less reputable boats: miners, ex-miners, chancers, ruffians, gamblers, ladies of the night – none of whom perhaps thought to use the name they were born with, and some of whom would not answer any questions at all. Regina joined them sometimes and her voice echoed out: *where have you sailed from? which ship?* Very occasionally she sang the twenty-third psalm.

On the East River, Inspector Rivers, helped by his trusted lieutenant Frankie Fields, worked day and many nights, doing for this daughter what he could not, not yet, do for other daughters. He checked every arrival and departure that he was able, checking imports and exports and gangs on the East River, as well as passengers arriving on the Hudson, giving his men special instructions, hardly coming back to Maiden Lane. Frankie Fields did not go home either: he had seen this girl, played poker with her, even received messages in her letters, been allowed to share the letters: he had thought of her often. The local gangs who had been eyeing Inspector Rivers and his lieutenants with more and more suspicion were now alerted fully: *what was all this extra activity?* Hadn't he got the message after the Astor Place riots? And more meetings were held behind curtains in Green-Grocers shops. Gold was coming through now. They had had one very successful raid. They were not going to be stopped. Even though they understood the unwritten law in the city, from the City Fathers, about not taking policemen.

Alfie Tyrone had not met this Gwenlliam, but he had studied her picture on the wall and now he carried it in his satchel; they talked about her to him over and over. And Alfie Tyrone knew more than almost anybody in New York about maritime traffic into and out of that wild port city. Alfie dispersed people to all sorts of places, made all sorts of enquiries, asked questions of the son-in-law who was a newspaper man. Alfie told the family about the new fast clippers that Gwenlliam herself had described to them, like the ships that had been sailing fast to China and India carrying opium and tea; now they sailed round the Cape, usually in less than one hundred days, clipping the waves, clipping the time, bringing mail and gold and, sometimes now, passengers. In the evenings Alfie and Arthur sat with their heads together over their notes and their lists.

'Well now,' said Alfie at last, putting his thumbs in his waistcoat pocket, in the attic room. 'Let's keep it simple, as simple as we can. If I was transporting somebody against their will, I think I would – specially if I could get a chance to board one of them new clippers – I would bring them all the way round the Cape. I wouldn't risk the Panama isthmus and cholera and crocodiles if I had an unwilling but valuable passenger, not till they find a way of making it safer – they will, mind!

'Mexico? Fast, yes, and a ship through the gulf, yes, but – not an Englishman, nah! Everybody knows there's bodies with throats cut of people who thought Mexico would be quicker, bodies that are left lying there in the sunshine still. And there's many groups now endeavouring to travel overland and through the mountains – but, nah, again too dangerous, too slow, too many deaths. If I was transporting someone against their will I think I'd most of all like to bring them safe and tidy in a fast, safe clipper sailing around the Americas.'

'The letter was given to Danny, the Irishman, the same day it was written,' said Arthur. 'He isn't really well enough to answer questions but tonight I had a very quick talk to him and he said the *charros* and Silas P Swift came aboard with the letter just before the steamer left San Francisco, lots of the miners knew Silas of course and Danny offered to take the letter when he heard the story of Gwenlliam. Peggy wrote on 14th May, and we received it three days ago. That means the letter took seventy-four days to get here. Danny got off his boat at Panama and travelled back over the isthmus, God bless him. No ship, not even a clipper, could have done the journey in the time. I think we might assume that our friend Mr Doveribbon is in a hurry, but will be sensible with so much at stake. I think we might assume also that he must've got out of San Francisco with Gwen the night before Danny left, and probably on one of those smaller boats Gwennie described plying to and from Panama all the time, or they would likely have been found, with so many people looking for them, and so many of them knowing her, from the circus.'

Alfie said: 'Okay, but what would happen to her when the small boat got to Panama? Now, I've been making some enquiries about Panama and the gold rush. Everyone says it is a hell-hole these days. Excuse me ladies, but I have heard too many stories! It's a famous old Spanish city of course, with its *camino real* across the isthmus, ha! Royal Road indeed, eh! Gwenlliam ain't calling it that! These days Panama's only a terminus you might say between the North and the South, or the Pacific and the Atlantic. People get stuck there now, as your daughter described in her letter, Cordelia: Americans, English, French, Italians, Chinese, Indians, Mexicans – all of them there crashing about the grog shops and the gamblers and the girls, waiting for boats; I've heard they trample over each other to get on to anything that floats. There's only one sure way up the Pacific Coast to San Francisco and that's by sea, and I'm told there's not enough ships making that journey even now, for the people who still want to search for gold. *Therefore*: many of the boats coming from San Francisco only go as far as Panama and then turn round and go back again. *Therefore*: not such a lot of ships going around the Horn if that's what she's doing. And we can't be certain, but we think that's what we're looking for.'

Arthur Rivers spoke very quietly. 'Mr Doveribbon is an Englishman with access to money presumably, and he had time to make his plans. So if there happens to be a clipper arriving in New York soon, we might, we just might, find our girl.'

Danny the Irishman, the messenger, had begun to slowly recover – almost wholly due to the ministrations of Blossom and Maybelle (although they called in Jeremiah, the large barman, to bathe him and make him bearable). They fed the Irishman soup and very much chicken and rice and gave him a little Irish beer; whenever he opened his eyes one of them was there, indistinguishable. At night he called out and cried and tossed and turned: when he sat up suddenly in his bed one of them was there, Blossom or Maybelle; even if they had been dozing in the chair they at once went to him, and smoothed the blankets and murmured that he was safe. During the day he found it hard to talk without getting dangerously upset: he wept often and every time he wept he vomited and, still, Blossom or Maybelle had put kind arms about his shoulders. Having, like most of his fellow countrymen, a particular disdain for the Negro (which was reciprocated in full measure) he had nevertheless never been so very comfortable and cosseted in his whole life, having come as a child from Ireland and settled in Cherry Street by the river: he was suffused now in their slow singsong way of talking and their kind black arms trying to sit him upright sometimes, although he thought they smelled strange. La Grande Celine intimidated him slightly with her black eye-patch and her loudness, but he saw that she was kind.

Now Cordelia came to see Danny.

She had lain awake again almost all of the previous night, trying to think how they could know more; she must speak to the Irishman even if Arthur had said he was too ill for questioning, *I must,* he was the only connection they had from California. Again Arthur had not come home. She had tossed and turned in the hot humid night.

Aunt Hester was very wise in the ways of the world. 'Ellis may set you up somewhere, pay. But never give up your career, for he will not be there always.'

'I am not going to be "set up". That is not what I want.'

'Ellis will not marry you, Cordelia. He is the nobility. One day he will be the Duke of Llannefydd, it would be impossible for him to marry an actress. You must not build up dreams that are impossible to fulfil.'

'He loves me! He loves me!'

Her aunt tried again. 'Cordelia, you do not understand the difference between their world and ours; the barriers of class are unassailable – appearing on his arm at respectable events is nothing, nothing at all: allowances are made for impressionable young lords. You cannot marry someone so far above you – I do not mean above you as a person, for there is nobody in the world above you in my eyes' – that fond, ironical look of hers – 'but I mean in society. It is impossible, Cordelia, and you are only storing up future trouble for yourself.'

Now Cordelia came to the small room. Blossom was there, she tried to sit Danny up. 'This here done be the mammy,' she told him gently. 'This done be the mammy you brought the letter for.'

Danny, trying hard to sit upright, was taken aback. Mothers to him were old. Cordelia was beautiful.

Cordelia was taken aback also. She had seen him so briefly the night of his arrival, and now, without matted whiskers and dirt, he was so thin and pale and young. She tried hard to hold back all her own anxiety. 'I want to thank you, Danny. For bringing news of my daughter. Without you we would know nothing at all about what has happened to her.'

'Like I say, 'tis an angel that she is. So 'twas me duty to get here.'

'Why do you say that?'

'She is the one who held me brother. She's the one who calmed him and stayed with him till he died. She didn't move away and care that he had the fever or whatever, she held him and spoke with him till he died because she is an angel. That's why I said I'd bring the letter.'

Cordelia suddenly gave a small cry of surprise as she understood. From a pocket in the side of her gown she quickly took the small oddly-shaped nugget of gold that she carried always with her. 'Was it you, Danny, who gave this to Gwenlliam?' He looked in amazement at the small piece of gold, he held out his hand and she gave it to him. He turned it over and over in his hand. And then he began to cry.

'Twas my brother Johnny's. Yes. We thought it looked like a little snail. I gave it to her. How have you got it?' and his pale, tear-stained face looked confused. 'Is she found again after all?'

'No, she is not yet found. She sent it to us inside a Bible, and her letter told us the story of your brother and of you. And thanks to you and your determination and your courage we have a lot of information and we hope we shall find her in the end.'

He handed the nugget back, tears in his eyes again. 'That's a sweet tale,' said Danny, 'about it coming to you in the Holy Book.'

'You crossed the isthmus, we know that.'

'I did.'

'It took you a shorter time than any ship, Danny. We know that.'

'It took all me life, that's what it felt like. All we wanted to do was get home. Never in me life do I want to see California, or Panama, or any place ever again, so I don't.' All the agitation that the negro maids tried so hard to calm came back, Blossom tried now to sit him back against the pillows, he spoke so fast and his accent was so strong they had trouble understanding him. 'Me brother Johnny died in Sacramento, and then me two best pals died in the stinking Panama rainforest and I wanted to just die meself but I had the letter about the angel so I had to keep going – all the cheating Indians and the leaky boats and the heat and the snakes and the crocodiles and monkeys and the ugly steam, all the horrible, evil steam rising from that stinking river like devil ghosts – in the end 'twas just me, just me left at Chagres waiting to be picked up by any rotten boat, giving them a nugget for me fare. I promised the circus-man that I would deliver the letter for the sake of the angel, that's why I put one foot in front of the other, never stopping, otherwise I think I would have lain down at Chagres and died.'

'How long were you in Panama?' She saw how much he did not want to talk any more about this but she must not stop, it was the only thing she could think of. 'I would not bother you, Danny, we just might get a clue about my daughter, for it seems to me you may have been in Panama at the same time. You are the *only* person, Danny, who can tell us anything.'

He nodded slowly, understanding. But he shook his head. 'Tis dates you mean? We didn't take notice of dates. I didn't see the angel, course not, I would have said.'

'Did you leave straight away? Were you there for a while? In Panama?'

He shook his head. 'We stayed a while. I wish we hadn't. Me pals and me – we stayed some days, we did – we thought to drink ourselves silly before we made the journey.'

'Will you try and think?'

He nodded again, but doubtfully. 'What about?'

Cordelia tried to pull herself together. She was being ridiculous. *What am I asking him to think?* 'Where's your home, Danny?'

'Cherry Street, by the river. You wouldn't know it.' Cordelia had heard from Arthur Rivers of Cherry Street by the river. Wasn't that where he'd seen human ears kept in alcohol? She swallowed.

'Would you like me to contact somebody there, from your family?' He actually laughed, made a funny little sound in his chest.

'I don't think it's a place for you, missus.'

'I'll willingly go and fetch someone, and bring them here, if you would like me to.'

'I'll go meself, you wouldn't be able to go, you couldn't go there.' He began to try and get out of the bed: Blossom pulled him gently back.

'No, Danny,' said Cordelia, 'the doctor says not yet. You have been very ill.'

'Why ma'am, I always look like this!' He thought for a moment. 'If me mammy and me brother came, that is if they're still living, I've been away nearly two years, but if they came, they could take me home.' He was biting at his lip. 'I have to tell them about our Johnny dying, it would be better to do that at home,' and she saw that he was very distressed again. 'And me pals,' he said. 'I'll have to tell their folks.' He was crying again.

'I'll go right now,' said Cordelia gently. 'Maybe you won't be able to go home just yet, but at least you could all see each other. Where in Cherry Street?'

'Paradise Buildings. Cherry Street. Ask for Bridget O'Reilly and Kenny O'Reilly.' But his head was in his hands.

'I'll go right now,' she repeated, going to the door. 'Bridget and Kenny O'Reilly, Paradise Buildings. And will you think while I'm gone? About Panama? Anything, *anything*, just in case. It would help us so much.' And then suddenly, seeing his anguish, she forced herself to put away her own. She said: 'You know what you saw my daughter do in the circus, the mesmerism, do you remember?'

He looked up then. 'Yes,' he said. 'We used to fight for a turn.' He wiped his nose with his arm. 'Me brother Johnny' – he began to talk very fast again – 'Johnny was in a terrible way and she just sort of stroked her hands above his face and he became quite calm, even when he woke again and we knew he was dying, that's what I mean about an angel. She made his dying better, she did, so I had to bring the letter,' and his whole body became distraught again and Blossom tried to calm him.

Cordelia went back and stood beside the small bed. 'Listen a moment, Danny,' she said. '*Let yourself rest in my care.* She took a long, deep breath and then over the thin, anxious, un-still body she made long, strong passing movements, over and over, over and over the long passes, concentrating only on Danny, on his pain, over and over and slowly, slowly, he became quite calm and after some time, Cordelia never stopping her actions, his eyes closed and he fell asleep.

Blossom looked at her with round eyes. 'Are you a witch?' she whispered.

'You know I'm not a witch, Blossom! It's – it's like going to the doctor. It is called mesmerism,' she said. 'It – helps people sometimes, calms them. He might sleep for a while and I'll try and bring someone back who knows him.'

41

Inspector Rivers was down on the docks. Monsieur Roland was down on the docks. Rillie and Regina were down on the docks: Cordelia had said she would join them there. La Grande Celine was down in the kitchen helping Maybelle while Blossom was taking her turn with Danny. So Cordelia went alone, to Cherry Street.

She walked along the street where George Washington (Arthur had told her) once danced. She walked towards a dark alley between tenements: she did not know, would not have believed, that the narrow dirty opening was called Paradise Alley. She stepped over garbage. She did not know that hot ash was thrown on strangers, and all their possessions robbed. Her light-coloured cloak went in and out of dark and light and shadow as she came to a huge, sagging tenement block with windows broken and hanging, she saw an opening where a door had once been. PARADISE BUILD-INGS it said in broken letters. Arthur had told her many things about the city: she thought he had told her of Paradise Buildings, perhaps? Was this the one with all the water clos-ets in the cellar? She refused to be frightened, *why should I be frightened? It is just a tenement building, it's people's homes and I am looking for Bridget O'Reilly.* She refused to think of anything at all but getting Danny O'Reilly well so that he could think clearly of Panama City, although if he hadn't seen Gwenlliam what else could she hope for? *Am I insane to come alone? No. For Gwennie.* She walked on. At a doorway she saw that she could go ahead, or take steps that went downwards into dark, stinking cellars.

People from high windows stared in amazement as the lone woman walked through the dark doorway. It was the smell inside that hit her first: a fetid, rank, disgusting smell of bodies and shit and old food and decay: it seemed to come up through the floorboards, from the cellars: she felt sick. She saw door after door, narrow passages as black as midnight; she was aware of breathing in the darkness: the only light thing was the cloak moving through the darkness as she moved deeper and deeper into the building, trying to find someone, anybody. 'Hello,' she called, but her voice stuck in her throat and she kept feeling she would vomit, finally she held her glove to her nose. Her heart was beating unpleasantly. Light shone somewhere: she heard voices shouting, children crying; she moved forward and she saw a small high staircase leading upwards. Broken banisters swung, there was a long pole there seeming to half hold the staircase up; there was light: there was some sort of skylight above: a shaft of daylight shone down now on to the staircase. She saw something run over her feet, gave a small muffled scream. Again she heard breathing somewhere near her in the shadows, *maybe this is where they slice ears off, how could I have thought to come?* 'Hello,' she called again, and her voice was terrified.

Men finally, suddenly, barred her way further. She gasped: she would have sworn one of them materialised in front of her from beneath the floor: in the daylight that shone down above the broken staircase he seemed to emerge upwards from the floorboards out of darkness, with slime falling from him, like a big fish. Her eyes were adjusted to the gloom and there was that strange shaft of sunlight from the roof: outlined faces stared. Dirty, sullen, *young* faces, breathing, danger, the flash of earrings, a sound of water, and the stinking smell. But she breathed very deeply, to still her racing heart.

'I am looking for Bridget O'Reilly or Kenny O'Reilly.'

The men stared. 'Why?' said one.

'Is this where they live? I was told this is where they live.'

'Why?' said another voice.

'I have a message for them.' She swallowed. 'A message for Bridget O'Reilly from her son.'

'Name?'

'Danny.' She swallowed again. 'And Johnny.'

Now one of the men did come forward from the others, the man who had emerged from the floor, slime and water still fell from him. 'Where are they?' he said. He seemed to be the leader; the daylight shaft from above shadowed a cruel face; his one earring shone, menacing and golden, and yet he seemed almost no more than a youth, not much older than Danny O'Reilly, his voice was almost that of a boy.

'I have to speak to their mother.'

'You've got a high-falutin' cheek just walking into our house, lady. See us walking into yours?'

'Yes. Yes, I see that. I am so sorry. Danny is very ill – he needs to see his mother. I said I would come and find her and take her to him.'

She felt them looking her over. Perhaps a knife flashed. She knew then she had made a most terrible, terrible mistake. And then that young man who seemed perhaps to be the leader stepped forward further to look at her more carefully. He stared at her: something, something in his face, some look, she saw some recognition: *do they know perhaps that I am a policeman's wife?* her thoughts screamed, *how could I have thought I could do this?* The man still stared. 'I've seen you before,' he said slowly. And he repeated the words, uneasy: 'I've seen you before.' He stared at her in the gloom. 'Were you in that circus?'

A strange voice suddenly came out of darkness. 'Charlie!'

And then a tall figure materialised behind them all. 'English, ain't yer?'

'Yes.' The tall figure spat, spittle landed on Cordelia's arm. 'I'm the only acceptable face of buggering England in Paradise Buildings.' The voice was deep and smoke-filled, crackling like fire. And the voice delivered a tirade of filthy cursing about buggering England and the men half-laughed, half-listened. The tirade ended with: 'Where d'you live, English circus lady?' and Cordelia heard the click of a gun: he was going to shoot her.

Some terrified instinct of preservation, for the others if not for herself: 'I have arrived from California. Danny O'Reilly is ill, he has nearly died, I said I would bring a message.' Sweat pouring down her body: *I have to get out.* 'I apologise for intruding. Please tell his mother, or his brother, I will wait at the Bowling Green Park, by the fountain.'

'By the broken statue of George, that we made into bullets to kill his soldiers!'

'Yes, there. My name is Cordelia.'

'*Cordelia?*' The tall figure in the shadows looked at her carefully and in some surprise. 'Did you once drown?'

Cordelia could feel the hairs rise on the back of her neck,

could feel the pounding of her heart. But something, some instantaneous instinct, made her say, 'No. No, that was Ophelia.' The tall, wild figure laughed, a very strange sound.

'Well, well, well. A lady who knows her Shakespeare,' and without the pause of a beat the deep, smoky voice of the tall figure declared:

> Methinks I should know you, and know this man;
> Yet I am doubtful; for I am mainly ignorant
> What place this is; and all the skill I have
> Remembers not these garments; nor I know not
> Where I did lodge last night. Do not laugh at me;
> For, as I am a man, I think this lady
> To be my child Cordelia.

and without a pause of a beat, Cordelia answered:

> And so I am, I am.

And the tall figure laughed again and moved forward into the shaft of sunlight and there was a sound of steel, and it was then that Cordelia saw it was a woman: a cold, hard, savage face and braces stretching down over her bosom to hold up her skirt: a woman. And she had a pistol in her hand, and knives at her waist.

'Saved by the Bard, Cordelia!' said the woman. 'Just this once. Get out.'

'Thank you,' murmured Cordelia and she turned and walked down the long, narrow, dark passage not knowing if she was really saved because she knew some lines of Shakespeare from *King Lear* or whether a bullet or a knife would pierce her back. She could see the light of the day, there, there through the open doorway if she could get to it, if she did not fall, or faint, in fear. She kept walking, she did not allow herself to run; she got to the door, still alive. Along the muddy path by the doorway and in the shadows of the alley between buildings she kept walking, she did not allow herself to run. All along Cherry Street she kept walking. She did not dare to find Arthur, there was surely someone following her; she did not dare to go back to Maiden Lane. As the sun beat down Cordelia Preston walked and walked and walked: at last she found herself in Pearl Street; she stopped there and bought ale from a store. She came to the bottom of Broadway, walked past the iron railings and into Bowling Green where indeed there was only the plinth remaining of the statue of George III. She sat on an iron seat under the blessed shade of a tree and wept and wept, great sobs of relief. Then she opened the ale, and drank it all.

And then she waited.

They came when the sun was directly overhead: she saw them at once: the old lady (who was probably younger than Cordelia) limped as she half-walked, half-ran towards the green and the man was young, like Danny. Cordelia stood, and raised her arm.

'Is it you that came?'

'Yes. My name is Cordelia.'

The man said roughly, 'Well. Where are they?'

'Hush now, Kenny.' But she looked up at Cordelia and repeated the question. 'Where are they?' she asked anxiously. 'Where's my boys?'

Cordelia was so tired from lack of sleep, and fear, and the ale, and rage at herself for her ridiculous stupidity in getting

392

involved in all this when she should be down on the docks with the others, that she wanted to just march them into Maiden Lane and out again but she looked at the worn face of the woman, and remembered what her son had done, and knew she could not.

'Please,' she said, 'Bridget, Kenny, sit down here and let me explain to you what has happened.' They sat slowly, suspiciously. As clearly as she could she told them the story. Very gently she told them that Johnny had died months ago, on the mining fields of Sacramento. The mother let out a long, loud sound, like an animal, crossing herself, keening: people in the gardens stared.

'But Danny is alive, Bridget! And he needs you.' She explained that Danny had got back to New York, that he was ill, but that he was getting better and she would take them to him. She told them that she was here because Danny had brought her an important letter all the way with news of her daughter in California; she did not say what the letter told. She saw again the filth and squalor of Paradise Buildings. 'The people who are looking after Danny are happy to keep doing so. But he needs you both.'

'Come on then,' said Kenny, standing quickly. His mother's face was dark with misery: she did not speak.

'I told you Danny's story,' said Cordelia, 'because – I think he cannot speak of these things easily yet.' And in silence they made their way to Maiden Lane.

'A nigger!' said Kenny when he saw Blossom.

'Mammy!' whispered Danny when he saw Bridget O'Reilly.

'I have told them what happened, Danny,' said Cordelia as she ushered Blossom out of the little room, and closed the door on the family.

Celine was in the dining-room; she quickly explained about

Danny's family and Paradise Buildings. 'I must go back to the docks,' said Cordelia. 'Any new news?'

'No new news,' said Celine. 'You look like death warmed up!' she said to Cordelia. 'At least drink coffee before you go. You too Blossom, you and Maybelle have looked after Danny damn good.'

'We done do what anybody done do,' said Blossom shrugging, 'even for the dirty Irish,' and she flashed her teeth in a half-smile. 'I'm going to Maybelle,' and she was gone down the stairs to the basement kitchen.

Cordelia closed her eyes. When she opened them again with a jerk, she thought it was the woman with the suspenders on her skirt: Celine was standing there with the coffee. 'Did I fall asleep?'

'You did. Only five minutes but you're having nightmares! Cordelia Preston, did you go by yourself to Paradise Buildings?'

Cordelia nodded. 'I know, I know, I must've been mad. I was terrified out of my wits almost.'

'The police don't go there alone, Cord!'

'Nor will I, I assure you, ever again. Don't tell Arthur.'

A little group appeared in the doorway: Bridget and Kenny each holding an arm of Danny. Kenny was carrying Danny's little broken satchel with the nuggets, holding it to him.

La Grande Celine turned to them: Cordelia saw how Bridget and Kenny stared at the black eye-patch. 'Oh please, let him stay a little longer, we are happy to look after him!' said Celine.

Danny gave a half-smile. 'I want to go home with me mammy,' he said. 'And,' he gave a quick look round the dining-room, 'tell them funny little leprechauns that looked after me I'll say a prayer for them to the Holy Mother.'

Cordelia went to Danny and kissed his cheek. 'Thank you for your bravery and your courage and your speed,' she said.

'I had to do it for the angel,' he said. 'I'll pray for her too.' He was leaning heavily on Kenny's arm. 'I tried to think about Panama, missus, but I'm putting all those things out of me mind. We did stay some days,' he looked briefly at his mother, 'as I told you. It was full of people all fighting to leave one route or another; we met people going to the gold-fields, all starry-eyed, poor fools. We were glad to get away, Panama City makes people mad, made us mad. The only beautiful thing I saw – you know the big ships have to dock way out because of the bar? – was a big, white clipper ship out there anchored at the bar, bound for home.'

'Clipper?'

'We knew it was bound for home because we talked of going with her, being fast and that and me with my precious letter, but of course they take cargo as well as passengers and there was no room.'

'Clipper?'

'Beautiful. Sails like snow in the distance.'

'Did the clipper have a name?' asked Cordelia very quietly.

'Sure and we had telescope eyes!' said Danny. His mother was on his other side, holding so tightly to his arm: there was colour in his cheeks. They walked slowly towards the big front door.

'Wait!' said Cordelia. There was colour in her cheeks too. She pulled the nugget shaped like a snail from her deep pocket. She moved to the mother.

'Bridget O'Reilly.'

'We're away home now, missus.'

But Cordelia held out her hand. 'Here, Bridget.' And she placed the small gold lump in the woman's hand, a hand which may have been younger than Cordelia's but was engrained with grime and age, the fingernails were black-rimmed and broken. 'Danny will tell you the story of this piece of gold, it belonged to Johnny and it came to me. I would like you to have it. If my daughter is found it will be thanks to your son, Bridget O'Reilly.'

'I've just remembered, missus,' said Danny, as his mother wept, stroking the gold. 'That clipper we was admiring. I reckon it was called *Sea Bullet*. We liked that name. *Sea Bullet*.'

And Cordelia was gone, down to the docks.

'Are there – what would they be called – shipping calendars? Time-tables?' asked Monsieur Roland, standing on an East River wharf with Alfie and Arthur and Cordelia with her news. In his pale old face now his old eyes seemed to shine. 'A calendar that might tell us of clippers?'

'Shipping schedules,' said Alfie knowledgeably. 'Shipping schedules are only guides of course, but they carry valuable cargo these clippers: not big cargoes, you understand, but valuable cargo for us: spices, jewels, tea – and certainly, from California, gold. So we keep our eye on their whereabouts as best we can. And of course everyone is so proud of the speed of these new clippers that we are forever checking records.' As usual Alfie brought out multifarious papers from his satchel. 'I've just checked again after Danny's story, we know there is a clipper due, it's carrying passengers as well as cargo, and it is almost certainly *Sea Bullet*, but we've had no message when: it hasn't sailed past Washington, or there would have been a telegraph.' Alfie spoke as if he owned the maritime affairs of New York.

Arthur said: 'I've had another read of Peggy Walker's letter. If we can get an idea of Mr Doveribbon – we're English! of course we can! – I think he's a man who would definitely have found *when* a clipper was leaving San Francisco to do the journey faster, and timed his taking of Gwenlliam accordingly. It was too risky to board at San Francisco, everybody looking for her. But if he could have left San Francisco in a small boat much earlier and timed things well, they could have picked the clipper up in Panama. Danny said the *Sea Bullet* was anchored, so it must have stopped to take on passengers or provisions, but it could have got provisions in San Francisco. Mr Doveribbon complained, Peggy wrote, about the length of the sea journey, but said you wouldn't catch him going through rainforests. Good old Peggy – she told us more in her letter than she realised. Or perhaps she did realise,' he amended.

'But we must still check the ships from Chagres,' said Cordelia. 'We cannot *assume* anything.'

'Of course. But Cordelia, we *can* assume that Mr Doveribbon is fairly carefully looking after Gwennie's welfare, and I think you should hug that knowledge to your heart.' Arthur came home briefly every evening, so that they could all exchange news: that was all they saw of him if they didn't meet on the docks. Although he was quartered at the Police Headquarters they knew he had not slept for several days: if he was not vigilant Gwenlliam could be lost to them; his face was pale and lined. 'We must hope and pray Gwennie is travelling on that ship,' said Arthur, and he saw his wife's white face and glittering eyes. She had not said she had been alone to Paradise Buildings. She did not tell them about the wild woman who had asked if she had drowned. 'We will be ready for her, Cordelia. If she is aboard the *Sea Bullet* we will find her. If she is not aboard the *Sea Bullet*' – he sighed at last as weariness and worry seemed to overwhelm him. 'Well, if she is not aboard the *Sea Bullet* then we must just go on checking every other arrival.'

They had reckoned without the sensible and spirited girl they were searching for, and without the most inventive support of Mrs Ray, star of *The Bandit Chief*, from the Royal Theatre, New Zealand.

42

Every time a ship left California it was murmured that thousands – maybe millions! – of dollars' worth of gold was being shipped out. Certainly cargo consisting of large boxes and containers had been loaded on to the clipper *Sea Bullet*, along with big quantities of mail, and the crew, and a number of passengers, and water and food, and live animals to be killed on the journey. About the decks and cabins of the *Sea Bullet* rumours and lies and dreams flew concerning the contents of the hold: *perhaps we are carrying great fortunes of gold, yes, I wager we are carrying gold fortunes.* And the *Sea Bullet* sailed away from San Francisco harbour and disappeared into the fog. The lucky ones among the departing passengers, of course, had gold in their luggage also.

Further exciting rumours flew through the decks and cabins when the *Sea Bullet* sailed away from Panama some weeks later, for the departure had a little touch of Grand Opera about it. The anchorage at Panama was the only scheduled stop: the clipper was then heading non-stop for New York but for reasons that were not clear to anybody but the captain, the *Sea Bullet* could not leave Panama until the *Moe'uhane* arrived, and the smaller vessel (for neither large nor small sailing ships could arrange the weather) was a day and a half later than expected. The Captain was furious and as soon as he saw the *Moe'uhane* approaching he dramatically shouted orders for the *Sea Bullet* to hoist sail. Unbeknownst to herself, Gwenlliam was to have been discreetly taken aboard the *Sea Bullet* in darkness: as it was all the passengers and crew caught a theatrical glimpse of a pale, unconscious girl being carried aboard in the sunshine, just as the clipper sailed away.

Somehow Gwenlliam, when she had once more awoken to those same, silent horses that carried her over fields of dreams, was in a small cabin of her own (to keep her from intercourse with other female passengers, many of whom shared sleeping space). Somehow, this time, Mr Doveribbon had the key (so that she was now, in truth, a prisoner). Somehow, someone had delivered clothes and linen.

Mr Doveribbon did not have everything his own way, however. Despite his long-ago mutually-beneficial arrangements with the captain in the Broadwalk saloon, the *Sea Bullet* was not a vessel where Mr Doveribbon could order things absolutely to his satisfaction: there were people everywhere on board who had seen their dramatic boarding, and in particular the ministrations and concerns of the ship's doctor made Mr Doveribbon deeply uneasy. For all her pleasant calm aboard the *Moe'uhane* he did not trust Gwenlliam in this more public and therefore dangerous situation; there was something odd in the way she had not asked any more about her fortune and her future. The Doctor, intrigued, had offered his services at once: who was to say Gwenlliam would not confide in him? Gravely Mr Doveribbon asked that the girl be left alone: his 'cousin' had suffered a terrible trauma, and was suffering from periods of wild insanity. She needed peace. (He did not want the ship's doctor to smell any sign of chloroform but he did need the doctor because he wanted laudanum for the patient: he had acquired a small amount which he had already used but he realised he needed regular supplies to keep her as quiet as possible at all times, on a vessel with other passengers, and such a long journey.) So another intriguing rumour was around the ship in fifteen minutes: there was a mad person aboard, possibly drug-crazed.

One of the female maids washed the pale, pretty girl and dressed her in fresh clothes while she was still drifting in and out of sleep.

'What ship is this?' murmured Gwenlliam. 'Where are we?'

'Why, this is the clipper, *Sea Bullet*, miss,' said the maid. 'Left Panama this midday. My, we are proud of her. It will only be a few months to New York, less than three, if we are lucky.'

Three months! How am I to survive three months? She tried so hard to focus her drifting thoughts, asked for water, tried to sit up.

'Where do we call?'

'We don't call anywhere, miss, we are non-stop to New York. And you are in a first-class cabin. Next to the Captain. And your cousin next door to you on the other side, so you are quite safe.'

Drifting, sleeping, trying to wake, drifting again: the only thing that she could think of to say was: 'Does anyone play poker on board the *Sea Bullet*?'

'Oh – all the gentlemen play,' said the maid. 'To pass the time. And already they fight and we only left San Francisco a few weeks ago! Sometimes they fight big over money. Many of them are coming back from California with money from the gold fields!'

'Good,' murmured the now much cleaner passenger, and fell asleep again.

'She's not *that* mad!' said the maid kindly to Mr Doveribbon, 'I'll wash her things and return them to her as soon as I can so she can dress properly. We could only find our own clothes to give her and they're too big and don't do a pretty young girl like that no favours!'

'Burn her own clothes at once!' ordered Mr Doveribbon: he immediately arranged for another maid to replace the first one: what had the girl said?

So now a second maid brought meals, and Mr Doveribbon always accompanied her. Sometimes Gwen ate, sometimes she didn't. 'I need fresh air,' she said. Mr Doveribbon pointed to the small port-hole, which the maid had opened; they could see the Pacific Ocean. He went out again, locking the door behind him.

The biggest difference to Gwenlliam, after Panama, was her rage. On the *Moe'uhane* she had felt quite calm because she knew she was capable of getting back from Panama to San Francisco, especially with her extra poker winnings; she had consoled herself she would soon be back with the circus. But now she was sailing non-stop around the Americas whether she liked it or not. She knew he had somehow given her lau-danum on top of chloroform: she knew exactly what laudanum was: tincture of opium: the midgets had taken lau-danum also, and the Indian chief, and several of the clowns. Gwenlliam had tried it: *high-low*, the midgets had called it: it made them smile before it made them sleep. Her rage was not only that she was kidnapped and now had no hope of escaping, but also that her kidnapper was using medicines in a dangerous manner. *How dare he use chloroform a second time and now add other sedatives? I will speak to the captain, they say he is in the next-door cabin, and he can imprison Mr Doveribbon and drop him off along the coast, preferably where there is much violence.*

Gwenlliam had in her heart, as Monsieur Roland had noted long ago, a presence of kindness. Her strange life – kidnapped by the nobility when she was six years old – might have made her unkind, but it had not. Her rackety life in the circus – and the gambling and the nitrous oxide experiments that were part of it – might have made her unkind but, they had not. She thought the best of people, she had a calmness of spirit, and she was kind. But a sliver of steel entered her heart, after Panama: once before this hateful Welsh family of her father had changed her life: she would not let them destroy her a second time. She was, indeed, her mother's daughter.

When the doctor was at last allowed to come with more laudanum she heard Mr Doveribbon murmuring: still with her eyes closed she strained to hear what he was saying.

'We must give her laudanum at once. She has been delirious, and she is having bouts of rage and insanity, you must take absolutely no notice of what she says.'

The doctor came near, so near she smelt the pomade from his hair; she heard him place the bottle of laudanum on the table beside her bed. 'What is troubling her so terribly?'

'She has lost her brother and her sister.'

Gwenlliam was so angry at this distortion of her private, personal pain that she sat upright very quickly: she was unable to contain herself. But then she saw the alarmed face of the doctor as he bent to her, she saw Mr Doveribbon. She also felt extremely dizzy. Very slowly she lay down again and seemed in a moment to have fallen asleep.

In and out went the deep breathing.

'You see!' said Mr Doveribbon triumphantly. 'You can see for yourself she is deeply, deeply disturbed! I think the best thing I can do is keep her taking laudanum very regularly, until I can get her to her family in Great Britain.'

'I do see,' said the doctor. 'Hysteria. We find it so often, in women. They are so weak, in so many ways.' His voice was pompous and English and deeply self-satisfied: no doubt he and Mr Doveribbon deserved each other. In and out went the girl's deep breathing. 'We try various treatments. Hot tubs. Cold sponges. Vibratory massage. Nevertheless, a little exercise and fresh air when she wakes will not go amiss. I never under-estimate the bracing qualities of sea air.' Gwenlliam made a little sound, opened her eyes again slowly.

'I would very much like some fresh air, doctor,' she said in a voice as gentle as soft rain falling.

'Exactly what I was suggesting,' he said. 'A little fresh air and a daily walk. It is not good for you to remain in bed all day, my dear young lady! Not healthy. But you must – I am so sorry for your sad trouble – take the laudanum when you return.'

'Of course,' said Gwenlliam, and, very slowly this time, she sat up.

'Just a moment!' said Mr Doveribbon very quickly. 'We must not rush things.'

'I do feel the need of air, Mr Doveribbon,' said Gwenlliam, so very humbly, so very sweetly. 'Perhaps though, one of you gentlemen will give me your arm, for I feel greatly in need of support.' And she smiled a very lovely smile at them both and as Gwenlliam was a very pretty girl the doctor's heart was touched. 'If I might just wash my face and join you both on deck?'

'Come along, old chap,' said the pompous doctor.

'Now look here –' Mr Doveribbon began.

'A lady must have a few moments' privacy, and she sounds sensible, although she is extremely pale.'

'The laudanum,' said Mr Doveribbon quickly, moving to the bottle beside the bed. 'Perhaps it would be better . . .'

'I have it here,' said Gwenlliam quickly, grabbing the bottle and holding it to her bosom as if it was the most valuable thing in her life. 'I shall take some as soon as I return. In fact I will be most glad to.' Mr Doveribbon could hardly scrabble at her bosom in the doctor's presence; unwillingly he allowed the doctor to lead him on deck. Quickly Gwenlliam emptied the laudanum into the slops bucket and then raised her skirts and sat on the slops bucket, covering the laudanum with other matter. (Mr Doveribbon would be, she correctly estimated, far too fastidious to *ever* investigate her slops bucket.) She washed from water in a bowl. The glass of the laudanum bottle was green and dark and would not give away secrets: she refilled it with water from the water bottle the maid had left on a shelf. She put the bottle back on the table beside the bed. It was only then she observed properly what she was wearing. Clean clothes, that was the main thing. But they appeared to be very unbecoming and not quite well-fitting. *I feel like an orphan!* But the word drew her up short, *I am not an orphan*, and at once she was suddenly overwhelmed with a longing to see her mother so powerful that she gasped and bent over, holding her arms about herself. *I will see her before very long. All will be well, in the end. I am on my way back to Maiden Lane after all.* She stood up briskly then, hitched and folded the clothes where she was able. There was no looking-glass in the cabin, she had no idea how she looked. She did not care. She was going out of this cabin at last.

On deck she took a deep, deep breath, let the air and the wind blow everything away for a moment as she stood there.

There was nothing to be seen: no land, no other ship, as far as the eye could see. The wind had filled the sails of the sleek and beautiful sailing ship, it flew through the waves and over the water: she realised she was on one of those clipper ships she had admired so much, *the fastest way home by ship*. Then Gwenlliam very quickly took note of everything around her: the size of the ship, the other passengers: surely they *would* help her when they heard her story – *where is the captain?* – but her demeanour and her behaviour were impeccable. Mr Doveribbon relaxed slightly. She took the doctor's arm; Mr Doveribbon walked closely beside, bowed at other passengers also promenading, who stared at Gwenlliam (she herself observed at once) with great interest. *I may presume that they have been told I am insane!* The doctor made conversation, asked questions; Gwenlliam remained silent, Mr Doveribbon answered for both of them: 'I am her cousin, she has been ill.' There was no sign of the captain. After several turns around the rising and falling, moving deck the doctor said: 'I think that is enough for the first day, young lady.'

Her heart sank but she spoke demurely: 'Might you escort me again tomorrow, doctor? I do feel a little better in the air.'

'With pleasure,' said the doctor, and he removed his hat and bowed. 'You see, sir, your cousin has a little colour in her cheeks already. But please take the laudanum now, young lady, and calm yourself at all times.'

'Thank you, doctor,' said Gwenlliam, smiling again her lovely smile.

'Do not bother to plan anything, Miss Preston,' said Mr Doveribbon, back in her cabin, 'by your little forays on to the deck.' She stood beside the bedside table: she did not want him investigating the laudanum bottle. But – foolish Mr Doveribbon – she saw that he had relaxed and was smiling slightly: all had gone as well as could be hoped for in public; there was even something triumphant about his smile. 'I must inform you that there has been a great deal of talk about you, and nobody will believe anything you say – and I hope you have observed your clothes, Miss Preston. You may have been the little Princess in Sacramento and San Francisco, but that was then, and this is now! A ship is a fine place to send rumours flying and everybody on the ship knows there is a young lady aboard who has periods of insanity – including the captain – so do not expect to be taken seriously by anyone at all.' She looked down so that he would not see the anger in her eyes. She breathed very deeply: perhaps he thought it was a sigh. She took the laudanum bottle from the table and held it to her.

'Mr Doveribbon,' she said coldly. 'You have kidnapped me. I have done exactly as you have ordered since we left San Francisco since I can do no other. I will not forgive you for using chloroform, about which, I believe, I know more than you. However, this ship they say is non-stop to New York. I do not intend to jump into the sea. I do intend to take this laudanum for I would not sleep otherwise after all that has happened to me. The least you could do, as a gentleman, is give me a little time on my own now, and also, while we are aboard this ship, some freedom to walk and talk.' And he saw her take a large drink of the laudanum straight from the bottle, place the bottle on the table beside her, and climb back on to her bed and close her eyes. At last he was satisfied, and left her, locking the door behind him.

She heard the click of the lock, opened her eyes again at once. The small porthole and the Pacific Ocean looked suddenly inviting: she did, briefly, consider throwing herself out.

*

And so several days passed: the doctor came every day, laudanum was provided when required; Gwenlliam emptied it into the slops bucket which the maid took away each morning, and drank long from the dark bottle each evening to the satisfaction of Mr Doveribbon. Gwenlliam's own clothes had disappeared, no amount of questioning could recover them. She caused no fuss, ate in the cabin, stared out the porthole as the blue sea rushed by. *I have to endure this. I have to. I am not actually in danger, except from chloroform. The captain of this ship will help me when he understands the truth. I am in the cabin next to the captain – perhaps I can knock on the wall when I hear him.* She listened carefully. Sometimes a cabin door slammed somewhere. Otherwise she heard nothing. Once she banged and banged on the wall, a dull, muffled sound. There was no reply.

Every afternoon the three of them strolled on the deck, the young woman closely escorted by Mr Doveribbon and the doctor. People stared surreptitiously at the pretty girl in the odd clothes and her companions. On the fifth day they came near to the captain for the first time: he looked an intimidating, slightly unpleasant man and was shouting at some of his crew but she decided she had to risk it. She broke away from the two men and ran towards him in her flapping ill-fitting gown.

'Captain, you must help me!' she cried. 'I am kept prisoner next door to you, against my will!' Other deck promenaders stopped and stared. '*I am kept prisoner!*' she cried, scrabbling almost at his jacket, surely he could understand?

'Yes, yes,' said the Captain in distaste, pushing her away from him. 'I have heard all about you. Be a good girl,' and he indicated to Mr Doveribbon impatiently to take her. That little miscalculation meant that the story was around the ship in moments: now everybody would believe she was mad. She felt a knot of pain inside her, as if anger was curled up into a hard, tight ball. She did not even get up on deck the following day: when walks with the doctor finally resumed she did not repeat her mistake. The *Sea Bullet* sailed on. Her shoulders became hunched as she walked, although she did not know it: in her ill-fitting clothes she looked a sad figure.

'*Gwen!*' All three strolling passengers stopped short at the very loud voice. 'Gwen, what are you doing here? Why haven't I seen you! We left Panama well over a week ago! I thought I knew everyone already and here you are walking with the most handsome man on the ship! O my God, you're not – you're not the one, are you, they say is quite mad?'

She recognised the voice at once and her heart leapt up as she turned and saw the voice's owner. 'Colleen!' She addressed the gentlemen on either side, almost dazzled with relief as she saw Mr Doveribbon's appalled face. 'May I introduce Mrs Ray from the Royal Theatre in New Zealand! Mr Doveribbon and Dr Barker.' The gentlemen bowed, impressed despite themselves, for Mrs Ray's hair was almost as flame-coloured as La Grand Celine's and Mrs Ray's bosom had made strong men tremble. Mrs Ray's eyes dismissed the doctor fairly quickly but her eyes lingered on the very good-looking Mr Doveribbon and she smiled.

'I have seen you walking alone on deck,' she said to him. 'Who could forget such a romantic sight!' Gwenlliam's mind flew like the wind in the sails above her: *what is the best thing to do right now?* Colleen waited expectantly for more explanation, taking in the strange ill-fitting attire.

'I have been ill,' said Gwenlliam quickly before Mr

Doveribbon could hurry her away. 'I am better now and am on my way to Great Britain.'

'Well, hallelujah!' cried Colleen. 'That you are better, of course, but also that we can play some poker to while away these tedious hours! I'm on my way to re-stage "The Bandit Chief" in Baltimore. The others are already ahead of me, I was delayed by – by an *amour.*' She sighed, her beautiful bosom heaved, and the Doctor was attacked by a little *frisson* beside her; even Mr Doveribbon, deeply shocked as he was by this unfortunate turn of events, was not unmoved.

'Colleen and I played a great deal of poker when we met in Sacramento,' Gwenlliam explained to the gentlemen. 'Perhaps we could play, all four of us? For money, of course,' she added, smiling so sweetly. She ignored Mr Doveribbon's alarmed face, turned to the smitten Doctor Barker. 'I feel a hand of poker would do me the world of good.'

'It may possibly be too exciting, young lady,' he said, but his eyes were twinkling as he smiled at Mrs Ray.

'Oh, doctor!' said Mrs Ray, putting her hand on his arm. 'Gwen here was the calmest poker player in Sacramento, that's why she kept winning!' Mrs Ray smiled dazzlingly back at the doctor, and he was lost.

'Partly it is being locked all the time in her cabin that *makes* the patient prone to hysteria,' he said portentously and the patient could have hugged him; then Doctor Barker, Mrs Ray smiling up at him, again insisted to Mr Doveribbon, in front of other passengers, that this interest in something outside herself was a good sign in the patient.

Mr Doveribbon acquiesced with a bad grace.

They played then, the four of them, in a quiet corner most evenings. Gwenlliam may have been mad, as the rumour went, but she was the best player: she and Colleen were better players than the men, and Gwenlliam's winnings were the largest. And even as she raked her pile towards her, *I must acquire all the money I possibly can*, her face was blank: Chief Great Rainbow would have been proud of her. And then, night after night, Mr Doveribbon would take out his watch, then rise and take Gwenlliam's arm, and thus, night after night, the evening's entertainment would be over.

Locked once more in her cabin but refreshed by this human intercourse, and by her winnings, Gwenlliam pondered: could she somehow mesmerise Mr Doveribbon to get away from his constant presence and explain things to Colleen? But Monsieur Roland had always made it clear: *our patients must always be willing, only hysterics can be mesmerised despite themselves*. And Mr Doveribbon would never be willing. And although she now considered him a criminal, hysterical, she thought, he was not.

So they had well passed, so it was said, Valparaíso to the east, Santiago, islands, archipelagos (all spoken of, hardly ever glimpsed) before Gwenlliam got a chance to talk to Colleen properly, for Mr Doveribbon never, never left Gwenlliam's side except when she was locked in her cabin; she was locked in there for a great deal of every day; there were no writing materials so she could not even write an explanatory letter and conceal it about her person until a moment presented itself at poker.

But as the clipper finally approached the Magellan Straits, providence at last intervened: the winds caught them and tossed them around and around; finally the *Sea Bullet* had to turn again from the Straits and endeavour to round Cape Horn instead – where the weather was almost as dangerous. And Mr Doveribbon was laid low: indeed to Gwenlliam's joy he vomited above deck and below, not always succeeding in locking her in securely as he made for slop buckets: he considered for some days that he was dying. Gwenlliam, who did not suffer from sea-sickness, was so delighted at his malady, so delighted to move freely that she did a little dance on deck in the wild wind – only proving to any hardy passing passengers how mad she indeed was. Mrs Colleen Ray, meeting her there as requested, applauded. 'That's more like you, Gwen!' she said.

Only a few brave souls had ventured on deck. Very briefly at last, the two women standing clinging to the boat's side as it rose and fell on the waves with the wild, wild wind blowing across its bows, Gwenlliam explained, the words whipped away from her by the wind almost as she uttered them, what had happened. Colleen's mouth fell open in surprise.

'Well, why didn't you tell me at once, you idiot?' she shouted above the noise of the wind and the sails. 'I thought you had to stay in your cabin because you had been so ill!'

'I have *not* been ill!'

'You told me yourself you had been ill! You said it, the first day on deck that I saw you! And I saw this poor little figure being carried aboard!'

'I haven't been ill at all! Not at all! He stole my clothes! And he kidnapped me by putting chloroform over my face!'

'What?'

'Chloroform!' The wind blew the words into the sky.

'Did you say chloroform?'

'Yes!'

'The bastard!'

'*Exactly!*'

Their words sang and shouted and disappeared. 'You do look very peculiar in those clothes, I did think – but you sound the same, and you can still play poker. Oh Gwen, you poor thing! Whyever does he want to dress you like that and take such a risk in public and kidnap you to England?' And then she laughed into the storm. 'He is madly in love with you – is that it?'

'Certainly not! He thinks I am an heiress. He apparently has to present me in person in London.'

Colleen laughed again in delighted fury, her wild hair dancing. 'This is America!' she cried, as if they were still on land. 'You can't kidnap heiresses here! We must tell the captain. "Clap that handsome gentleman in irons!" we will say. Then I can visit him in the night and drive him crazy and make him confess his guilt!'

'It's no joking matter, Colleen! I *tried* to tell the captain but Mr Doveribbon has told the captain that I am ill and deluded.'

'He had told me that too!'

'Yes, yes, he has told everybody that! And even you do imply I *look* odd!'

'Well, let us un-tell that whole story and explain! Now that I know!' The *Sea Bullet* suddenly reached upwards, and then fell down again into the ocean; even bigger waves suddenly washed over the railings, taking them by surprise, covering them with sea water so that they gasped and screamed, and swallowed and spat, half-terrified, half-exhilarated. Now nobody else was still on deck. They clung tightly to ropes and rails.

'Will they believe an actress and an acrobat, or will they believe an English gentleman?' Gwenlliam shouted. 'And the doctor will confirm he has been giving me enough laudanum to tranquillise an elephant!'

'Have you been taking laudanum as well?'

'No! I've been disposing of it in the slops bucket.'

413

'Don't do that! Give it to me! I love the stuff!' Again a large wave crashed down over the deck. 'O God, I'm soaking wet! Hold very, very tight, Gwen – this could be our final hour!'

'I'm fine, I'm an acrobat!' answered Gwenlliam, balancing with the ropes. 'But the doctor thinks I've been taking large amounts of laudanum for weeks of my own free will. I must seem to him to be some kind of mad addict. Also have you *heard* the captain? He shouts at the crew all day long! I have tried – he dismissed me without even listening to me. He is not likely to listen again, even to both of us – even with you on my side.'

'Yes. He's a bully, the crew do not like him at all.' The sea heaved upwards; Colleen held quite desperately on to a sail rope, grabbed for the deck rail again. She turned to look up at the helm, bravely made one hand free and waved up to where the Captain and the helmsman were pulling at the wheel. The captain saw them in surprise, indicated to them urgently and angrily to go below at once.

'Shall I seduce him?'

'The captain or Mr Doveribbon?'

'Whichever you like. I am usually found to be irresistible. Certainly that beautiful helmsman above us – just look at him! – I can tell you for certain, finds me so. I bet you five precious dollars I shall meet with him in a lifeboat on a calm night before long.' Despite herself and the now extremely dangerous waves rolling over the deck, Gwenlliam laughed. Above them the captain gesticulated wildly in their direction.

'Do you know that's the first time I've laughed since I left San Francisco? O Colleen, I am so glad that you are on this ship. Hallelujah, hallelujah!'

'Hallelujah indeed! We'll outwit him, I'll help you get safely off this ship and away from him when we get to New York. I'll have hysterics and scream the docks down, actresses have useful skills – and we'll make sure he gets arrested as well! What a bastard! But listen, I have no money if we are to have adventures – I came aboard with only enough money to get from New York to Baltimore – although poker has helped! My *amour* paid for my passage and I did not like to say I had no money at all about my person as we parted.'

'Nor have I much! But I have won quite a lot at poker also.'

'I know, I see you!'

'We will share everything. Just keep winning!' And with their wet clothes clinging to them, and holding tightly to railings and ropes, one hand over the other, they slipped and slid precariously on the wet deck, making their dangerous yet exhilarated way towards the door that led below. A white-faced Mr Doveribbon was looking for Gwenlliam frantically.

'But my dear Mr Doveribbon, it is my fault, I didn't realise it was dangerous, I thought the wild air would be good for her, brush away the cobwebs! You lock her in again, and I'll help you back to your cabin, you look so terribly, terribly pale and interesting.'

And locked back in her lifting and falling cabin, the porthole tightly locked now and the sea wild outside, Gwenlliam thought how glad she was that Mrs Colleen Ray had not, for even a moment, even when they were talking about their penury, suggested that being an heiress was worth the loss of freedom.

The days slipped so very slowly by. The boredom on board was unspeakable: for everybody, and in particular for Gwenlliam locked so often in her cabin. But the days had to be passed somehow. *I will be home soon,* she said to herself every single day. She counted the poker winnings over and over.

She counted the minutes to her daily walk; she worked out how many seconds had to pass before her door would be unlocked again and she could play poker. Out of desperation she began to embroider: tablecloths and napkins and needles and coloured cottons had thoughtfully been made available for the ladies: the finished products, they were told, would be used on the dining tables of the *Sea Bullet*. So Gwenlliam embroidered flowers, as she had been taught by noble ladies so long ago; she sat always near the small porthole watching the sea and the sky. On deck sometimes she observed strange birds, saw how they swooped low, appearing unexpectedly out of nowhere between the white sails; here, locked in her cabin she saw only how they soared back upwards into the far, blue sky, *where do they go?* Through the small porthole she watched porpoises playing, jumping and seeming to smile. She saw how the skies changed colour: blue, yellow, iron grey, red, orange: once she saw a full moon so low beside the horizon that she felt she could stretch out with her hands and almost touch it.

'May I not just visit Gwen briefly?' Colleen said beguilingly to Mr Doveribbon, leaning slightly against him in the morning wind. 'You do seem to lock her away for very long periods. Can it be good for her?'

'She has been very ill,' he answered, so smoothly. 'She surely isn't the girl you knew in Sacramento.' Colleen did not answer. 'If –' he looked at her carefully, 'she has been saying anything different, you must not believe her. They become very sly.'

'Who do, Mr Doveribbon?'

'Hysterics, Mrs Ray. Drug addicts. Speak to the doctor, he will enlighten you.' Colleen thought (as she smiled as if in acquiescence and her alluring bosom rose and fell beside him) how very unattractive this handsome Englishman had become to her. But there was only the sea in every direction: she did not see how to change things as the days passed: they lived in a little sea-bound world where the captain was king. But Mrs Colleen Ray had seen Gwen crossing high wires in the air and mesmerising miners. Gwen was stalwart and brave: they would have to dock in New York eventually and then they would make sure she escaped. Colleen leaned further against Mr Doveribbon and took his arm, and smiled again.

Through all the long, interminable hours Gwenlliam would ply her needle like any respectable lady and watch the sea – and conjure up her unrespectable family into her mind.

She thought so often of her brave, beloved mother: her mother who had endured so much because of the same, destructive family, her father's family. She thought of Arthur, the step-father who she loved: if she couldn't jump off the *Sea Bullet*, it would be Detective-Inspector Arthur Rivers she thought, as the ocean flew by below, who would find her. *Arthur will know what to do.* Arthur. Her mother was light, and bright, with Arthur. Gwenlliam knew her mother held something back from this man: something to do with her past and her pain. Sometimes Arthur's eyes were dark with loss.

Gwenlliam stared out for a long time, at the blue-grey sea: she had seen her mother alight with love and joy.

She conjured up the pale, beautiful old face of her beloved Monsieur Roland; she thought of dear, kind Rillie, her mother's best friend. And Regina's rough, kind way too, when they shared a small bedroom in Maiden Lane; 'I'll tell you a story, girl,' she used to say, to put Gwenlliam to sleep. And she thought of dear, deluded Mrs Spoons and sometimes in her lonely cabin she sang to herself the song that Mrs Spoons had remembered:

> *O whistle and I'll come to ye, my lad,*
> *O whistle and I'll come to ye, my lad,*
> *Though father and mother and a' should gae mad*
> *Thy Jeannie will venture wi' thee, my lad.*

And very occasionally she even allowed herself to think, day-dreaming, of the tall, fair-haired policeman called Frankie Fields, who had equalled her at poker and who, just sometimes, appeared in her dreams at night.

Days, and days, and weeks, passed. Sailing well up the South Atlantic coast now, past Montevideo, Rio de Janeiro – romantic names but out of sight – the passengers got more and more bored and fractious. Most people shared cabins: they fought with their companions, and became childishly cantankerous over a small piece of soap. It was no use telling them how lucky they were to be sailing on a clipper, clipping off the time, clipping through the waters up the east coast of South America: the journey may be one of the fastest but it was *interminable*. The passengers put on amateur productions in which Mrs Ray starred with much success. And then, having been inflamed by Mrs Ray, certain noisome passengers started insisting that they too join the evening poker school; the quiet corner became louder; in the evenings Gwenlliam and Colleen collected serious winnings from the men from California with money in their pockets.

'Good,' whispered Gwenlliam.

*

On and on and on went the days. Just occasionally, locked away for so much of the time, Gwenlliam wondered, with a beating heart, if she would really go insane and make Mr Doveribbon's stories true after all. In her locked and lonely cabin she plied her needle.

Thinking of her family, she knew it was peculiar the way she thought about her dead brother and sister and herself: she never thought of what they had all become after they had been kidnapped away to their new, hated world of cruel, cold hearts: she thought only of them as children when their beautiful mother waved to them from the meadows of dancing flowers and called them home in the dusk from where they played for hours on the long, long sand. Because the time after that was too painful to recall.

But once, one bad day locked in her cabin with the sea grey and nothing on the horizon but grey sky, the terrible memories did win: Gwenlliam thought of Manon weeping wildly, walking round and round one of the grand rooms in her nightgown (her beautiful nightgowns for her new, beautiful life). *I HATE being married, nobody told me it would be so terrible, Gwennie, so terrible and so ugly – he tries to do such disgusting things to me, he hurts me and he laughs – never marry, never marry, it is a trick!* and afterwards potassium acid that burnt stomachs, and the wedding dress. And Morgan, her beloved little brother with his headaches, rampaging and stealing her jewellery and painting wild pictures of rage. But when he was fifteen Morgan had also painted a most beautiful picture of three fair children in the distance on a long shore; they bent to the shells and the seaweed and the driftwood, you could see the tide, far out in the distance. That beautiful, beautiful painting, Gwenlliam knew, was kept locked away now in one of her mother's old battered travelling trunks. But wild, uncontrollable Morgan had still kept the memories too: *I know Morgan had not seen that long shore of Gwyr since he was five years old he simply painted it from his memories.* And, quite suddenly, tears fell down Gwenlliam's face, the embroidery dropped to the floor and she wept and wept in the locked cabin as the years of unhappiness rolled over her: her perfidious father who tried to smile and her cold step-mother and her drunken, bullying grandfather. She wept and wept: in desperation she put her head right outside, through the small porthole space; the wind whipped and burned at her skin but she would not move. She would not move until the shuddering, uncontrollable weeping had stopped. Even then she did not move: breathed in the sea, in and out: just the old song still: *when that I was a little tiny boy with a heigh ho, the wind and the rain*, and two small ghosts seemed to hover there, in the grey, louring, endless sky.

Shshshshshshshshshsh called the sea outside her little porthole that night as the clipper sailed on. *Shshshshshshshshshsh* called the sea in her dreams.

Someone started a ship's newspaper, interviewed passengers. Open, inquisitive Americans asked handsome Mr Doveribbon all sorts of personal questions: about his journey, about the mad girl, asking him if he was rich, making him extremely irritable and uncomfortable. A plain girl travelling with her mother fell in love with him, followed him wherever he went, making him more irritable still. When she wept and declared her love he was most unkind. And the bored passengers now gambled on everything, not just on cards: on how much gold was languishing in the hold of course; on the date the clipper would get to New York; on the time of day the clipper would get to New York; on what dastardly food would be served for dinner as the meals became less varied the longer they were at sea. If fresh fish was caught it was a triumphant occasion shared by the whole ship: much money was bet on the weight of the catch. The depths of boredom were reached when in despair they gambled large sums on who amongst them could hold their breath the longest: a man who had owned a dry goods store in San Francisco and made his fortune who nobody liked because he had charged even more than the usual Californian high prices, held his breath, had a heart attack, and died, which at least enlivened things briefly; he was wrapped in canvas and buried overboard somewhere in the huge Atlantic Ocean and the captain asked that God might have mercy on his soul. Gwenlliam, locked in her cabin, shared none of these activities; snippets were recounted by Mrs Colleen Ray at the poker school.

And the *Sea Bullet* sailed on: past islands, romantic place-names again that they could not see: they passed Martinique it was said; Guadaloupe.

They were coming near to North America: Gwenlliam and Colleen, in their few moments free of Mr Doveribbon's atten-tion, talked and planned as best they could. 'If only this ship would call somewhere!' muttered Gwenlliam to Colleen between her teeth as they spent precious time during her after-noon walk leaning together on the deck rail, Mr Doveribbon not far away, keeping an eye on them while discussing matters in the city of London with the doctor. 'I am an acrobat! I could seize a rope, swing onto a pier and be gone! That's my work! That's what I do!' Yet all the time she kept her voice low and her face blank. They thought that it was not definite, but prob-able, that her family somehow knew by now what had happened to her: Gwenlliam trusted that Peggy Walker had somehow sent a letter the fastest way possible, across the isthmus. It was even possible, she said, that her step-father might be even now boarding all sorts of ships with police re-inforcements (perhaps – though she did not say this to Colleen – even with the tall Frankie Fields who had equalled her at poker and intruded into her dreams). 'But there is no way they could know which ship I am on: how will they find me?'

'But maybe you can just jump off on to the pier, as you say, when we arrive in New York!'

'*Of course* I am planning to do that. While you are screaming and having hysterics! But – as long as he can't – when I'm locked in the cabin he could do anything – Colleen he *mustn't* get a chance to chloroform me again!'

'Is there more chloroform? The bastard!'

'I do not *know!* That's what I worry about most. But how can I get into his cabin when he locks me in mine?'

'Leave it to me. What does chloroform look like?' Gwenlliam began to explain but Mr Doveribbon approached: luckily the captain called to him, and he turned away again to the bridge.

'Have you smelt chloroform?' said Gwenlliam quickly.

'No!'

'It is – it is slightly sweet, not unpleasant, it doesn't have any colour – I remember we saw it at the hospital and it was in a glass bottle with a stopper,' she kept her eye on where the two men were talking above them, 'though who knows how Mr Doveribbon transports it or where he keeps it.' Above them white sails billowed, a sailor was up on one of the masts, untying a tangled rope.

'We'd be looking for something a bit like a bottle of water then?'

'Ye–es, a bottle of water with a sweet smell. And – I think I remember the surgeon in the hospital brought it out of a dark cupboard – the midgets told me that some of these things have to be stored in the dark.'

At that moment Mr Doveribbon came down the steps from the bridge, he was smiling slightly.

'Leave it to me,' said Colleen again, she was smiling slightly also; that very afternoon she caught a handsome steward in an embrace in a dim passageway, asked for a favour, promised one in return. The steward used his passkey to pass into Mr Doveribbon's cabin while poker was being played upstairs; the sweet colourless liquid was found and thrown into the dark, night sea; the bottle was filled with water and replaced; when that was accomplished the steward passed the poker school and nodded: later that night he was given a favour in return, as promised. In the night the handsome steward told Colleen Ray he had seen something else also: he had found a parcel of hair, a woman's hair. *I didn't touch it,* he said, *it seemed a bit spooky.* This information un-nerved even Colleen: she decided not to mention this part to Gwenlliam.

Mr Doveribbon complained loudly some days later (he had been checking the chloroform for its next outing) that his cabin had been entered and private matters stolen. But when the handsome steward asked in concerned tones what he had lost, Mr Doveribbon did not specify. Of course he suspected Gwenlliam, but Gwenlliam was with him at all times when he did not lock her in her cabin. He wondered: could chloroform turn to water if it was thrown about in a storm as he himself had been thrown about? Or could Mrs Ray have entered his cabin and searched his baggage? He regarded everybody on board with great suspicion and malice; this treacherous man concocted stories in his mind of treachery by others.

But for Gwenlliam it seemed that the worst part of her

ordeal was over: *no more chloroform!* She hugged Mrs Colleen Ray: her eyes began to recover their old sparkle. Now she had often to look down demurely as she thought of being so soon with her loved ones: how much she longed to see them again: she pictured them all waiting at Battersea Gardens, or down on the East River docks.

And Gwen and Colleen had at least one fail-safe plan should all else fail: Mr Doveribbon had no authority over, or key for the cabin of, Mrs Ray of the Royal Theatre, New Zealand, who when the *Sea Bullet* docked at last, would go immediately to Maiden Lane before she rejoined 'The Bandit Chief' in Baltimore.

However. The conversations between the sea-captain and Mr Doveribbon, begun so long ago in the Boadwalk saloon, were now coming to their extremely mutually-advantageous climax. And their plans did not include Mrs Colleen Ray of the Royal Theatre, New Zealand.

43

If the star of 'The Bandit Chief' had not been intimately involved for some time with the beautiful helmsman of the beautiful clipper, Gwenlliam would never have known what was to happen to her next. However one warm, balmy evening (cushions in a secluded lifeboat in a secluded corner), the helmsman, off the wheel for four hours, confided in the actress that the *Sea Bullet* was making a brief detour into the port of Norfolk in Virginia in the next few days.

At once she was alert. But she stroked his chest lazily, in great admiration. 'Why is that, my handsome, handsome young man? I thought we were non-stop to New York.' She yawned, relaxed and fulfilled – and wide, wide awake.

'The captain says the diversion is to drop two passengers who are going direct to Boston.' Colleen sat up slowly and carefully, partly at the information, partly because the lifeboat swayed and squeaked if they were overly energetic.

'Two passengers?'

'But I know him, the old braggart, he would never divert when speed is of the essence, records are being broken – not for a passenger anyway. I think – I'm not so bright but –'

'You are very bright to me,' she said, kissing his cheek, extremely wide awake now.

'–but I just wonder, just wonder you understand, I'm guessing, but I've got no proof, if there might be some transference of gold.'

'Gold?'

'I heard the rumours before we left California. They don't tell the man at the wheel, you know! But we're carrying a huge amount of gold, that's sure. They wouldn't be able to get up to any shenanigans in New York, not a clipper, and everyone waiting for her, coming to admire her. But: unscheduled, Norfolk, Virginia . . . some of it could be dropped off, papers fiddled with – it happens all the time.'

'Norfolk, Virginia,' said Colleen thoughtfully. He lifted the long hair slowly, ran his hands through, pulled her to him.

'Yeah. I've heard all the passengers guessing about our cargo, betting money on it! But if I know for certain that we *are* carrying gold, pal, there'll be others who'll know too. I don't know what the plan is and maybe I'm being a mite suspicious, but something funny is going on.' Mrs Ray smothered the beautiful, beautiful helmsman with her hair, and bent to him as the *Sea Bullet* sailed on.

'Don't laugh, but I think I have uncovered a plot more unlikely than "The Bandit Chief",' she said quietly to Gwenlliam under the cover of a particularly violent poker game. Tempers frayed almost every day now as passengers knew their destination was approaching, counting the days: luckily someone had accused the doctor of cheating, voices were raised, Mr Doveribbon could hardly not go to the doctor's aid as gentlemen stood menacingly. Colleen quickly explained what she had learned. 'But never mind the gold, do you think the

426

disembarking passengers might be you? Two passengers going direct to Boston, he said it was.'

'I should think it is almost certainly us,' said Gwenlliam slowly. He knows I have family in New York, and he is always plotting and planning with the captain, they seem to be great friends.'

'Well, I could disembark in Norfolk also and see what happens to you, Norfolk's not so far from Baltimore anyway,' offered Colleen. 'He can hardly kidnap us both!'

And Gwenlliam's eyes glittered. 'And no chloroform!' she said. 'We can't fail! God, I'm glad we have accrued money! I will divide it in half tonight, and give you half tomorrow when we play.' She thought for a moment. 'Listen, listen!' she suddenly almost hissed under the noise of the still-shouting card-players: 'I'm *not* going to Boston!' Two men were being held apart now, the doctor looked as if he had been punched right in the eye. 'If we actually dock, and it is us who are being transferred, I will jump.'

'Into the sea?'

'I'm an *acrobat* remember! And now that there is no chloroform he can't stop me physically – because I'll bite him – except –' and somewhere in amongst the noise of the nearby melee Mrs Ray's laugh could be heard because Gwen suddenly sounded so like an English lady, '– except that quite frankly I could not *bear* the taste.' Stewards were now being called for, or the captain. 'Listen, Colleen, if we dock, I can get off, I'm sure of it. And another thing: whatever happens, *we can surely send a telegraph from Norfolk, Virginia!* It's near to New York, it's not like being across the other side of America! Listen, listen, I've thought of something else: I know of a man who everyone knows, everyone on all the New York docks, and he knows my step-father the policeman. I'll divide the money and whatever else happens one of us can send him a telegraph: George Macmillan, New York Docks.' There was nearly murder now in the group of gambling men: in strode the captain, shouting, and at last the crowd dispersed and the doctor was saved from further pugilism, and the next night Gwenlliam managed to put eighty-seven dollars into Mrs Ray's hands, wrapped carefully in the *Sea Bullet* tablecloth she had embroidered.

'It's a present for you, Colleen,' she said at the poker table. 'Some of my own embroidery.'

'Thank you, Gwen! How charming!' said Mrs Colleen Ray and she placed the parcel very carefully beside her as the poker game went on.

Then, that same evening, after the poker school had disbanded (Mr Doveribbon looking at his watch and taking his charge away as usual), the sails began flapping in a different way; it became clear that *Sea Bullet* was changing course. Gwenlliam stared out of her porthole in excitement; after some time she thought she could see lights. Quickly she put her poker winnings in the bottom of her cloak pockets. In less than an hour Mr Doveribbon suddenly came into Gwenlliam's cabin carrying his luggage: he quickly put her meagre belongings into a small bag: she rather pugnaciously added one of the ubiquitous embroidered napkins. 'For a souvenir,' she said shortly, 'for wherever we're going next since we seem to be going somewhere.' He gave her no more information.

'Come along,' he said shortly. 'Don't think of trying anything.'

'What do you think I'll try?' she answered quickly, putting her cloak about her. 'Do you think I'll jump!'

'Did you think I did not remember, Miss Preston, that you told me you had family in New York when we first met? I do not wish to go to New York.' (He certainly did not want Gwenlliam to ascertain that her mother had drowned long ago.) He looked quickly about the cabin, took her arm tightly and half-pulled her on to the dark deck. Several fussy little Norfolk lighters had already appeared with lamps, helping the big vessel into the harbour to dock, moving about the water as the clipper furled sails, throwing ropes upwards. A voice from one of lighters called up, 'Name. Business.'

'Clipper *Sea Bullet*. Passenger transfer to *SS Scorpion*,' called the captain with a loud hailer. 'Docking briefly.' There was great excitement among the passengers as the ship made to tie up at long last; people wanted to get off, in fact insisted on getting off no matter what the captain ordered: *Land!* they had shouted in delight as the coast came nearer and nearer: they could see civilisation: *Land!* Gwenlliam, on deck, caught Colleen's eye, stared at ropes and poles; the captain shouted orders; under the sound of his voice she whispered to Colleen, but very, very firmly: GEORGE MACMILLAN, NEW YORK DOCKS.

Ropes were now thrown down on to the wharf. On the other side of the wharf they could see the shape of the side-wheel of a steamer, and its funnels. '*SS Scorpion*,' called the steamship's captain now, from his loud-hailer. 'Direct to Boston. Been expecting you, *Sea Bullet*. Leaving for Boston in the morning.' Passengers on the deck of *SS Scorpion* waved upwards to the tall, shadowed beautiful clipper.

'Passengers for you, *Scorpion*,' called the captain again. 'And some luggage,' he added.

On deck Mr Doveribbon was very thrown to see that Mrs Ray from the Royal Theatre, New Zealand, surrounded by cabin trunks and carrying a lamp, was preparing to disembark also, but then it became clear that several passengers from the

Sea Bullet were taking advantage of the unexpected stop and had decided immediately, whatever the captain said, to carry on their journey by land; some others asked if they too might board the *Scorpion* and go straight to Boston. There was a great deal of negotiating, and shouting about luggage, and to-ing and fro-ing of people and boxes and large containers in the night, ropes being tightened, men running, carrying things, a gangplank for the disembarking passengers was being wheeled along the wharf towards the clipper, lamps swinging, voices calling. Colleen saw Gwenlliam's glittering eyes as she watched the dockmen and the ropes carefully: Mr Doveribbon was holding her arm but Gwenlliam was taut, like a spring.

Colleen kissed Gwenlliam goodbye, quickly whispering into her hair. 'Be careful. I'll shine the lamp on the rope as best I can. If you don't get away I'll send the telegraph.' And then she wept loudly as she kissed her friend goodbye again very publicly and theatrically, 'With whom shall I play such poker again!' – she was an actress after all – and a little smattering of passengers leaning on deck cheered and reached out their hands to say goodbye to the flame-haired Colleen Ray who had brightened up their journey and Mr Doveribbon was forced to move back slightly and at that moment Gwenlliam broke free from his grip, climbed on to the deck rail nimbly, and jumped towards the tightened rope that reached down to the wharf: the rope could be seen clearly in the light of several lamps, including, very quickly, Colleen's. Afterwards, passengers on both vessels were not sure what they had observed: everything happened so quickly but there was a glorious moment when the mad girl who played such excellent poker flew downwards, caught the rope as her cloak and her skirts billowed out behind her, poised for a second like some beautiful shadowy bird as she looked about her, and then quick as a flash she had slithered easily down the rope and was on the wharf. The captain leapt across to the still moving gangplank first, followed by Mr Doveribbon: they were both shouting. 'STOP HER! SHE IS INSANE AND DANGEROUS!' Gwenlliam ran, the people on the wharf didn't stop her, even parted in amazement as they watched. Along the wooden wharf she ran fast. And then in the darkness her skirt caught on a cargo hook, she stumbled and fell forwards as the hook pulled the skirt: even as she picked herself up the captain caught up to her and grabbed her, Mr Doveribbon took the other arm and it was over: coins fell on to the slatted wooden boards of the wharf, some rolled onwards, some fell into the water in the darkness as Gwenlliam was bundled – fiercely dragged, you might almost say – on to *SS Scorpion* on the other side of the same wharf. It happened so quickly that Colleen was greatly taken aback: she could hardly believe it: still on the *Sea Bullet* herself she saw at once that the captain and Mr Doveribbon held Gwenlliam in a vice-like grip between them, Gwenlliam's feet seemed not to touch the ground until she was aboard the other ship, bound for Boston.

'It was the mad girl,' Colleen heard people say all around her. 'Did you see her fly?' and their voices carried a hint of admiration.

Down on the wharf herself now a few minutes later, people milling about in the darkness, the last of the boxes being transferred between the vessels, Colleen stared up but could not see if Gwenlliam was on the deck of the *Scorpion*; she supposed they had taken her quickly below: she was shocked at the vicious way they had held the girl. *Bastards.* She waved upwards and called out in a voice that travelled easily upwards: 'Goodbye, dearest Gwen! Goodbye, dear Mr Doveribbon! May you travel safely to Great Britain!'

'We're off again!' called the Captain of the *Sea Bullet*, back on board the clipper. People watched the dark and beautiful shape move quietly away from the dock with the help of the lighters, and heard the sails rise and the wind catch as the *Sea Bullet* put out to sea and turned towards New York.

The helmsman looked heartbroken as the woman with the long red hair waved her arm to him, in farewell.

Colleen Ray then stood holding her lamp so that she could be easily seen by the men on the wharf and hopefully by Gwen on the steamship. 'Can someone take me to your best hotel!' she called loudly. 'I have all my luggage here,' and there were many acquiescent replies.

'Just on the corner here, pal,' they called and they lifted her trunks cheerfully on to their shoulders and walked back along the wooden wharf. 'Just follow us. What's your name? What are you doing in Norfolk? Are you married?'

She bent to pick up her smallest bag and follow them, looked back once more at *SS Scorpion* to see if she could catch a last glimpse of Gwen – and heard two men talking quietly just as they went aboard the sidewheeler.

'Everything on ok?'

'Yeah.'

'We're calling it a coal stop,' one muttered. 'Midnight off Sandy Hook.'

44

They heard Alfie running up the stairs to the attic before they saw him because, as well as the heavy pounding footsteps which sounded as if they belonged to a giant monster, he kept calling: 'CORDELIA! ARTHUR!' in a voice that would have awakened every one of the boarders living in Celine's House and probably the doctor next door as well. La Grande Celine with her black eye-patch was striding upwards behind him, anxious not to miss a thing. They burst into the attic like musket balls.

'I can't wait to meet this girl of yours,' Alfie cried. 'Clever! Intelligent beyond words! I want her to work for me! I'll pay her whatever she wants!'

'What? *What?*'

'She's so clever! She remembered the name I use, not Alfie Tyrone but George Macmillan! And she wasn't even here when Queenie and I found each other! Without her cleverness, we'd have lost her!'

'What is it?' cried Cordelia. She was actually pulling at his waistcoat.

'What have you got, Alfie?' asked Arthur, holding Cordelia to him.

'Somehow she's managed to use the telegraph! A young girl who's been kidnapped if we understand things, using the telegraph! From a port: Norfolk in Virginia. It came through this morning.' He pulled out a paper, but instead of reading it himself he gave it to Regina to read.

GEORGE MACMILLAN, NEW YORK DOCKS
TELL ARTHUR SS SCORPION DIRECT BOSTON,
COALING MIDNIGHT SANDY HOOK LEAVING
NORFOLK AM 19 G

'AM 19 G,' Regina repeated uncertainly.

'G! It's Gwennie! Where's Norfolk?' Cordelia was again pulling at Alfie's waistcoat in a most uncharacteristic manner.

'Norfolk, Virginia!' cried Alfie. 'Just down the road. Leaving there morning of the 19th, it's on its way now! And do you know what is just coming in to Battery Gardens? The clipper *Sea Bullet* that young Danny O'Reilly saw in Panama! Our guesses have been fortuitous!'

'AM 19 G, yes, yes I see.' Now Regina nodded sagely.

'She's alive, she's nearly here! *She's nearly here!*' Now Rillie held Cordelia; Arthur was suddenly gathering papers together.

Alfie shouted again, waving his papers. 'We hadn't thought young Doveribbon might be so clever! Off the *Sea Bullet*, which must have stopped at Norfolk for some reason, they must have been on her, they couldn't have got here so quick elseways. Then direct to Boston, by-passing New York where very likely he has ascertained Gwenlliam has a family who might be looking for her! So what a bit of luck for us, eh, Arthur, that it's coaling at Sandy Hook!'

'And then direct Boston–Liverpool,' said Monsieur Roland. 'Many ships take that route of course – we took that route!'

'*She's nearly here!*' cried Cordelia again, and tears of relief poured down her face.

'Wait a minute,' said Detective-Inspector Arthur Rivers slowly. And then loudly: '*Wait a minute!*' Till now he had said nothing after he heard Alfie's news. Everybody was immediately very quiet. 'Wait a minute,' he said softly a third time. 'There is coal in Norfolk, quite enough coal to get to Boston – nothing wrong with Norfolk coal, Norfolk is a port like any other.' They saw him thinking aloud, marshalling the facts, trying to join them together even as he uttered them. 'Why would a steamship require to be coaling again off New York harbour – at midnight – only a short time later? And something else: why would a clipper stop at Norfolk? The clippers are always competing, flying up the coast trying to break each other's records, not stopping off at smaller ports.'

'It could have broken down?' said Monsieur Roland.

'It could have.'

Alfie said: '*SS Scorpion*, I know her, plies up and down to Chagres, large side-wheeler. Hmmmm. Some of those sea-captains are a law unto theirselves, let me tell you. I know stories about autocratic sea-captains that would make your hair stand on end – Arthur, you know as well as me a lot of them are near enough pirates! If they want to stop outside Sandy Hook, they'll stop outside Sandy Hook.'

'Exactly,' said Arthur Rivers. 'And we wouldn't necessarily know about it then, would we? I wonder – I just wonder what cargo, apart from our dearest Gwennie, might have been also transferred in Norfolk from the *Sea Bullet* from California to the sidewheeler *SS Scorpion*.'

'It doesn't *matter!*' cried Cordelia. 'As long as we somehow get her off.'

'I think it matters very much, Cordelia,' said Arthur.

'Stop thinking about cargoes and smuggling and gangs! How can you! *It doesn't matter!* We just have to find Gwennie. Where are you going? You can't go until we've decided what to do!' Cordelia's face was pale, her skin icy in the hot humid attic. Arthur had already picked up his hat.

'I have decided what to do, Cordelia, and I think it would be a good idea if you tried to get some sleep.'

'Arthur, please, *please*, there must be some way I can be on a police boat at Sandy Hook with you!'

'No way at all. Go to bed now.'

'*I have to be there!*'

They all saw how Arthur Rivers, on the edge of total exhaustion himself, tried to control himself now. 'Listen, Cordelia,' he said. 'Listen to me carefully. The reason *SS Scorpion* is planning to stop at Sandy Hook is possibly, not definitely but possibly, because the captain – if he has had any dealings in Norfolk with the cargo of the *Sea Bullet* from California, which would almost certainly be gold – because the captain is in some sort of cahoots with the Daybreak Boys from the East River, or some other criminal gang. Even involving damned coal-lighters! Excuse me. That's a new one. Somehow Gwennie has obtained that information – and when we meet her again I shall be extremely grateful to find out how. In the meantime we *have* to stop the *Scorpion* to get Gwennie off. So I will get the authority and enough boats and men to stop the *Scorpion* by saying I suspect gold smuggling from California – I don't know if it *is* gold smuggling: but even the City Fathers will not countenance gold smuggling under any circumstances – and that way we will get Gwennie off whatever else happens. But it may be unpleasant and it will certainly be dangerous. There could be guns and ugly tempers and it will – I am certain – all take place in darkness.'

'I'm not afraid of guns and darkness!'

'It will be dangerous for Gwennie too!'

'Then I must be there!'

'You will hinder us!' He turned and went down the stairs.

As Alfie moved to follow, he said kindly to Cordelia: 'If I were you, my lovely, I'd get some rest before tomorrow, your daughter will need you when she gets here and you are very tired,' but Cordelia did not hear.

It was the greatest of ill-luck for very many people that Mr Doveribbon had chosen the *SS Scorpion* to continue the journey.

45

There were six police boats waiting. None showed any light; each held ten men crammed into the space available. The police boats were waiting behind the narrow peninsula, Sandy Hook, at the far end of the harbour of New York.

There were six police boats waiting, none showing any light (hidden by the spit of land), as several sets of muffled oars, almost silently, dipped in and out of the dark water in the harbour, making for Sandy Hook also.

The moon came and went from behind hot, louring night clouds; sometimes the sea caught moonlight, then the clouds rolled over and the sea was in darkness once more.

There are all sorts of sounds across water at night: sometimes fish jump; always the sea washes *shshshshshshshsh* against the shore and then pulls back: in and out gently in the darkness if the night is calm, as this night was calm, *shshshshshshshsh*. Voices can often be heard clearly across the water at night. Muffled oars could be fish, or the sea touching the shore; voices could belong to boatmen or then again to people on the dark land: it is often hard to tell.

The moon came out from the clouds again, catching tiny ripples, making them shine.

And then they heard it, far out. The sound of the side-wheel ploughing through the water: the sound of the steamship.

In the dark, secreted police-boats they made signs but not sounds.

In the rowboats, oars pulled in now, bobbing up and down on the water, they made no sound as they heard the ship they were waiting for. Coming nearer. The rowboats could not see the police boats. The police boats behind the spit of land had no view of the rowboats.

The only other sound was the calm *shshshshshshshsh* that still went on and on, the tide ruffled by small night winds as it approached the shore and drew back again: *shshshshshshshsh*: the sound of the sea.

And then, lamps could be seen from within the harbour, coming towards Sandy Hook. As it drew nearer, not in anyway hiding itself, they saw that it was a coal-lighter indeed. In the middle of the night.

Still the moon drifted in and out from behind the clouds.

The sound of the side-wheel grew louder and the shadow of *SS Scorpion* came nearer and nearer – and then the sound of it was dampened down and it drifted quietly. There was a splash as it dropped anchor.

As the coal-lighter approached, calling to the *Scorpion*, as if to go about its odd night business of feeding coal, the rowboats came silently out of their resting place, oars moving so very quietly in the water, undetected under the shouts of men on the coal-lighter and the answering shouts of the men on the *Scorpion*. Shadows moved across water.

Unexpected shadows: shadows of men climbing from small rowing boats on to the anchor ropes in the darkness, not yet seen by the *Scorpion* or by the coal-lighter but seen now by Detective-Inspector Arthur Rivers.

It was only then, seeing the shadows, that Arthur Rivers understood quite how dangerous this all was. He gave a low, low whistle. Not one gang. But two. Instead of boxes being quietly transferred from the *Scorpion* to the coal-lighter, the unexpected Daybreak Boys in their rowing boats had their own plan: they were going to do battle with whomsoever had arranged the coal-lighter: *another gang was invading their territory.*

Inspector Rivers felt his heart pounding, *Gwennie in all this*, motioned the new information to his men: the small police boats held ready. Frankie Fields, in the same boat as his boss, felt his heart beating fast also: this is not where he would have chosen to have his next meeting with Miss Gwenlliam Preston, who had remained in his heart and sent him messages from the other side of America.

Each of the police boats carried a very large oil lamp. Arthur Rivers muttered instructions and then his boat set out alone in darkness to the far side of the *Scorpion*. The noise from the coal-lighter drowned the sound of the police boat. When his vessel was in the shadows he gave the sign: a loud whistle. At once five oil lamps flared as the other five police boats moved forward and shone light on to the *Scorpion*: the scenes on the water became clear for there was no coaling, certainly: men climbing ropes like monkeys to board the *Scorpion*; other men passing boxes into the coal-lighter; wild shouts as the gangs realised there were two gangs present, not one; as two men met who did not like what they saw when they saw each other, a knife gleamed, a body fell into the water. The police shouted, moved closer to the vessels, began battle, a shot rang out from one of the rowboats.

There were several rope ladders over the far side, boxes were being lowered; while three policemen wrestled with a box and two men, Arthur Rivers and Frankie Fields, quickly climbed aboard the *Scorpion*.

He had to risk it. 'Gwennie!' he shouted, *'Gwennie!'*

The sound of running footsteps, of men fighting, but no Gwenlliam.

He ran down iron steps to passages and cabins: *surely it will be a first class cabin, otherwise Gwennie would have had to share with other women, he would not have allowed that surely? Or was he himself sharing her cabin?* Passengers either emerged in terror or locked their doors: all looked fearful at whatever was happening above and below them: no Gwennie.

First class cabins: this passage, it had to be this passage. He yelled: 'Gwennie! *Gwennie!* Where are you?' He heard, at once, a frantic knocking further down: as suddenly the knocking stopped and then he thought he heard a muffled cry. Somewhere in this narrow passageway. *'Gwennie!!'* he shouted again, 'I need to know where you are!' and from a cabin towards the end of the passageway there was a dull thud. *There? Maybe?* With Frankie beside him he did not stop to consider further, he used his bulk to crash against the cabin door. It gave partly the first time, Frankie added to the bulk and the small door splintered and crashed open and there she was: Gwenlliam: held by a man wielding an iron bar and a knife. She was gagged with something that looked like a table napkin tied by a man's cravat, and her face was bleeding and her eyes were wild and terrified: she saw him: she tried to escape, to throw herself towards him, tears ran down her face, she was trying to say something to him but he could not understand: it was Frankie who at the very same moment tackled Mr Doveribbon: he threw himself at the man and the bar: the knife flew across the cabin and Mr Doveribbon screamed, fell heavily against the bed, and was then silent: knocked out by his own iron bar and Frankie Fields.

'Take her!' said Arthur to Frankie, untying the cravat and the table napkin, '*Mama!*' she screamed as soon as she could speak, 'Where is Mama? *I have found her hair! He's carrying her hair!*' Quickly he held her.

'She is alive, she is well, she is waiting for you at Maiden Lane!' but he saw that she looked at him in disbelief: 'They took her *hair*, not her life, Gwennie,' he said gently and only then could she throw her arms around him, sobbing and shaking, this beloved girl. 'Just get her safely ashore,' he said to Frankie, 'don't think of anything else. Go with him, dearest girl,' he said quickly to Gwenlliam and Frankie needed no second instruction although Gwenlliam looked back at Arthur in confusion. But Arthur had already picked up the inert Mr Doveribbon's iron bar, motioned them away.

He moved back on deck where pandemonium reigned: crewmen fighting gang members fighting other gang members, fighting members of his force, all in half darkness and lamp-light and shadows. The captain of the *Scorpion* saw the Inspector, shouted to him: 'Get these criminals off my ship!'

Inspector Rivers blew his whistle loudly so that it could be heard everywhere above the fighting and the crashing and somewhere then a gun fired again; he leaned on the deck-rail out of the lamplight and called out to his men below to board the coal-lighter and take her ashore to be searched; he called for his men aboard the *Scorpion* to surround the gang-members and the crew. Some of the brawling men headed for the deck rail, jumped into the dark water. 'Scupper the rowboats too,' called the Inspector. 'Someone down there has got a gun, let them swim.' And then to the captain of the *Scorpion*: 'I must ask you to bring your ship ashore also, sir.'

'I am on my way to Boston!' shouted the captain. 'And to Boston I shall go. There is no law against refuelling!' and he fell upon the Inspector in a rage.

'There is nevertheless a law against smuggling, Captain,' and the iron bar came down heavily on to the captain's shoulder. 'My name is Detective-Inspector Rivers,' and he showed his badge. 'Order your ship into the harbour, Captain,' he repeated calmly. 'It will be released in the morning if there has been a mistake.'

A crowd of passengers had finally gathered on deck, saw clearly the situation. 'Anything we can do to help you, Inspector?' said a young man keenly.

'This is piracy,' screamed the captain. 'I am being attacked!'

'Thank you,' said Inspector Rivers. 'Just persuade the captain here that there must be a short detour into New York. I do apologise for the drama on your journey – if the captain co-operates you will not be delayed long.' And he stepped over several inert bodies on the deck and gave the iron bar to the keen young man. It was suddenly very quiet on the *SS Scorpion*.

Just as quickly as the violence had begun, it was over.

Or so it seemed.

The coal-lighter and the *Scorpion* slowly made their way into the harbour towards the East River docks. Arthur Rivers counted the police boats escorting the little flotilla, their oil lamps showing the way: six: one of them far ahead, almost at the docks. He sighed with relief: Gwennie was safe. He suddenly staggered against the deck rail, understood how exhausted he was, but it did not matter. The gangs had been stopped till next time but in the end that did not matter either.

Gwennie was safe.

He sent someone below to arrest Mr Doveribbon.

*

The ships were tied. Various crew members of both ships were escorted up to the prison. Several gang members – some of them still screaming obscenities at one another: Daybreak Boys versus Dead Rabbits and Plug Uglies combined – were now in cells. And a pale-faced Mr Doveribbon was introduced, down in the cells also, to Detective-Inspector Arthur Rivers.

Mr Doveribbon was obviously terrified but trying to hide behind a mad, wild bravado. 'You cannot hold me here in this dangerous madhouse!' He indicated the sounds of the gang members. 'This pig-pen! You have no jurisdiction over me. I am an Englishman!'

'I am an Englishman also, and you had no jurisdiction over my daughter.'

Mr Doveribbon for all his bravado was now shocked. *Cordelia Preston had married a policeman.* But – thank God – an Englishman at least. 'Listen, man, wait till you understand. I did everything for her, *everything*.'

'Including drowning her mother?'

'I don't know what you are talking about,' but the policeman silently held up the satchel of hair. Mr Doveribbon panicked, his voice rose into a scream as if Arthur was hitting him, although at that point he was not. 'I had nothing to do with that, I was sailing to America, I can prove it. Listen, listen, you're British, you understand these things. She will be one of the richest women in Great Britain! Everything I did, I did for her.'

'No, you did not. You did it for yourself.'

'Do you know the fortune that is involved?'

'My daughter made it plain to you she is not interested in that particular fortune.'

'Your daughter, your daughter! You have got above yourself, man.' Mr Doveribbon bravely called on all his English *hauteur.* 'She is the daughter and the grand-daughter of British noblemen.'

'And you will be tried for kidnapping and attempted murder, Mr Doveribbon, I do assure you. It will do you good to spend some time in America, as I am afraid is going to be your fate, and sample their feelings about nobility.'

'I do not believe it. I simply do not believe that any person can refuse half of Wales if it is there for the taking. She obviously does not understand.'

Arthur Rivers suddenly felt very tired.

'Goodnight, Mr Doveribbon,' he said quietly and he left the police cell and locked the door, exactly as Mr Doveribbon had been locking the door, all around the Americas.

As Arthur came upstairs Frankie Fields had just arrived back at the Halls of Justice, almost weeping himself at the joyous scenes in Maiden Lane. 'They are waiting for you at home, sir.'

It was almost morning.

46

Dawn light turned into morning light turned into the midday
sun: all the attic windows were open; the room was hot, sti-
fling, but nobody cared: shoes, jackets, hats all discarded and
ice acquired by Celine and Rillie from the iceman on the corner
as soon as it was light. They had put ice on Gwenlliam's
bruised face, too, Mr Doveribbon had attacked her when she
began to scream when she found the hair as he tried to lock
them together away from the fighting; he hit her again when
she tried to let Arthur know her whereabouts on the *SS
Scorpion*.

At first Cordelia and Gwenlliam had just held each other,
literally unable to speak. After some moments Gwenlliam
put up her hands, smoothed her mother's head. 'I *saw* it!
The black and the white. I knew it was your hair.' Tears poured
down her face, Cordelia tried to wipe them away: 'I'm here,
darling, we're both here!' and Rillie poured large glasses of port
and they all cried and laughed together at last and Gwenlliam
hugged Monsieur Roland, hugged Rillie, hugged Regina, hugged
Celine.

And then Gwenlliam said suddenly: 'But – where is Mrs
Spoons?' Looking round the familiar attic she had dreamed of,

knowing something was different. And then she looked quickly at Rillie. And then just as quickly understood, from Rillie's face: quick tears came to her eyes again as she hugged Rillie tightly again. 'Ohhhh,' breathed Gwenlliam: it was a sigh and a cry, combined.

'You have been away over a year, dearest girl. And she was a very old lady.' Gwenlliam was silent, she had thought so much about being with all her family, had not expected anything to change.

'I thought it would all be exactly the same and –' she looked again at her mother's head, '– nothing is the same at all.' She wiped at the tears on her face. 'I used to sing her song, Rillie, when I was locked in my cabin.'

'She could still sing,' said Rillie smiling, and for a moment it was almost as if they could hear that high, frail voice: *Whistle and I'll come to ye, my lad*.

Regina, who never cried in normal life, cried too, and hugged the girl again; then read out the headline from the morning newspaper: '**NEW YORK POLICE FOIL GOLD SMUGGLERS!** Well, that'll make our Arthur proud!'

Gwenlliam took off at last her strange orphan clothing, knowing – as she had always known – that with all the people of her odd family around her – although one of them looked different and one of them was gone – she was not an orphan at all.

La Grande Celine, unwilling to miss a single word, had actually decided not to open her dining saloon: an action unheard of; Maybelle and Blossom and the waitresses Ruby and Pearl kicked up their heels among the empty tables in the large empty room, Pearl played the harmonium, and sang.

> *Gin a body*
> *meet a body*
> *coming thru' the rye*
> *Gin a body*
> *kiss a body*
> *Need a body cry!*

The lively, carefree song echoed out into Maiden Lane. A notice on the unopened door read:

DINING SALOON CLOSED TILL TONIGHT
DUE TO UNEXPECTED (HAPPY) CIRCUMSTANCES.

Monsieur Roland was quiet but his pale old face radiated warmth and life and – quite simply – happiness; Celine, looking at him, thought what a privilege it would be, to be loved by this old man. Even Alfie could not tear himself away to go to his business; he had arrived, hugged Gwenlliam too and told her she was a clever girl, sat next to Regina, and smiled and smiled.

In no coherent order, Gwenlliam recounted the whole extraordinary story: her terror when she found her mother's hair as Mr Doveribbon grabbed everything when the fighting began; the gangs and the brawling at Sandy Hook and Arthur arriving with Frankie Fields, rescuing Gwenlliam, sending the flotilla of boats in to New York docks. Cordelia closed her eyes for a moment as she remembered how she had tried to insist on going too, and her own stupidity. Then Gwenlliam had to describe over and over the whole kidnapped adventure: Mr Doveribbon, San Francisco, the *Moe'uhane*, chloroform ('He used *chloroform?*' Monsieur Roland suddenly raged), Panama, the *Sea Bullet*, the neverending locked days, watching the sea

448

and the sky, the Magellan Straits – and Mrs Ray from the Royal Theatre, New Zealand.

'She's a sort of version of you, Celine, I wrote about her in one of my letters. I think you must be related. It was her who sent the telegram when I was hustled away again on the *Scorpion*.'

'My, I am proud! I will be glad to be related to such a heroine!'

'I will employ you both!' cried Alfie. 'The cleverness of that telegraph!'

'It was paid for by poker winnings!' said Gwenlliam, and then had to describe the quiet little poker school that had drawn bigger players to its side, thanks again to the charms of Mrs Ray.

'However would she have known that the *Scorpion* was to call at Sandy Hook when she sent that telegraph?'

'I don't know! But Colleen Ray moves in mysterious ways,' said Gwenlliam smiling to herself.

'I want to employ her!' said Alfie again. 'Both of you! Intrepid!'

'Will she visit us?' Cordelia spoke at last. 'I would like to hug that Colleen Ray!'

'You can't tell with her where she'll turn up next, but I think she will find us – even just to hear about whether Mr Doveribbon got his retribution.' And they saw the sternness in their girl's face, something new. 'They tried to kill you, Mama!'

'Yes, and now I understand – to get me out of the way, no doubt, so that they could have you. They have spent many years of my life trying to get me out of the way because they wanted my children!'

'What *has* happened to Mr Doveribbon?' asked Monsieur Roland angrily.

449

'He was unconscious when I last saw him; if he's not dead I hope Arthur has him locked in the police cells!' said Gwenlliam, suddenly fierce. 'I hope they keep him there. Let's see how he likes it,' and they heard again the different, harder sound in her voice.

And all the time, as the attic got hotter and hotter, Gwenlliam and Cordelia still sat close together, leaning into each other as they spoke. Sometimes Cordelia would smooth the hot, damp curls of her daughter; Gwenlliam did the same to her mother's short hair almost without noticing, talking still: they sat as if they were conjoined, as indeed, because of the events of their strange life, they were. Gwenlliam heard of Danny O'Reilly bringing Peggy Walker's letter overland, of the chance of the gold nugget shaped like a small snail; they all spoke at once and questioned and shouted and laughed and wept and ranted at the Welsh nobility.

'*I do not want to be their heiress!*' cried Gwenlliam.

'You are an heiress already,' said Rillie dryly. 'Thanks to you we have enough money to live comfortably for years.'

'It is not of course my business, but are you sure, dear Gwen?' said Celine slowly at last. 'If you were an heiress it would change your life entirely and give you other freedoms.'

'*This* is my freedom!' said Gwennie, in a very firm voice. 'I've been locked up for months! They tried to kill Mama! I know the importance of money, we all in this room know the importance of money more than many people.' She turned to face Celine directly. 'I am not being romantic, I am being sensible, I never had one happy day after they took us away from Mama: my sister died, my brother died, Mama was arrested for murder – that is not freedom. Nothing at all good came to us from that family after my father betrayed us all and I *do not want* my life to be conjoined to theirs again!'

'*Ah oui, ah oui*, that is my girl that I know,' said Monsieur Roland matter-of-factly, and somehow they all laughed and Celine bowed her head in acceptance (even if she herself might have been more pragmatic had the problem been her own). And then she suddenly looked up again.

'Gwen, tell me, how is *Pierre l'Oiseau*? And is he still married?' she asked, and her one eye danced as Gwenlliam reported that there seemed to be no wife at present.

They expected Arthur. The sweltering afternoon drew down. He did not come. 'Frankie Fields said it was a huge operation: sixty police,' they kept saying to each other over and over. 'There will be so much to do still.'

'He usually sends a message,' said Cordelia in an uneasy voice as the afternoon wore on. 'Surely he would have sent a message today of all days. He would have wanted to hear your story. He hasn't heard your story.'

'And Frankie,' said Gwenlliam. 'He said he would bring him back.'

'And Frankie,' said Rillie. 'What a brave young man.'

They were all totally exhausted but they could not rest till Arthur came. Cordelia again remembered how they had parted: something caught at her heart.

Celine needed to go downstairs at last, to open the dining saloon. 'Come and eat!' she called as she finally dragged herself away and down the stairs; she came up again almost immediately with a large basket full of fruit.

'She is a very good woman,' said Monsieur Roland.

'Is she still in love with you?' teased Gwenlliam.

'Of course she is!' chimed Cordelia and Rillie together.

451

'She gave him that purple jacket!' said Rillie. 'But also, to Monsieur Roland's great relief, she showed signs of heart palpitations every time Pierre-the-bird's name was mentioned in your letters – we know you did it on purpose Gwennie! – she has other plans perhaps, if Monsieur Roland remains obdurate!'

'Pierre-the-bird needs someone like Celine. He was a great big baby about the *mosquitos*!'

'But where is Arthur?' said Cordelia.

'Frankie Fields would have come and told us,' said Gwenlliam, 'if anything was wrong. Wouldn't he?' The attic room was completely quiet for the first moment since Gwenlliam had returned; they could hear all the carts on the cobbles outside. And then very suddenly it was Gwenlliam who stood. 'But – *he* said he would come back too.' They stared at each other. 'Come on, Mama, let us at least go to the Police Department. Just in case.' Cordelia's heart caught again oddly as she stood. She tried to pull herself together.

'But I'll go, Gwennie,' she said. 'I'll look for Frankie too, you can't go anywhere, dear heart, after what you've been through. Stay here.'

'You can't go anywhere, girl,' echoed Regina to Gwenlliam. 'You've just come back from an adventure! Look at you!'

'What do you mean "look at me!"? You saw what I *was* wearing! I'm freeeee! I'm home! Mama is here. All that will sustain me, Regina. And I'm wearing a gown that fits me for the first time for months!'

'I'll go with them,' said Rillie. 'I'll look after them.'

'I'll go with them,' said Alfie. 'I'll look after them all.'

'Shall we play poker for money, Monsweer?' said Regina dryly. 'Till they return? Seeing as we're old? Someone's got to stay here in case he turns up.'

Monsieur Roland, always so undemonstrative, put his arms around Gwenlliam and held her for just a moment. 'Take care, dearest, oh dearest girl,' he said.

That morning, just before dawn, Arthur and Frankie and two other policemen, tired but all relaxed, job successfully completed, had strolled down in the darkness through the pleasant gardens by City Hall. Inspector Rivers was taking them all home to Maiden Lane for breakfast.

The gardens with the fountain, where others were waiting also.

Arthur was the first to be jumped upon; as he tried to retaliate he could see: there were at least ten of them: the policemen were already crashing on to the ground. 'Cunting spoiler! Cunting English cunting spoiler!' A heavy object smashed down on his head.

47

The four of them walked in the hot dusk: Cordelia and Rillie and Gwenlliam and Alfie all walked, trying to feel nonchalant, up beautiful Broadway lit by its beautiful gas lights; Gwenlliam could not stop herself exclaiming with pleasure as she saw it all again: the lights and the luxurious stores after the Californian tents: the people and the buildings and the brightness and the hope: *free*. People rushed past about their own energetic business, as they always did on Broadway, even in the heat. It was almost dark by the time they reached City Hall, past the park with the fountain. Behind City Hall they came to the Halls of Justice that people called *The Tombs* because of its odd architecture; here were most of the police department offices and the prison below but not for one moment did any of them spare a thought for the Englishman Mr Doveribbon, locked up somewhere near. Their footsteps echoed as they came to the empty reception hall: a man and a desk, some chairs and a long wooden bench in one corner. They presumed the man at the desk was a policeman although he was reading a penny paper and hardly looked up as they stood there. 'We're closed,' he said lazily, without standing up or directing his gaze in their direction. 'The watch-house is outside,' he said, 'if you people have been robbed, though it's probably closed by now also.'

'We're looking for Inspector Rivers,' said Cordelia firmly.

'Well, so am I,' said the policeman, still turning pages of his paper. 'We've been waiting for him and his cohorts all day. There's big reports to be filed and they ain't been done, and there's journalists wanting a story and he ain't here to satisfy them.' He still did not stand. The three women were now looking at each other in consternation.

'Listen, mate,' said Alfie and he walked right up to the desk and stood over the young policeman. 'Inspector Rivers is a blooming hero after last night and where is he? He's not at home and he's not here and we're worried about him and your mother should've taught you to stand when there's ladies present.'

'This is America, pal!' said the policeman. 'Different rules.' He sighed and unwillingly closed the paper. 'The Inspector and his special pal, Mr goodie-goodie Frankie Fields and the other goodie-goodie boys went off into the dawn when it was all over. We're not their guardians! They probably went off and got properly drunken! There's nothing else I can tell you.'

The visitors were taken aback by the unfriendliness. Hadn't Arthur just foiled a huge robbery? They did not move. 'Where is your superior? We are not leaving. This is Inspector Rivers' wife.'

The policeman, glancing vaguely in the direction of the women for the first time, looked at Alfie, surprised. 'Well, well, well. I thought it was his wife sending him all those letters,' he said. 'All those letters from London.' And he looked rather sly, indicated a pile of papers. 'Maybe he's got two wives, then, Mr goody-goody Rivers. This afternoon we decided to break open the drawer of his desk, see if we could find any clue as to his whereabouts. Just found these letters.' It was Rillie who tried quickly to gather the pages: but they all saw words on papers:

Come home . . . aren't you ashamed? . . . Elizabeth, after your beloved wife . . .

we are fine really Father, don't worry . . .

how could you do this? . . . grand-children . . .

we are fine really Father, when you can Father, I miss you father

. . . raging epidemic . . . fancy woman . . . we are in receipt of financial contributions.

'He was very secretive about them!' said the policeman jauntily. And only then did the unmannered officer look at the wife in front of him properly. She was holding one of the pages in her hand but not really reading it; a long scarf had fallen from her head, lay about her shoulders. And he did stand then, that policeman. He saw this woman (he told afterwards) and there was something, something about her, the short, spiky hair with the white bit in front, something strange. *Her eyes were glittery*, he told afterwards.

This time Alfie banged the desk. 'What's the matter with you, pal? Wotcha doing opening a man's private papers? And wotcha being so unpleasant for when you can see these ladies is so worried?'

'Inspector Rivers isn't a hero here, mister, that's all.' But he was disconcerted by the glittering, pale face.

At this moment a gasping, gulping officer ran in: he could

hardly breathe to tell his news: he garbled it out: a message had just arrived: four policemen had been taken to Cherry Street hours ago.

'What?' said the desk policeman sharply before the messenger could finish.

'*Who?*' said Cordelia.

'Please keep out of this, ma'am,' said the desk policeman, suddenly officious, 'this has nothing to do with you.'

'Oh, yes it has! I am the wife of Inspector Rivers and he seems to have disappeared.'

'Who?' said Gwenlliam.

Cordelia saw Gwenlliam's face. 'Inspector Rivers is my husband,' she said to the still breathless messenger. 'Frankie Fields is our friend. They have been missing all day. Are they in Cherry Street?'

'Yeah!' The messenger breathed in and out heavily, 'God, it is hot! Yeah, so we hear, yeah, yeah. They are both in Cherry Street. We knew there'd be a retaliation after the gold plan went so wrong. We've been waiting all day for something – but it had happened already! Only,' he flicked a glance in the ladies' direction but then addressed the desk officer, '– only there's something else. They say Jem has been killed, Jem Clover!'

'Jem? Jem *killed*? How do you know?'

'Somehow the news has got out. Apparently the *b'hoys* picked them up early this morning, as soon as they heard the gold raid went wrong, I suppose. There was a quiet little fracas down in City Park we hear now, Inspector Rivers and Frankie and Jem and Thomas, all taken away by the Daybreak Boys. You should see them,' he said to the visitors, '– nasty-looking young fellows with rings in their ears.'

Cordelia felt the floor moving underneath her as the desk

policeman suddenly leapt into action: she had been to Cherry Street, *I know the nasty-looking young fellows with rings in their ears*, the desk policeman was blowing a whistle, shouting loudly, dispatching the messenger to the captain, sending a message to the Aldermen. A policeman killed: that meant everything was different. Other policemen appeared having heard the whistle, some half-asleep, some pulling on jackets, running footsteps. Rillie and Gwenlliam and Cordelia and Alfie were pushed back into the corner by the wooden bench, no-one took any notice of them in the noise and confusion, Rillie put Arthur's letters into a deep pocket in her cloak.

'Cherry Street,' someone shouted. 'Jem Clover's been killed. They've got Inspector Rivers and Frankie and Thomas, that's all we know of, who knows who else?'

'The *b'hoys*'ve got no sense,' muttered one of the policemen to another, as they sat on the bench, slowly pulling on boots. 'They know we'll leave them alone if they leave us alone, they've got no sense. Now we have to do something! And that goddam Cherry Street at night is goddam hell. Let's wait. We should wait till the army gets there.' And Cordelia who had heard every word suddenly loomed over the policemen as they sat there each with one boot on.

'How *dare* you say "wait", you little cowards! Don't you dare *wait*, it's my husband, Inspector Rivers, who is missing and if you don't find him I will, and I'll shame the whole New York Police Force and its brave men!'

'Excuse me, ma'am,' said one policeman, abashed, getting up and hopping.

But the other one answered at once as he pulled on his other boot; he hadn't even looked up at Cordelia. 'If you don't mind me saying so, lady, he puts his nose in where it's not always wanted. There's a danger in that.'

'There's a danger to you in not finding my husband!' Cordelia cried out, shocking the second policeman into standing at once, and all the running, calling policemen slowed for a moment in their tracks, distracted by the raging light that seemed to catch at them from the woman with the strange, short hair, from the eyes of the woman who was looking for Inspector Rivers, and Rillie found herself thinking, *my God, there she is, the old, wild Cordie, I haven't seen her for years*.

But Captain Washington Jackson suddenly appeared, in charge of the police officers; he told them the Seventh army regiment was already on its way, and any recalcitrance was at once put aside. The police contingent and the Seventh army regiment met up on the way to the docks, marched on together. There were some unwritten rules in amongst the corruption and the chaos of New York and one of the unwritten rules was: don't kill a policeman. Cordelia and Alfie and Gwenlliam and Rillie attached themselves to the marching men in the darkness, moving nearer and nearer to the front.

'Go home, Gwennie,' said Cordelia suddenly, thinking of all that had happened this day, 'you must go home, this is too dangerous.' Cordelia knew where they were heading. 'Don't do this, Gwennie, you don't understand what it will be like, you can't go through this as well, after all that has happened to you!' But Gwenlliam just shook her head in the darkness.

'I can, Mama,' she said fiercely. 'I'm not a child. I want to see Arthur and Frankie Fields.'

The streets around the Cherry Street area were deceptively quiet that night. And no-one was as quiet now as Cordelia Preston, who had been here before: quiet like explosives are quiet before they erupt: Cordelia Preston. The soldiers moved in groups, with lamps, with their guns held ready, along strangely silent Water Street: even in the speakeasies the music was soft, as if not to draw attention to itself; some of the soldiers kicked at the door of the strangely empty saloon on the corner where a bottle of human ears stood behind the bar; came out again, turned into strangely empty Cherry Street. As she came along the muddy, narrow alley she remembered so well, almost with the front soldiers now, something made Cordelia look above her. In the hot, humid night there were people on the roof of this most notorious place of all trying to get some cooler air, odd lights flickered; they watched the army and the police arriving in a strange, languorous silence so that the only noise was the feet in the alleys; some of the policemen who had been here before looked up apprehensively. Finally the contingent arrived at the gaping doorway: the broken sign announced PARADISE BUILDINGS.

'They'll probably be in the cellars if they're anywhere,' called Washington Jackson loudly to all the men, indeed to anyone who wished to listen, 'but let's go in and see who's in charge of this little meeting first, because I have no doubt they'll have heard we are on our way and they're expecting us,' and a group of policemen and armed soldiers crashed inside of Paradise Buildings.

That smell. It came upward into the main building from the vaults and lay everywhere: the fetid, stinking, disgusting smell of humanity and its garbage, one policeman turned away retching even as lamps were shone into every corner. Irish, Negroes, Germans, Italians, Americans, Mexicans, a Chinese man with a pigtail, many women and children: people inside and outside every room. A warren of seemingly disconnected, crowded, narrow, dark corridors leading to other narrow dark corridors, leading to where? Upwards by a broken staircase? Downwards to vaults that perhaps even led down to the docks eventually? Who would really know except the inhabitants, or some of them: no sane man, including policemen and soldiers, would willingly be here, especially on a night as dark and hot and fraught as this one. This was not ordinary over-crowding and debauchery: these (or so people like Mr Charles Dickens had described, in books read all over the world) were animals, not people; this was living hell only streets away from Broadway with its fine shops and houses and its gas light and its sycamore trees.

Police and soldiers, sweating profusely now, moved together down narrow corridors, shining their lamps through small doors that led into room after room: if they kicked a door it didn't just open, it fell down; if a soldier pointed a gun it was not to warn but to kill: already they had fired several shots, already a body lay on the dirty floor, the body of somebody who had foolishly attacked a soldier with a knife. The crowds of inhabitants congregated now in groups in narrow passage-ways: stared, surly. Several of the police officers pushed past, stepped over the dead body, moved ahead with lamps, calling, followed by soldiers. One group went to the end of the building, pushing people out of their way; one group went up the high broken staircase, pushing people out of their way: up there their shadowed heads were caught in shafts of moonlight that shone in from above. A name echoed up the stairs and down the stinking corridors and around garbage-piled corners: 'ARTHUR RIVERS! ARTHUR RIVERS!' Cordelia and Gwenlliam slipped forward also; somewhere a child screamed over and over; rats, huge rats like cats, scurried from under the piles of rubbish, caught in the light of lamps for a moment and then gone. 'ARTHUR RIVERS!' the voices called and still the child screamed, another joined in: women shouted at the children: *shut up! shut up!*

'ARTHUR RIVERS!' called the voices.

Gwenlliam flicked her eyes round all the corridors, over all the people, automatically, just as she did over the crowds at the circus: suddenly she saw a man standing insouciantly, arms folded, near the staircase: *this young man is in charge*. She indicated to her mother standing near, the way they used to indicate something when they worked together in the circus, but she did not have to speak because Cordelia at once saw too: the man in charge was the young man who had recognised her in some way when she came to find Bridget O'Reilly: Charlie, the woman with the men's braces had called him: Charlie. Charlie standing nonchalantly where passageways met, near to the broken staircase. And where was she, that woman? The woman who they said bit off ears, and who thought Cordelia had been drowned, the woman who quoted Shakespeare?

Charlie stood slightly apart from all the other tenants of Paradise Buildings who had gathered around now: Charlie was watching, smiling slightly, the golden earring caught and lost as lamps flickered; he was chewing tobacco, his arms folded across his chest.

'Where are they, Charlie?' Captain Washington Jackson folded his own arms also. 'You can't get away with this. We know you brought them here.' Guns prodded at Charlie. He kept slowly chewing, and slowly smiling.

'Don't know what you're talking about, pal.' That light, boyish voice that she remembered, the young cruel face.

'Hell, it's Charlie Pack!' whispered Alfie almost to himself, and then he said quietly to the others: 'One of the leaders of the Daybreak Boys. He's a bad, violent little bugger, make no mistake, I've always thought he was a bit mad in the head. Don't be fooled that he looks so young, he's dangerous.'

The groups of soldiers with lamps came back from dark corners, from the staircase. 'Nothing,' an officer muttered to Washington Jackson. 'We'll go below to the water closets, God help us,' and they went out again into the night, and then immediately disappeared downwards.

'ARTHUR RIVERS!'

And the voices called fainter: 'ARTHUR RIVERS!' Cordelia had to fight to stop panic enveloping her, *he cannot be dead he cannot be dead!* She saw the high broken staircase very near, with the long pole holding it up, tied to the banisters: a shaft of moonlight slanted down from the skylight in the roof, breaking up the blackness. Shadowy figures stood on the staircase: could he be somewhere up there? If she could partially climb the staircase she could look upwards and she could look downwards, see more in the light of police lamps; she edged herself further towards the stairs and into the darkness as Charlie stared the soldiers and the police officers down even as they pointed their guns straight at him.

'Don't know what you're talking about, pal,' said Charlie.

'ARTHUR RIVERS!' she heard from somewhere far below, the cry was even more distant: it seemed now – and her heart caught in fear – more like a far-away lament: ARTHUR RIVERS.

She reached the shadowy, steep staircase: *remember it is half collapsed:* quickly she half-climbed, half-scrambled upwards, *I'm only fifty-one, I know about balance,* feeling for broken steps: once her foot went through a hole and jolted her, she clung to broken banisters; she heard breathing on the staircase, there were people somewhere near. The shaft of light from the summer moon shone down across one of the banisters and one of the broken stairs higher up as if to guide her further: the pole was tied to that moon-lit banister, roughly supporting the whole staircase. Her eyes were now accustomed to the dark and the light, she moved upwards, she knew there were people there but she moved upwards. Just as she made to turn back to look below she thought she caught sight of a tall figure looming much higher up still, she thought moonlight gleamed on the braces holding up the skirt: *O God! that's her!* but as she stared the figure disappeared completely: Cordelia wondered if she was seeing visions: stared up again but could see nobody at all; she turned; she held on to the pole by the banister to steady herself, and her wildly-beating heart, half-expecting a knife or a bullet in the back as she balanced on the broken stair: she heard now her own terrified breathing.

The scene just below was like some sort of dark painting of a netherworld. Heat rose up: she could see it, like a miasma. In the murky light of the swaying lamps and the beam from the moon far above she could see people huddled in doorways of small rooms: lifeless, even as soldiers kicked doors; energyless, as if they did not care what happened. Soldiers stood tensely pointing their guns; police officers barked out questions to which nobody gave an answer; she could see Charlie clearly; she could see Gwenlliam looking around for her. She raised her arm as Gwenlliam looked her way: the flash of the light colour of her cloak caught Gwenlliam's eye: from that moment Gwenlliam only looked at her mother.

Some of the soldiers came back. 'He's not down there,' they said.

'As I told you,' said Charlie, in that young boy's voice that she remembered. 'Can you leave us be now.'

'No,' said Washington Jackson, 'no, we won't be leaving you be, Charlie Pack, we'll all be going down again to the vaults. You do your dirty business in the vaults, don't you, Charlie Pack? And it's not just your bum dirty business is it, Charlie Pack!'

464

And then from Cordelia's vantage point – as the police lamps shone on Charlie and he did not move –

But of course!

She knew: *hurry*: she suddenly knew she had to stand, or balance, so that the moonlight caught her cloak, if she could stand on the banister by holding the pole she would catch the light perfectly: *I'm an acrobat, for God's sake! And Silas has taught me about lighting. Charlie recognised me from the circus and it made him uneasy.* Gwenlliam was watching her mother carefully: Cordelia indicated Charlie: Gwenlliam saw her mother wrap her long scarf quickly about her head and then – Gwenlliam watched aghast – use the tall pole to pull herself upwards until she was precariously balanced on to the stair rail – and Gwenlliam understood. Her mother, partly caught in the shaft of moonlight, looked like a ghost.

Gwenlliam stepped forward from the soldiers towards the young man with the earring and tapped him lightly on the shoulder: the slight smile disappeared; taken by surprise, he spat his tobacco, not quite at her, it landed on split, broken floorboards; his hand was on the knife at his hilt. A soldier, uncertain, cocked his rifle, everyone heard the sound. Gwenlliam simply pointed upwards and then moved back beside the soldiers.

Charlie! came a voice that seemed to be in the night sky. Charlie, suspicious, frowned, held his knife, half turned to where the girl had pointed – and saw the ghost on the steep staircase: not on the stairs but somehow flying, half-in-half-out of light from the moon. He stood stock still, staring. Nobody moved: not the soldiers, not the police: they all saw the figure above: moonlight shone down, lighting this apparition.

'*What is it?*' whispered the young man with the gold earring, and Cordelia said, *Look at me, Charlie*, in her strange, low, carrying voice and the man couldn't help it: he looked up at her, frozen. Like many of the wild, uneducated, half-mad men of Cherry Street Charlie Pack was superstitious: he believed in witches and the evil eye: he could feel Cordelia: he could feel her holding him with his eyes: *he knew her, he had seen her before.*

Wait there for me, Charlie.

She waited until she was sure he was caught, then she quickly moved out of the light from the moon: no time for fear: *I've been trained in this!* and she jumped down to the darkness of the staircase, catching the banister to balance. Lights flickered immediately as the police pointed their lamps upwards: Washington Jackson stilled any other movement in his men, put up his hand in warning: his instincts told him something was going to happen that he did not yet understand. Almost at once the figure could be seen again in the light of the lamps, moving slowly down the dangerous staircase: *Charlie*, called the strange voice: the figure in the light cloak and the scarves moved in and out of the light as she moved towards the man with the gold earring. He himself did not move: his knife glinted in his hand. *Charlie*, said the ghost.

'I know you,' he said and his young voice was hoarse. 'I know you.' Still he did not move. He could not take his eyes from her.

She approached Charlie, she was the same height as he, and she stood before him, staring at him with her glittering eyes. Without taking her eyes from him she drew her hands down over him, near not touching; he moved as if to duck, as if she would strike him, but he did not stop staring back at her. Her hands did not touch him, only her hands moving over and over, around him, over and over, long deep strokes, and he stared at the ghost-lady, she seemed to flicker slightly in the moving light of the lamps. Staring, thrown, he was suddenly caught off-balance, was down on his knees still holding the knife, it was inches from her breast. Yet everybody, everybody – the soldiers the policemen the crowds who lived in Paradise Buildings – was still as if transfixed. The woman leaned down to the man who was on his knees holding the knife: she calmly moved her hands over and over, just above his head, round his shoulders also: over and over, the long rhythmic strokes. Breathing: only the sound of breathing everywhere, Cordelia's breathing, the soldiers breathing, and the heavy unhealthy breathing of people who seldom saw sunlight. And the breathing of the man who held the knife. Still Cordelia moved her hands and seemed perhaps to murmur something to the man, she bent her head to him, others near heard her voice but not the words.

And then his eyes closed, still there on his knees.

For a moment still Cordelia drew her hands down over the man, over and over. The policemen and the soldiers and the people who lived in Paradise Buildings and were called animals never forgot what they saw that night. Her cloak was light in the half-darkness, police lamps caught it and lost it. She did look, they all said later, like a ghost. The knife dropped down, clattered dull on rotten wood, Charlie fell forward.

At once the soldiers surrounded the man, 'Jesus, ma'am!' said one of them and perspiration was running down his face.

'Move him,' she said.

They looked blank.

'There is some sort of door beneath his feet that leads below, maybe to the cellars or maybe to somewhere else,' she said. 'I once saw him climb up from there, covered in water. They will be down there. My husband will be down there.' *This has to be true, I have to believe it is true.*

There was a gasp, an intake of breath from a woman in one

of the groups of huddled people, and a moment of understanding from Captain Washington Jackson: the ghost woman was English, and she was Arthur Rivers' wife: he had never spoken of a wife. Charlie was dragged aside, beginning to stir. In the gloom it might not have been seen if you did not know what you were looking for, and then a lamp shone downwards and they saw: the floorboards were a door.

'No, missus,' said an urgent voice. And then there was some loud whispering in a group of the people who lived here, in this place, and then the person who owned the urgent voice shook off the restraining hands of others, moved forward. 'Don't be going down there if 'tis your man.'

It was Bridget O'Reilly.

'What is it?' said Cordelia, her heart beat like a thousand drums as she moved to Bridget and grabbed her shoulders. 'What is down there? What will I find?'

'I'm sorry, missus.'

'*What will I find?*'

Bridget O'Reilly looked at the woman who had taken her to her son, and given the gold piece of her other son. 'I'm sorry, missus,' she said again. ''It leads to the sewer and the river. 'Tis where they throw the bodies.'

It was Gwenlliam, not Cordelia, who screamed.

And that scream seemed, at last, to break the spell that had lain, for those few strange moments, on Paradise Buildings. The soldiers moved, the police moved, Charlie came out of the mesmeric trance, looked confused for a moment, then roared like a wild animal to find he was secured and surrounded by soldiers and policemen and had been moved from where he had leaned with such insouciance; now they pulled at the boards that made the trapdoor he had been standing, so carefully, on top of.

A sharp-faced wild little boy, seeing the man with the ear-ring was powerless called out to Cordelia. 'Ghost Lady! I'll show you if you give me a dollar!' It was Rillie who quickly, so quickly, found a dollar in the pocket of her cloak and held it up. The eyes in the thin feral little face gleamed, he reached up but Rillie pulled it away.

'Show first,' she said gently, but her face was taut with tension.

The boy disappeared downward through the doorway in the floor, downward into airless dark: soldiers, police, includ-ing the captain, followed with light, Cordelia somehow with them, Gwenlliam prevented by Rillie and Alfie. They disap-peared into a dangerous-looking, home-made construction that looked as if it could fall in on them at any moment; putrid water ran along the bottom. Inside Paradise Buildings soldiers looked towards the crowd, guns ready, but even now the crowd remained listless, energy-less, watching the man with the gold earring and the police surrounding him.

Down, down, hot as a roaring oven, no air, some of the lamps flickered out; down further into the mud and the filth of this vault, the smell almost overpowering now, unbearable: the policemen shone their lamps. There was a crack now in a con-crete wall, and moving lights: Cordelia quickly looked through and understood they were in a separate vault altogether, they were *behind* the vault containing rows of water closets which were reached from the outside alley. Now they were walking behind the boy in foul oozing filth, breathing in foul, oozing filth: someone, understanding what the filth was, vomited: it was not Cordelia. One of the soldiers fainted, fell into the sludge, one of his colleagues pulled him upwards: but it was not Cordelia who fainted. The boy was leading them on, they could hear something: *water*: *they could clearly hear water rushing by:* were they beside a sewer now? Or was it the rushing water of the East River they could hear? Right at one far corner of this vault there was another trapdoor leading downwards. It was much too heavy for the boy: four soldiers heaved, then lamps shone downwards.

In a narrow, putrid, stinking tunnel there were dead bodies. First the police officers recognised the body of Jem Clover. He was handed outwards. One ear was missing. Then another body: they reached further down from the edge: Thomas Duggan, murmured the policemen. He was handed out. One ear was missing.

'She's been here,' said Washington Jackson. 'Gallus Mag.' The boy stared. Cordelia kept upright. The sound of running water was louder; they shone their lamps into narrow darkness. Now there was only emptiness. Cordelia pushed right up to the opening of the tunnel, past the captain, past the soldiers; she knelt down in the mud and looked down, down inside the tunnel. She could see only darkness.

'Arthur!' she called in anguish above the sound of water, leaning right down into the tunnel. 'Arthur! Can you hear me?' Only her own desperate voice echoed back.

'Don't go any further, lady,' said a policeman, 'you could be swept away down. Your clothes will drag you downwards.' He held up a lamp, tried to look also into the blackness.

'Arthur!' she called again, and one more wild time: '*Arthur!*'

She thought she saw something move in the deep darkness, the policeman with the lamp saw it too, moved closer.

'**ARTHUR!**'

Not Arthur but Frankie Fields rolled himself somehow from a bend in the tunnel, towards them.

'It's Frankie!' Now policemen and soldiers pushed her quite roughly aside, moved quickly around the tunnel entrance, one

470

of them had found a long thick plank of wood, pushed it down, felt it held: more of Frankie appeared. He held on to the plank and very slowly, very carefully, the soldiers pulled. Frankie was completely covered in ooze and slime but down there where they shone the lamps they thought they could see eyes. He was near to them but still in the tunnel, he vomited mud, he was exhausted, could not move further in any direction.

'Where's Arthur?' called Cordelia downwards to Frankie and he could not answer because he could hardly breathe.

They heard the river.

Cordelia felt a flash inside her head, like a blow, at first she thought someone had struck her and then the flash came again: *my past blocked my love.*

Frankie's voice when it came was full of mud and water. 'He's there,' choked Frankie, 'beyond the bend. I'll go back, he might be able to grab my feet.'

'No, pal!' shouted a soldier. 'You won't get up. We'll never get two of you up at once! You come up first!'

Again they had to wait for Frankie to be able to speak. 'But they tied him,' he half-called, half-choked towards where he could see light. 'I don't know,' and they heard him vomit again, 'I don't know if he's still alive,' they could hear his choked, laboured breathing. 'He freed one of his hands and he held my head above the water even though he was tied. They threw – they threw us two in just before the woman came, we heard her, she got the others.' The soldiers thought he was delirious, *woman?* but the captain understood: Gallus Mag. And Cordelia understood: the woman who knew Shakespeare. Frankie vomited mud, spat, but still tried to speak, 'Call – call down to Arthur.' Perhaps he saw Cordelia, perhaps he did not. 'Tell Arthur – tell him he has to grab at my feet with his free hand.

He has to.' She knelt down into the darkness, towards the loud sound of running water, called past Frankie's body, her voice echoed down and down.

'Arthur! Arthur!' She only heard her own voice echoing back to her, and the running water. 'Arthur! Grab Frankie's feet! He's coming back towards you! *You must hold on to his feet!'*

And very slowly, slitheringly, Frankie Fields went back. But this time four soldiers held the piece of wood at one end and sent it down with him, he held the plank tightly as he was lowered. The boy who had led them down into the tunnel stared from where he stood, spell-bound.

'That's the wood they push the dead men down with,' he said to one of the soldiers, indicating the plank. 'Not pull them up!'

Four soldiers were lying flat now in the filth, leaning down into the tunnel, together they held one end; when the wood moved, they held it tight, trying to go with the movement so that the wood wouldn't break. It moved and pulled and still they held it. Then the wood was still. Nothing. A policeman shone the lamp downwards into blackness: all that could be seen was the mud-covered plank, reaching into darkness and nothingness.

And then Cordelia and the four soldiers heard a faint, extraordinary sound above the water. They heard someone whistle.

'That's Arthur,' Cordelia half-whispered. And then louder, 'The whistle! *I know that's Arthur!* Pull now!' The soldiers pulled and pulled; a small length more of the plank appeared upwards; other soldiers joined them now, pushing Cordelia away again from the edge of the tunnel entrance; five, six soldiers now, pulling carefully upwards; they heaved and swore and spat and then heaved again: *slowly! It will splinter!* And then the top of Frankie re-appeared: the mud and the ooze and the whites of his eyes. Arms pulled, lifted: it was as if Frankie found some supernatural power inside himself to heave himself upwards with the plank, against the side of the oozing tunnel. And there, at last, clinging tightly to Frankie's ankles with one free arm, swimming somehow with the rest of his body, half in and half out of the putrid, stinking mud and water, they could see a shape: a tied-up body. Quickly now the soldiers pulled: *gently, careful now men . . . gently, gently . . . easy, easy.*

First Frankie Fields and then Inspector Rivers were laid down for a moment right there in the mud, the ropes around the Inspector were untied. As Arthur Rivers lay in the filth they saw him move very slightly; then under the coatings of mud and sewerage they thought they saw two eyes looking upwards at the figure in the mud-blackened cloak, who bent over him.

'Whistle and I'll come to you, my lad,' whispered Cordelia.

They carried the two live men back through the vault, up into the home-made tunnel, through the trapdoor and into Paradise Buildings, lay them beside the bodies of their two dead colleagues, preparing to carry them all out: everybody saw the dead men and the half-dead men and the black, filthy mud. Gwenlliam quickly knelt for a moment between the bodies of Arthur and Frankie: she was weeping, an arm on each of them. The boy pushed past, cocky, claiming his dollar from Rillie.

The man with the earring, handcuffed now, humiliated by a ghost woman in front of everybody, betrayed by his own nephew, made an almost superhuman effort, as Frankie Fields and Arthur Rivers had done in the sewer not long before. As the boy passed, looking only for Rillie and the dollar, the man somehow managed to pull away from the police, leap forward, grab the boy between the handcuffs, and thrust him with a roar of rage straight against one of the walls of Paradise Buildings.

'*Cunt!*' he screamed.

The boy bounced off, they heard him fall; the soldiers tied the struggling man up tightly even as he screamed more obscenities. The boy did not cry, still came towards Rillie, grabbed at the dollar, blood pouring down his face. As Rillie gave the dollar to him, she tried also to hold him for a moment. 'I'll help you,' she said gently. He snatched the dollar, punched at her arm at the same time and ran, shouting, 'Fuck off you old cunt-face, quink-goose, ugly, fuck old ugly, old cunt-arse, ugly quink-face, fuck off old ugly old . . .' The words echoed back from the hot, filthy darkness along the alley outside Paradise Buildings, on Cherry Street, where George Washington had danced.

To be replaced by another word, echoing upwards from the darkness beneath the still-open trapdoor in the floor:

Cordelia!

Cordelia froze: she knew the deep, rusty voice at once. So did Washington Jackson: quickly he moved to the trapdoor, cocked his gun, and fired downwards. A bullet flew immediately back out of the darkness, grazing his shoulder, he moved back, holding his bleeding arm, shocked.

Cordelia! called the voice again and it was Alfie who quickly pulled Cordelia away from the trapdoor and into the shadows: not a bullet but the voice echoed up out of the stinking black.

Hear me, recreant; take thy reward.
Five days we do allot thee for provision
To shield thee from disasters of the world.
And on the sixth to turn thy hated back
Upon our kingdom; if on the tenth day following,
Thy banished trunk be found in our dominions,
The moment is thy death . . .

The words echoing and disappearing now into the recesses of the foul filth of the black vault, leading to trapdoors and passages and the sewer, and the river.

And nearby, on Broadway, the fine houses were lit up and shining after the Italian opera at Astor Place, the soaring, thrilling music.

48

Finally they left the hospital, walking from Anthony Street and on to Broadway. The two surviving policeman, both of them floating in and out of consciousness – sometimes shouting out loud, sometimes shaking as if they lay on ice – had been washed, and examined, and were at last lain in white, clean sheets (which perhaps seemed ice to them), and given long draughts of laudanum.

Outside it was now another hot, late-summer day. Slowly, almost in a dream, Cordelia and Rillie and Gwenlliam and Alfie walked home. Gwenlliam and Rillie exchanged a few words about Frankie Fields whose mother had appeared: *You're the poker girl who went to the gold-rush!* she had said to Gwenlliam and had hugged her. Cordelia's cloak and scarf were gone, unsaveable: still her face and her gown were mud-covered but the hustling, bustling New Yorkers did not stop, hurried by, money to be made. Gwenlliam took her mother's mud-encrusted arm, they walked close together and slow. All along the way Cordelia did not speak: it was as if she had been struck dumb by all that had happened. Alfie wanted to call a cabman but he saw – and he felt it too – they needed the blue sky, and sunshine, and warmth, and normality, and peace. So Alfie Tyrone held his peace, until they arrived back in Maiden Lane: a message had already been sent to Monsieur Roland and Regina; La Grande Celine was waiting with them in the attic with muffins and corn-cakes and coffee.

It was Alfie who told the story; it was Alfie who recounted the terrible nightmare events of the last hours, Alfie in his usual chair by Regina, but up and down as he spoke, the terrible adventure. Rillie and Gwenlliam and Cordelia were squashed together on the small sofa, white with exhaustion, taut with tension still. Although they tried, and showed their gratitude with polite half-smiles, the muffins were not eaten.

But, having told the story, Alfie could hold his peace no longer.

'You have to leave New York at once, Cordelia. You and Arthur. You ain't safe, not in New York, not any more.'

She looked at him blankly, as if she hardly took in his words. Gwenlliam said quickly: 'But they are caught. The Daybreak Boys are caught.'

'The Daybreak Boys are a shifting, snaky, devious, ever-changing, amorphous swarm of dangerous violent hooligans. Frankie Fields can't stay either. I don't know if even you and Rillie can feel safe. You heard Gallus Mag.'

Cordelia said expressionlessly, 'It was Shakespeare. She was quoting from *King Lear* because she knew my name. Cordelia is one of the characters in the play.' It was so long since she had said anything at all that her voice was even lower and huskier than usual.

'I know it was Shakespeare,' said Alfie patiently. 'She's famous for using Shakespeare instead of her own cruel words. She was giving you a warning, my lovely. The gang is disarrayed and shamed by all that stuff that happened in Paradise Buildings. People like you and Arthur and Frankie ain't going to be forgiven and you gotta get out of here!'

'What about you then, Alfie?' Regina suddenly sat up very straight indeed. 'You was there!'

'It's different for me,' said Alfie. 'They know me.' They all looked at him in incomprehension. 'I've been working on the docks for years and years,' said Alfie in the same patient voice. 'They know me.' A taut, hot silence. Sunshine shone into the attic, just like all the other late-summer, sunshine days. And then at last Monsieur Roland stood; something in his manner made everyone look up.

'I think,' he said, 'I think this is enough for now. Everyone is exhausted, nothing can be decided at this moment. Everyone must rest.'

Alfie stood at once; Celine saw that all of them, even Alfie, were so shocked by what had happened, and by what was happening still, that they obeyed the tall, frail old man who spoke so gently, as if they were children. She heard Regina saying to Gwenlliam: 'Come on girl, put your head down and I'll tell you a story,' and Gwenlliam put her arms around Monsieur Roland for a moment and then allowed Regina to lead her away. Rillie kissed Monsieur Roland's head as she passed his chair. Cordelia touched his arm briefly.

Alfie was retrieving his hat. Celine had collected up some plates but then she did not go downstairs. Instead she pulled some papers from the big pocket of her apron. 'There's something else,' said Celine to Monsieur Roland and Alfie in a quiet voice. 'Perhaps this is not the right time, but perhaps it is, while the others are not here. For this is about Arthur also and I don't believe Arthur will ever show it.' She cleared her throat as if she was embarrassed (which was a very unlikely scenario for La Grande Celine). 'Arthur dropped this, the night Danny O'Reilly arrived. When I found it next day under the chair I thought it was from Danny's satchel, of course I picked it up and started to read it. It is a letter. Or two letters it seems.' And she began reading the pages to both men.

Marylebone
London

Dear Arthur,

You write and enquire why there is no letter! Well here is the answer: little Arthur died nearly two months ago, you remember him? The grand-child you knew? Or have you forgotten? His small coffin went alone into the earth, and no husband to comfort Faith, nor no father either. Live with that, Arthur Rivers, if you can.

I entreat you to return to your duty in London.

The Lord has seen fit to visit me with much further tribulation, my head aches all day and night, if it were not for Millie I do not know what would happen to me. All doctors are useless. I am no longer able to attend properly to your house in Marylebone, there is no money for any servant. Millie suggests that they should ALL come and live with me! Seven children! I am too ill and in too much pain, each part of me aches and swells and of course I cannot have those wild children here. As for Faith's husband, the drunkard, the less said about him the better.

Nobody cares what happens to me, yet I gave up my own

479

life to look after your family, yours, Arthur Rivers, <u>yours</u>.
London is topsy-turvy, foreigners everywhere, all the
preparations for Prince Albert's Exhibition, one cannot go
anywhere (not that I do) without falling over foreign
people, they are opening brothels all round Hyde Park, the
foreigners.

       I remain your dutiful sister-in-law
       Agnes Spark (Miss)
PS We are in receipt of five payments.

Oh Father, I am so <u>sorry</u> for the long silence, everything here is more
and more difficult. It was so so sad about little Arthur Father. It was
not the cholera, which is over, but another fever and Faith without the
support of a husband, that was hard for her, drunk old Fred
disappeared and has never been seen again. We are so glad of your
letters, and the money, but life is so exhausting. O Father could you
come home now, perhaps just for a short while and sort things out
somehow, just a little? I tried to talk to Aunt Agnes as you suggested
but she is so adamant. We will be much kinder to Miss Preston now that
we have grown up ourselves, Father, how horrible we all were then.
Nobody remembers all that scandal now, there are newer and bigger
scandals every week – a man cut up two women in Islington yesterday
and put the pieces in a railway carriage and the penny papers say
15,000 aliens deluged London last week, who immediately set about
hiring houses to set up brothels and gambling dens to cater for the
millions who will attend, they say, Prince Albert's Great Exhibition next
year but Charlie says `if you believe everything in the newspapers you
would never leave your house' (like Aunt Agnes.) Shall you insist that
we all move to Marylebone father, despite Aunt Agnes's
protestations? it would be cheaper – we all eleven of us live now on
Charlie's wage from the Water Board and your kind money, (without
which we would have drowned long ago Father) Perhaps – perhaps you

<u>could</u> come home for just a little while just to sort out things? I am at my wits' end trying to please everybody and manage the money, thank goodness for dear Charlie who helps and supports me always. Faith is living with us now, and I cannot dare leave any of the children with her at the moment, she lost her job at the pickle factory, she is very sad and low and weeps very much and we found little Arthur's pictures that you drew him, he had kept them always, in the larder, at the back of all the jam and pickles, I did cry when we found them, dear little boy. O dearest Father, I miss you so much – I cannot write it. But I know too that you have a life of your own now, and I am so glad you are happy. So if you cannot come home just now then – well, well when you can dear Father, it would be so lovely, but we will manage till then.

Love from Millie.

Celine's voice ceased. 'That's all,' she said and they were back in Maiden Lane, New York. For a while they all three sat in silence.

'Poor old Arthur,' said Alfie at last.

Monsieur Roland bowed his head for a moment and did not speak. They saw that he too was exhausted.

'I'll go, Monsweer, you rest too, and I'll call in at the hospital and I'll get all the news I can and I'll come back tomorrow morning. We'll talk about things then.' And Alfie picked up his hat and put his old hand, for a moment, on the older man's shoulder.

When Alfie had gone, still Celine lingered.

'I'll leave these,' she said to the Frenchman, putting the letters on the table. 'You will know what best to do with them.' But even now she did not go: instead she sat down beside him. 'Dear, dear Monsieur Roland,' she said quietly, or as quietly as it was possible for La Grande Celine to be.

481

Outside, Maiden Lane was as busy and clattering and noisy as it always was, hot air shimmered outside the open windows.

Inwardly, but not outwardly, the exhausted old man sighed. He sensed from her tone that Celine was about to make a proposal to him that would make him very uncomfortable and he did not want to hurt this entertaining, good woman with the jaunty black eye-shade and the business sense and the kind, inquisitive heart.

And he was right: Celine had a proposal. It was just that it was a slightly different proposal than the one he had feared.

La Grande Celine said: 'Monsieur Roland, I've been thinking. These letters. Do you know anything at all about this Great Exhibition in London that they've written about?'

In the early evening the first shadows fell across the attic room as the sun moved downwards in the sky. Monsieur Roland still sat at the table. He had his pen and paper there: he was working on a project he had begun: he was writing down everything he had thought about memory, and loss of memory, and the blocking of memory, and about the failure of TALK TO THE MESMERIST. He would deposit the papers in some hospital or library perhaps: they would gather dust, but one day they might be useful to another.

But perhaps Monsieur Roland slept also.

When he looked up he seemed to sleep still. Hester, his beloved Hester stood once more before him.

'I did not mean to wake you,' she said quietly. She sat beside him, as if they were young again.

He rubbed his eyes. It was not Hester. It was her great-niece.

'Can you not sleep, dearest Gwenlliam?'

'Yes, I have slept but I woke just now and I did not know where I was.'

'I am not surprised, my dear girl. So much has happened to you! It is not very long ago that you were locked up on the Atlantic Ocean.'

'That *seems* long ago after what has happened since.' And she gave a very small smile. 'But just now for a horrible, horrible moment I half-woke and heard footsteps and I thought it was Mr Doveribbon outside the cabin on the *Sea Bullet*,' and she shook her head slightly, 'but it was Mama, walking about in her room. Oh – oh –,' and he saw that she could not catch her breath easily, '– oh, I am so glad it is over, I am so glad Mama is alive, I am so glad I am not locked in a cabin, I am so glad to be home.' But he saw that she shook slightly as if she was cold, although it was so warm. 'I hope Arthur will recover. I hope Frankie will recover.' And then the little anxious question that she had come into the room to ask him: 'They will recover, do you think?'

He nodded. 'I believe they will,' he said, for himself as much as for her, and she smiled at him then, as if she was sure that if he said it, it must of course be true.

'Where's Rillie?' she asked. 'Her room is empty.'

'I believe she has walked down to St Paul's Chapel. To talk to her mother. She tells me she does that when she has something to think over. Regina went with her.'

'Oh. Dear Rillie. Dear Regina. Dear old Mrs Spoons. All those months and months I – I could not think that – one of you would not be here when I returned. And then I saw the hair – her hair in the satchel. And now I am home and . . .' She let the words drift, wandered over to the empty rocking chairs. She pushed one slightly, watched it until it was still. And then she turned to him.

'Was it mesmerism?' she said suddenly. He understood at once.

'Yes,' he said. 'I think it is a kind of mesmerism.'

'I seemed somehow to – to hold them in my arms, the miners. I used to say: *All will be well*. For comfort's sake.'

'I think, sometimes, the energy can work that way,' he said slowly. 'It is your energy and their energy and it comes together for a moment.'

'I could feel it,' said Gwenlliam.

'Yes,' he said.

She was silent, and, then she gently pushed the rocking chair again, he heard a tiny sigh. 'When I was locked in that cabin I used to think of these rocking chairs!' Backwards and forwards went the wooden chair; it creaked slightly. 'Do you think we will really, really have to leave?'

'We'll think about that later, dearest girl, not today. Too much has happened for us to make decisions today.'

'You really do think they will recover?'

'I really do think they will recover,' he said, again for there was no other answer.

'I will think about Silas and the circus and how to find them tomorrow then. But I do so hope I have seen the last of that golden wand – I am an acrobat and a mesmerist, not a fairy!' and they both even laughed slightly. 'But now that I am clear where I am, and safe, and now that *you* have said *all will be well*' – and Monsieur Roland smiled at her – 'I will go back to sleep!' and she kissed the old, dry cheek.

Voices called from the street but he did not hear. He slept again.

When he woke Cordelia was sitting at the table near to him and it was dusk: all the mud was gone from her now: in the darkening light he saw the drawn, pale face, huge eyes, still the white streak of hair, she sat hunched and still. She held the letter Celine had left on the table. 'There were many more of these at the police station,' she said, and then, as if they were in the middle of a conversation: 'It wasn't my *memories* that were blocked.'

He waited.

'It was my love. *It was my love that was blocked!*' She looked up at him. 'Don't you understand? *I thought love was a lie.*' She held her arms about herself, as if for comfort. 'In a way I was like Mrs Spoons, I was there, and I was not there. For so long.' The letters to Arthur lay upon the table between them. And the words burst out. 'How could Arthur *bear* it! Me there beside him, but not there. He understood everything and was so always kind, and I took the kindness as if it belonged to me, as if it was no more than my due. And lived with my memories, on and on.'

'Your memories were stronger than your life perhaps?' he said, smiling a little.

She tried to smile back. 'Yes, you tried to tell me. But I did not hear.'

He nodded, and then he spoke. 'Cordelia, my dear. You know how I wanted to help people unblock, or unlock, memory – not you, it was never about you, you did not lock your memories away; although, perhaps because of them, you may have locked your heart. The reason I still think my ideas are correct – despite our Herculean failure with TALK TO THE MESMERIST – is because I have come to believe that people cannot move on, grow, until they have given memory its due.' And very, very gently he said: 'I think perhaps you have done that now.'

She got up quickly, that way she had. 'Yes,' she said. 'I think perhaps I have done that now. They will always be there inside my head, Morgan and Manon, how can they not be?' And she looked at him. 'But love is not a lie. And I am going to the hospital, and I'm not coming back without Arthur.'

And Monsieur Roland said a most surprising thing. 'You might consider this,' he said mildly, 'which might interest Arthur when he awakes. La Grande Celine has been talking about Prince Albert's Grand London Exhibition. If the gold rush in California is coming to its natural end, as the newspapers seem to intimate, I wonder if Mr Silas P Swift is fully apprised of the details and opportunities of such an occasion?' She half-laughed as she went towards the door: she thought he was joking.

At the hospital nobody asked her business so she simply walked into the room where the men had been placed. Both men were asleep: Frankie Fields' chest moved deeply and regularly and there was colour in his young, bruised face. But the older man seemed to have difficulty breathing and his face was grey; there were dark bruises all over his body also. There was nobody there, no doctor or orderly. Her heart beat fast as she looked at his face, known but unknown; the dear face, bruised and grey. Cordelia Preston closed her eyes for a long, long moment: then she stood beside her husband and drew her hands down, over and over, over and over, all her energy into her hands as they moved over him, all her energy moving over and over. And as she worked she spoke to him softly. 'Don't you *dare* die, Arthur Rivers, I have things to say to you, things I should have said long ago. And there are so many things for us to talk about and do together still, and share. Don't you *dare* die now.' Over and over him the long, steady strokes of her own energy to heal him, over and over and over.

49

All about London people published Poetic Rhapsodies at their own expense.

> *What a Shop! What a Show! What a wealthy Exchange!*
> *What strange-looking men, and what products more strange!*
> *O what a collection from Earth's farthest shore*
> *In this Palace of Industry, Taste may explore!*
> *The tribute of trust to Britannia's worth,*
> *By the East and the West, and the South and the North;*
> *What a Gathering of Nations to witness the smile*
> *Of Order and Plenty, in this favour'd isle!*
> *Here thousands of traders are come from afar,*
> *To exhibit their wares in this mighty Bazaar!*

It had been predicted in certain circles that the Wrath of Almighty God would, without doubt, strike down such a brash, arrogant, provocative, insolent, providence-tempting edifice as the one made of glass that stood, like a shining miracle, in Hyde Park, London. However God must have stayed his hand because the Great Exhibition of the Works of Industry of all Nations opened as planned, on May 1st 1851.

Lo! They come! On Britain's happy shore
The locust horde of foreign nations pour,
Ripe for sedition, prompt to lend their aid
And teach John Bull the arts of Barricade.
Turn where you list, what strange costumes arise,
What outré figures glad our gamins' eyes:
Turk, Russian, Russ – good reader if you will
Scan the gay front of Jullien's new quadrille:
And there behold them, turban, tunic, skirt;
*And better still, **without their native dirt**.*

THE CRYSTAL PALACE, the erection was called by every-body (although as aforementioned it was made of glass, nor was it a palace but an exhibition hall) and it was a wonder of design and beauty: people gasped as they stepped inside and saw elm trees growing upwards and flowers blooming and palm-trees waving and fountains playing and the light shining down through the two hundred and ninety-three thousand, six hundred and fifty-five panes of glass.

Unfortunately sparrows had found the edifice beautiful also (and warm) and had got inside the vast space before the roof was finished. Despite the Duke of Wellington's valued suggestion of sparrow-hawks, some of the exhibits had been somewhat befouled. So there was much final polishing and cleaning around certain of the hundreds and hundreds of British and foreign offerings that were placed inside the huge, bright, light building, before Her Majesty Queen Victoria and Her Royal Procession arrived at the official opening. There was particular difficulty with the silent alarm clock: a bed which awoke the sleeper by turning upon its side: some particular cleaning of appurtenances was required for the invention to work as spectacularly trumpeted in all the advertisements. It was unfortunate also that the Russian exhibits would not be there for the opening: the ship they were being transported upon had been iced in somewhere far north of England for weeks (but was now said to be on its way carrying it was rumoured, among other exhibits, a cloak of silver fox fur belonging to the Tsar). There were, it was true, an unaccountably large number of statues to be found places for, and Queen Victoria's face stared up, not just, many times, from marble, but from multitudinous jugs and teapots and tong-handles and tapestries. But at last, on the morning, the printing press of the *London Illustrated News* could be seen right there inside the Crystal Palace, turning out five thousand copies an hour, and all was ready – all the wonderful steam machines and statues and jewels and the replica of Liverpool docks with all its ships, and the machine for turning over the pages of music and the china and the chandeliers and the maps and the portable baths, and the crimson satin quilted eiderdown from Heals and the Colman's Mustard and the Reckitt's Starch and the diving-suit and the snuff-boxes and pianofortes large and small, decorated and plain (including a collapsible piano for gentlemen's yachts).

And thanks to the attention of Detective-Inspector Arthur Rivers and his colleagues, the great Koh-i-Noor diamond from India remained safely locked inside its large gold bird-cage: a plan by some visitors described in the newspapers as 'foreign agents' to steal it, foiled just in time, by Scotland Yard.

But all the flags of all the nations flew and the fountains inside the Crystal Palace sent water shooting upwards (confusing goldfish in the pools below); organs echoed magnificently in different parts of the huge structure; massed choirs sang; the trees and flowers and tropical plants blossomed in the warmth of such a stupendous green-house; bands played; and, waiting for their Queen on the opening day the crowds (said to be half a million people), were in a frenzy of excitement.

Alfie Tyrone, inside the Crystal Palace, waiting with all the thrilled visitors, laughed. 'What a mad trove!' he said to Detective-Inspector Arthur Rivers and his new London assistant, Sergeant Frankie Fields. 'You seen that bed that tips people out? And the collapsible piana? And that famous blooming diamond ain't even shiny! I wonder what the Daybreak Boys would make of all this!' But Arthur wryly indicated all the uniformed English policemen (six thousand extra) everywhere about and informed Alfie that London was also surrounded by soldiers in case of trouble, which no doubt would deter even the Daybreak Boys (should they have been interested), and just then there was an extremely loud, echoing salute of cannons. The panes of glass did not, at the sound, shatter and cut a hundred young ladies into mincemeat (as had been warningly foretold by the *Times* newspaper) and the glorious Royal Procession entered the Crystal Palace and the people cheered and that old republican Alfie Tyrone looked about him and felt a tear in his eye to be here, even just for a visit, among the pomp and the circumstance of the city of his birth that he had seen the last of over fifty years ago. *Oh Home! Oh London!*

The two daughters of Arthur Rivers, Millie and Faith, ecstatic to have their father home again at last, were nevertheless so nervous about re-meeting their stepmother, Miss Cordelia Preston, that Faith developed the hiccoughs and could not be cured, and Millie spilt raspberry jam (meant for the scones) on to her gown just as the visitors arrived and looked as if she was bleeding most rudely. In the small parlour of the house in Marylebone where they lived again now, the display of pinned butterflies, that had once pierced Arthur's heart even though he had been told by Agnes that it was a polite occupation for young ladies, still hung on one wall. Aunt Agnes herself bowed once, and then played endless hymns, grimly, on the pianoforte.

But Arthur, having spent many rejoicing hours with his family and the grand-children he had not before met (*you probably think I'm biased but they are so* intelligent, *my grand-children!* he kept saying to Cordelia), was now confident all could be resolved. And he had several secret weapons for the momentous meeting. First of all, like everybody who met him, the three Marylebone women were entranced by Monsieur Roland who bowed low over their hands and spoke to them in his odd and charming accent, and had cured Faith's hiccoughs in three minutes. Aunt Agnes' hymn-playing faltered as she saw the frail and beautiful old man sitting in her armchair. Gwenlliam, the step-sister they had never met, was rehearsing with the circus (received back into the arms of her colleagues, not to mention Mr Silas P Swift's, with cries of delight) but kind, warm Rillie Spoons bustled in with circus tickets for all, including the grand-children, and, as if a miracle-maker, had an apron about her person that looked very pretty over Millie's strawberried gown.

'They're trying a new acrobatic thrill for the London season!' Rillie told them all. 'Pierre-the-Bird, he's Gwenlliam's acrobatic partner, is working with her to throw her much further *upwards!* That is not the same as throwing her downwards, it requires different strength. Isn't it dangerous, I say, but Gwennie only laughs and says it is magic! They've always wanted to do this, and then Silas had an idea with the lighting, and now they believe they can! It's not *very* far up he throws her, she tells me, but it *looks* very far.' Everybody, not only the children, listened with wide, round eyes. To Aunt Agnes it sounded immoral in the highest degree.

'Pierre-the-Bird can do it!' cried La Grande Celine (another of Arthur's secret weapons) with her one eye flashing. 'He has the muscle to throw her to the roof! I have met up with him again most fortuitously and interestingly, and I assure you he has lost none of his strength!' and she laughed and shook her flame-coloured hair and Arthur Rivers' grand-children stared at the lady with a black eye-patch, thought she was certainly the most exciting person they had ever seen.

Yet perhaps Regina was the oddest secret weapon of all. Hearing Aunt Agnes' dour and heavy piano-playing, Regina, in her old and loved celebratory-feathered hat, nevertheless stood beside the piano and sang whichsoever hymn was played. She may have looked rather odd but Regina could sing and no matter what hymn Aunt Agnes played, Regina knew the words and Aunt Agnes, despite herself, finally joined in:

> *Amazing Grace, how sweet the sound*
> *That saved a wretch like me!*
> *I once was lost, but now am found*
> *Was blind, but now I see.*

They sang in unison and in truth it sounded melancholy, but rather fine.

And there, at last, Millie and Faith saw, was the still-beautiful Miss Cordelia Preston, with the odd, fascinating, translucent face, a strange new hair style with still the one

492

white lock of hair, and those huge eyes. Somehow, she made their hearts jolt when they looked at her, as if she was not quite real. However she smiled at them, just like a real person, and gave them a very fine daguerreotype of their father in America: they both cried, and hugged their father again.

But then Millie looked more carefully. 'This is beautiful,' she said. 'All the lights and the shadows on Father's face. This is better than any other picture I have seen. Aren't they clever in America!'

'Cordelia took that picture herself,' said Arthur. Millie looked at Miss Preston in amazement and then back at the daguerreotype.

'How did you learn?' she finally said, shyly. 'I would like more than anything else to learn to make pictures like this.'

'Well. Well, well. It just so happens that I would like to teach you,' said Cordelia, smiling. She looked at the others in the visiting party with bright eyes and then said to Millie and Faith: 'We have an enormous plan. And we would like you to be part of it, if it interested you.'

'You too, girl,' said Regina to Aunt Agnes. 'We need everybody. And I ain't heard such good piana-playing for a while.' Nobody had called Aunt Agnes *girl* for forty years.

In Oxford Street flags were aflutter to welcome visitors, especially above a new eating establishment. They had thought long and hard about the flags: French and English, yes, but also the American flag: all up there fluttering together over London.

CELINE'S LONDON HOUSE OF REFRESHMENT said a brightly painted sign (Alfie had had some hand in the brightness; when he arrived with his wife and his sister to his homeland, one week before the Exhibition was to open, he had insisted that the sign be not only larger, but scarlet).

Alfie's wife Maria, who had never been to London before, had been over-awed by the old buildings and the history and the age of London. 'It's the *ancientness*,' she said over and over again. 'Ah declare, in America we don't know the meaning of that word! *Ancientness*.'

'Ancient maybe, but the old city is dull compared to New York,' Alfie had said bluntly. 'And here it is, full of foreigners all here for the Exhibition, and this is not a time for English niceties in eateries! It's only for six months, this Exhibition, and then all them foreigners will go home and if you want to stay, Celine, you can get as respectable as you like for the British. But for now, I'm telling you: advertise! Advertise!' And his advice had proved admirable: CELINE'S LONDON HOUSE OF REFRESHMENTS was full from morning to night with extremely diverse visitors from many climes: the same long, shared tables as in New York and the food in the middle: the food was good and the service was fast. Every single available member of this strange and now extended family had been called in to assist. The most unusual and captivating reception hostess was none other than Alfie's wife, Maria, with her fluttering fan and her Southern American accent: customers were charmed to be shown to their seats by such a fascinating woman (who would speak French if required). And then – *what an interesting place!* people said – there was also the red-haired lady manager with the eye-patch who looked like a beautiful pirate. Celine and Rillie took turns sitting in the high cash-desk in the centre, in charge of proceedings; when they were not in the cash-desk they were in the kitchen or waiting at the tables. They had employed two cooks, and also serving the guests were Millie and Faith, delighted after some shyness, with their new jobs and their new family. Faith, who couldn't hold down the job in the pickle factory (poor Faith whose drunk husband disappeared, poor Faith the mother of little deceased Arthur) had been taught that ladies never took employment; never in her life would she have believed that paid work could be *agreeable*. As she waited on tables she talked for the first time in her life to people of many countries, to *foreigners*, even *black and brown* people: laughing, even flirting a little. The customers from all over the world didn't look down on her as she served them: they *liked* her, she understood after while, and especially the Americans talked with her as an equal, laughed with her about their adventures at the Great Exhibition.

'The Exhibition is all such fun!' the visitors said, advising Faith of the silent alarm-clock and the diving-suit and the replica of Liverpool docks and all the marble statues. 'Even if it is for nothing else in the end, it is such *fun!*' and there was much laughter and much devouring of Celine's corn-cakes and oyster pies, and often expansive visitors left an extra three-pence.

There were two large advertisements just inside the door of the dining-room.

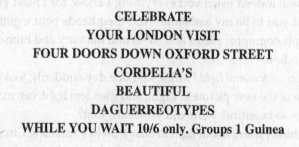

**CELEBRATE
YOUR LONDON VISIT
FOUR DOORS DOWN OXFORD STREET
CORDELIA'S
BEAUTIFUL
DAGUERREOTYPES
WHILE YOU WAIT 10/6 only. Groups 1 Guinea**

Millie only worked for Celine in the evenings; all day, four doors further down Oxford Street, on the top floor, she and Monsieur Roland helped Cordelia run her daguerreotype studio.

'Could – could I learn properly, do you think?' said Millie shyly, once she had seen how Cordelia knew everything, not just the taking of the picture but the developing also in a small dark room off the studio. 'I have seen some of the modern English photographs but I think the daguerreotypes are much more beautiful. They have more atmosphere it seems.' Millie was puzzled, tried to work out the difference.

'I will indeed teach you everything I know, for I need you! I need you to be my assistant!' And their heads bent together over photographic plates and silver and mercury and bromide and iodine.

'You *understand light*,' Millie said one day suddenly, looking at one of the new pictures. 'Light, and then less light, can make things so beautiful. How did you learn that?'

'I think I learnt about light in Silas P Swift's Amazing Circus,' said Cordelia, laughing. 'Silas understands light, he can change the look of everything with light,' and she showed Millie how to use the mirror to direct brightness to shine in the eyes of their sitters.

And at the studio entrance who should sit at a small desk, and stand graciously to welcome the customers, but Monsieur Roland. He spoke with his old-fashioned French charm to the customers who crowded in, and told them where to put their hats and cloaks and where the mirrors (to enhance themselves before they faced the camera) could be found. And he took ten shillings and sixpence when the daguerreotypes were completed; a guinea for a family photograph. They kept making more and more money. It was all madness: the daguerreotypes were part of the madness of the times: of the money being taken everywhere in London; they could have made more daguerreotypes than there were hours in a day: it seemed that everybody wanted a picture to commemorate this time, this year, this city and the Great Exhibition.

Monsieur Roland laughed at his strange new temporary career. 'I consider my involvement as a Daguerreotypist's Assistant as a most interesting experience in my long life,' he said to Rillie. 'For in all my days I did not think to end up selling likenesses in Oxford Street! And Cordelia calls me The Manager and pays me handsomely and I am earning more money than I ever earned before!' And he gave most of it to Rillie. 'I need so little,' he said when she demurred. 'I don't need money. Take it now, for the time when my income falls again!' And yet – and yet – already some of his old customers had somehow found Monsieur Roland on his return: a member of the government; a famous doctor. Mesmerism might have become old-fashioned but there would always be some customers for Monsieur Roland's particular healing skills. And Rillie knew that most of all the old man would be glad when the Exhibition was over and he could work with his books and papers again, and ponder, still, over memory. Already one of his concise hand-written manuscripts had been deposited modestly in the British Museum: his hope was that perhaps one day there would be more knowledge and someone else interested in memory would find his papers of use.

'And you still will not marry Celine?' Rillie said to him teasingly.

'I do not think I would be a suitable person for Celine,' he said to her gravely, but his eyes twinkled. 'And you know she has found someone much more suitable – and I do thank the heavens for that! But I continue to admire her, and am more grateful to Celine than she can ever know, for it was her enthusiastic plans and ideas and energy that got us all safely home again.'

Just once Celine had confided in Rillie. Her one eye was frank: the pearl on the black eye-patch caught the lamp-light. 'I know I fall in love very often. Jeremiah says it is a character failing. And of course, I had *already* fallen in love with *Pierre l'Oiseau*, years ago! And –' she laughed her loud, infectious laugh, 'it is true I *did* hope that Pierre might come to London with the circus when I first had these grandiose ideas about our contribution to the Great Exhibition!' For just a moment she became serious. 'When I first met Monsieur Roland, I had thought about how much he could do for me, for my happiness, for that was what love has been, for me. I had not realised, then, how much I could do for him – and not just the purple jacket to make him look like Dr Mesmer.' She had sighed, just a little, but then she had tossed back the flaming hair and laughed again. 'I am an improved person, even *Pierre l'Oiseau* says so! I would not have missed knowing dear Monsieur Roland, not for the world.'

Also often at work in the kitchen of CELINE'S LONDON HOUSE OF REFRESHMENTS was Regina who enjoyed nothing better than peeling pots of potatoes and singing – sometimes the twenty-third psalm, sometimes rude old murder songs from London penny papers years ago, sometimes *Whistle and I'll Come to Ye my lad* which reminded her of her old friend Mrs Spoons and their times in London in the days that were gone. Sometimes Alfie came and peeled potatoes with her early in the mornings (later he was often off on mysterious business at the East India docks) and their voices echoed upwards, where tables were being laid for the day's business, as they sang the songs they used to know when they were young. When the pounds and pounds of required potatoes were prepared Regina would rise, her joints would creak, and she would then proceed upstairs to the always crowded dining-room where the most unusual employee of all was in full swing. It was Regina who had somehow cajoled Arthur's sister-in-law, Aunt Agnes, to play the piano in the dining-room. It was Aunt Agnes who now at certain hours sat on a special stool and pounded the pedals and performed melodies for the diners, who often even joined in. *O Susanna!* Frenchmen and Germans would sing, *Don't you cry for me.*

And sometimes late at night, Alfie's wife Maria would stand beside the piano and sing 'The Last Rose of Summer'. And a hush would descend on Celine's House on Oxford Street, and diners sometimes (in a comfortable, sentimental way) wept and enjoyed themselves.

And finally there was what Rillie denoted The Child Arrangements. 'We need their mothers,' she said firmly, 'so we will all have to help. It's only temporary.'

Millie had four children and Faith had, after the death of poor little Arthur, three; they all lived now in Arthur Rivers' house in Marylebone with the pierced butterflies and the small back garden. So seven children had somehow to be catered for. Millie's husband Charlie, who entertained everybody with malicious stories of the Water Boards of London and their responsibility for epidemics, worked very long hours, but he looked after the children whenever he could and his frail, funny, one-legged old father sat with him often, and cracked old jokes. The children were good and naughty and loud and silent and rumbustious and clinging and kind and unkind, like most children. Celine took her turn and told them stories of fire-eating and circuses and they always assumed she was a pirate because she had a black eye-patch and they screamed with delight. Arthur Rivers wangled what time-off from Scotland Yard he could in this busy period, to spend with his intelligent grand-children. Rillie told them stories of New York and removed the horrible dusty, pierced butterflies without anybody's permission: she replaced them with the daguerreotype of the children's fine-looking grandfather. Cordelia made them cardboard cameras and promised they would soon all be daguerreotyped and put on the wall also. Monsieur Roland had some strange hold over the children: for him they were the most well-behaved, and brought pictures for him to peruse that they had drawn for him themselves, with chalks provided by Rillie.

Everybody then, all of them, worked extremely hard and never had enough sleep, they were exhausted, and yet they were jubilant: everyone knew that it was just temporary: the Exhibition would close in October. But at the moment more and more daguerreotypes were required daily; more and more people came to the circus; more and more people ate at, and praised the excellent food and service and music of, CELINE'S LONDON HOUSE OF REFRESHMENT. 'All you needed was my crimson sign to start you off!' said Alfie jubilantly. They were all earning a lot of money, like many people in London at this Great Exhibition time.

Celine received regular epistolary accounts of her House of Refreshment in Maiden Lane, New York, written by Blossom (who had been taught to write in a church school) but dictated by Jeremiah, the ex-strongman. Business was going well; Pearl and Ruby and Maybelle and Blossom were all helping; but *when was she returning?*

'I am considering,' said La Grande Celine grandly to the others, 'that I may first open CELINE'S **PARIS** HOUSE OF REFRESHMENTS. Don't you agree dear Monsieur Roland? I am discussing it daily with *Pierre l'Oiseau*,' and Monsieur Roland looked gravely delighted.

Mr Silas P Swift also was doing a roaring trade in his little corner of Hyde Park, near Oxford Street, that he had somehow been able to rent (after much negotiating and difficulties, and letters of apoplexy to the *Times*), for the duration of the Exhibition: till October. The Crystal Palace was always closed and locked at dusk, and what better place to end a wonderful day than the Circus! The Big Top stood with its bright advertising pennant waving from the roof: **MR SILAS P SWIFT'S AMAZING CIRCUS**, and the strange, exciting, flickering lights and shadows inside the huge tent called the audience like a siren, as night fell over London.

Silas P Swift had excelled himself for his London visit. He had acquired extra acrobats, extra horses and a baby orang-utan who was very charming but in fact deeply disoriented (she clung to Manuel, one of the *charros*, and cried and bit people if separated from him). Silas particularly encouraged Gwenlliam and Pierre-the-bird in the new upward-throwing sensation: he saw how magical it could look, assisted the effect cleverly with lights and mirrors and smoke. Silas had also acquired an Indian snake charmer, who kept a long and extremely dangerous-looking snake in a decorated pot: he played a flute and the snake emerged, flicking its terrifying-looking tongue and reaching up and up and swaying to the music. All the circus ladies, who patted the lion sometimes, were almost prostrate with fear at this, until the Indian assured them that all the poisonous sacs had been removed: then the ladies became quite fond and eventually allowed the snake to wind around their arms, screaming the while nevertheless.

The most popular – that is not necessarily to say the most tasteful – exhibit in Prince Albert's Great Industrial Exhibition in the Crystal Palace was not after all the diving-suit or the replica of Liverpool Docks or the steam engines or even the large but lustreless Koh-i-Noor diamond but, without doubt, the teasingly titillating, carefully-draped but nevertheless nude, statue in the American Section called The Greek Slave. People crowded about this particular exhibit from morning to night: it was as well Sir Joshua Reynolds, the first President of the Royal Academy, was long dead: he had extolled sculpture, almost the last word he uttered was said to have been *Michelangelo*: the rather (to be truthful) vulgar rendering of a naked, chained female would have offended him mightily. But it did not offend the Exhibition visitors: on the contrary it excited them (although there were several letters to the *Times*). And so now, Silas P Swift excelled himself further. He saw the thrill engendered by The Greek Slave at the Crystal Palace, he therefore invented his own Greek Slave for the Big Top. A voluptuous, scantily draped figure, standing in the same exact pose as the statue further along Hyde Park (a triumph only an actress could have accomplished), appeared in a gold cage drawn into the circus ring by four horses. The crowd exploded as the statue stood there: The Greek Slave: untouchable, unknowable: a statue just as in the Crystal Palace – though perhaps just a little more maturity and colour (the hair in particular a little redder perhaps). But – *did the bosom heave just a little? Did the glance flutter?* The crowd surged into the Big Top to see this phenomenon and Mrs Colleen Ray, late of the Royal Theatre, New Zealand and 'The Bandit Chief' (for it was she), became the second-highest-paid performer in the circus.

How they welcomed Mrs Colleen Ray to London, Gwenlliam's family. How fortuitous that she was in London at this time, at the invitation of a minor prince who had offered her a minor palace. 'It is not my *usual* work,' she had said of her latest employment with Mr Silas P Swift, but Gwenlliam and her family did not care what Colleen Ray did: she was their heroine, and Alfie Tyrone said, 'Don't trust English noblemen, lovely, come and work for me in my New York office.'

'It depends on my Minor Prince,' she said and she laughed, and she and Celine compared their flame-coloured hair, and their secrets for maintaining it so.

And Gwenlliam bloomed because she was back at last with her beloved family and her beloved circus, and because she was in love.

On the steamship back to England she and Frankie Fields often leant on the deck-rail in the moonlight; she told him of other decks and other moonlights. He told her of being thrown into the sewer that led to the river, and of hearing Gallus Mag and the screaming of his companions. And of the sound of Cordelia's voice echoing down into the dark stinking tunnel when hope was gone. And how Arthur, tied up, had saved

Frankie's life by pulling him further down into the tunnel before Gallus Mag could reach him as she had reached his colleagues, and then somehow held Frankie's head above the stinking water, and how he, Frankie, had perhaps returned the compliment by helping to heave Arthur up again.

'Thank you, Frankie,' said Gwenlliam, her eyes shining up at him, 'thank you, thank you, thank you!'

Then for several days the Atlantic weather was wild and stormy: Frankie and Gwenlliam clung to the deck-rails and laughed. She told him of clinging to other deck-rails with Colleen, and making plans, and once she told him of remembering her brother and her sister and weeping and putting her head out through the porthole. And as she told him that part, Frankie put his arm gently about her for comfort and her tears were blown into the Atlantic sky. And then she told him about the terrible, worst part of all: seeing her mother's hair, that night aboard the *Scorpion*, and when she told him that, great sobs convulsed her and then he held her very tightly and the ship ploughed through the waves and the wind blew. 'She is alive,' he said, 'dear Gwen.'

'I know, I know, it was just the shock and I am so happy,' and she realised she was talking nonsense and that Frankie Fields was holding her tightly and that the waves were breaking over the bow and she lifted up her head and kissed him hard. And then Frankie Fields told Gwenlliam Preston above the sound of the waves that although he was going to continue to try to best her at poker, he loved her very much. And so, at last, she admitted that on other ships, in other oceans, she had dreamed of him. And then on this ship in this ocean, the rough and wild Atlantic, they stood together, held very tightly in each other's arms.

*

504

Frankie absolutely loved working at Scotland Yard where the police rules and the police men were so different from those he was used to. He was proud of his uniform; he came to the circus as often as his work permitted, in his uniform gladly if he had to. He sat in the audience and watched his beloved with anxiety and pride, mixed. Sometimes in the early evening if he was free they would walk down Oxford Street together to Hyde Park, as crowds streamed in excitement towards the Big Top.

Foolish, foolish, *foolish* Mr James Doveribbon to ever *ever* show his face again anywhere near **MR SILAS P SWIFT'S AMAZING CIRCUS**. In fact he thought it deeply, hugely unwise himself, but his father would not hear because Mr Doveribbon senior, the well-known London lawyer who often worked for the nobility arranging many private matters to their satisfaction, was about to be declared – the scandal was too much to contemplate – bankrupt.

The more and more ailing Duke of Llannefydd's promised open purse: *All Expenses. Any bills paid. High Fees*: remained closed, because whatever they told him of their expensive endeavours, they had not produced his grand-daughter. 'I said I would pay if you brought my blood, my grand-daughter. Do I see her in front of me? No!' and whisky slurped and spilled. 'No, I see the horrible whore's hair and nothing more. How do I know it is *her* hair? It could be anybody's!' But he knew it was hers and he did not touch it, it un-nerved him, the white streak which he remembered so well from the days in court when Cordelia was almost convicted of his son's murder. He could not bear it, now that it was so clearly here beside him: something malign and dank and black and white. 'Take it away!' he cried, and he felt cold. 'I want my grand-daughter to look after me,' he said piteously. 'It is her duty. Then she can have Wales. I know the son of my despicable second cousin haunts my halls and waits for me to die.' He lay in his big house in Mayfair that stank like a brewery, bullying his servants. Cordelia's hair lay there, in a satchel, in a far corner of the room where she herself had never been made welcome, all those years ago. The duke refused to sign any papers or pay any promises unless his grand-daughter stood before him. Mr Doveribbon senior was beside himself: the fee alone required by his son to bribe his way out of a New York prison and get the parcel of hair out of the police safe – for it was true of course that anything could be bought or sold in New York if the price was right – had finally tipped the family over the financial edge into penury and social disgrace.

The duke's doctor was brief. 'I give him another week, no more. He has stopped eating, drinks only whisky, and most of that misses his mouth.' The doctor's lip curled in unprofessional distaste. 'I must insist you lawyers stop bothering him and coming to the house so often.' (The doctor himself stood to receive a very large payment for his services: that paper had been signed, and he wanted no interference.)

And then Mr Doveribbon junior had understood – as who in London would not, so great was Mr Silas P Swift's skill at publicity – that **MR SILAS P SWIFT'S AMAZING CIRCUS** had come to town.

'I suppose it is possible she has rejoined them,' he said to his father reluctantly. 'They advertise a Clairvoyant Ghost, it may be her.' He was very, very unhappy and nervous to be in any way involved further but he was even more unhappy to find himself penniless, and he awoke sweating in the night as a future without ready money loomed and Edgware Road mismanagement promised further debts.

Mr Doveribbon senior made the decision at once. He was in a high state of panic: distasteful as it may be, they must immediately attend a circus performance: the younger man would accompany him, alert his father as to whether the heiress was present; then he (the elder Mr Doveribbon) would present himself and his credentials and simply politely ask that the girl come with him at once to Mayfair: it was after all simple: a cabriolet ride away, nothing so vulgar as kidnapping necessary. 'I do not believe there is a person in this world who is immune to riches, and after all she is, for all her "blood ties", a common little acrobat. You simply went about the matter clumsily. Hurry, hurry, we cannot wait another day, we must succeed now where you failed before, or, to put it to you bluntly, we are utterly and totally ruined!' and Mr Doveribbon senior's hand shook badly as he pulled at his cravat.

To the Doveribbons' misfortune therefore, they were attending the circus ticket office when Gwenlliam and Frankie were hurrying down Oxford Street, late for once (because they had not noticed the time when he had proposed marriage to her in Cavendish Square, and she had accepted, as one lone sheep grazed dispassionately beside them). The newspaper boys always shouted as they displayed their wares, they always shouted the news just out: for just a second Gwenlliam slowed as she heard the cry: **DUKE GONE TO MAKER! ONLY ONE PENNY! DUKE GONE TO MAKER!** And she stopped. And she took a penny from her cloak. And so Gwenlliam saw what the Doveribbons had not: the Duke of Llannefydd was dead.

For a moment, she did not move, stood there among the hurrying crowds of Oxford Street. They were even later now, but she did not say anything, or move in the direction of Hyde Park. Kind Gwenlliam Preston had only one sliver of steel in her kind and loving heart. Finally she spoke.

'I am glad,' she said to Frankie, and he saw that her eyes glittered coldly as she threw the newspaper into a rubbish-filled gutter.

Peggy Walker had the Clairvoyant Ghost costume in her arms and had been looking anxiously through the crowds for a sign of Gwen from the step of the wardrobe caravan. At last she saw her, running now with Frankie Fields. 'Gwen! Where were you? It is so unlike you! They've been holding the band, quickly!' Gwenlliam stopped at the caravan, tried to catch her breath. 'Come along, pal,' Peggy scolded. 'You ain't been late since you vamoosed in San Francisco! You had me real worried!'

For now Gwenlliam had only time to hug Peggy Walker as she quickly pulled on her costume; she disappeared into the shadows at the back of the Big Top as the band played at last and the crowds, now joined by a beaming Frankie Fields in his police uniform, cheered in anticipation and spat their tobacco.

It was Chief Great Rainbow who caught sight of Mr Doveribbon first: Mr Doveribbon (junior), sitting with his father on the end of a row in the audience, far towards the back. (James Doveribbon had actually placed himself there carefully – where he thought it unlikely he would be noticed by any circus performers – right at the back of the Big Top where there was less light, just in case he needed to make a quick exit.) The Chief came cantering on with all the horses: exotic, foreign; the big feathered headdress and the scarred and painted face. But to the Indian Chief the audiences in Hyde Park were foreign and exotic also: the clothes, the voices, the ladies' hats: an elegance: nothing could have been more different from the wild, murdering audience in California. His poker-face – eagle-eyed, alert, one of an ancient, watchful tribe – observed everybody just as they observed him as he cantered round the ring: of course he saw Mr Doveribbon, remembered well the man who had hung around the circus in San Francisco paying court to their girl, then disappearing with her. He gave an Indian war-whoop – alerting all the circus performers that there was something or someone interesting in his line of vision. The Mexican *charros* heard, exchanged information with Great Rainbow, passing it on as they galloped round the ring; the lion-tamer took the news out to the acrobats and the snake charmer and The Greek Slave in the shadows. *CRACK!* went the whip as the *charros* galloped faster and faster. Within minutes every performer in the circus, including The Clairvoyant Ghost who was just beginning her climb up to her waiting-place in the roof in the darkness, knew that Gwenlliam's kidnapper was quite coolly sitting there at the back of the Big Top, on the right. Frankie Fields, watching for his girl Gwenlliam, was not a policeman trained by Arthur Rivers for nothing: sitting in the audience he was conscious of a *frisson* of excitement among the performers: something had happened: he looked up apprehensively to the circus roof. If he had not been so happy that she had agreed to marry him; if he had not been so thrilled, yet always so anxious, about his girl's adventures up in the air, he would of course also have seen the man he hit on the head with an iron bar aboard the *SS Scorpion*, off Sandy Hook. Near to Frankie, sharing ginger beer with him in fact, excited too, sat Arthur Rivers' daughter Millie and her husband Charlie: they had met their stepsister at last and this was the third time they had been to the circus.

The clowns muttered the news together as they smiled their huge smiles; there were some younger clowns now: three of the older men had been fired in San Francisco (*sorry boys,* said Silas firmly, giving them twenty dollars extra each, for long loyalty). But the younger clowns too knew the story of

Gwenlliam: now they ran around the ring tripping and dancing, they laughed and laughed and the audience cheered and called back, children screaming with laughter at the big oversized shoes and the big, over-sized red noses and at the clown that was being bounced up and down in the big net and the band broke into another fine British march and the lion roared as the trainer (back in his toga) cracked his whip against the cage door and ladies screamed and the snake charmer ran on with his flute and his coiled serpent.

And up high now, in the shadows, with the steel in her heart, The Clairvoyant Ghost swung, backwards and forwards in the dark, waiting.

Now the lion and the trainer had done their thrilling act, the trainer had gone inside the cage and then removed himself after a young wag had called (as usual) *Eat him boy!* to the lion; now the midgets had juggled and the cheeky monkeys had swung on bars, the acrobats had soared, and the baby orang-utan had charmed (although the Mexican cowboy, Manuel, was exhausted: he could go nowhere, do nothing, without this small orang-utan clinging to him: *estoy enfermo!* Manuel complained, but then could not help comforting once again his needy, neurotic little charge). The fire-eaters had run about the ring, breathing fire in and out; the *charros* had pyramided themselves on the horses, again exchanging whooped messages with the Indian Chief as they ended their race around the sawdust circle.

'LADIES AND GENTLEMEN!' called the circus master in his red coat, 'WE PRESENT, STRAIGHT FROM THE GREAT EXHIBITION: THE STATUE OF THE GREEK SLAVE!' and the whip sounded once more, **CRACK! CRACK!** and the golden cage appeared out of the shadows. The tuba and the trumpet had a special tune that was played when The Greek Slave appeared. It was a piece that the bandmaster (who was besotted by Mrs Colleen Ray) had composed. The tune at first seemed dignified, as befitted the delicate sad subject, but all the time the tuba played a tiny background of *oomp-pa-pa* as if it was laughing, slightly naughtily, behind its hand: Silas P Swift was very approving of this composition.

The crowd gasped as the contents of the golden cage came further and further into the light, and then roared, literally roared, its approval. Immobile, tragic (albeit definitely tinged with vulgarity, like its original), the statue did not move as the cage was drawn around the ring, coming to a halt in the middle. The chained hands (the rather unusual red hair and the perhaps slightly more mature look), the bowed, submissive gaze: still as stone as it stood there. And the statue as nude as the favourite statue in the Great Exhibition Hall (well, just a very small gossamer drape where cover had to be made). As always, the crowd stared and whispered and nudged: *look!* men whispered to each other, *look! the bosom! did that bosom heave?* And then in the excited, whispering stillness, suddenly breaking all rules of propriety (and no doubt legality) The Greek Slave not only moved, but spoke.

She raised one beautiful, graceful arm from her chains and cried. 'I knew him! I see him!' pointing: that is, accusing their quarry to the whole circus: Mr James Doveribbon. Who sat with his father minding his own business (you might say) at the end of a row, at the back.

The crowd, shocked, turned, strained to look at the now half-standing-in-alarm Mr Doveribbon (who the very moment he heard the voice understood the statue was Mrs Colleen Ray); then the crowd looked back to the ring, puzzled: *did we imagine that?* for there stood the buxom, naked Greek statue, posed and passive, unmoving. But the Indian Chief was already riding up the wide planked steps of the centre aisle, he gathered up the terrified Mr Doveribbon (junior) from the guardianship of the terrified Mr Doveribbon (senior), as if they were in a war in the Wild West of America, and turned his horse. How alarming and thrilling for the audience (how further terrifying for James Doveribbon) as the horse's legs lifted high for a moment as it stopped as ordered by its rider. And then it turned and clip-clopped delicately back down the wooden steps into the ring; Chief Great Rainbow then deposited Mr Doveribbon neatly straight into the clown's net, and the clowns cheerfully bounced the shouting Mr Doveribbon up and down. This whole drama had been carried out so skilfully that the audience – *what magnificent horsemanship!* – thought it was part of the show – and then, as they applauded, the drums rolled, a different note.

And suddenly THE CLAIRVOYANT GHOST could be seen, suddenly appearing in the murky, smoky gloom above. She flew like a white bird from trapeze to trapeze, lower and lower, till she stood poised on the bottom trapeze, nearest to Mr Doveribbon but still shadowy because of Mr Silas P Swift's clever use of the oil-lamps always at the first moment of her appearance. She swung backwards and forwards for a moment, quiet, eerie; the drums rolled.

I have a particular aversion to snakes, Mr Doveribbon had said as they sailed towards Panama.

She jumped from above straight into the bright light and the arms of Pierre-the-Bird: *HOUP-LA! HOUP-LA!* How the crowd roared yet again, how Millie and Charlie clapped and shouted in relief, how the crowd now stamped their delight (how Frankie Fields in his policeman's uniform had suddenly stood, ready to blow his police whistle – for was it not he who had felled Mr Doveribbon in New York harbour?). In a moment

Mr Doveribbon could be surrounded by constables, for at this moment Hyde Park was the most policed spot in Europe.

But The Clairvoyant Ghost, balanced now on the shoulders of the huge French acrobat, held up her hand: Frankie saw: it was not yet finished. The ghost turned to the snake charmer and made a sign: the plaintive, eerie foreign sound of his flute began and the snake uncoiled itself from the pottery jar and stretched up, up, upwards, hypnotised by the music, up, up towards Mr Doveribbon held in the net – the long tongue flicked in and out. Mr Doveribbon cowered, screamed and screamed in terror as the snake swayed nearer and nearer. And Gwenlliam thought coldly: *how stupid he looks, screaming in his gentleman's suit.* This arrogant Englishman who strode over ships with chloroform and keys, hiding her mother's hair. She watched, unmoved, as the snake stretched closer and closer to him, and he screamed. And then she turned away.

The Duke of Llannefydd could do no more harm. It was enough.

At a sign from The Clairvoyant Ghost the clowns simply tipped the net upside down. Mr Doveribbon fell, stumbled, and ran (and Mrs Colleen Ray, poised and naked in her golden cage, suddenly remembered Gwenlliam stumbling, running in the dark on the Norfolk wharf and the men grabbing her so viciously and the precious poker coins falling from her cloak through the wooden planks of the wharf, and into the sea). Tonight Mr Doveribbon stumbled and ran: ran right into the arms of Sergeant Frankie Fields: they were gone: the moment was over.

HOUP-LA! HOUP-LA! HOUP-LA! cried Pierre-the-bird, grabbing the wrists of the Clairvoyant Ghost and the drums rolled and the lights lowered and then Gwenlliam called to him: **NOW!**

And somehow the Clairvoyant Ghost seemed to fly upwards, right up into the murky shadows, and it seemed like magic: they were seeing real magic: the Clairvoyant Ghost flew upwards, up, like a ghost-bird: it was against the laws of nature and the law of gravity but there she was: up, up: then she caught a dark trapeze with one hand. She swung herself – and she stood there, swinging slightly, and the audience could not take their eyes from her and then very slowly, balanced, she stood with her arms outstretched, as if she held the audience to her in some magical way.

'Listen,' said the shadowy Clairvoyant Ghost above them *and there was not a sound, not a sound from all the people: and yet there was the sound of tears as she held them all.*

'Once upon a time,' (and the audience leaned forward to catch the words, as if she was telling them a fairy story, as indeed she was) 'once upon a time, on a long, long shore where the tide goes out very far, there were the ghosts of children who could never leave: *shshshshshshshshshshsh.*' And the audience, so silent, caught in her arms, thought they heard the sea. And Mr Doveribbon senior who had not dared to move from his place in the Big Top heard it too, much against his inclination: he heard the sound of the sea.

'And, tonight, this special night, those little ghosts have been set free.' And the shadowy figure held the crowd for one moment more in her arms, perfectly still. Then she added softly, as though the tears they had heard had been ghost-tears, yet everyone could hear the words: 'And all will be well.' And then she swung herself somehow into darkness – and she was gone.

The bandmaster, who had been as transfixed as everybody else, pulled himself together and required his band to at once play 'GOD SAVE THE QUEEN', and the crowd, collecting themselves also, sang, as they always sang to their dear monarch. But nevertheless: they understood something had happened: something. And as the circus performers paraded around the ring, the people cheered and smiled and they looked up to the roof of the Big Top. But there was no-one there. And the crowds poured out at last into the night from the circus tent, in a kind of excited puzzlement, breathing in the summer night air in Hyde Park, happier without quite knowing why, something had – they weren't quite sure how to say it – touched their hearts – how thrilling it had all been, this circus. And not thinking for a moment of the man in the net who had been taken away by a policeman.

At the house in Great Titchfield Street, near Oxford Street, that Cordelia and Rillie had found and rented when they first arrived back in London, there was room for everyone. The daguerreotype of them all in New York hung on the wall, and near to it, a beautiful painting of three children playing by the sea. They all met at the house in Great Titchfield Street late at night after their various activities, always exhausted, always full of stories of foreigners and food and business and the Exhibition, and Cordelia and Rillie poured glasses of red-port for everybody, just as they had in the old days, and Regina had immediately commenced her habit of reading aloud from the newspapers, just as she had in the old days.

'I see the English still think they're best,' she said dryly, 'listen to this.'

> *The more I think, the more I must admire!*
> *Surely we soon shall set the Thames on fire!*
> *Oh! What are Egypt's Pyramids of old,*
> *What that Colossus, that the vile Turks sold*

Or what Rome's Colosseum, wide and vast
Unto our Crystal Palace, built to last?
They are but ruins – they shall pass away;
Swift be their fall, unsorrowed their decay!
Once they were famed – their name is now a farce
Extinguished by the rays of English glass!

And then Gwenlliam and Mrs Colleen Ray and Frankie Fields burst in through the door.

'The Duke of Llannefydd is dead, the newsboys were calling it,' said Gwenlliam matter-of-factly, although her voice caught unexpectedly. And then there was just one sound: Cordelia dropped the port bottle to the floor. It didn't break, simply rolled, spilling some of its contents as it went, came to rest underneath a table; Cordelia stared at her daughter.

'And tonight we caught Mr Doveribbon in the clown's net during the performance.' And those words sounded so unlikely and ridiculous that everyone, already stunned, half-laughed: a kind of astonished laughter and then all had to be explained, although Gwenlliam herself did not say anything else, left it to the others to recount the events. But, ever practical, she bent to the port bottle, retrieved it with a little left inside, poured the liquid into a glass, and handed it to her mother. And she and Cordelia looked at each other. *It is over at last.*

Frankie described the Indian Chief and The Greek Slave and the snake charmer and their contributions; Colleen described how The Clairvoyant Acrobat bewitched the audience. And Cordelia and Monsieur Roland both saw Gwenlliam's face as she smiled at Frankie Fields: Gwenlliam's eyes shone with joy as she looked at Frankie, and there was something else in her eyes too: something lost, something found.

'Pierre-the-Bird said he would be waiting at the usual address,' said Mrs Colleen Ray to Celine and the two flame-haired ladies laughed, and Celine waved and disappeared.

But Celine had first delivered corncakes from her House of Refreshment: there was food, there was port, there was talk and laughter. Gwenlliam, with Frankie talking still, *he's safely locked up tonight, sir, believe me!* (but saving their own news for another night), set up their poker school with Alfie and Rillie; Monsieur Roland sat at his little corner table with his books and his papers. Maria fanned herself in the heat, enjoying all the excitement, her feet up on the sofa, Regina read on from the newspapers.

'Listen to this,' she said, rattling the *Times*.

> *'Why is there such a lack of conveniences for visiting foreigners – who are not particular, when certain calls of nature press, **where they relieve themselves**.'*

Mrs Colleen Ray also had an assignation, and had kept her cloak on; she was to meet with her minor prince near the Marble Arch. 'He'll be cross that I'm late, but I had to come and help tell the story of that bastard, oh, to see him bounced up and down gave me great pleasure!'

'Wait,' said Arthur, 'we'll come with you' and he murmured to Cordelia who still had not spoken: 'Come for a walk down to Hyde Park, I want to show you something,' and Cordelia put on her cloak also; just as she left she put her arms around her daughter tightly and her arms said: *the whole nightmare is over at last.*

The three of them walked from Great Titchfield Street in the moonlight, Colleen still recounting the events with gusto; they passed a night newsboy and he shouted the headline the way they did: except he could not pronounce the Welsh name, but they all saw the headline: **DUKE OF LLANNEFYDD DIES**.

And Arthur immediately took Cordelia's arm; she leant close to him, they did not need to speak.

But Mrs Colleen Ray gave an odd little shiver. 'She used to weep sometimes in her cabin. She thought I didn't know. I never saw a braver girl than her, flying from that ship like a bird, to try and get away. I'm glad all those adventures are over,' and Cordelia gave her a sudden warm hug in Oxford Street. And Colleen thought she felt tears fall in her hair.

And there at the Marble Arch was the noble, waiting minor prince; he was relieved and delighted and cross and in love, all at the same time. Explanations and apologies were given; Arthur and Cordelia waved them goodnight and turned into Hyde Park.

The Big Top was hushed and empty after its adventures that night; a duty constable saluted the Detective-Inspector as he passed. Cordelia looked up at the pennant that fluttered gently from above: **MR SILAS P SWIFT'S AMAZING CIRCUS**.

'Do you miss it?' said Arthur.

'With my *knees*?' said Cordelia firmly and they both laughed. As they walked through the park a small wind blew a newspaper along a pathway, it danced ahead of them, and then was still, caught on the twisted roots of an old oak tree. **DIES** was the only word they could see. In the distance now the beautiful Crystal Palace glittered in the moonlight.

Another duty policeman saluted and let Arthur and Cordelia in by a side door, into the big, almost-empty building. The occasional voice called, one to another, as other duty constables padded by in big, silent slippers so as not to scuff the wooden floors further, checking the east wing and the west wing, the south wing and the north wing; all the exhibits shadowed and hushed: all quiet now in the night and the Koh-i-Noor diamond safely locked away inside the pedestal of the golden birdcage.

Arthur and Cordelia wandered down big, empty aisles as the light of the moon shone in through the glass roof. They passed storm-detectors and engines and anchors; they passed busts of Shakespeare, busts of the Duke of Wellington, busts of Queen Victoria; they passed the diving suit, and the crimson satin quilted eiderdown from Heals and the statue of The Greek Slave. They walked towards the silent glass fountain, the centre-piece where the nave met the high transept. They sat together on the steps that led up to the throne under the captive elm tree, from which Queen Victoria had made her opening speech about beneficent Providence and the happiness of mankind; Cordelia's cloak caught moonlight in its folds and there were strange looming shadows, and palm trees, and the scent of flowers.

And for some time they sat alone in this huge, empty, extraordinary, beautiful, temporary, moonlit crystal palace.

And as she leaned into his warm shoulder, and stared at the way the moonlight fell through the glass, *this would be the most beautiful daguerreotype in the world,* and as she felt the warmth of Arthur's body next to her, *o how lucky I am, after all,* somebody, one of the slippered policeman, began to play one of the pianofortes. The music drifted down the aisle to where they were sitting.

'Arthur, are they really going to take it all away somewhere else, the whole Crystal Palace?'

'So they say.'

She shook her head, almost disbelievingly. 'And I suppose the grass will grow again and this beautiful building, that has been crowded with so many people from all over the world, it will be as if – how strange to think – was never here in Hyde Park, never here at all.'

'But you and I will remember this night,' he said to her quietly. And because the tiny shards of dangerous glass between them had been swept away at last she knew he was also saying to her, *we have learnt from the old man: it is our memories that make us who we are* and she buried her shorn, damaged head for just a moment next to his loving heart, and kissed him; he held her tightly to him.

They stood to go at last, walked down the long aisle, and they heard the music still: jaunty, sliding, waltz music that might have been disapproved of, but was all the rage.

And he put his arm about his wife, and she put her hand in his, and in the huge, empty, beautiful Crystal Palace, in the moonlight, they danced to a tinkling, distant piano.

I am indebted to the writers of the following books:

New York Past, Present and Future (2nd Edition) by Ezekial Porter Beldon (GP Putnam, New York 1849)

Valentine's Manual of the City of New York edited by Henry Collins Brown (The Valentine Co. New York 1916)

The Diary of George Templeton Strong (Volumes 1 & 2: 1835–1859) edited by Allan Nevins (Macmillan, New York 1952)

American Social History as recorded by British travellers edited by Allan Nevins (Allen & Unwin, London; printed in USA 1924)

American Notes for general circulation by Charles Dickens (Chapman and Hall 1842)

Gotham: A History of New York City to 1898 by Edwin G Burrows and Mike Wallace (New York; Oxford University Press)

A History of the Circus in America by George L Chindahl (Caxton Printers; Caldwell, 2nd printing 1959)

Step Right Up by LaVahn G Hoh and William H Rough (Betterway Publications, White Hall, Va. c.1990)

The Development of Inhalation Anaesthesia with special reference to the years 1846–1900 by Barbara M. Duncum (Oxford University Press 1947)

Cops and Bobbies by Wilber R Miller (University of Chicago Press 1977)

The Blue Parade by Thomas A Repetto (Free Press, New York; Collier Macmillan, London 1978)

Paddy Whacked: the untold story of the American Gangster by T.J. English (Regan Books, New York c.2005)

Gangs of New York: an informal history of the underworld by Herbert Ashbury (Knopf, New York 1928)

Gold Dust: the Californian gold rush and the forty-niners by Donald Dale Jackson (Allen & Unwin, 1980)

The American Leonardo: a life of Samuel B. Morse by Carlton Mabee (A.A. Knopf, New York 1943)

Talking to the Dead: Kate & Maggie Fox and the Rise of Spiritualism by Barbara Weisberg (Harper Collins, San Francisco 2005)

The Spirit Rappers by Herbert G. Jackson jnr (Doubleday, New York 1972)

The American Daguerreotype by Floyd and Marion Rinhart (University of Georgia Press, Athens Ga. c.1981)

The Origins of American Photography 1839–1885 by Keith F. Davis (Yale University Press, 2007)

1851 and The Crystal Palace by Christopher Hobhouse (John Murray, London 1937)

Crystal Palace Exhibition Illustrated Catalogue with introduction by John Gloag (Dover Publications, New York; Constable, London 1970)

I am also grateful for the assistance of Joshua Ruff, Curator, New York City Police Museum: any mistakes about the somewhat convoluted police systems of that time are nevertheless my own.

Thanks also to Barry Creyton, Kitty Williston, Vanessa Galvin Buist, Lynne and Chuck Woodruff, Danielle Nelson Tunks, and John Agace. And to Professor Graham Smith, and the staff of Te Whare Pukapuka, at Te Whare Wananga o Awanuiarangi.

And lastly, but most importantly, gratitude to the city of New York itself, where for the first time in my life I actually wore out a pair of shoes walking and walking and trying to find what was left of 1845–50, in that wonderful, energetic city.

If you would like to hear audio clips of the songs featured in *The Circus of Ghosts*, and for more information about Barbara Ewing and her novels – plus reviews, exclusive material and video clips – please visit

www.barbaraewing.com

If you've enjoyed reading the wonderfully evocative
The Circus of Ghosts, why not pick up one of Barbara Ewing's
backlist? Details of her books are included in the following pages.

Also by Barbara Ewing:

THE FRAUD

Barbara Ewing

1763. As candles flicker in the falling dusk along Pall Mall,
Filipo di Vecellio, fêted portrait painter from Florence, and his
beautiful wife Angelica entertain the cream of London's art world
in their fashionable London home, with Joshua Reynolds and
Thomas Gainsborough among the guests, and William Hogarth
a disapproving observer. Little is known of Filipo's past
or his family except in the shadows sits his sister,
Francesca, who watches, and listens, and waits.

For beneath the opulence and success, the house in Pall Mall
conceals a swarm of secrets, corruption and lies. Filipo's ambition
has meant numerous, terrible sacrifices for Francesca, but Filipo is
not the only painter, nor the only one capable of fraud. And as the
great wild city of trade and business expands its grasping, avid
tentacles, a climax erupts involving love and passion –
and the quiet sister who has waited so long . . .

'In this engaging and enlightening novel about artistic ambition
and fraud at the nascent Royal Academy, Ewing is an
accomplished storyteller who puts the pleasure
of her readers first' *Independent*

'Ewing is particularly good when painting in the background of
18th-century London with all its colour and filth . . . the character
of Grace is compelling and there is some fascinating stuff about
the ruinous effects of 18th-century beauty products, but what
really makes this book worth reading is Ewing's skill at
unfolding a story' *New Zealand Herald on Sunday*

THE MESMERIST

Barbara Ewing

Mesmerism, the genesis of today's Hypnotism, is all the rage in England in 1840 and out-of-work actresses Cordelia and Rillie decide to set up their own fake Mesmerism business in London's Bloomsbury, to keep themselves out of the workhouse. But Cordelia finds she actually has the Mesmeric gift – and then the past, and a murder, intervene . . .

'A compelling storyteller, Ewing puts on a masterly performance in recreating Victorian theatre land. Even when the body count starts to mount, she keeps us believing' *Independent*

'Ewing's depictions of the theatre world, the battle between mesmerists and physicians, her portrait of the London streets, are all first-rate . . . she has produced a consistently entertaining, amusing and enlightening novel – what more can one ask?' *Sunday Telegraph*

'Written with insight, intelligence and style, a highly engaging and entertaining read with a complex plot and a cast of believable and mostly loveable characters' *Sydney Morning Herald* (Book of the Week)

The Mesmerist was chosen as Westminster Libraries' 'ONE BOOK FOR WESTMINSTER'

ROSETTA

Barbara Ewing

At the end of the eighteenth century young girls fall in love
with handsome men, get married, and believe – of course – that
they will live happily ever after. In the middle of the Napoleonic
wars, in search of a lost child and lost love, one young girl travels
to Egypt, through Cleopatra's old city of Alexandria, to the little
town of Rosetta at the mouth of the Nile. There the Rosetta Stone,
that will unlock the Egyptian hieroglyphs and tell the secrets
of the world, has just been discovered. And, there,
other discoveries are made also . . .

'A brilliantly evocative and superbly researched re-creation of
a period fascinated by the Rosetta Stone and the decipherment
of Ancient Egyptian hieroglyphs. For Barbara Ewing, history is not
merely a decorative background for romance, but the very centre
of a passionate and enthralling intellectual adventure' Dr Richard
Parkinson, Assistant Keeper, department of Ancient Egypt and
Sudan, the British Museum, and Keeper of The Rosetta Stone

'A delightful plum pudding of a historical novel' *Sunday Times*

'[An] engrossing saga set in 1795, following Rose and Fanny
from their innocent childhoods and premature marriages . . .
The feminist agenda of rebellion and enlightenment mirrors one
of the major preoccupations of the Romantic age and there are
some fascinating historical details . . . absorbing' *Time Out*

'A convincing and stirring period epic' *New Zealand Herald*

THE TRESPASS

Barbara Ewing

A cholera plague in Victorian London heightens the dark secrets
in the house of a well-to-do English family. Every month small,
brave sailing ships leave for the outer regions of the new British
Empire and on one of those small ships a desperate young girl
hides, knowing very little about this new country New Zealand
and what she might find there. And not knowing that she will
be followed to the other side of the world by people who –
each for their own reasons – cannot live without her.

'A detailed and extremely readable novel. Full of well-realised,
interesting and believable characters' *Good Book Guide*

'Compelling storytelling and an exquisitely detailed evocation
of Victorian London. Barbara Ewing's cholera-ridden London
is so vivid you can smell it' Clare Boylan

'Ewing writes accessibly and tells a ripping good story,
but her passion is also for ideas . . . Ewing keeps the pace up
right to the dramatic ending' *New Zealand Herald*

'Packed with period atmosphere . . . a stirring tale' *Woman and Home*

A DANGEROUS VINE

Barbara Ewing

Long-listed for the Orange Prize

In the 1950s, when people who had never left New Zealand still called England 'home', New Zealand prided itself on being The Greatest Little Country in the World, where there were no racial problems and everybody lived happily together in God's Own Country. Was it that way? A novel of love and pain and laughter and music. And loss.

'A vivid sense of the era, with its swirly skirts, box brownies and the last tram home' *Sunday Times*

'Rich, vivid and interesting and woven into a plot that has a ring of verisimilitude and plenty of fascinating detail' *The Times*

'Ewing's absence from New Zealand over a long acting career has perhaps given her a clearer view of New Zealand society than we who live here can have. In showing us how much we believe we have changed, she reveals to us how much we have yet to understand' *Waikato Times*

THE ACTRESSES

Barbara Ewing

A class reunion at a London drama school in the 1990s triggers
a series of dramatic events that leads to a celebrity court case
in the Old Bailey, and shows the successes and the failures –
and the past and the memories – of a group of famous
(and not-so-famous) actors and actresses.

'This is an excellent account of the late middle-aged antics
of the class of '59 . . . a terrific insight into actors' childish psyches.
Ewing understands the different kinds of love and friendship,
and the denouement on a Hawaiian island is pure
Jilly Cooper' *Sunday Times*

'Excellent . . . Ewing, herself an actress, weaves a plot as complex
as fair-isle knitting, darting teasingly between past and present,
and fastens off all the threads so that the pattern is
satisfyingly complete' *Daily Telegraph*

'Ms Ewing is herself an actress of distinction, and knows how
to create believable yet memorable characters, to evoke place
and to tell a story which takes hold of the reader and holds
them enthralled – through tears and laughter –
from the first page to the last' *Gay Times*

Other bestselling titles available from Sphere: